Blood Bond

by

Shannon K. Butcher

BOOKS BY SHANNON K. BUTCHER

THE SENTINEL WARS

Burning Alive
Finding the Lost
Running Scared
Living Nightmare
Blood Hunt
Dying Wish
Falling Blind
Willing Sacrifice
Binding Ties

THE EDGE

Living on the Edge
Razor's Edge
Edge of sanity
Edge of Betrayal
Rough Edges

DELTA FORCE TRILOGY

No Regrets
No Control
No Escape

AND MORE

Go to www.ShannonKButcher.com for details.

Blood Bond
The Sentinel Wars, Book Ten
By: Shannon K. Butcher
Published by Silver Linings Media, LLC
Copyright © 2018 by Silver Linings Media, LLC
ISBN: 978-1-945292-18-7

This is a work of fiction. Names, characters, places, and incidents either are the products of the author's imagination or are used fictitiously. Any resemblance to actual persons, living or dead, businesses, companies, events, or locations is entirely coincidental.

Cover art: Dar Albert
Editing: Julie Finley

DEDICATION

For all the readers who didn't give up on me.
This one is for you.

CHAPTER ONE

Justice had encountered a wide variety of scumbags in her line of work, but this kind was her least favorite—entitled, arrogant, self-important assholes who thought they should have whatever they wanted simply because they could afford it. They didn't care who they hurt so long as the object of their desire was in their greedy, little hands.

A walking case of 'roid rage in a suit escorted her past the nurses' desk, down a bland, beige hallway back to the waiting room.

While a vacant doctors' office wasn't exactly the normal meeting spot for black market dealings, the setup did offer some benefits. The place was a rats' nest of turning hallways and small rooms. Only the thugs working for Chester Gale knew which room their boss was in, forcing any would-be attackers to check behind door after door for the right one.

Justice could have turned around and gone back to exam room six where she'd met him moments ago, but her guess was the man in charge had already moved from one whack-a-mole hole to the next, just in case. That's what she would have done if she had a pile of people looking to kill her.

Too bad she wasn't one of the would-be assassins. At least not today.

If she'd been here to kill the black-market crime boss, God, karma, the fates, or whoever the hell controlled her, would have already forced her to take him down, armed or not. That the entitled asshole still breathed was proof that she still needed the link to dark dealings his scumbag ways could provide.

The suited thug escorting her reached behind the giant, u-shaped nurses' station and handed over a clear plastic shoebox.

Justice retrieved Reba first and checked her Glock to make sure it was still loaded and ready to deliver deadly force. No way was she trusting these goons not to fuck with her only sure way of taking them down.

Once she was satisfied that Reba was unmolested, she tucked the .40 cal. in the back of her jeans.

Next, she grabbed the small, leather-clad box and flipped it open. Inside was the majority of her payment in the form of a silver ring. The surface was etched with a chaotic jumble of lines that might have been some kind of bizarre writing, but just as easily have been the scars of a garbage disposal gone rogue.

She had no idea what the ring was for, but now that she had it, she waited for that gnawing itch at the back of her brain to fade, indicating her task was complete.

It wasn't. The powers that had sent her here weren't done with her yet, which worried her. Who knew what the fates wanted if the ring wasn't it.

The brown paper sack was next. She peered into it and saw a banded stack of cash. There was no sense in stopping to count it now. If the remainder of the fee she was owed for services rendered wasn't all there, the only way she was getting the rest was by spilling blood. No amount of cash was worth that kind of trouble—not when her task wasn't yet complete.

No rest for the wicked.

The meaty thug held the empty plastic shoebox and stared at her with a blank expression only hard drugs or incurable stupidity could create. "We're done here."

It wasn't a question. It was a dismissal.

Justice tucked the ring in the bag of cash and shoved it in her back pocket to leave her hands free. Again, just in case. Then she turned and went past an empty check-out desk and down the hallway that led to the waiting room. She caught a fleeting glimpse of another guard near the door she'd come through earlier. He was poised inside the last room along the hall, peering through a gap no wider than a pencil. The space behind him was dark, and the only reason she'd been able to see him at all was because a glitter of fluorescent light from the hallway caught his eye.

She didn't stare. There was no point in it. She knew this guy was here to make sure she left—under her own steam or by force. The dead look in his eye said he wouldn't really care which.

At least he wasn't bloodthirsty, like some of the assholes she dealt with.

Her escort punched in a code on the electronic lock and opened the door that led into the waiting room.

"Next," he said, bored.

Justice gripped her sack of loot tighter and kept walking. The itch at the base of her skull was starting to buzz.

Whatever the fates had sent her here for, it was close.

When the thug saw who waited, his tone perked up. "Boss has been waiting all day for you. Quite a lucky find you have there."

Justice walked past the young man whose turn it was to offer up his prize for cash. He still had pimples and hadn't yet managed to fill in the patches in his scraggly beard. A baseball hat hid his eyes, but his eager grin was unmistakable. "When you're as good as I am, you don't need luck."

"She'd better be the real thing, or that fucking grin will be missing a few teeth."

"She is," said the young man, all confidence and swagger.

It wasn't until Justice passed him that she saw what it was he'd brought to sell the entitled scumbag Chester Gale.

A little girl trailed behind the punk, sucking her thumb. She was too old for the habit, maybe four or five, but the stark look of fear on her tear-stained face made the childish trait completely forgivable.

Her blond hair was a mess, and her big blue eyes stared up at Justice in a silent plea for help.

The buzzing in the back of Justice's skull turned to a full-out roar. Jet engines and rock concerts screamed through her head, nearly driving her to her knees.

This child was the real reason she was here trading trinkets with men who were best used for fertilizer.

Justice was no hero. She had done a lot of shitty things in the ten years of her life she could remember. Chances were she'd done even more before that. But never once had she looked the other way while entitled assholes traded money for terrified children, screaming fates or not.

She couldn't stand the thought of adding that to her long list of sins.

Instincts took over before a coherent plan could form in her mind. As she passed the man, she scooped up the little girl in one arm while pulling Reba from her waistband.

The child let out a startled squeak, then started to wail. The punk who'd been ready to sell her spun around to see what had happened to his prize. The armed guard pulled his weapon and aimed it at Justice.

Before the barrel of his handgun had steadied, Justice fired a round in the center of his meaty head.

Red pulp blasted open the door behind him so hard it banged against the wall. The child-stealing fucker in front of her had his own weapon in hand now.

She acted without hesitation. The only thought in her mind now was how to get her and the girl out of here alive. Whoever else had to die to make that happen, well, just add them to the pile of bodies in her wake.

Justice squeezed the trigger of her Glock again just as the punk fired.

She felt a punch of force shove her back, but no pain. It would come. Soon. Been there, done that. She had only a few seconds before it did.

The little girl screamed louder. A ragged, gaping hole appeared under the punk's left eye as Justice's bullet tore through flesh and bone. He crumpled where he stood, like a puppet with the strings cut.

She backed up toward the exit. Her car was parked outside. All she had to do was make it that far. Ricardo, her beloved Maserati, would do the rest of the heavy lifting.

The armed thug previously in hiding had come out to do his job. Only a couple of seconds had passed since she'd snatched the kid, but it was long enough for him to have steadied his aim.

"Stop," he said, his tone as cold and still as a frozen pond.

She didn't waste her breath. Nothing she could say would change what he was about to do.

Justice spun around so that she was between the gun and the girl, then sprinted out the door, toward Ricardo.

Another round slammed into her body, hitting just above her hip. Her leg seized up for only a split second, but it was long enough to send her sprawling onto the sidewalk.

Late afternoon sunlight hit her face. Cold winter air swirled around her head. The little girl had rolled away and was screaming even louder. The building was by itself, separated from the nearby restaurants and gas stations—likely by design. Traffic slid by a few hundred feet away, but if anyone noticed what was happening, she couldn't tell. No one blew their horn or screamed for someone to call the police.

Blood wet her clothes now, and the pain of her wounds began to slip in between the cracks in her adrenaline. She'd been shot before. She knew what was coming.

But not yet. Just a few seconds more…

The door had shut behind her—a single, thin sheet of glass between her and the next round aimed her way.

The armed guard stepped close enough to the door that she could see his thick head and shoulders through the tinted glass. Her hands were shaking now, but Reba would make up in power what Justice lacked in aim. Her target was big and close.

And a fraction of a second too slow.

Justice fired again. Glass shattered. She didn't pause long enough to see if her aim had been true. If it wasn't, she was already as good as dead.

She scrambled to her feet, grabbed the little girl's arm, and bolted for her car on unsteady legs.

Ricardo welcomed her with a heated embrace. Sun-warmed leather seats cushioned her fall as she tumbled in behind the wheel. The little girl was unceremoniously pulled in over Justice's lap, dumped over the console, and into the passenger's seat.

"Get on the floor," Justice barked, just as the first wave of searing pain washed over her.

She gritted her teeth and punched the ignition on her Maserati.

Blood welled from her abdomen. More slickened the seat beneath her. Already she could feel her strength fading.

She had to get the girl away from here—as far away as she could manage. Nothing else mattered, not even the lingering itch at the base of her skull compelling her to do whatever the fates demanded of her next.

As far as she was concerned, the fates could go fuck themselves.

With one hand pressed against her abdomen to slow the bleeding, she gunned the engine and tore out into early rush hour traffic.

The little girl cowered on the floorboards, sucking her thumb between snuffling sobs. Spit and snot leaked down her face to mix with her terrified tears.

"Everything is okay now," Justice lied in a ragged tone. "What's your name?"

The pain had reached its zenith and was currently burning through her guts like fire.

The child stared up with big, blue eyes and mumbled something around her thumb.

"Take your thumb out and try again." Justice did her best to keep her voice gentle, but she knew the pain had given it a growly edge.

The girl did as she was told. Her pudgy hand gripped the seat and left behind a smear of slobber across the handstitched leather. "Pepper."

"Where are your parents?"

Pepper's face melted into the kind of agony only death could create. "He hurt mommy." Once the words left her mouth, the thumb went right back in and she started rocking as she cried.

Justice didn't dare ask about the girl's father. She didn't have the strength to torture the poor kid all over again.

The itch at the base of her skull began to spread and strengthen.

Whatever it was that made Justice do the things she did had the worst timing. Didn't the fucking fates know that she was bleeding, hoping to outrun armed killers, and toting a child who was probably a recent orphan? A child who had some value to a man who valued only a very narrow subset of objects?

Ancient, magical objects.

How the hell did a kid barely out of diapers qualify?

Justice had no idea.

Another wave of dizziness spun her head, and she knew she was running out of time. She briefly thought about going to a hospital but knew the fates wouldn't allow it. They never had.

She was going to have to keep going and hope Ricardo kept her from running into any of the cars crowding around her.

The itch began to burn. She was going the wrong way. Wherever it was she was being compelled to go, it wasn't north.

Justice took the next exit heading east. As soon as she did, the burning at the base of her skull faded. Her guts still felt like they were being ripped out through her navel, but even that was dying down to a manageable level.

It was her growing weakness that scared her.

If she ran off the road and killed the girl or passed out and left her stranded on the highway, things could go from bad to worse.

Miles slid by in a foggy daze as Justice tried to get her shaken brain to come up with a plan.

Pepper had worn herself out crying and was now curled up on the floor, asleep. Sundown was coming soon, and with it, all the snarly, fanged Synestryn would come out to play. She was bleeding enough to know they'd come sniffing around for a bite.

She had to get rid of Pepper before that happened. But who could she trust to take the kid off her hands?

Ronan's beautiful face entered her mind as if begging her to reach out to him. Instead, she shoved the image away with a feral snarl.

Even if she did want to contact him—which she didn't—there was no way she could. It's not like she had his phone number. He was the one who chased her, not the other way around.

And if she did find him, then what? No way was she handing a child over to a man who drank blood.

She wished she had a friend—just one single person she could trust.

But friends weren't something Justice could have. The one time she'd tried had taught her that lesson so painfully, she'd never tried again. The only things she could count on were her gun and her ride. So she, Reba and Ricardo were going to go find Pepper some help before she ended up in a place worse than whatever Chester Gale had in store for her.

Justice searched her mind for a solution, but her head was foggy and her body was fading. The bleeding had slowed, but she couldn't tell if that was because her wounds had begun to close, or if she was almost out of blood.

Thoughts of Ronan filled her thoughts again, and this time she was too weak to shove them away.

She could feel him somewhere east of here. She didn't understand how she could tell where he was—maybe because he'd drank so much of her blood a few weeks ago—but his presence was like a glow against her skin she could feel but not see.

To him, she was prey. Food. And yet she couldn't seem to get him out of her mind. How screwed up was that?

Finally, when she was too dizzy to drive straight, even with Ricardo's help, she exited the highway at a rest stop miles from anywhere interesting.

Two semis sat in the upper lot for truckers. The lower area was for smaller vehicles, and completely empty. Justice parked near the bathroom and simply breathed as she waited for someone trustworthy to stop. No way was she handing Pepper over to a couple of truckers who might or might not be involved in human trafficking. It was better to wait for a family with kids or an elderly couple to come by and hand over Pepper to them.

Justice was almost out of strength to do anything. If she moved, she was sure she'd start bleeding again. Based on the puddle at her feet, she didn't think she could lose much more.

Pepper was still asleep on the floor, curled up in a space the perfect size for her tiny body. Now that she wasn't screaming, she was adorable, with soft, blond curls and chubby cheeks.

Whatever those scumbags were going to do with her, Justice was glad she'd stopped it. Maybe saving a little girl wasn't her usual job, but she didn't care. If saving an innocent child was her last act on this spinning ball of dirt, then so be it.

That was the thought that filled her mind as the last of her strength faded and the lights winked out.

CHAPTER TWO

Ronan jolted awake, certain that something was wrong.

The sun hadn't yet set, leaving him weak and groggy. He searched the small, windowless basement he'd taken shelter in for signs of what had startled him but found nothing. He was alone. There were no sounds of intruders or smells of danger nearby. He was as alone now as he had been when he'd laid down at sunrise to rest.

He lay motionless on a narrow cot and concentrated on the deep feeling of unease that rippled through his limbs. Had it been just a rare dream? Was this lingering wrongness some strange figment of his sleeping mind?

He waited to see if the feeling would dissipate, but instead, it grew stronger, deeper.

The need to get up and move buffeted against his left side, as if whatever had caused his unease was screaming at him from the direction of the setting sun.

The minutes ticked by in agonizing slowness. His nearly constant hunger swelled as his usual feeding time neared.

Normally he slept through the worst of the day's hunger, but he was awake now, too rattled to fall back asleep.

Just a few more minutes. That was all he had to endure before he could leave and go hunting for the blood he needed to sustain him. He'd already located a young couple nearby who contained the traces of ancient magic he craved.

His work on Project Lullaby had brought these two together only a few months ago. They were madly in love, and with a bit of effort on Ronan's part, they would soon be expecting their first child—another life to keep him and his kind from suffering the slow death of starvation.

The idea that the couple would never have met without him, and that he was taking away their freedom to reproduce as they saw fit, no longer bothered him. There was a time when he would have been loathe to interfere with the free will of blooded humans, but that day was long gone, right along with the deaths of too many of his kind.

The three races of Sentinels were at war with Synestryn, and Ronan was far too pragmatic to concern himself with what a handful of humans wanted or didn't want. If he and his kind died off, the Theronai would soon fall. Once their swords were no longer protecting humankind from the influx of hungry demons who used humans as food, then petty concerns like whether or not a single couple fell in love or had a child in their own time would hardly matter.

Everyone had their place in this war, like it or not. Ronan's was to ensure that the bloodlines his Sanguinar brothers and sisters needed to survive were strengthened. Cara's and Doug's job was to have as many children as possible. In exchange, Ronan would make sure that their family lived long, healthy, happy lives.

Whether or not they agreed to this arrangement was irrelevant. At least that's what Ronan told himself whenever his dying conscience let out one of its few remaining gasps of outrage over his meddling. He wished the thing would just die and leave him in peace. Manipulating lives was so much easier without it.

Another flutter of urgency buffeted his side, and this time, he knew it was no dream.

Someone was in trouble—someone whose blood bond to him was strong.

Ronan forced his weak body to move and retrieve his cell phone from his pocket. It shifted around inside his too-loose jeans before his cold, clumsy fingers could corner it.

He looked at the screen. No calls. No texts. He had email, but it was all offers for products promising harder, longer erections and people wanting to give him millions in exchange for his bank account number.

He opened the app that showed him the location of all known Theronai, Slayers and Sanguinar near him. Nicholas had created the program to help foster cooperation between the races, but with so many people now at Dabyr, there were only a handful of Sentinels still outside of the fortress walls.

Ronan saw only three dots on the map that spanned from the eastern edge of Kansas City to the western side of Columbia. Two of them were moving along I-70, east of him, and the other was curving along rural roads, heading north toward home. All of them were Theronai, and none of them had called to ask for help. Not only that, but none of them were to his west.

But someone he knew was.

Justice.

He'd fed from her recently, though the savage way he'd ripped at her skin and sucked out her blood was far too violent an act to be considered merely feeding.

He'd brutalized her. Used her. She'd saved his life and he'd nearly killed her in the process.

No wonder she'd kept well out of his reach since that night.

He could feel her presence glowing and warm, like he imagined the forbidden sun would feel against his skin. At dawn, when he lay down to wait out the weakness of day in some dark hole, he would position himself so that he was broadside to her and able to absorb as much of her warm presence as possible.

She was always on the move, constantly running toward something or possibly away from him. He'd tracked her for weeks, and rarely gotten closer than a dozen miles.

She wasn't hampered by daylight. She rarely stayed in one place for more than a few hours. He wasn't even sure she slept.

What he did know was that every night when he woke, she would always be moving away from him, her head start ensuring that he could never quite catch up with her before he was once again trapped by the sun, weak and exhausted.

Except today. That thread of her that remained inside of his cells, connecting them, was still. She wasn't moving. She wasn't running from him. In fact, she was closer than she'd ever been before at this time of day—close enough he might be able to find her. Touch her.

The mere idea sent a heady rush of excitement sweeping through his wasted body. It was too good to be true, and perhaps even another trap that would leave him bleeding and unconscious like the last time he'd met her.

In a sudden wave of fear, he realized that the deep stirring of wrongness he'd felt was coming from the same direction as her. It was *her* blood that had woken him.

Justice was in trouble.

Panic set in and stole what little warmth he possessed. His body was slow and stiff, but he forced his thin limbs to move and push himself upright.

He couldn't see the sun, but he could feel it sucking power from him and sapping his strength.

How much longer until sunset? He wasn't sure. Only minutes, but too many. Too fucking many.

He managed to stand upright, but the effort left him shaking. He hadn't fed well since Garet a few days ago, and his work sapped his strength.

There was always someone who needed healing—the injured and sick—and he was responsible for the health of a lot of innocent children. He'd helped create them, but they were still too small to repay him in blood.

One day they would be fully grown and become a source of power, but for now, they were a fragile crop not yet ready to harvest. Until they were, Ronan and his kind had to suffer in the hopes that their future would be better than their present.

He only hoped that in the meantime his weakness didn't cost someone their life.

Hurry!

A sense of urgency flapped around his head like raven wings and made his heart beat faster. He didn't have time to wait for the sun to set. He had to move now.

On joints that felt old and brittle, Ronan climbed the basement stairs into the two-story house above. It was vacant—a safe house meant to serve as refuge for those who fought the war against Synestryn.

The wooden floors were scarred and gouged with use, but clean. The air smelled of disinfectant and the remains of a meal cooked days ago.

He'd made sure the curtains were drawn before he'd gone to sleep, but even the filtered sunset blazing against the western windows was too much for him to stand.

His eyes burned. Tears streamed down his cheeks. His skin seemed to shrivel as if looking for a place to hide.

If even one single ray of that light touched his bare skin, a Warden would be summoned and Ronan would be killed. There was no way he could fight one of those giant, crystalline warriors as weak as he was.

Each breath was a struggle, as if he were sucking in air through a mile-long straw. His lungs were tight and aching, and his heart raced in an effort to spread his weary blood through his body.

He stumbled on the leg of a kitchen chair and spilled to the cracked vinyl floor. It was cold and stole what little heat he had left.

Even the constant warmth coming from Justice seemed to fade.

That was the thought that got him moving again, despite his pain and weakness. She might not like him. Hell, she might even hate him. But she was the only hope he had in an otherwise hopeless life.

He barely knew her, but if anything happened to her, he wasn't sure he'd survive it.

He needed her blood, her power. He needed her warmth. He needed *her*.

It took several more tries before Ronan was able to get back on his feet.

His van was parked in a garage that had been added to the century-old house a few decades ago. The space was small, but he'd managed to cram the van in and rush inside just as the first rays of sunrise had peeked above the eastern horizon.

Small windows in the east-facing garage door let in the golden glow of sunset, but nothing more. No direct rays from the west could touch him here. He was safe. Weak, but safe. And once he got behind the wheel of his van, the magically-enhanced windows would make sure he was protected from Wardens, if not weakness.

He hit the button to raise the garage door but would have no way to lower it once he pulled out his van. He'd call a gerai to come secure the house later, but now his complete focus was on dragging himself the last few feet to his ride.

Climbing up into the high vehicle was exhausting. His loose clothes drooped on his frame as if he were no more than skin-covered bones. A deep, constant ache thrummed in his chest now, but he couldn't tell if it was his heartbeat or his instincts begging him to hurry.

Justice's glow was fading fast.

He lurched out of the garage into the last few blinding rays of sunlight. He wasn't sure how he managed to steer onto the gravel road through the stinging tears blurring his vision, but he was speeding away toward the closest highway, a trail of dust billowing behind him as the last tendrils of light were swallowed by the rolling hills in the west.

With the remains of the toxic sunlight fading, his strength returned, and with it, more fear.

She wasn't dead. That was the thought that kept him sane. Whatever had happened to her had left her still and weak, but she wasn't dead.

Each mile that passed seemed to take a year. He broke every speed limit, uncaring about the consequences. His van wasn't sexy, but it had been designed to be a workhorse, carrying the weight of tradesmen and all their heavy tile, carpet or tools. With only a small amount of medical equipment and supplies in back, all that power went into speed. He rushed onto the interstate and into the trailing end of rush hour traffic between Kansas City and Columbia.

With a brutal push of compulsion, he forced human drivers to get out of his way. Even the highway patrolman he passed gave him plenty of room as Ronan shoved the man's mind full of an image of flashing ambulance lights and sirens where the speeding van had been.

Even though he grew closer to Justice, he didn't feel the blood bond they shared getting stronger. It was as though she were getting weaker at the same rate he got closer to her.

He was going so fast, he missed the rest stop exit. It wasn't until he felt her presence sliding past him that he realized where she was.

He turned hard, into the wide, weedy median, then crossed oncoming traffic and all their blaring, angry horns to slew onto the exit ramp.

When he saw the sleek, red Maserati, he knew it was hers. She had an affinity for speed, and there was no question where he would find her.

Ronan parked beside her car and jumped out of his van without bothering to shut off the engine. It took only seconds to run to her door, but those last few feet seemed to stretch out like an eternity.

· Her head was slumped sideways at an awkward angle. Her loose, black curls obscured her face. Still, he knew it was her. If he'd seen only a single strand of her hair or one inch of her caramel colored skin, he would have known her.

She was his. She didn't want to be, but that changed nothing. He didn't know how he knew that she was meant for him, but every cell in his body screamed the truth.

And if he lost her, there would never be another woman like her, no matter how many more centuries he lived.

Her posture was limp and wrong. Not asleep, but unconscious.

Her engine was running, but the door was locked.

"Justice," he said, filling her name with a strong compulsion to respond.

She didn't, though he couldn't tell if it was because she couldn't, or because his power of compulsion didn't work on her. It never had.

Without hesitation, he slammed his pointy elbow into the glass. The window broke into blocky, sticky bits that glittered in her hair like snowflakes.

A child's terrified scream assaulted him, and it was only then that he realized that Justice wasn't alone.

Curled up on the floor on the passenger's side was a little, blond girl. Her mouth was stretched on a wail of fear, and her blue eyes were just as wide. Blood smeared her clothing but didn't soak it the way Justice's clothes were soaked.

"It's okay," he said in a low, gentle voice. "I'm not going to hurt you. Hush now."

This time, the gentle compulsion laced around his words worked.

The girl quieted suddenly, her cries turning to strangled sobs and little sniffs.

"Are you hurt?" he asked, his power urging her to respond truthfully.

The child shook her head and sucked her thumb. She looked scared, but unhurt.

Justice wasn't as lucky.

The smell of blood rose out of the sports car. Lots of blood. Rich, intoxicating blood filled with magic and power.

Ronan's fangs lengthened, and the hunger in his belly bloomed into a ravenous pain. A snarl escaped his throat before he could stop it, which made the child's soggy sobs grow louder.

He ignored her, jerked the door open and crouched to inspect Justice's wounds.

Blood soaked her shirt and pooled on the floor beneath her seat. He could hear her pulse, weak and too fast as her heart struggled to keep oxygen flowing through her empty veins.

She didn't have much blood left to spare, but he had no

choice but to take more. He was too hungry and weak in this state to do anything but watch her die.

Before he could waste seconds she didn't have, he brought her wrist to his mouth and bit deep.

Only a few drops. As powerful as she was, that was all he needed to jumpstart his system. At least that's what he told himself.

But the second her sweet, potent blood hit his tongue, he knew a few drops would never be enough. He could drink an ocean of her power and still want more.

His chest thickened with muscle. His scrawny arms regained their natural shape, growing as strong and healthy as they had been in his youth. Clothes that had been baggy stretched to fit perfectly, and all the weakness and lethargy of starvation disappeared.

He became a mindless animal, consuming her sweet elixir in heavy, loud gulps. It was only when he felt her heart flutter that he realized just how far he'd gone.

She was on the brink of death, hovering on the razor-thin line between this life and the next. Even one more drink, and he feared the damage would be irreversible—Justice, gone from this world forever.

That was the thought that caged the hungry animal side of him behind thick, sturdy bars, clawing and biting to get free.

He willed the puncture wounds in her wrist closed, then sent part of his essence into her body to find the source of her bleeding.

She'd been shot twice. The bullets were still lodged in her flesh. One had chipped away a fragment of hip bone. The other had nicked the blood supply flowing to her kidney. That was where most of the blood was coming from.

Ronan gathered his power and sent it out into her to mend her torn flesh. He shoved the bullets from her skin and healed the damage from the inside out. He fused that chip of bone back in place and stayed hovering inside of her to make sure he hadn't missed anything.

As soon as the damage was repaired, he sped the process

of replenishing her blood supply. She'd need fluids to make the magic work, but once he'd issued his demand to her cells, they would obey and keep doing so for days.

The warmth of her mind curled around him and lured him to go deeper, but he didn't dare. She was too weak, and he worried that if he started unraveling the mystery of who she was and where she'd come from, that he'd never stop.

He'd already violated her once. He wouldn't make the same mistake again.

When he was satisfied that her flesh was mended, he backed out of her body and into his own.

Normally, he was always relieved to return to his own flesh, but this time it was different. His own skin seemed colder, thinner. All he wanted was to be back inside her, basking in her warmth.

The child watched him with wide, untrusting eyes.

"What happened to her?" he asked.

"The bad men shot her."

"Why?"

Her pale brow wrinkled in confusion, as if Ronan were an idiot. "Because they're bad."

That was as good an explanation as any, and probably as much of one as he was going to get until Justice woke.

They couldn't wait here. The smell of her blood would draw demons to them. And she needed more medical attention than he could provide in this too-public rest stop. There weren't many people here, but there were a few truckers in the second parking lot, and plenty of traffic on the interstate. Some nosy driver could see something suspicious and come investigate at any moment. If that happened, Ronan would have to use the precious power he'd gained from Justice's blood to send them away with no memory of the event.

He didn't have enough strength to waste even a drop—not until he was sure Justice was going to be okay.

Ronan picked up Justice's limp body. A bloody paper sack fell out of her back pocket, but he didn't stop to see what was in it. He set her in the back of his van on top of a narrow, waterproof mattress. This wasn't the first time he'd had a bloody patient to tend, and cleanup was far easier when one took a bit of precaution.

Her beautiful face was lifeless and slack. The hot vitality she normally exuded was gone, leaving her looking far too young and helpless—too weak—which didn't suit her at all.

He couldn't let her die. No matter what it took, he was going to nurse her back to health until she was strong enough to battle monsters singlehandedly again.

Maybe this time she wouldn't bash his head in with a flashlight just so she could escape his company.

He looked at the terrified child and offered her a smile. "Come with me. Everything is going to be okay now." He powered the words with a trace of reassurance and a desire to trust him.

The last thing he needed was for the child to run off covered in smears of Justice's blood. Not only would she draw human attention he didn't want, she'd also draw the attention of any hungry demons in the area.

The child got out of the car and came around to stand beside him.

"Get in and sit down," he said.

She did as he asked.

Ronan closed the van's door and started an IV to feed Justice the fluids she so desperately needed. He fastened thick woven straps over her body to keep her from rolling around, and to make sure that if she woke, she wouldn't fling herself out into traffic just to get away from him. Once that was done he moved Justice's overnight bag from her car into his.

Ronan called Dabyr as he wiped off his hands and pulled a clean shirt from the store of clothing he kept in the van. Nicholas, an unbound Theronai and all-around tech guru, was manning the phones.

"I need someone to come fetch a Maserati," Ronan said as he stripped off his bloody coat and shirt.

"Why? Did you kill a speed demon?" Nicholas's deep voice lilted with good humor. After all the man had been through, he'd managed to hold onto the core part of himself that could still laugh.

Ronan had no idea how he managed such a magical feat.

"I found Justice," he said as he wiped the blood from his long, black leather coat as well as a few smudges on his chest where it had soaked through his shirt.

"The concept, or the woman you've been chasing after for weeks?"

"The woman. She's injured. Lots of blood. Public place. I need to get her away from here before any demons show up."

Nicholas's tone went serious. "I see your location. I'll send Slade and Vance that way now. Leave the keys."

"But they're human."

"I know. But Joseph has ordered all the sword arms to stay close to home until the babies are born. He's not taking any chances with a surprise attack."

Nika's child was the first offspring of a Theronai couple to be born in two centuries. The baby was due any day. Iain and Jackie's child would come soon after. No one wanted to take any risks with either mother or the children. Nearly every fighter available was poised inside Dabyr, ready to defend the newborns with their lives.

"I understand," Ronan said. "But there's blood. I had to break the window to reach Justice, and it's only a matter of time before demons smell it."

Nicholas grunted in agreement. "I'll make sure the boys know that they need to proceed with caution. They've both been training a lot and aren't half-bad with a sword."

"They're still human. The car isn't worth their lives."

"Seeing as how they're young twenty-somethings and said car is a Maserati, I'm not sure they'd agree, but I'll give them a stern warning."

"Thank you."

"Are you coming home?" Nicholas asked.

"As soon as Justice is stable. And I'll be bringing a child as well."

"A child?"

Ronan pulled on the clean shirt and buttoned it. "I don't know who she is or why Justice has her, but until I do, I'll keep the girl close."

"Good luck. Safe travels."

Ronan hung up.

He caught the mistrustful gaze of the little girl. She sat on the floor by Justice's head, petting her curls as if she were a beloved puppy.

Ronan stretched out his arm toward her. "Take my hand," he ordered with a faint wisp of compulsion.

The child put her chubby fingers in his, and as soon as she did, he sent a thin tendril of himself winging through her limb and into her mind.

The blood covering her clothes wasn't hers. She had been terrorized, but not physically harmed. She'd seen her mother die, though she had no understanding of what death meant. She'd been forcefully taken by a man with blurry features under a baseball hat. He'd shouted at her and scared her. She remembered something about him telling her she had to be good on their trip, that he was taking her somewhere fun.

Even at the tender age of four, she still hadn't believed the killer.

Ronan couldn't figure out where the young man had taken her or why, but as soon as the child's memory lit on Justice's beautiful face, she'd thought she was meeting a princess.

The girl was jerked away bodily by the princess. Then there was more gunfire and screaming. The child was shoved into a car. After that, she saw nothing until the sound of breaking glass woke her.

Whoever she was, Ronan wasn't going to learn why she was here until Justice woke.

"You're going to come with me now," he told her gently. "I'll make sure the bad men can't find you again. Buckle up. We're going to take the princess somewhere safe."

The child nodded and did as she was told.

Ronan left the bloody Maserati behind and merged onto the highway headed west.

The little girl had buckled herself into the passenger's seat, since there were none in the open back of the van. He didn't know if she was big enough to be riding up here without a booster seat, but it was the best he could manage under the circumstances.

Her little feet stuck out straight. One of her sparkly pink shoes was missing, the other untied.

"I'm Ronan. What's your name?"

"Pepper."

"Is that your last name or your first?"

"Pepper Louise Sullivan. That's all my names, but don't say them."

"Why not?"

"Because it will make you mad. Mama always gets mad when she says all my names."

A twitch of a smile played about his mouth. He checked the rearview mirror to glance at Justice.

Blood smeared her chin. Her smooth skin was waxy and sallow. Even so, she was still the most beautiful woman—human or otherwise—he'd ever seen.

He wanted to stare at her and drink her in, but Pepper pulled his attention back to the road.

"How many times can Mama die?" the girl asked.

Ronan glanced at her in confusion. "What do you mean?"

"I can die three times in my game before I have to wait to wake up. How long will Mama have to wait to wake up?"

His heart squeezed hard, leaving a dull ache in his chest. This poor girl had seen her mother die but didn't realize it was forever.

He was going to have to explain it to her soon, but for now he'd let her hold onto her childish hope that her life as she knew it would somehow miraculously keep going on as it had been. These were the last few moments of peace she'd have before reality crushed her spirit under its heel, and he was going to let her have them.

"Do you know why you're here, Pepper?"

"Because you told me to get in. Your van is bigger than

Mama's. Where did your chairs go?"

"I'm like a doctor," he said. "This is my doctor's office. I had to take out the seats to make room."

She wrinkled her nose at that. "You don't look like a doctor. Where are your glasses?"

"We don't all wear glasses."

"Oh. Ok." She wiggled her sparkly shoe.

He drove a few miles down the road and parked outside a nearly abandoned outlet mall.

It was fully dark now, with only the orange glow of security lights slipping through his front windows. The back of the van was lightless out of necessity so he could sleep in here if there was no other shelter to be found.

"After this, can we have dinner?" Pepper asked.

"You're hungry?"

She nodded. "The bad man said I was loud so I couldn't have lunch."

Ronan found a granola bar and a bottle of water and gave them to her. "I need to help Justice now. You stay in your seat and eat, okay?"

She nodded and ripped the foil wrapper open with her teeth. As she did, her sleeve shifted and he saw a ring-shaped birthmark on her wrist.

Shock rippled through him, but he kept it from showing on his face. Years of keeping secrets had taught him to control his expression as well as the best poker players on the planet.

This tiny child was a female Theronai—a rare and precious creature that had the power to save countless lives.

If she lived long enough to do so.

At least now he knew why bad men wanted her. In the wrong hands, she could be a formidable weapon. In worse hands, she was simply a rich source of food and power.

And in the worst hands…there were unspeakable things that could happen to a girl her age if the demons got their claws on her. Ronan had seen it before.

Little Tori had been taken when she was eight and fed toxic blood that altered her body so she would be capable of carrying the offspring of Synestryn. She'd spent a decade in the dark, poisoned, starved, tortured and raped. When his people finally found her, she was no longer a sweet, little girl. She was violent, bloodthirsty.

His kind had spent gallons of precious blood in an effort to fix her. Cleanse her body. Heal her mind. Every effort failed because there wasn't enough left of the girl she'd once been to save. She was twisted and dark. Irrevocably broken.

She'd been sent away to another world for her own safety as well as that of the innocents living at Dabyr.

As far as Ronan was concerned, even that distance wasn't far enough.

He looked at Pepper and made himself a silent promise to keep this child from the same fate. Whatever it took.

"You will be my lookout," he told her. "If you see anyone coming toward us, tell me right away."

She nodded around a mouthful of granola.

Ronan slipped into the back of the van to check on Justice.

Her pulse was stronger and slower, thanks to the fluids. She was going to need more, but it was a start.

He laid a hand on her forehead and sought out her mind.

The feel of her skin under his fingers was its own kind of magic. How often had he dreamed about being close enough to her to touch her? She was so smooth and soft on the outside, which warred with her prickly temper and complete lack of trust.

He would have been content to spend the night tracing his fingers over her skin, but that wasn't going to heal her. He had to focus, no matter how much he ached to get lost in the smooth softness of her body.

Ronan gathered himself and sent a trickle of himself into her mind to check on her.

Lethargy and confusion still swamped her thoughts, but she was drifting quickly upward, out of the thick swamp of unconsciousness.

He needed to get rid of the bloody clothes—hers and Pepper's. Until he did, the scent could draw countless nasties to them. And while he was now strong enough to take on a small number of demons, he didn't want to waste the energy he needed to heal in battle.

He undid the restraints holding her on the mattress, unlaced her leather combat boots and pulled them from her feet. They went into a black trash bag, along with her bloody socks. He tried to keep a professional distance as he unbuttoned her jeans and slid them down her long, curvy legs, but the task proved to be impossible.

She was simply too beautiful. He couldn't put her in the untouchable category of patient, but rather she stayed firmly fixed in place as his deepest, darkest fantasy.

He eased off her jacket then extended a claw and sliced away her shirt, rather than jostle her to remove it over her head. Before he could strip the bloody fabric out from under her, she opened her eyes and grabbed his hand.

Pale, silvery-green eyes stared up at him in shock and anger. "Don't."

Her voice was weak, but the look of challenge she gave him was anything but.

"It's okay. I'm just getting rid of the blood," he said, flicking a glance to the front seat where Pepper sat munching on her snack. "The demons will smell it and come for her."

Justice's grogginess seamed to fade from one instant to the next. She sat up and took in her surroundings in a sweeping glance.

"Where are we?"

"Not far from the rest stop where you passed out."

"I need to go. Take me back to my car. Now."

"You're in no shape to drive. Or make demands."

Her grip on his wrist tightened. Her voice was quiet but filled to the brim with the promise of violence. "Listen, bloodsucker. Either drive me back to my ride, or I'll shove you out in the dark and take yours. Your choice."

"I saved your life, and healed your wounds, and this is how you thank me?" he asked.

She closed her eyes and let out a long breath. The grip on

his shirt loosened and she leaned back against the wall of the van. "You should have let me die. I was so close to escaping this bullshit."

The child stared at them with wide eyes. Her mouth went slack and a chunk of oats fell from the corner.

Ronan gave her a reassuring smile. "It's just a game we play. Don't worry. She's not really mad." That last bit was laced with a strand of compulsion meant to ease Pepper's nerves and calm her fear.

She nodded and started chewing again.

He jerked his hand free from Justice's grasp and pulled the light-blocking curtains closed. It wouldn't do much to block sound, but at least the child didn't have to see the defeated look on her princess-turned-rescuer's face.

"You don't mean that," Ronan told Justice. "Tell me what's going on. Maybe I can help."

Her breasts swelled beneath her modest bra as she sucked in a resigned breath. "There's nothing anyone can do."

"Why do you have the child?"

"Hell if I know. I haven't been told yet."

"Told by whom?"

She closed her eyes. "No idea."

"Where did you find her?"

"Some asshole was selling her to some guys I know."

"Selling her?"

"Yeah. I knew they were lowlife scumbags, but I didn't know how low. Guess I'll need to kill Chester Gale now. No way I can let him live." That last part was delivered with the kind of sigh meant to accompany a distasteful chore, like mopping up a after a leaking toilet, or cleaning up the mess left from a broken trash bag.

"Who are they? What did they want with her?"

She let go of his wrist and waved a hand. "Doesn't matter. I'll deal with it."

"You're in no shape to deal with anything. And we really do need to get rid of those bloody clothes. You need to change."

Ronan cleaned his hands on a wet wipe, then pushed her overnight bag toward her.

"You brought my clothes?" Her tone was skeptical, mistrusting.

"Would you rather wear mine?"

Instead of answering his question, she motioned toward her arm and the tube feeding fluids into it. "You should know that human drugs won't work on me."

The idea that she knew that bizarre fact posed more questions than it answered.

"There are no drugs in the bag. Just saline," he said.

She started picking at the tape holding her IV in place. "So this raging headache I have going is all my own, huh?"

"Dehydration. It will pass if you leave the IV in. So will some of your weakness."

Another heavy sigh burst out of her and she slumped back against the wall, eyes closing.

Ronan couldn't help but stare at her body. Even with the bloody bra and panties, even with smears of sticky rust staining her smooth, dark skin, she was stunning.

She was all long and lean, like a predatory cat. Smooth, slender lines curved into sinuous shapes that drew his eye to the swell of her breasts and the shadows between her thighs. Curving, feminine muscles hugged her frame, lending another layer of beauty and intrigue.

She was built like a warrior maiden of old, hard where she had to be and soft everywhere else. She bore a few scars to mar the perfection of her skin—including puncture wounds at her neck that he'd inflicted but had never been given the chance to heal—but even those he found alluring. They made him want to delve into her mind and bathe in her past, to see all the things she'd faced that made her the woman she was now.

He didn't know why he was drawn to her so completely, but since she'd saved his life a few weeks ago and fed him her blood, he'd spent every waking moment working to find her again so he could say what needed to be said.

"I am so sorry I hurt you, Justice. There's no excuse for savaging you like I did, but I promise you it will never happen again."

As he gave his vow, a heavy, comforting weight settled over him and bound him to his word.

She cracked open one pale green eye and studied him. "That was a stupid promise to make."

"Not stupid. Necessary. I'd take back what I did to you if I could, but—"

"You were starving," she said matter-of-factly. "And I was food." A heavy sigh, then a mumbled, "Fucking fates. They're the ones to blame. They sent me to you that night to be your meal, though I guess to be fair, I let it happen."

"Fates?" he asked.

She waved a hand. *Nothing to see here. Move along.*

Justice nodded to the IV. "Can I take this out yet?"

"I don't suggest it. That's the fastest way barring magic to get you back in fighting form."

"Fine. I'll leave it in until we get back to Ricardo."

"Who's he?"

"My Maserati."

"It's probably already gone."

She sat up, expression tight with anger, fists tighter. "Gone?"

"I had to break a window to reach you. Blood was everywhere. I couldn't leave it sitting there to draw demons, so I had some gerai come get it."

"I don't know who or what gerai are, but they'd better be damn careful not to hurt my baby."

Ronan wasn't sure how careful two young twenty-somethings would be behind the wheel of a car like that, but he decided to keep that worry to himself. "I'm sure your precious car will be fine. If not, I will replace it."

"Where are they taking him?"

"Him?"

"Ricardo," she said, as if here were brain damaged. "Where are they taking my car?"

"Dabyr."

"Your home? Was this all some elaborate trick to get me behind the walls where you could hold me prisoner?"

If only Ronan had met her under better circumstances, if only he hadn't hurt her, used her.

But he had, and now he had to pay the price for his actions, no matter how little control he'd had over them at the time.

He gathered up his patience and forced it into his tone. "Dabyr isn't a prison. It's a safe place. A stronghold against the Synestryn. You'll be safe there."

Another wave of weariness crossed her features and she sagged. "I don't get to stay in one place. Already the fates are nagging at me to get moving."

"What are you talking about?"

"Wish I knew," she said with a longsuffering sigh. "All I know is that I get this itch to do things. If I don't obey, then the itch turns into a burn, and that turns into searing pain. I've learned my lesson enough times to know that obedience is the only way to keep from suffering. So that's what I do."

"Which do you do? Obey or suffer?"

She let out a long sigh. "Depends on my mood."

Ronan had never heard of such a thing, but it sounded horrible. To never be in control of your own actions? To never be able to simply choose to be still? His life often sucked, but that, he couldn't imagine.

"And these fates?" he asked. "What do they want you to do now?"

She shrugged. "Who knows? All I know is that I need to get back to Ricardo so I can go wherever they want, whenever they want."

Ronan nodded. "Okay, then. I'll take you home, to Ricardo. Then we can figure out what needs to come next."

"You can't get involved," she said.

He kept his gaze on her eyes, rather than letting it float down to her sweet breasts, or the mysterious shadows at the cleft of her thighs.

It had been a long time since he'd had energy to waste on

wanting a woman, and he'd never wanted one the way he did Justice. Resisting the need to soak in the sight of her was almost more than he could stand.

"I already *am* involved. And until you're strong enough to go alone, I'll take you wherever you want."

"How do I know you won't turn vampire on me again?"

He flinched at the use of the derogatory term but kept his hatred of it to himself. "I gave you my word not to hurt you. If you know anything about our kind, then you know that's binding."

She studied him for a long time, as if sizing him up. Finally, she gave him a single nod. "We'll try it your way, but only because I'm too woozy to drive. But it's only fair to remind you that while you made a promise to me not to hurt me again, I didn't do the same. One wrong move, and I'll kill you as easily as I did the ten men before you. Understand?"

Ronan did, and for some reason he couldn't name, the defeated look on her face broke his heart.

CHAPTER THREE

Justice couldn't remember the last time she'd been this tired. Her whole body ached, and her joints felt like they were made out of spun sugar. One sudden move and she'd shatter.

She'd nearly died. She would have died if not for Ronan.

She wasn't sure if she should thank him for that or curse him.

The wall of his van held her weary body upright. The rumble of the highway beneath her was a familiar vibration but felt strange when she wasn't behind the wheel.

She hoped Ricardo was okay. She had a few more vehicles to serve as backup if something happened to him, but he was her favorite. The way he cupped her body and held her close while he cornered made it possible to pretend he cared, that he was her friend.

After a few minutes of gathering her strength, she pulled the curtains behind the front seats shut to give herself some privacy. Then she stripped out of her dirty underwear, scrubbed the caked blood away with a wad of baby-scented wet wipes, and dressed in clean jeans and a button-up shirt from her overnight bag. The IV was going to have to come out soon, but she was grateful for it now.

She didn't have the energy to drink anything and didn't think her sloshy stomach would let her do so even if she could.

That last mission had gone wrong. Goat-fuck wrong. And

now she had a little kid to deal with on top of everything else.

Maybe that's where the fates were sending her now—to a safe place for Pepper. That would be nice, if such a place existed.

Then again, with Justice's luck, wherever they were headed might be the intended end for the little girl's life— some snarling demon or sacrificial altar. There was simply no way to know how it would end until it did.

Justice promised herself that if the fates made her hand over the girl to a killer, she wouldn't watch the outcome. She'd turn her back and keep that sight out of her nightmares. She might not deserve that sliver of luxury after all the shit she'd done, but she'd fight and claw for it all the same.

The simple act of covering her naked ass and shoving the bloody mess of clothes and used wipes into a trash bag wore her out. She slumped back on the bare vinyl-covered mattress and simply breathed.

On the other side of the curtain, she could hear the steady drone of the little girl's voice as she asked a string of questions. Ronan's deep rumble was patient and kind, despite the fact that this interrogation went on for the better part of an hour.

He didn't seem like a monster now. He had once—the night she'd met him, all gaunt, starving and deranged. He'd been chained up, taped up and trussed like a Thanksgiving turkey. In the darkness of that basement where he'd been imprisoned for his own good, his blue eyes had literally glowed.

The eyes of a killer, a monster.

She couldn't forget that. Just because he had this strange pull on her, just because she always seemed to know where he was, didn't mean she should let her guard down. He may have promised not to do to her what he'd done before, but there were many ways to hurt someone besides drinking their blood.

Justice knew that all too well.

She checked Reba, who had miraculously ended up in the van—perhaps a peace offering from Ronan. She was all but empty, so Justice fed her the wicked Ranger-T rounds until she was full.

That made her feel better. More normal.

The van turned, and the itching in the back of Justice's skull woke up to tell her they were going the wrong way.

She pushed aside the thick, black curtains that separated the front and the back of the van. Four blue eyes hit her face— two big, innocent and round, two narrow and glowing.

"How do you feel?" Ronan asked.

"Fine," she lied as she knelt between the seats. "But we're going the wrong way. Ricardo is north of here."

"The road north ended. We'll jog east for a bit, then hit the county road that leads north, to Dabyr."

"They have ice cream there," Pepper added. "And books. Mama likes books."

The pained look that crossed Ronan's face mirrored her own worry. Pepper's mother was dead. If she hadn't been, she would have fought the man who'd stolen her. At the very least, she would have contacted the police if she'd lived. Amber alerts would have screeched through phones everywhere, warning the public to be on the lookout for a girl matching Pepper's description.

None of that had happened.

Justice couldn't bring herself to tell the girl the truth. She wasn't that strong.

The itching in the back of her skull intensified until Ronan turned left on a narrow blacktop road. There were no street lights this far out in the rolling rural countryside. A few deer looked their way, their eyes reflecting back shiny silver dots in the dark.

The forest was winter bare. The sky was thick with stars. The pavement sparkled under the brilliant white headlights. Inside the van was warm, but outside, it was cold enough to squeeze a few stray snowflakes out of the dry air.

Her coat was too bloody to wear. Pepper didn't have one, plus, her clothes were smeared with blood.

How the hell was Justice going to take care of a child, even long enough to take her wherever it was the fates demanded? She didn't know the first thing about kids.

Out of nowhere, a hidden memory swelled as it tried to surface. She went still, willing the thought to finish its journey and show her some lost sliver of her past.

Instead, as always, the sights and smells associated with the memory faded back into the black sea of her unknown history, leaving her aching for something she couldn't quite touch.

Ronan was watching her in the rearview mirror. His expression was one of speculation and curiosity.

"Are you going to tell me what just happened?" he asked.

"What are you talking about?"

"I saw the look of anticipation on your face. I smelled a surge of hope coming from you, followed by disappointment. Something happened, didn't it?"

"If it did, I can promise it was none of your business. You're just the cabbie."

He lifted a raven-black eyebrow at that. "I'm more to you than that, and you know it."

"Is he your boyfriend?" Pepper asked with a strange giggle, as if the idea was both hilarious and disgusting.

"No," Justice snapped a little too loudly. Then more gently, "He's…a friend."

"And a doctor," Pepper added with a nod. "But he doesn't wear glasses."

Ronan took another turn onto a narrow strip of road that passed through dense trees and brush. Several low evergreens had been planted in neat rows, obscuring what lay beyond even in the dead of winter. There was no street sign or indication that anything was here, but Justice could feel a hum of power all the same.

About a mile down this lane, a clearing opened to reveal a massive, brightly-lit structure made entirely out of stone and metal. Towering, ancient trees dotted the area to cast the manicured lawn into pools of shadow.

"This is Dabyr," Ronan said.

High stone walls wrapped all the way around the building, which looked like the bizarre love child of a castle and a sprawling hotel. The center section was several stories tall, with two huge wings jutting out from it to shield what was behind. Lights were on in several windows, but they were too far away for her to see more than a warm glow and movement inside.

Ronan rolled up to a metal gate and turned to face a camera. "I've got two guests. Please ask Joseph to meet me at the entrance from the garage with a change of clothes for a little girl, size four."

A light near the camera turned green and the thick bars blocking the entrance began to roll open. As soon as he was clear, the gates closed right behind them.

Justice studied the area, making note of the measures she'd have to take to bust out of here if the need arose. She couldn't see any obvious guns or weapons on the walls, but there were lots of cameras and plenty of big, serious men roaming the grounds. She didn't doubt for a second that each one of them was armed, even though she couldn't see any bulges under their coats.

As if reading her mind, Ronan said, "You're free to leave whenever you want. Those walls are to keep things out, not in."

"From the looks of it, you all are expecting a fight."

"We're just being careful," he said, though she could hear the lie in his tone.

For a moment, she wanted to know what was going on, but then she remembered that she didn't care. She wasn't going to be here long enough to care. All she was going to do was pick up Ricardo and maybe find Pepper a coat and shoes so she didn't freeze off any toes. A barefooted child in winter was the kind of thing that raised too many questions—questions Justice couldn't answer.

They pulled into a massive garage—the multi-level kind used at hotels and shopping malls. By her estimation, there were hundreds of cars here. Ronan parked a few slots down from where Ricardo sat, seemingly unharmed.

Two young men were scrubbing the interior. One was wringing out bloody suds into a five-gallon bucket, and the other was unwinding the hose of a shop vac on the driver's side.

The bag of saline dripping into her vein was empty, so she ripped out the IV. Ronan opened the side door just as a drop of blood welled from her arm.

A faint blue light hit her skin, and when she looked, she saw it was coming from his eyes.

He swallowed hard, then lifted his gaze from the blood to her face.

"May I?" he asked as he held out his hand.

A strange, soft, relaxed feeling washed over her as she stared back at him. He was such a handsome man, but that word was so insufficient to describe him, it was laughable. He wasn't just handsome, he was beautiful, perfectly formed, temptation incarnate. He was the stuff of fantasies, a walking shiver of pleasure and the answer to all the questions she was too afraid to ask.

Justice put her hand in his, and even though she knew the act was one of madness, she couldn't help but enjoy the way her skin felt against his.

He bent low over her arm. She didn't realize what he was going to do until she felt the wet heat of his tongue glide gently over her sensitive skin.

A powerful shiver raced through her and shook her to her core. Tingling warmth swept up her arm and lodged just under her heart. The next breath she took smelled spicy and sweet and gave her a rush of strength she so desperately needed.

She didn't know him—not really—but he was so familiar to her. She felt like she *should* know him, the same way she knew the texture of her hair gliding between her fingers, or the way her own voice sounded in her ears.

For a woman with no family, friends or ties, that feeling of familiarity was potent.

He straightened, and held her gaze again, only this time,

all she saw in his eyes was an odd combination of hunger and satisfaction.

"Can I have ice cream now?" Pepper asked from nearby.

Justice had all but forgotten the child was here, which only served to prove just how off her game she was. She was usually keenly aware of her surroundings and everyone in them, because there was no way to know who might want to kill her. Or who she'd have to kill.

His touch on her skin lingered. The tip of one finger slid over her skin in a light caress.

The hair along her arm lifted in response as if each strand was straining to get closer to him.

She pulled her arm away slowly, grieving over every inch lost. She tore her eyes from Ronan's, but she could still see him there, his image vivid and fixed in her mind. If she didn't distract herself, she was going to reach for him again just to feel his fingers on her skin.

Justice busied herself with retrieving her things from his van.

"Thank you for the ride," she said. "Will you let the person manning the gate know we'll be leaving now?"

"But your car isn't clean yet," Ronan said. "The blood will draw Synestryn and uncomfortable questions. Why don't you let Slade and Vance finish detailing your Maserati, and we'll get Pepper something to wear and something to eat. She needs a proper meal, and it shouldn't take more than an hour or so to get Ricardo spic and span. We'll even call someone to replace the window I broke so you won't freeze to death."

Justice opened her mouth to refuse, but what came out was beyond her control. The fates were behind the wheel again, steering her life in the direction they chose. "That would be nice. Thank you."

That's when Justice realized that the itch was gone. She was doing exactly what was demanded of her, and it felt amazing, almost like she was free of the shackles that had caged her all her life—at least the part of it she could remember.

Ronan took Pepper's tiny hand, leaving Justice to trail behind. As she passed the two young men cleaning Ricardo, one grinned at her said, "Sweet ride. We'll do pickup duty for you anytime."

They looked like brothers, both with squat builds, heavy brows and flattened noses. They were in their twenties and had the air of young men working for an important cause they believed in deeply.

She wasn't sure how cleaning a car was an important task, but they went at it as if it were a matter of national security.

The bloody paper sack that had been filled with cash was in a trash bucket, along with several bills spotted with red. The rest of the money had been stacked neatly inside a clear zipper bag on the hood, along with the ring box. She didn't know if they'd taken her earnings or put them back, but she was curious to see which it was.

Were these people thieves? It seemed like the kind of thing she should know, and this was as good a test as any. She didn't need the cash and had no idea why the fates had demanded she earn the ring. Maybe bringing it here was part of her mission all along. She had no idea.

"Don't worry," said the other kid, whose face looked smooshed as flat as if he were pressing it against a pane of glass. "We'll wash the bloody bills and put them back. If we can't clean them, Joseph said he'd replace them for you."

She gave the young man a nod and trailed after Ronan and Pepper.

They passed through a pair of glass doors, into a long hallway about ten feet wide. Waiting just on the other side of the doors was a tall man with dark hair going gray at the temples. He held a soft wad of purple fabric in his hand. His hazel eyes dipped to Pepper, then shot back up to Justice.

"I'm Joseph Rayd," he said. "Welcome to Dabyr."

She noted that he didn't extend his hand in greeting, which suited her just fine.

As he spoke, two more big guys stepped up behind him, eyes hard and mistrustful. Both wore strange, iridescent necklaces that hugged their thick throats. She didn't need any introductions to know that they were Joseph's backup, and even if they didn't have the empty-eyed look of the men she'd killed earlier, she would bet they were just as deadly. Probably even more so.

"This is Justice, the woman I told you about," Ronan said. He nodded to the child. "This is Pepper Louise Sullivan, who is in need of a proper dinner, but is also quite fond of ice cream." He crouched beside her and in a low voice asked, "Will you show him your special mark?"

Pepper pulled up the blood-smeared sleeve of her shirt to reveal a red, ring-shaped birthmark on her inner wrist.

Instantly, the mood of the men shifted from mistrust to shocked disbelief.

Protective instincts Justice didn't even know she had rose up and had her taking Pepper's hand. She pulled the child behind her and demanded to know, "What does that mean?"

"She's a Theronai," Ronan said. "Like these men and many others here. She's one of our own."

"Does that mean I can have ice cream?" Pepper asked from behind Justice.

Joseph looked Justice square in the eyes—something most men never could manage without flinching. "We would never hurt her. Every man here would die to keep her safe. You have no idea how precious she is and how grateful we are to you for finding her."

"She stays with me," Justice said.

"Okay," Joseph agreed. "I imagine you could use a meal as well. Why don't we talk over dinner?"

She almost told him that she didn't have time to waste but realized there was no itch in the back of her skull, no pressure to keep moving on to the next task.

The sensation of being free to linger was both odd and heady. Not to mention the fact that she was starving. She couldn't remember the last real meal she'd had, and she was certain that it had been crappy fast food eaten behind the wheel, flying down the highway at ninety.

"Okay. Dinner. But then we're out of here."

"Is Mama coming?" Pepper asked.

Justice's heart lurched in her chest and bled. She knew there were things an adult should say to a child whose mother had just been killed in front of her, but Justice didn't know what those things were. She wasn't good with kids. Or adults. Or people in general. She was better off alone.

But what about Pepper? Could Justice really leave her here with strangers? Just because they hadn't done bad things yet didn't mean they wouldn't.

Justice checked in with the fates, searching for their opinion, but they were uncharacteristically silent, leaving her to figure things out on her own. The bastards.

Ronan crouched beside Pepper and took her slender shoulders in his big hands. "Your mother isn't coming, honey. But it's okay. We're going to take care of you. You don't have to worry about anything."

"But I want Mama." Her chin trembled and tears magnified her big, blue eyes.

Ronan slid a finger over her brow to brush her tangled hair away from her face. "Of course, you do. But everything is going to be just fine. You'll see. Would you like to meet some of the other kids here?"

The tears dried up as the tension drained from her face. "Okay."

"Let's see who might be in the dining room. Maybe you can make a new friend," he said.

"She needs to change first," Joseph said, holding out the soft purple dress. "She shouldn't be around the other kids with blood on her clothes. Most of them have seen more than their fair share already."

"For me?" Pepper snatched the dress and hugged it as if in love.

Joseph showed them to a restroom toward the end of the hall. He looked at the child. "Do you need help to change?"

She wrinkled her nose at him in response, then rushed into the bathroom and closed the door behind her with an independent flourish.

Joseph caught Ronan's gaze. "How bad?"

"Her mother is dead, but Pepper is not yet able to understand what that means. She thinks it's temporary. I've been easing her fear and worry, but it's not healthy for me to numb her for long."

"What about a father?"

Ronan shook his head. "There was no memory of one in her mind."

"You read her mind?" Justice asked, appalled.

"How else was I going to learn what happened? She's too young to make sense of what she saw. She still thinks her mother will wake up, like in a video game."

"You stay out of her head," Justice warned. "I don't want you fucking with her mind."

A flash of hurt flickered in his pale blue gaze, then vanished. "All I'm doing is helping. She needs to eat and sleep so she can face what's happened and begin to heal."

"This isn't the first orphaned child we've dealt with," Joseph said, his tone defensive. "Ronan knows what he's doing."

Did he? Justice had no idea. She did, however, know that she was clueless when it came to kids. Hell, she couldn't even remember *being* one.

Pepper came out, pleased with her new dress and tall, striped socks. The fabric was a soft jersey knit. The dress that fell to the top of her socks and sported some cartoon character Justice didn't recognize. To her, the blonde could only have been called Princess Glitter Bomb based on the amount of sparkly paint and plastic gems covering the front. Still, Pepper seemed to love it, so who was Justice to judge.

Maybe these people did know what they were doing when it came to taking care of orphans.

A pile of bloody clothes lay on the tile floor in the bathroom, completely forgotten, along with one sparkly shoe stuffed with rumpled socks.

Pepper needed shoes and her hair was tangled, but all

traces of blood were gone.

"You are beautiful," Joseph said with a wide grin. "Let's go find you some friends. We'll let you try on shoes after you eat. We even have some that light up."

Pepper clapped her hands in anticipation and gave a little jump.

Joseph led the way to an open dining area that was big enough to feed at least two or three hundred at once. Tables were covered in cheery checkered cloths and flickering tealight candles in colorful jars. The ceiling overhead was glass, which reflected the warm, earthy tones beneath. The smell of rosemary and garlic filled the space, along with something sweet and citrusy.

Dozens of people sat at the tables, talking and laughing as if they were out at a casual restaurant with friends. Several tables were filled with children, who'd segregated themselves by age. Teens took up three tables, their plates piled high. Tweens gathered at another pair of tables, watching the teens with open fascination. The little ones sat lined up on benches along a long, low table sized just for them.

Some of them were smiling and talking animatedly, while others were quieter and more sedated. They were all bigger than Pepper, but not by much. As soon as she saw them, her face lit up.

"Can I eat over there?" she asked Ronan, who looked at Justice for permission.

How could she say no? The poor kid had been through hell, and while she might not have been able to grasp what had happened, one day she would. Maybe one of the kids over there had been through the same thing. Maybe one of them could help her cope with the loss of her mother in ways Justice never could.

Besides, it wasn't like she could drag Pepper along with her, into the chaos and gunfire that was her life. It had taken Justice a minute to realize it, but her life was no place for a child.

She couldn't get attached, and this place, with its thick,

high walls and laughing kids was as good as any to drop off an orphan.

Wasn't it?

"Sure," Justice said. "Go ahead."

Pepper raced off on stockinged feet and squeezed into a seat beside the youngest girl there—a redhead with fuzzy braids and a wash of freckles across her pale cheeks. She offered Pepper a smile and half of her sandwich.

Joseph led them to a table a few yards away, but well out of earshot of the kids. His two silent guards didn't join them, but she could feel them hovering nearby, watching her for signs of violence.

Little did they know, she was doing the same, only with a lot more people. The place was bustling during the dinner rush, with at least a hundred bodies present.

"Are they all orphans?" Justice asked as she watched Pepper make herself at home.

"Most of them, but not all," Ronan said.

"Too many," Joseph added.

A middle-aged woman with rosy cheeks and a sweaty brow came over to their table. She read the short list of options for dinner.

Joseph ordered coffee, Ronan asked for a salad, and Justice opted for a ribeye with all the trimmings.

If they were going to kill her, she at least wanted to be well fed when it happened.

The waitress bustled off. A second later, a stunning woman with feline features and yellow-blond hair came to their table. She was tall like Justice, but with a delicate build. She sat close to Joseph, who offered her a welcoming smile full of shared secrets.

"This is my wife, Lyka," he said. "Lyka, this is Justice...what was your last name?"

"Don't have one," she said.

Lyka extended a slender hand across the table. "Nice to meet you."

Justice saw no reason to be rude before her steak arrived,

so she shook the woman's hand.

Her skin tingled, like it carried a faint electrical charge. Her pale golden eyes went distant for a second before she let go and turned to her husband and nodded. "We're good."

"You're sure?" Joseph asked.

"Positive. The only thing she wants is freedom." Lyka frowned. "I'm not sure from what, but she means us no harm as long as we don't strike first."

Irritation raked beneath Justice's skin. "That handshake was some kind of test? Why not just ask me if I'm here to screw you?"

Joseph's hazel eyes held hers. "We do what we must to protect our own. Lyka has a gift for knowing what people want. If she says you don't want to hurt us, I trust her."

"Well, I don't. What I want or don't want is my own damn business. Next time you decide to pull some magical mindfuck, why don't you just ask me to leave first. I don't need to be here anymore than you need me to stay."

"I need you," Ronan said. His tone was clipped and angry.

She turned to him and saw that his ire was aimed directly at Joseph.

"Do you really think I would have brought her here if I wasn't sure it was safe for her to be around the children?"

"All I know is that you've been searching for her for weeks, and that you've disobeyed orders to return home to do so. After Connal's betrayal, and after what happened to Rory, you'll have to forgive me for needing a second opinion."

"I am not Connal," Ronan growled.

Justice didn't know who Connal was, but she was oddly curious to find out.

The middle-aged waitress brought Pepper a bowl of macaroni and cheese. She grinned up, then dove in with relish. The little redhead sitting next to her picked up a spoon and joined in the feast. Both girls were chatting nonstop between bites, uncaring that they were talking with their mouths full.

It was so...normal. So innocent. Justice's world was stuffed full of blood and violence, full of compulsion and an endless string of tasks she had no hope of understanding. And yet here, inside this stone fortress filled with orphans, vampires and women who knew what you wanted with a single touch, Justice felt at peace for the first time she could ever remember. Literally. There had not been one true moment of quiet in her mind until now.

It was a gift she would relish for as long as it lasted.

"Are there other people here like me?" she heard herself ask before she could think better of it.

"Maybe. What are you?" Lyka asked as casually as if she were asking if Justice liked chocolate.

"I don't know," she answered honestly.

"I think she's like Hope," Ronan said with a kind of reverence in his tone she didn't understand.

Both sets of eyes on the other side of the table widened in shock.

"Who is Hope?" Justice asked.

"Are you sure?" Joseph asked at the same time.

"Not yet," Ronan said to Joseph, then his gaze fell on her and his next words were clearly meant for her alone. "But even a man like me can dream."

***

Ronan had revealed too much. He'd let his excitement get the best of him and told Justice about Hope before it was time.

Their food arrived, but Justice hadn't touched hers yet. Instead, she'd watched him with those silvery-green eyes as if she could see all the way through him.

Maybe she could.

"I want to meet Hope," she told him.

"Of course," Ronan said.

"I don't know if that's a good idea," Joseph said. He sipped his coffee, then slid the mug over to his wife to share.

"Why not?" Justice demanded.

Lyka laid a hand on her husband's arm. "I told you she's no threat."

"No, you told me that she wants to be free. From who or what is still a question. For all we know her freedom comes at the price of lives here."

"It doesn't," Justice said through clenched teeth. "I may have been forced to do some bad shit, but none of it was by choice."

"She brought us that live demon a few weeks ago when we needed one," Lyka reminded him. "And she found Pepper. We owe her."

Joseph's mouth tightened. "I owe a lot of people a lot of things, but these kids are at the top of my list. Everyone else can get in line behind them."

Ronan set down his fork as he fought a sudden surge of anger. He ignored Joseph and turned to Justice. "Who forced you to do bad things? What did they make you do?"

Her expression shut down hard and fast, leaving him guessing her emotions. "It doesn't matter."

"Tell me."

She sliced into her steak and filled her mouth and mumbled, "Can't talk. Eating."

"I'm not letting this drop," he said.

She ignored him.

Joseph recovered from the daggers his wife was staring at him and let out a long sigh. "Fine. Tell us about yourself, Justice. Let me get to know you a little, then we'll decide if meeting with Hope is a good idea or not."

"Nothing to tell," she said.

"Why don't you have a last name?" Lyka asked.

"Didn't have a first one either when I woke up."

"When you woke up?"

Justice stopped eating and toyed with the buttery innards of a baked potato. "I woke up ten years ago with no memory, no clothes, no nothing."

The quiver in her voice made Ronan's heart clench. "That must have been scary."

"I managed."

"How did you manage?" Joseph asked, though his tone was gentler now than it had been before.

"I had help. Kind of."

"Care to elaborate?" Lyka asked.

"Not really, but apparently that's the price of admission to see Hope. So, here goes." She pulled in a long breath and took a while letting it out, like she was putting off the inevitable for as long as she could. "I get these feelings, like someone needs me to do something. I never know why and sometimes don't even know what I'm supposed to do until I'm doing it. I've tried to fight the urges, but I can't. Whoever is calling the shots makes me suffer if I don't play along."

"Who is it?" Ronan asked.

"Not a damn clue, but whoever they are, I'd like to kick them square in whatever is between their legs." She trailed off with an angry, "Fucking fates."

"You think it's fate?" Joseph asked, skeptical.

"Or karma, or God, or little green men on Mars. Who the hell knows? All I know is that if I don't do what they want, I suffer."

"What kind of things do they want you to do?" Ronan asked.

"This last time, I thought I was trading a dusty old book for some cash and a ring, but it turned out that the real reason I was there was Pepper."

"These fates, or whatever they are, knew she would be there?"

"I guess. It's not like I can talk to them. All I get is the urge to act and punishment for resisting. And the assholes always want something. I can't remember the last time I had a day to myself."

Ronan couldn't imagine a life like that. It was no wonder she was so nomadic, flitting from one task to the next without any time to rest between.

He kept his voice level out of sheer willpower. "What kind of punishment?"

"Pain, mostly. My brain will itch, then if I ignore it, the headaches come, then dizziness, nausea and the general need to curl up and die." She finally looked at him, and when she did, he saw desolation there. "I nearly killed myself trying to run away from you. Guess the fates want to rope you into their twisted games too."

He put his hand on hers in an effort to comfort her, but instead, he got swept up in the smooth softness of her skin.

She flinched, let him touch for a second, then pulled away and steeled her spine.

"It's fine," she said. "I cope. But it would be really nice to meet someone who's been through what I have and come out on the other side. If this Hope chick can tell me how to get the fates to back off, maybe I could have something vaguely resembling a life. That's all I want."

Joseph's posture softened, as did his tone. "I'm sorry, Justice, but Hope hasn't faced what you have."

"Maybe not," Ronan said, "but she did wake up with no memories of who or what she was. Brenya told us there were more women here like her. It's not a stretch to think Justice is one of them."

"Who is Brenya?" asked Justice, frowning.

"A powerful woman from another world," Ronan answered.

Joseph scowled at him for speaking so openly. "Forget about Brenya. What proof do you have that Justice is like Hope, beyond amnesia, I mean?"

"Her blood," Ronan said. "It's powerful beyond anything I've ever experienced—the way Logan describes Hope's blood."

Justice turned to him, frowning. "Is that why you chased me all over the country? For my blood?"

There was more to it than that, but Ronan wasn't about to spill his guts in front of Joseph and Lyka. He wasn't even sure he understood why he felt so possessive of her. All he knew was that he needed her. She was his. He'd kill anyone who tried to get in the way of that.

She already thought he was a bloodsucking leech. Saying that he wanted to claim her for his own was going to make him sound like a bloodsucking *barbarian* leech.

He settled for, "Your blood was only part of it."

Joseph looked at Lyka. They spoke no words, but it was clear some kind of silent conversation had passed.

"Okay," he said. "She can meet Hope, but not until she and Logan are done with their work. Nika and Jackie come first, then the kids who need healing, then Justice."

Ronan nodded as Joseph stood and helped his wife up.

Justice stared at her plate. "Thank you. It's been a long time since anyone offered to help me. It's nice to know there are still people on this spinning rock that still give a shit about someone other than themselves."

Joseph nodded once in acknowledgement. "Stay with Ronan. He goes where you go, understand? I don't want you roaming around unescorted."

She nodded. They left.

Ronan stayed seated next to her. He liked feeling her warmth against his side, having her close enough to touch. He'd like it more if they weren't surrounded by so many people, but he'd take what he could get.

"Joseph is a good man," he said. "But we've been through a lot lately. He has reason to be mistrusting."

"It's okay that he doesn't trust me," she said. "I wouldn't trust me, either."

"Give him time. He'll warm up."

"I really don't care if he does or not. I won't be here that long."

"You need to recover. Rest."

"I'm fine. Whatever you did to patch me up worked wonders." She lifted her head, and her eyes hit his with the force of a meteor. "Thank you for that, by the way. I'm not used to saying those words, but it seems I'll be getting some practice with you all."

She was so amazingly beautiful, he almost lost track of the conversation. The full curve of her lips made his blood heat.

The warm caramel color of her skin contrasted with her pale eyes until they seemed to glow. Her dark curls framed her face, swaying and bouncing as she moved. Everywhere he looked, she was smooth and silky, and all he could think about was how he was going to find an excuse to touch her again.

"You should eat," he said, because he didn't hear a word she'd said as he'd stared at her, and food seemed like a safe response. "You need to rebuild your strength."

"I feel fine."

"Because I set in motion your body's natural healing mechanisms. But if you don't feed the process, all that effort will go to waste and your speedy recovery will grind to a halt."

She shook her head in wonder. "How the hell do you do that? Is it magic?"

"I suppose. It's more about the transfer of energy than anything."

"How does it work?"

She genuinely wanted to know. He could see the inquisitive spark lighting her eyes, so he explained it the best he could.

"There's power in blood—Athanasian blood to be specific."

"What's Athanasian?"

"Athanasia the source of all magic, another world that's linked to ours through a series of gateways. They came here, mingled with humans, had children. The gates were all closed long ago—we thought permanently—but the bloodlines remained. Human descendants and Sentinels held the magic of that world in their blood, and as they had children, they passed it down. Now, centuries later, that power spread out among humans until only tiny traces of it remain in some people."

"That's why you drink blood?" she asked. "You can somehow harness the magic in it?"

Ronan nodded. "I'm able to extract power from blood cells and convert it into other forms of energy. Healing, strength, speed, stealth," he caught her gaze, "restoring lost memories.

I may even be able to find a way to block these fates as you call them from compelling you to act."

She went still. "You think you can fix me?"

"I don't know. Maybe. Logan was able to restore Hope's lost past."

She was silent for so long his ears began to ache for her response.

"So this whole time, you've been chasing me because you want to help me?" Some childlike desperation filled her gaze, as if his answer could undo a lifetime of wrongs.

"Partly," he said. "But that's not the whole story."

"Then what is?"

"My people are starving. When I tasted your blood, I was blown away by the sheer power you hold. A single drop from you is like a gallon from someone else." He swallowed, hoping he didn't sound desperate, but knowing he was. "One drink from you, and I was no longer starving, no longer weak. I was as I was born to be."

Her voice was quiet but determined. "Do you want to kill me? Drain me dry?"

"Never. I won't lie to you and tell you that your blood is not a dangerous lure. It would be easy to go too far, but if I kill you, the source of all that power would be gone. I'm far better off if you live a long, happy, healthy life."

She stabbed an uneaten bite of steak. "Milk from a cow, rather than beef."

"Exactly."

"You think you can use my blood to drive the fates out of my head?"

"Perhaps. I could try."

She lifted her eyes and what he saw there startled him.

She was exhausted. Desperate.

"All I want is to be free, to make my own choices, go where I want, when I want. If you can do that, you can have as much of my blood as you want."

Maybe she hadn't meant it to be a promise, but it was one all the same. He felt the weight of her vow wrap around him and hold him tight. It gave him hope for a future free of starvation and weakness. A future so much brighter than his past, he couldn't help but accept her offer with a smile.

"It's a deal."

CHAPTER FOUR

Joseph kissed his wife and left her to get in a few more hours of work before he called it a night.

Dabyr was filled to the brim with people, and every one of them depended on him to keep them safe, clothed and fed. Thanks to Lyka, he was able to focus on his duty now, free from pain and so deeply in love, he knew he'd never surface.

He was the luckiest man on the planet, and despite the challenges they faced, he'd never felt stronger, never felt more whole.

When he opened the door of his office, Sibyl was waiting for him.

Not long ago, she'd been a small girl with ringlet curls, dressed in frilly lace and satin. Since the death of her parents a few months ago, and the destruction of the curse that kept her looking perpetually eight years old, Sibyl had aged rapidly. She now looked to be in her mid-twenties.

No matter how old she looked, her appearance had always been a lie. With over two centuries under her belt, she was a formidable ally with the uncanny ability to see into the future.

She sat across from his desk, wearing jeans and a pale blue T-shirt that perfectly matched her eyes. Her blond hair was a bit darker now but hung all the way to her hips in loose, casual curls. She was as pretty as her mother had been but would be stunning if she ever smiled.

She certainly wasn't smiling now.

Joseph sat behind his cluttered desk, covered with maps, suggestions and complaints from Dabyr's residents, and an endless string of purchase orders for food and supplies.

"What can I do for you?" he asked.

"Something is wrong," she said in a quiet, husky voice so unlike the childish one she'd had only last spring.

"What's that?"

She shook her head slightly and gave him a troubled frown. "I'm not sure."

"You're going to have to elaborate if you want me to help."

Sibyl tilted her head to the side. "There's nothing you can do. I simply thought you should know."

"Know what? All you've said is that something's wrong. I hate to tell you this, Sibyl, but something is always wrong."

"Not like this."

Impatience prowled beneath his skin. He knew she wasn't the type to jump to conclusions, but vague worry wasn't going to help anyone. "Tell me what's going on. Why are you here?"

Sibyl stared out through the window behind him. It overlooked the training yard where Theronai practiced combat, lifted weights, and kept their skills honed for the next battle.

He feared it would come sooner rather than later.

"My sister has always been impatient," Sibyl said.

Maura, Sibyl's twin sister, had long ago shunned her people and gone to fight on the side of their enemy. Rumor had it she was some kind of queen among the Synestryn now, but no one knew for sure.

"Have you heard from her?" Joseph asked.

"Not for a while. I tried to convince her to come home, but she believes she is where she belongs." The sadness in Sibyl's voice helped Joseph gather his patience and give her a chance to speak.

Paperwork, bills and defense plans would all wait a few more minutes, even for a man who was anxious to be back by his new wife's side.

"She's made her choice," he said. "I know it breaks your heart, but you can't dwell on it. You have your own people to think about. Have you had any luck finding a compatible male?"

Anger sparked in her blue eyes, turning them cold. "I told you not to rush me. I will take a mate when I am ready and not a moment before."

"I'm sorry. Rushing you wasn't my intent. I know you're aware of your duty and will step up when you're ready." He only hoped that she didn't take too long to do so. They needed every bonded pair of Theronai they could get. With luck, one of the men under his command would be compatible with her.

"I will, but *I'm* not even used to this body yet. I certainly am not ready to invite a man to share it with me."

That image made Joseph's cheeks heat. Even though she hadn't truly been a child for a long, long time, he had seen her as one his whole life. That kind of sudden shift was hard to make.

It was probably much harder for the person living it.

"Fair enough," he said. "Let's talk about why you're here."

"As I said, Maura has always been impatient. Our gift of sight is shared between us. We each take turns. Usually, when it's my turn, I wait to use the gift until absolutely necessary, denying her access to it for as long as I can."

"So, she can't see the future and use her visions against us," he guessed.

"Exactly. She's always quick to act, as if eager for the next tidbit of the future. Then it's my turn again, and I hold out as long as possible so that our power remains with me."

"Seems smart."

"Only this time, she's waiting. It's as if she's using my own tactic against me."

"Maybe she learned some patience when her body aged."

Sibyl shook her head. "No. It's something else. I know her, Joseph. I shared a womb with her. We are part of each other, split from one whole."

"What else could it be if she's not simply making you wait?"

Her eyes narrowed in speculation. "She's hiding something, or planning something—something she doesn't want me to see coming."

"Do you have any idea what that might be?"

"I've been thinking about it for days but am no closer to an answer now than I was before."

"I'm sure there's nothing to worry about."

Sibyl rose to her feet in an angry rush. "If you believe that, then you are a fool. Worry and the action it causes is the only thing that might keep us alive. I suggest that whatever protections you have in place for the birth of the infants, you do more. Much, much more, Joseph."

"I've been calling in everyone for months. Nearly every man and woman, human or Sentinel, who can swing a sword or channel magic is here. We have armed men patrolling the grounds every second of the day and night, and everyone is on high alert. I know that these babies are targets and have taken every precaution to see that they come into this world safe and sound."

She paced in front of his desk, agitation clear in every step. "It's not enough."

"What more would you have me do?"

"I don't know. That's the problem. If Maura would just use our gift and give it back, I'd know what else we should do."

"Maybe she's just screwing with you. If she knows you so well, she has to know that withholding your ability to see the future would drive you crazy. Sisters do that kind of thing, right?"

Sibyl's glare was almost painful to witness. "My sister commands armies of demons and thirsts for power. She doesn't have time for silly games."

"She's never once come after us here. She knows where we are. If she has so much power and hates us so much, then why hasn't she marched on Dabyr and tried to destroy us?"

Sibyl shook her head. Her long hair swayed around her hips in a quiet whispering caress. "When the future is your domain, when you spend your life seeing the possibilities that await those around you, you learn that there is a time for everything. My fear is that Maura has now found her time to act."

Joseph knew that Dabyr was one big, juicy target right now. Their walls were filled not only with blooded humans who needed their protection, but also with dozens of Theronai, Sanguinar and now several Slayers whose homes had been recently destroyed. His wife's people had come here so they could recover from attack, regroup and plan to rebuild. But with so many blooded souls under one roof, and with the added bonus of the impending births, this fortress was a giant glowing sign inviting Synestryn everywhere to come take a shot.

Already, they were fighting off nightly skirmishes at the walls as small groups of demons tried their luck.

Lexi had done her best to reinforce the walls with magic, but she was only one woman. Centuries ago, a dozen female Theronai would pool their magic to seal even the smallest cracks from invaders. But they didn't have a dozen women, much less a dozen skilled in the defensive arts. Lexi had exhausted herself warding gerai homes, then gone down to Africa, helping them rebuild a fallen Sentinel fortress there. And even though her work wasn't yet done, she and Zach had still returned home as soon as they'd heard they were needed.

After all, Jackie was about to deliver Lexi's niece. She wasn't going to hope for the best when she could be here working to strengthen Dabyr's defenses.

Joseph didn't know how to ease Sibyl's worry. He wasn't even sure if he should. They all needed to be on high alert. "We're doing everything we can, Sibyl. If you can think of something else we should do, then we will. But until you know more, I'm not sure what other measures we can take."

"Maura is cunning. She is convinced she has no soul and

has acted accordingly. She lived with us for years. She knows our ways, our preparations. She'll look for a weak point and exploit it."

"That's what I'm trying to tell you. We've spent the last several months shoring up every weak point we can find. The walls are as strong as they've been since we first erected them. We've relocated everyone living out in the cabins inside the main building. Security is tight, with one of my strongest men always monitoring the gates to avoid any dabbling with human minds. We have cameras watching every inch of the grounds beyond the walls. There are traps and sensors every few feet to alert us of approaching armies—which is what it would take to breech the walls."

She didn't look relieved.

"And if our walls do fall, we have men and women constantly poised to fight. We're well-stocked, we're armed and we're as ready for a fight as we can be."

Sibyl's shoulders drooped and she let out a defeated breath. "Without the gift of sight, without knowing what's coming, all we can do is pray that will be enough."

***

The more of Dabyr Justice saw, the more impressed she became.

These people were ready for war.

From the grounds outside, well-lit and swarming with armed men, to the cameras inside that kept a vigilant eye on entrances and public areas, to the low hum of readiness she felt in the air itself, it was clear that these people knew that the shit was about to hit the fan. Even the teens were outside, drilling with swords under the watchful eye of big, burly men who corrected their form and pushed them toward perfection.

With only a few exceptions, the adults who didn't carry blades carried guns. Even a wizened old lady with a stooped posture and a wispy bun held up with a yellow pencil had a semiautomatic pistol on the table next to her coffee and her open book.

Ronan led Justice from the dining tables, through an open recreation area overlooking the grounds outside. They went into what she thought was the south wing, then down a long hallway that led to an elevator. He had to swipe his ID and press his finger to a touch screen in order to make the doors open.

Once inside the polished steel box, he had to go through yet more layers of security before the elevator started downward—security that involved him shedding a drop of blood to identify himself.

"Where are we going?" she asked.

"My suite. All we Sanguinar live belowground, below all the public areas. No sense in risking a broken pane of glass during the day."

"Because you'll burst into flames?" she asked, only half-joking.

He rolled his eyes. "Hardly. Despite what Hollywood would have you believe, we bloodsuckers don't go in the sun because of what it does to us, but because of what it summons."

"Summons?"

He nodded. "The Solarc—who rules Athanasia with as much mercy as a hungry shark—hates the Sanguinar. He's able to see through sunlight, and if even a fingernail sliver of it touches our skin, he can see us and sends one of his assassins to destroy us."

"Harsh. Why does he hate you?"

"Because our birth was not pre-approved by his majesty and therefore, blasphemous. He doesn't believe we should exist, so it is his mission to wipe us out."

"Sounds like this Solarc guy is a whiney bitch-baby."

Ronan's grin was slight, but still had the power to take his appearance from stunning to mind-numbingly gorgeous. Drool-worthy. Completely scrumptious.

Not that she was into that kind of thing. She'd never been with a man that she could remember and wasn't about to start the bad habit now. She didn't have time for that kind of bullshit.

Still, that didn't mean she couldn't enjoy the show.

The elevator was large enough to move a couch, but it was still small enough that she could smell him. She wasn't sure if he wore cologne, or if it was his natural scent, but he smelled sweet and spicy, like fresh cinnamon raisin bread.

A small, irrational sliver of her mind wondered if he tasted half as good.

The elevator dinged, and the doors slid open to reveal a hallway that looked much like those three levels up. It was lined with numbered doors. Lights ran down the center, though they were much dimmer down here.

Ronan led her to the third door on the right, then swiped his ID in the lock to open it.

He walked into the dark space. "Come in. Make yourself at home."

She couldn't see a thing past the faint pool of light coming in from the hallway. After a second, he made a noise of realization, then flipped on the lights.

"Sorry. I forget others can't see in the dark."

"That must be handy."

His suite was bigger than she'd expected. The ceilings were high—maybe ten feet—and space was open. A living room, complete with a couch and a recliner was decorated in soothing grays with accents of deep midnight blue. There was a miniature kitchen in one corner that looked like it had never been used. Next to that was a dining space just big enough for two that also looked unused.

On the far side of the room was an area bracketed by two adjacent bookshelves that went all the way to the ceiling. A scuffed side table and an overstuffed leather chair sat on a plush rug, giving the reading nook a cozy air. Every shelf was lined with books, and most of them looked to be old. Really old.

To the right was a short hallway that she guessed led to a bedroom since there was no bed out here.

A few personal items dotted the space—books, trinkets, several throw blankets. But what caught her attention most was the drawings framed and hung on the walls.

Sloppy crayon art and crooked drawings were treated like the finest masterpieces, lit and labeled as if in a museum.

"What's all this?" she asked as she studied the artwork.

Some were sweet images of kittens with pink noses and suns with smiling faces. Other were darker, drenched in blood and covered in frenetic scribbles. One was completely black except for a pair of mismatched green eyes in the middle of the page.

Each piece had the name of the artist and the date on a small metal tag.

"Gifts," Ronan said. "From the children I've helped."

"Helped how?"

He shrugged as he came closer. She'd been able to feel his presence since he'd taken her blood, but when he was this near, that feeling was more defined. Almost like a touch, rather than a shimmer of heat.

She could still feel his hand on hers, feel his tongue flicking over her arm, feel his mouth at her throat. Everywhere he'd touched her, he'd left behind ghosts. No matter how hard she tried, she couldn't seem to find a way to rid herself of them.

Ronan pointed to the top drawing of the smiling sun. "Charlie was sick. Leukemia. He said that since I couldn't see the sun, he'd draw it for me." His long finger slid down to the next one. "Sidney got injured in an attack the night we found her. I healed her wounds and brought her here to live with her parents."

"And this one?" she asked, pointing to the green eyes.

"William drew this over and over. It was what he saw the night his parents were killed and eaten in front of his eyes. I worked with him for months, easing his fear and smoothing some of the sharper edges of his memory of that night. We replaced them with memories of his parents, before the attack. This was the last drawing he did of those eyes." He pointed to another wall with more framed art. In the center of it was a very lifelike pencil sketch of a puppy, mouth open, tongue lolling in a doggie grin. "He draws animals now, and he's quite good."

She didn't know what to say to that. This man she'd been evading for weeks was far more than she'd expected. He'd done good in the world. Helped people.

All Justice could think was how amazing that must feel.

"Would you like something to drink? I have coffee, tea, wine."

"Water," she said, mostly because she wanted something to do with her fidgety hands.

She felt out of place here, like she didn't belong. These people were fighters, heroes. They raised orphans for heaven's sake. She was just a pawn who stole, lied and killed when the fates demanded it of her. And sometimes when they didn't.

Ronan had a home, a family, people who loved and depended on him. All she had was an accumulation of stuff she named so she didn't feel so fucking lonely.

Reba was a poor substitute for drawings from a child who had once been broken but was now able to create art. And as nice as the hug of Ricardo's leather seat was, it couldn't compare to the touch of another living soul.

Suddenly, Justice felt the need to get out of here. As much as she wanted Ronan to help her the way he had those kids, she wasn't sweet and innocent. She didn't deserve his help.

Maybe her compulsions weren't the fates at all, but a punishment for something she'd done in the years she couldn't remember.

Whatever her crime, it must have been heinous.

"I think it's time for me to leave," she said.

Ronan stopped midstride, a glass of ice water in his elegant hand. "But I thought you wanted me to help you."

"I do. I did. But I think it was a mistake to come here. I don't suppose I can activate the elevator without your blood, can I?"

"It wasn't a mistake to come here, Justice. Whatever fears you have, let's talk about them. You don't have to run off."

She didn't want to talk. She didn't know how. She was used to being alone. The last thing she needed was some sexy, smooth-talking man outmaneuvering her in a battle of words.

No, the *last* thing she needed was another mission from the fates.

If she was going to have any chance at freedom, this was it. Ronan possessed magic. He helped people. He was willing to help her. That wasn't a combination she was going to find ever again. She could hardly believe she'd found it now.

He set the water down and closed the distance between them. She hadn't realized how near he was until his hands cupped her arms in a gentle squeeze.

Another ghost of a touch that would haunt her forever.

"I need you, Justice. You have no idea how much. Please don't go."

He needed *her*? That didn't make any sense at all. She was the one with the screwed-up head.

He looked at her like he was telling the truth. She didn't know how he could be, but to be gazed upon like she was more than a pawn—like she was important—was almost more than she could stand. It was too good to be true.

Indecision warred in her mind, armed with arguments for and against staying. In the end, the final blow was as simple as it was sad.

She had no choice. Just like always. If she didn't find a way to free herself from her tormentors, she was going to end up dead. Even worse, she might end up killing someone who didn't have it coming. How would she live with herself then?

She knew the answer to that question.

She couldn't.

"Okay," she said. "I really don't have much to lose."

Relief spread across his beautiful face like a wave. He didn't even try to hide it. His posture relaxed, as did his grip on her arms.

Long, elegant fingers slid over her thin cotton shirt. His

touch was cool, which gave her the oddest need to warm him.

The faint scar on her neck where he'd fed from her the first night she met him tingled. As much as his actions had shocked and confused her, she'd often looked back on that night, dwelling on the feeling of her blood flowing into his body.

There was an intimacy in the act of feeding someone—a deep closeness. She imagined it was the same for a nursing mother nourishing her child.

The feel of his mouth moving over her skin had never quite left her, and while there had been some pain, it was nothing compared to the heady rush of giving someone the very thing they needed to survive.

She reached for the scar out of habit, hardly even realizing she had until Ronan's gaze tracked her movement.

Sad lines creased his eyes and regret shone plain on his face.

"I'm so sorry I treated you like that," he said. "Had I been in my right mind, I would have healed you so that no scar remained."

"It's okay. I have worse scars. Some I can't even remember getting."

His pale blue eyes slid over her features, down her throat and back again. As they did, his pupils flared wide. "Would you like to see what we can do about that?"

She nodded. "Now, before I lose my nerve."

"You don't have to worry about a thing. Just look into my eyes and breathe."

Justice did as he asked. It was easy, just like falling, and a moment later, she felt herself do just that.

***

Ronan caught Justice before she could fall and eased her onto his couch. Her body melded against his perfectly, her dips and swells lining up exactly with his.

He'd tapped into his power to help her relax, but it had worked almost too well.

She was still healing, he had to remind himself. She looked healthy and whole, but her body was still rebuilding her lost blood. On top of that, she was in a constant state of exhaustion, always moving and going wherever she was compelled.

It was that compulsion that worried him the most, and the thing he was determined to fix. She could live without her memories, but she couldn't live at the mercy of a master she didn't know and couldn't escape.

He settled her languid weight in his lap and cradled her body like a lover. Perhaps he was overstepping boundaries, but he really didn't care.

She was his. It was his right to hold her close and feel the warmth of her flesh on his.

Wasn't it?

A sleepy, contented sigh escaped her lips as she nestled her head in the hollow of his shoulder. Her breathing was deep and even, and her pulse was a steady beat that slowed to match his own.

He could have simply held her like this all night, enjoying the feel of her against him and her warmth becoming his own. He would have preferred they both be naked, but that would have inevitably led to more than he intended.

Even the idea of taking her made his cock swell and ache. His nerves buzzed with anticipation, and his mind drew pictures of the two of them together, bodies entwined.

He was going to have her. Soon. But for now, his focus needed to be on his task.

Ronan gathered a trickle of power from his cells and sent it into Justice's mind.

He was good at this slow, delicate invasion. He had to be. Traumatized children were often sensitive to even the slightest signs of interference in their thoughts. But so many of them carried memories that would ruin their lives or get them killed. Synestryn were drawn to thoughts of them, and a child who'd been terrified couldn't help but play the memory of the event over and over until it wore a permanent groove in their mind.

One of Ronan's jobs was to ensure that those memories

were muted, foggy. He stripped them away completely when he could, but more often than not, that was impossible. Blooded children were strong, and removing those mental scars was often more damaging than helpful.

So, he'd learned the art of subtlety, the need to slip into a mind so slowly and carefully that the person rarely even felt his presence.

That was his intent with Justice—to ease into her and see what kind of task he had ahead of him. Instead, the moment he passed the fringes of her thoughts, he was sucked in. Consumed by her.

She was beautiful inside, but in such a different way than he'd ever experienced. He was overwhelmed by her.

She was like a chaotic piece of art, all swooping, tangled lines and brilliant colors. Strength looped around her insecurity. Confidence in her skills jumbled up with her constant, aching loneliness. The need to do good knotted in an intricate pattern with ties of honor around a thick vein of duty.

The longer he basked in her essence, the more he could see the churning, frenetic war she waged against herself. It was inspiring and heartbreaking at the same time. He had no idea how she'd managed to hold onto herself for so long, despite her weariness and total lack of companionship.

The only friends she allowed herself were inanimate objects. She'd given names and personalities to a few cherished possessions, as if cold steel and plastic could give her what she needed.

Ronan didn't understand why she'd isolated herself like this, but he wasn't going to let it continue. She was hurting herself, and that was something he simply couldn't allow.

He felt his strength fading, and only then realized that he'd been inside her mind for too long, soaking her in. It was time to concentrate on his task and see if he could figure out who compelled her and what had happened to her missing memories.

As soon as his own mind touched on his mission, a foggy wall appeared in front of him. He reached for it, but the thick mist simply bowed away from him as if repelled.

Experience told him two things: One, behind this wall was her lost past. And two, someone had done this to her intentionally. The work was better than any he'd ever seen—better than his own, even.

Whoever had done this was powerful, which only added to his evidence that Justice was like Hope. The powerful, otherworldly Brenya had shielded Hope's memories from her, and chances were she'd done the same to Justice.

Even with her blood flowing through him, Ronan wasn't strong enough to undo the work of an Athanasian queen. He was going to need to plan his attack more carefully or risk hurting Justice.

That, he wouldn't do.

Ronan turned away from the wall and searched for evidence of the fates, as Justice had called them.

A wide vein of something he thought of as duty trailed all through her essence. It pulsed with a deep crimson light that flared brighter in spots. As he followed the path it took, he saw it disappear through the foggy wall blocking her memories.

Whatever this thick rope was, she'd had it for a long time. The source of it was behind that wall, currently out of reach.

Experimentally, Ronan extended his power and just barely grazed the surface of that tree-thick vein.

Possession. Control. Unrelenting, merciless demand.

Pain exploded in his head as a presence screamed at him in a bellow of pure thought. Power unlike anything he'd ever felt flung Ronan out of Justice and back into his own mind.

Whoever or whatever had planted that thing in Justice wasn't fucking around. He couldn't even stand to touch it. He had no idea how she could tolerate toting it around inside her.

He opened his eyes to find her staring up at him. Her silvery-green gaze was dreamy as if she'd just woken from a long nap. There was no sign of distress or pain, which relieved him.

Poking around in her mind hadn't hurt her and he was grateful for that. As it was, he was shaking and sweating from his encounter with the presence inhabiting her.

And it was a presence. There was no mistake about that. Whatever was controlling her wasn't a spell or a curse. It was a person, though that description seemed inadequate for the enormous power of the thing he'd touched.

"What's wrong?" she asked.

She pushed up from his embrace and shifted from his lap to sit beside him. He took note that she put more space between them than was necessary. He didn't know if it was a sign of mistrust or a need for distance, but he instantly resented the cold air swirling around him where her body had just been.

"I don't know." The pounding in his head made his words more clipped than he'd intended. His guts twisted with nausea, and his hands were actually shaking.

Lethargy faded from her face and was replaced by a frown of worry. "You look like you're about to throw up. I felt you in my head. What did you see?"

He took several deep breaths to calm his body.

"There's a veil over your memories, which is what I expected. It's the kind of thing I do for the children who've seen their parents slaughtered."

"You think that's what happened to me? I saw my parents die and someone covered it up?"

"No. Ten years ago, where your memories stop, you would have been old enough to understand what you saw. None of my kind would have protected you from your past like that. At most we would have blurred whatever trauma you suffered so you could deal with it in your own time. What I saw in you was far more than that."

"What was it?"

"Someone intentionally cut you off from your past—completely—but that's not the problem."

"What is?" she asked.

"Those compulsions you have? The fates?"

"What about them?"

"Someone did that to you."

"What do you mean?"

"I felt a presence. Someone you knew before your memory was erased is calling the shots."

"Who?"

"I have no idea. And honestly, whoever it is, they're powerful enough that *who* might not be the right question."

"Then what is the right question?"

"*What* is it?"

Her gaze fell away from his and landed on her lap. He could practically smell the defeat wafting out of her.

"If you think that's the end of it, Justice, you're wrong. I'm not done yet, and I won't stop trying to help you until I find out how to get that thing out of you."

She shook her head. "This was a mistake. I can tell how hard this was on you, and all you did was take a look around inside my skull. I won't ask you to do more." She shrugged and stood as if the matter were settled. "I'm fucked. That's old news. Thanks for trying."

She couldn't leave without his help. She had no way to activate the elevators to the surface. There were too many helpless, sleeping Sanguinar down here for them to take risks with security. Only a few trusted Theronai could access this level. No humans were allowed. Their minds were too easily controlled by the enemy.

Ronan waited for her to realize she was stuck.

She was halfway to the door when she stopped, turned and sighed. "Are you going to make me beg?"

"Never. But we're not done here. Just because I wasn't able to free you in the last few minutes doesn't mean it's hopeless."

"Are you sure? Because you looked pretty damn hopeless a minute ago."

"Surprised," he lied. Truth was, he had been terrified. To be touched by anything as powerful as the presence in her mind was not the kind of thing a man dismissed as uneventful.

Ronan knew that there were things in this universe that made even the strongest Sentinels look like weak newborns, but he'd never *felt* one before. It was as humbling as it was intimidating.

He had no idea how he was going to inflict his will on that thing and force it out of her, but he knew he was going to try. No one deserved to suffer the way she did.

He still marveled that she was strong enough to withstand that presence on a daily basis without going mad.

She shook her dark curls. "I shouldn't have come here. What the hell was I thinking?"

"You were thinking about Pepper."

"And now that I know she's safer here than she would be with me, I think my work is done. Time to move on."

"Is that the fates talking?"

"No. They're uncharacteristically quiet."

"Then perhaps you're doing the right thing by staying."

"Is it right, though? Or just what they want me to do? I really can't tell anymore."

"All the more reason to stay and let me try to help you. You do want them gone, right?"

"More than anything in the world."

"Then why give up now?"

"Because if you fail, then I'm out of options. At least now I can pretend there's a chance for freedom."

"So, you're going to walk away from a chance just so you can pretend you have one? You realize that's a bit crazy, right?"

She stared at him for a long moment. Tension radiated through her body, and all he wanted to do was pull her close and soothe her. But if he touched her, he'd want more. He'd forget himself and do something that might drive her away.

There were at least a dozen ways he could think of to get her to relax, and most of them ended up with her naked and shimmering with pleasure.

The idea made his blood heat and his skin flush with need.

Finally, she spoke. "If I were to let you try to help me, what would you do?"

"I'd need to be at the peak of strength to take on the thing inside you. Once I was, I'd go back into your mind and try to drive it out."

"Have you done that before?"

"With Synestryn, yes."

"Is that what's inside me?"

"I don't know," he answered honestly. "I didn't feel the taint of malevolence I would expect of a demon. If it is one, it's the strongest I've ever encountered."

"Of course, it is. Just my luck." She sighed. "How long will it take you to get strong enough to try?"

"That depends on you, since yours is the only blood powerful enough to give me what I would need to combat the presence."

Her hand flew to her throat and the twin puckers his fangs had left behind a few weeks ago.

He crossed to her and tilted her head to the side to inspect them.

The marks were pink against her caramel skin—still fresh enough he could heal them if he tried. He wouldn't. He liked his mark on her far too much to remove it. Let any other Sanguinar see her and know that she was his.

Bloodsucking barbarian, indeed.

"You're still healing," he said. "But with a few days of rest and fluids, you should be able to give me what I need."

A tiny shiver coursed through her, but he saw it all the same. Just like he saw the way her pupils widened and her nostrils flared as if breathing in his scent.

He could smell her arousal, earthy and warm. Never before had any woman put off such an intoxicating scent.

Ronan bent his head to breathe in the air swirling beneath her delicate ear.

Sweet, womanly need. Pure temptation going straight to his head.

His lips brushed her skin. He hadn't meant to do it, but now that he knew just how warm and soft she was, he couldn't shake the need to press his lips against her flesh and kiss her.

Her pulse sped. The rush of blood through her veins made

his mouth water and his cock swell.

A puff of air escaped her chest as a whimper, so faint, he almost couldn't hear it over the hammering of her heart.

Her tentative fingers curled against his shoulder, twitching as if she wasn't sure if she should grab on or push away.

He knew which one he was going to allow.

One hand splayed at the small of her back and drew her hips closer to his. The other hand slid into her thick, springy curls and nestled against the heat of her scalp. He closed his fingers around the strands to hold her head still while his lips opened over her pulse.

Justice's body tightened in anticipation, practically quivering in his arms.

She wanted what he was about to do, but even he wasn't sure if he was going to kiss her or bite her. The need for both was raging inside of him, so loud he couldn't hear his own thoughts.

Her head tilted slightly, giving him better access. It was an invitation, a welcome, and one that made his fangs lengthen into wicked points.

The need to possess this woman was unlike anything he'd ever experienced before. He felt like she belonged to him— like she'd always been his—and yet she was also a precious, untouchable creature too good for a man who preyed on others.

Still, he'd craved her for so long, he knew he couldn't let her go without a taste—just a few drops to ease his hunger.

Her heart stuttered, tripping over a single beat. He might not have noticed if he hadn't been so close, but he was, and he did.

She was still healing from her injuries. As strong and healthy as she looked, he knew her body was working hard to replenish what she'd lost. To take more blood from her now was selfish. Weak.

She deserved a man who was neither of those things.

For someone who'd spent most of his life resisting the urge to feed, willpower came to him slowly, grudgingly, dragging its feet. But when he finally grabbed it and forced it to submit, he was able to do the right thing.

With a fleeting kiss that was barely more than a breath of air, he pulled away from her throat and let her go.

Her mouth was open. Her lips were stained a dark, aroused red. Thin rings of green surrounded her wide pupils, which she covered in a sweep of thick, black lashes.

He cleared his throat twice to loosen his voice enough to speak. "I'll take you aboveground now. We'll find you an empty suite where you'll be comfortable while you finish recovering."

When her nod finally came, it was small and tight. "That's probably for the best."

He wasn't so sure *best* was the word he'd use, but until she was healthy, it was safest for her not to be alone with him. Because for the things he wanted to do to her, she needed to be nice and healthy.

CHAPTER FIVE

Justice was relieved when she was finally alone inside a comfortable room that looked a lot like an upscale hotel. There was no kitchen, but she did have a stocked mini fridge and microwave tucked in one corner, along with a coffee pot and basket of snacks.

There was a small sitting area on one side of the space and a large bed on the other. A quarter of the suite was filled with a massive bathroom that had a freestanding tub inside a glass-enclosed, walk-in shower big enough to host small parties. She didn't know what anyone needed with a shower that large, but she did appreciate the gleaming white tiles with soft gray veins running through them.

The towels were thick and fluffy, as was the bedding. Someone had even gone to the trouble to place a real, live plant on the coffee table, along with several coasters to make sure guests took the hint to use them.

Justice turned on the TV to keep her company, then stripped off her clothes and made use of a small portion of the shower. There were more jets and nozzles than she knew what to do with, but she experimented with all of them before she got out and dressed in the softest clothes she had with her.

Ever since Ronan had kissed her neck, her skin had felt over-sensitized, as if her cells were holding their breath and waiting for him to finish what he started.

It wasn't like her to linger over thoughts of a man, sighing and mooning like some adolescent girl. She didn't stare into space, pining for another touch, and she sure as hell didn't grin like a fool when she thought about how good his lips had felt along her skin.

She flipped mindlessly through the channels until she found a bloody boxing match. The rapid-fire violence and mangled faces made her feel better—more at home in her own skin.

It was late. She'd been through a lot. She should have been tired, but her whole body buzzed like it was on the verge of an adrenaline high.

Ronan had done something when he'd touched her mind. She wasn't sure what it was, but she felt different. Altered.

She'd been able to sense him since he'd fed from her weeks ago, but now she felt like she was close, like if she closed her eyes and reached out her hand, his taut skin would be right under her fingertips.

The boxer in red shorts took another brutal blow to the eye and spun away from his opponent. Blood and sweat dripped from his jaw, but he came back for more.

Just like she would do with Ronan.

Maybe he could help her, maybe he couldn't. She wasn't sure about that, but she was sure that if he knocked on her door right now, she'd let him in—and it had nothing to do with wanting him to free her from her compulsions.

She wanted him. She'd never wanted a man before, but there was no question what she was feeling.

She wanted Ronan. Bad.

After ten years of rolling her eyes at women who threw themselves at men who were no good for them, she finally understood what made them such gluttons for punishment.

He survived on blood—her blood—and yet she knew that if he came to her now, hungry and desperate, she'd give him whatever he needed. Whatever he wanted.

If that didn't make her a fool, she didn't know what would.

There was a soft knock at the door. Justice jumped up with

the image of Ronan blazing in her mind, but it was a woman standing there instead.

Justice's first impression of the woman was that she was sunshine in a ponytail. Her hair was sunny-blond, her eyes were amber, and her skin was tan and gleaming with health. She was average height—a couple of inches shorter than Justice—dressed in faded jeans and a soft yellow sweater. Her grin was wide and genuine, and she smelled like a warm spring day.

"I'm Hope," she said. "Joseph said you wanted to meet me."

Justice wasn't sure what to do. She'd never had a visitor before. Hell, she'd never even had a home for anyone to visit.

She tried to think back to the times she'd been welcomed in someone's home, but it had happened so rarely, she was drawing a blank on what the protocol was. What did one do with an unexpected visitor?

At a loss, she simply stepped back to give the other woman room to enter. "I do. Thanks for coming."

Hope bounced in, all good cheer and swaying ponytail. "It's true, isn't it? I can see it in your aura."

"Is what true? What aura?" Justice asked.

"Joseph said you might be like me. You know, Sanguinar, but without the curse."

"What curse?"

Justice backed up in shock, but Hope took it as an invitation to come on in and sit down.

"The sunlight thing. You can go in sunlight, can't you?" Hope settled on the couch with her legs curled under her like they were girlfriends revving up for a nice, long chat. "I'm a bit of a sun-worshiper myself."

Justice had no idea what to do. Did she sit, too? Offer Hope a drink? Ask to braid her hair?

Instead, Justice stayed on her feet and moved closer to Reba, sitting next to a gleaming chrome lamp.

"Why wouldn't I be able to go in sunlight?" she asked.

Hope cocked her head to the side and narrowed her eyes.

Her ponytail swung like a pendulum. "Your aura is familiar. Not many people have bright starbursts like yours. You've got this massive war going on between duty and acceptance." She squinted. "I can't tell which will win."

"Uh," was all Justice could think to say to that. She felt like she was the victim of an involuntary CT scan on public display.

Hope waved her hand in dismissal. "Sorry. I'm freaking you out, aren't I? How about we try this again. I'm Hope, and once upon a time, I was just like you."

Yeah, right. The two of them couldn't have been less alike unless one of them grew a third arm.

"Like me how?"

"I came here with no memories of who or what I was. I was lucky enough to be taken in by a woman who loved me like a daughter, but without that, I probably would have gone crazy."

She probably would have turned inanimate objects into her friends or something batshit like that.

Hope continued, "I worked for years to recover my memories, but nothing worked. Until Logan. He helped me remember who I am. What I am." A sappy smile warmed her expression. "I remember how lonely it was to have no past. How frustrating. I want you to know that you're not alone. I'm here for you, no matter how long it takes for you to recover your memories."

"So, you think I can?" Justice asked with far too much desperation in her voice.

"I did. Maybe I can help. How about I tell you what I know and you see if anything strikes a chord?"

"I'd like that."

Hope beamed. "My mother is Athanasian. She snuck out of her world even though it was forbidden and came to Earth to find a man to give her a child. Because she couldn't be gone long without her asshole father noticing, as soon as I was conceived, she went to a world called Temprocia where time flows much faster than either here or on Athanasia. As soon as I was born, she had to go home, but I couldn't go with her. If her father knew I existed, I'd be cursed like the rest of the Sanguinar and never be able to go into the sunlight." A shiver of dread coursed through her delicate frame. "So, she made the ultimate sacrifice and left me with a woman named Brenya to raise me. There were a lot of other girls there just like me."

"Other girls?" Justice felt something in her mind wobble and shift, like Jell-O being sucked through a straw. She tried to grasp it, but it was gone before she had time to even realize what it was.

Hope nodded. "At least a dozen. We lived in these small villages in the jungle. Does that ring a bell?"

Justice waited for something else in her brain to wiggle, but everything stayed steady. "No. Sorry."

"Then I'll keep going," Hope said. "Once I was old enough, I was sent back to Earth to help fight the war against Synestryn. The only problem was that if I knew about the demons, they'd come for me before I was able to find safety and learn how to exist in this world. So, in order to protect me, my memories were stripped away, leaving me protected until I was ready."

"How did you know you were ready if you couldn't remember anything?"

"I had to have help. I never would have remembered anything without Logan. I think that was an intentional safeguard Brenya put on our memories so she would be sure we were with allies before we could draw Synestryn to us."

"Us?"

Hope nodded. "I think you and I are the same. I know you probably don't remember me. And the fact that I don't remember you means we were raised in different villages on Temprocia, or that you left before I was born. But when I look at you, there's something familiar there. I recognize parts of you that I've never seen in anyone who wasn't like me."

Justice sat then. She had no choice. After a decade of wondering who and what she was, this walking bit of sunshine was just handing over all the answers. Freely.

It was too good to be true. Wasn't it?

"I know it's a lot to digest," Hope said. "And until your memories return, you probably won't feel like it's real, but the longer I'm with you, the more certain I am that we're the same. We may even be cousins."

Justice looked at her dark skin, then Hope's sun-kissed tan. "I find that hard to believe."

"Our mothers were almost certainly sisters. Who knows who our dads were, though. That would account for how different we look."

"What makes you say our mothers were related?"

"Because the only people in Athanaisa who are strong enough to rebel against the Solarc and travel through a gate are his children. When his sons mate with humans, a Theronai is born. When his daughters do the same, it produces a Sanguinar."

This was all too much. Not only was there another world filled with magical people, apparently there were more than one. Justice was having a hard time with just Earth and the things creeping across its face. How the hell was she going to deal with more?

"I know it's a lot," Hope said as if reading her mind. "But Brenya taught us everything. Once you recover your memories, I'm sure it will all come back to you."

"And how do I do that?" Justice asked.

"You'll need help from your own kind."

"You?"

Hope shook her head. "I'm not skilled with that kind of thing. You need someone who is experienced with altering memories. Like Ronan. He's great with the kids. Very gentle."

Just like his kiss on Justice's neck.

The thought of Ronan being gentle with her made a delicious shiver slip down her spine. If a brush of his lips could rock her world, she wondered what he could do with his fingers, or his tongue.

"And there's something else that might help. It's kinda weird, but taking Logan's blood seemed to be the key for me."

"His blood?"

"Just a few drops. I know it sounds gross but trust me." A secret smile curved her mouth. "It's not. You'll see."

Justice very much doubted that. No way was she drinking blood, even if she was a Sanguinar the way Hope thought. Justice had never needed it before, and she didn't need it now.

Hope's phone chirped, and when she looked at it, her smile widened. "I need to go. Duty calls. But if you have any questions, just call me. I'm happy to help."

"Are you sure about all this?" Justice asked. "I mean, you didn't do hard drugs when you were young or something? Maybe make all this shit up?"

Hope laughed. "It won't feel real until it does. Be patient with yourself. Don't force the memories. All you'll do is make your head hurt." She rose and reached out her hand. "It was so great to meet you. I was beginning to think I was the only one of us who made it."

"How many of us are there?" Justice asked as she took Hope's hand to bid her farewell.

Whatever the other woman might have said was lost in a rush of agony screaming through Justice's head. She recognized the pain from all those times she'd resisted the compulsion to act, but never in her life had she skipped the warning itch and burn that usually came first.

This was an avalanche of agony, hitting her from out of nowhere.

She doubled over in pain, clutching her head so that it wouldn't explode in a shower of bone and brain. A harsh, strangling sound welled from her throat, when all she wanted to do was beg Hope to kill her. End the pain.

Maybe if Justice could reach Reba...

There were frantic words in the distance, well beyond her ability to understand.

The roar of pain slowly died down to a scream, then a whimper. When it was gone, Justice was on the floor, twitching and rocking.

She tried to breathe, but her body was too clenched to let

in any air. After what seemed like an hour, she was finally able to suck in little sips of oxygen between sobs.

Ronan crashed in through the door. "What happened?"

"I don't know," Hope said. "I barely touched her hand and she just crumpled, screaming."

Is that what had happened? Justice had no idea. She was still too shaken to form a coherent thought.

All she knew was that the fates were making demands, and if she didn't start moving, they were going to kill her for disobeying.

South. She had to go south.

Justice tried to pull her ravaged body in that direction, but she had no strength. She couldn't even sit up.

"I wanted to help her," Hope said, "but I was afraid to touch her again."

Ronan crouched beside her and pulled her upright against his body. He didn't ask her if she was okay, he simply slipped inside of her mind to see for himself. She could feel him there, like a warm spot of light hovering just behind her eyes.

Everywhere his glow touched, her pain disappeared, like he'd burned it away with his potent light.

She leaned into him and let him do what he wanted. She didn't have the air or the energy to protest.

His solid body felt nice against hers. Comforting.

She'd never been comforted by anyone before, and it was a strangely pleasant feeling—one she could quickly get used to.

He was moving around inside her thoughts. She wasn't sure how she knew that, because he seemed stationary. That warm glow never seemed to shift position, but he traveled to different parts of her all the same.

After a few moments, she felt him slip away from her, leaving her cold and lonely. His body was still holding hers, but the rest of him was gone.

She was utterly alone.

"I think I know what happened," he said, panting.

Was being inside of her hard on him? The thought

bothered her more than it should have. She should have been glad that he couldn't just waltz through her mind, willy-nilly, without some kind of consequence. Heaven knew she couldn't inflict any on him in the state she was in.

"What?" Hope asked, which was good, because Justice still didn't have the ability to speak.

"The walls of Dabyr are warded against all kinds of magic. I felt the presence inside of her trying to reach her, but not quite able to get through."

"Then what was that?"

"When you touched her, it somehow strengthened the connection to whoever or whatever is using her. I think they were able to reach her through you for a split second."

"Remind me never to touch you again," Justice finally managed.

Hope tucked her hands under her arms and took a step back. Horror painted her pretty face. "I had no idea. I'm so sorry."

Now that the rampaging storm in Justice's head was abating, she was able to voice the fading echo of what the fates wanted from her.

"I need to head south," she said, sure that was what was demanded of her.

"And leave the walls that are keeping this presence from controlling you?" Ronan asked.

"I can't stay here forever. The longer I wait to obey, the worse it will be when I leave." She swallowed hard at the thought. "I can't imagine it being much worse than that. It almost killed me. I can't wait and risk it."

He shook his head. "I don't like it. We don't know who the presence compelling you is."

Justice nodded to Hope and asked Ronan, "Do you trust her?"

"Absolutely," was his immediate response.

"If the fates could use Hope as a conduit to get to me inside these walls, then they must be someone she knows, right?"

"Maybe Brenya," Hope said. "She's certainly powerful

enough to compel someone worlds away."

Ronan didn't look convinced. "Even if that was the case, which I'm not sure it is, you're in no condition to travel."

"I've driven in a lot worse shape than this before. Ricardo has my back. I'm fine." She struggled to her feet, but the way she swayed made her wonder if her statement was true.

"You're not fine. I keep telling you that you're still healing. Do I need to remove the magic keeping you from feeling the effects of the damage you suffered?"

"No, thank you. I've got enough problems."

She needed to gather her few possessions and throw them back in her overnight bag, but she wasn't quite able to stand up without leaning on Ronan yet.

When he set her on the couch, she had no choice but to go there.

So much for being able to drive.

"We need to slow down and figure out what's going on," Ronan said.

"I'm screwed," Justice said. "That's what's going on. That's what's always going on."

He shook his head. "You're safe here. You should stay until we have a better idea what we're up against."

"I may be safe, but what about someone else?" she asked.

"I don't understand."

"If I'm not out there doing what is demanded of me, then who is going to suffer? Will there be another little girl like Pepper who gets sold to the highest bidder? Or will another man who's chained up and starving in a basement not get his midnight snack?"

Ronan's beautiful face darkened. "You're not responsible for saving everyone."

"Maybe not, but aren't you glad I saved you?"

His mouth twisted as if he tasted something vile, and he let out a curse. "Do you think that's what this compulsion is?"

"I have no idea," she answered honestly. "I rarely do until it's right in front of me."

"She has a point, Ronan," Hope said. "I know it's a risk,

but what choice do we have? I didn't feel any evil taint when I touched her. There's nothing bad in her aura. I think we have to believe that whoever is sending her these compulsions is trying to help."

"Help everyone but her, at least," Ronan said.

"It's not your choice," Justice said. "If I'm not a prisoner here, then I can leave when I want. I may not like the hand I've been dealt, but I've come to terms with it and learned that it's always better to obey."

Hope frowned in thought. "I knew someone who used to say that all the time—someone on Temprocia." She shook her head. "I can't recall a name, but I remember a woman who came to have a child when I was little. It was her third time there. I remember because it was a big deal for someone to be strong enough to go through three rounds of travel between worlds. Everyone was in awe."

Ronan turned to Hope. "Are you sure?"

The sunshiny ponytail bobbed. "Yes. Brenya was big on obedience, too. We were all very well-mannered children. Or else."

"Or else what?" Justice asked.

"Or else we'd get eaten by something. It was a wild place we grew up in. Plenty of predators, not to mention a mad king who would kill us on sight if he knew we existed."

Ronan looked at Justice. "I don't want you to leave, but if you do, I'm coming with you."

"What about the sun? It will be up in a few hours."

"We'll take my van. I'll sleep in back. The windows are warded to protect me from the light."

"I have no idea what I'll be walking into," she said.

"I know. That's why I don't want you to go alone."

She almost refused his help but stopped herself. Not because she was afraid, or because she hated the idea of him worrying about her. No, she was going to let him come because when he was around, she felt better, like she wasn't completely alone. She almost wondered if being with him was what happy felt like. She'd never been happy before, so she wasn't really sure. People talked about it a lot though, and she'd always hoped to experience the illusive emotion someday.

"Okay," she said. "Pack what you need for a few days and meet me at the van."

"Any idea where we're going or what we'll be doing?" he asked.

"Not a clue," she said, then added. "Welcome to my world."

***

Justice's world was a fucked-up place.

They'd been on the road for less than three hours when she hijacked a semi headed for a sporting goods store. She left the driver tied up a few yards off the road and called an Uber to come pick him up in an hour. Then she left a note taped to a mile marker post, telling the cabbie where to find him.

She ripped out all the tracking equipment onboard the rig, then took off with Ronan trailing behind her in his van.

Just before dawn, she pulled the semi into a building that looked like it had once been used as an aircraft hangar. There were no other buildings around. The metal structure was like a giant mushroom that had randomly popped up in the middle of the countryside.

He followed her inside the building and left his headlights on while she powered up the industrial lights overhead.

There were no aircraft inside, but the space was lined with rows of heavy warehouse shelving. Stretch-wrapped pallets of boxes were stacked nearly to the ceiling. Most of them held shelf-stable food, like crackers and canned goods. One whole row was filled with nothing but bottled water and sports drinks. Another section he recognized as medical supplies. The rest of the boxes were a mystery.

She shut off the rig and climbed up into a forklift, then proceeded to unload the back of the semi and stack the pallets on the last empty shelves remaining. A few of the unloaded pallets were put back inside the trailer, following some logic he didn't understand.

Next, she ripped open boxes until she found a gym bag and then proceeded to fill it with a seemingly random array of objects: a metal water bottle with a screw top, a small pocket knife, a flashing LED light one would wear while jogging or biking at night, and a few other items he didn't recognize.

While she searched through boxes, Ronan strolled through the building, openly staring at her collection. She didn't try to stop him, so whatever she had going on here wasn't a secret— at least not from him.

When she was finally finished unloading her stolen goods, the sun was above the horizon and Ronan was forced to take shelter in the back of his van. The warehouse had no windows, but he wasn't taking any chances that a missing rivet or rust hole would let in the one ray of sunshine that would hit his skin and destroy everything she'd worked to collect. And the two of them.

She found him in the back of his van, climbed in and handed him one of the bottles of water she carried.

"Where's your bag of loot?" he asked.

"Stashed in the truck."

"Any idea why?"

"Nope."

That was what he assumed.

"What is this place?" he asked.

"Stockpile."

"For what?"

She shrugged. "The zombie apocalypse, I guess. I really have no clue. I gather what I'm told to gather."

"What's with the sporting goods?"

Again, she shrugged. "Maybe I'll need a few yoga mats and tennis balls to kill the zombies."

She was so casual about the whole thing, like it was completely normal to have a random hangar filled with supplies.

Maybe for her, that was normal.

He must have been wearing his thoughts on his face because she shrugged at his unanswered question. "After a while, you get used to random acts of chaos and stop asking why. It's easier just to go with the flow."

He couldn't even imagine.

"Is this where you live?" he asked.

"I don't live anywhere. I have some clothes, cash, guns and ammunition stocked here, but I keep those things in all my warehouses."

He stared at her as he adjusted his estimation of just how crazy her world was. "How many of these places do you have?"

"Just three."

"Of course. Because four would be ridiculous."

She gave him a half-grin, but even that much of a smile nearly knocked him off his feet. If she ever beamed at him, he wouldn't survive it. She'd be too beautiful to gaze upon.

"You're making fun of me, aren't you?" she asked.

Weariness tugged at him, but he fought it off so he could be with her like this for a few more minutes. He'd have to sleep soon, but not yet.

"Maybe a little," he said. "You know your hoarding isn't normal, right?"

"I do. But I also know that no one is screaming in my head anymore, either. I'll take that silence over normal any day of the week."

"When will the next compulsion come?"

"Who knows. It doesn't usually take long, though. A few minutes. A few hours."

No wonder she was never in one place for long. "What will you do with the truck?"

"Add it to my collection. I have two more out back."

"Are you worried about the police finding them outside?"

She shook her head. "That's the thing with being fueled by otherworldly powers. They always seem know when the cops are coming and compel me to hide the goods."

"Handy."

"On occasion." She finished her water and leaned back against the wall of the van. She was close enough to touch, but he didn't. He was content having her here and knowing she was safe. If he touched her, she might retreat, and he didn't want that.

"I thought about you a lot when I was searching for you," he said. "I imagined what you did and where you lived."

"Did you guess right?"

"Not even close." His eyelids were heavy, but he wasn't ready to stop looking at her yet. "I wondered why you kept running from me."

She grunted. "Because you freaked me out."

"Says the woman with enough firearms to supply a small army."

"If I'd wanted to kill you, all I had to do was not give you my blood that night."

He could still remember her taste—how surprisingly sweet and potent she was. There was no blood on earth that was as intoxicating as hers, as addictive. Even thinking about it made his mouth water.

Her fingers trailed over the twin puckered scars as if remembering.

He could never forget. They'd formed a blood bond that night, and he doubted that he'd ever know another quite like it.

His eyelids drooped. His body began to weaken as the sun rose.

"I need to rest now," he said. "Promise me you won't leave."

"I can't promise anything, but I will tell you that I have no intention of leaving until I have to. I'm kind of exhausted myself. If the fates let me, I'm going to get a few hours of sleep."

He stretched out on the narrow mattress and patted the space next to him in invitation. "There's room for both of us. And if you're worried about me groping you while you sleep, I will be far too lethargic. You're safe with me."

She lifted her gaze from his hand to his face and said, "Somehow I doubt that."

"I promised I wouldn't hurt you again. You know I can't break my vow."

"It's not you feeding on me that worries me."

"Then what does?"

She lay down beside him, giving him her back. In a faint voice he wouldn't have heard if not for his heightened senses, she said, "What I might have to do to you."

***

Maura paced her chamber, willing the chill in her limbs to warm—a chill that had nothing to do with the temperature in the caves she inhabited.

Her room was a cold, damp hole in the ground with walls constantly wet with earth's tears. Small puddles formed at the base of the walls, and no amount of rugs or curtains seemed to warm the space.

She missed being aboveground. She missed being with creatures who walked in the sun and ate something other than raw meat and blood.

But most of all, she missed her sister, Sibyl.

They'd been apart for so long—a state that was unnatural to both of them.

She was good, kind and sweet, where Maura was not. Sibyl was eager to please and to serve the cause of the Sentinels—protecting humans and destroying Synestryn. Maura had been more interested in rebelling against her mother, who'd imprisoned her in a child's body out of fear and selfishness.

But now Gilda and Angus were dead. Maura had killed them.

It hadn't brought her satisfaction. It hadn't brought her peace. Just or not, all her parents' death had brought her was another empty, black spot in her soul.

She wanted to know what was going to happen to her

sister. She ached to grab ahold of the power they shared, taking turns telling the future. She could feel its presence like a vibrating ball in the center of her mind. All she had to do was reach for it and force it to do her bidding.

Maura didn't dare. Something dark and deadly was coming for the Sentinels, and if her sister saw it coming, the creature who ruled this territory would know Maura was a traitor.

Vazel was as powerful as he was ugly. He'd stepped up to take the place of the beautiful Synestryn queen who'd ruled before him. She was dead now, but her son lived on. When he was old enough, he'd take his mother's throne—a throne Vazel was keeping warm for him.

He'd warned Maura that his protection came with strings. She might be a Theronai with powers of her own, but in a world filled with beasts who craved nothing more than her blood, she needed more than the ability to see the future when it was her turn to play with the gift she and Sibyl shared.

Even Maura's ability to kill with a single touch did little good against monsters with no ability to reason. The things that lurked down here were often little more than animals with a thirst for blood. They didn't understand what she could do, and once she'd showed them, it would be too late to save her from becoming a deadly feast.

She needed Vazel and this weeping stone chamber to keep her alive. At least for now.

Vazel entered her chamber without so much as announcing his presence. He was a large creature, that was only vaguely humanoid. He had gray, almost reptilian skin with mangy patches of fur here and there. His head was bald and bulbous, nearly too big for his frame. His joints were swollen and knobby with extra flesh that sagged when he was tired. He had thin lips that showed off pointed teeth where they weren't simply missing. Every time he spoke, spittle flew, so she'd learned to keep her distance. And if the flying spit hadn't taught her that, the dirty, barely-there loincloth he wore would have.

There were some things a lady could never un-see. Vazel's genitals were firmly in that category.

Trailing behind the grotesque demon was a young boy who looked to be three or four years old, but had been born only a few weeks ago. Vazel called Mordecai his son, but the only thing they had in common was the loincloth.

Mordecai was a beautiful child, with thick, black hair and translucent black eyes. Rumor said that he was the offspring of the dead queen and a Slayer, but Maura had no idea. Nor did she care.

She didn't dare make attachments down here, when there were so many creatures who wanted her dead, and even more she could kill with a touch. She really didn't want Mordecai to be her next victim.

She squared her shoulders and channeled her mother's best disappointed frown. "Where are your manners, Vazel? Don't you know it's rude to enter a lady's chamber unannounced?"

"You think you're a lady?" Vazel asked in a spray of spittle.

She ignored the insult and held her haughty stance. "Why are you here?"

Vazel put a too-long arm around the boy's slender shoulders and pulled him close. "My son needs to go outside, into the sun. You will escort him."

"Why?"

"Because you can go into the sun and I cannot. And because I demand it."

"No, why does he need to go into the sun?"

The demon shared a look with the child he called his son, but clearly was not. Neither said a word, but some kind of communication seemed to have taken place.

"It's time. Go now," Vazel said.

She had nothing better to do than pace and fret and try not to play with the toy humming in the middle of her mind. "Fine."

The child held out his hand to her. Maura was wearing

gloves, but she didn't risk touching the boy. She really didn't want to watch him die, writhing in pain.

Vazel on the other hand...

"You must never touch her," he told Mordecai with gentle patience. "She is unclean. Dangerous."

Unclean? At least she changed her underwear on a regular basis. Vazel was still wearing the same grimy loincloth he'd had on for days. Maybe longer.

They wound their way through the complicated maze of tunnels and openings in the stone. The path led gradually upward until they reached a small hole in the side of a rocky hillside.

Sunlight streamed in from outside. Vazel held himself well back from the light and pushed the boy forward.

"If you let any harm come to him, I will eat you, starting with those pretty eyes."

Maura ignored his threat, stepped into the light and followed the boy outside.

The air was cold, but crisp and dry. The sky was clear, allowing sunlight to pour into her skin. It felt good. Clean.

Sometimes she forgot how much she missed the sun.

She moved a few feet away from the dank opening into the nest of demons and sat on a rock near a grassy patch.

Mordecai stood in the clearing, turned his face up to the sun, spread his chubby arms wide, and closed his eyes. Pure bliss poured out of him, like he'd been starving and was finally being fed a delicious meal. He didn't say a word, but he didn't need to. There was something otherworldly about his silence.

"Can you speak?" she asked.

He cracked open one eye and peered at her before going back to his sunbathing.

"I guess that's a no."

Then again, he was only a few weeks old. Maybe his voice needed time to catch up to his rapidly-aging body.

"I wouldn't trust Vazel if I were you," she said. "I know he acts all nice toward you, but he's not a good..." Man? Creature? Demon? "...father. All he cares about is himself."

Mordecai wore no clothing to keep the chill from his tiny body. The strip of fabric around his hips was little more than a dirty flag waving in the wind.

He lowered his chin and stared at her again, but this time, his eyes were no longer that translucent black, but a rich, golden brown. As she watched, plumes of black swirled within the depths of his gaze, hiding within the shade his thick lashes created.

He toddled to her on bare feet, faster and more nimble than he had any right to be. She half-expected him to backhand her for the insult to his father, which is something he could have learned from the demon on more than one occasion. Vazel ruled his little empire with violence and the threat of more.

Before she could skitter away, Mordecai touched her cheek.

Images flooded her mind of Vazel. He was smiling, his thin lips stretched grotesquely over pointy teeth. He cradled her in his arms. She stared up at him, through eyes that weren't her own as he sang her an off-tune lullaby and rocked her to sleep.

These things she was seeing were Mordecai's memories. Somehow, he was sharing them with her.

Was he trying to prove her wrong—that Vazel wasn't the monster she knew him to be? Or was he trying to change her mind?

Maura scrambled back off the stone and landed hard on her hip. "Don't touch me," she warned him. "Don't ever touch me."

Mordecai didn't seem afraid. In fact, he showed no sign of emotion on his little face at all. It was as still and calm as it had always been.

It struck her then that she'd never seen him smile. Never heard him cry.

What kind of child did that? Then again, what kind of child could make you see what they wanted you to with a mere touch?

Maura rose to her feet and donned a protective layer of

haughty irritation. "Touch me again and I'll take off these gloves and show you why your father warned you to stay away."

Mordecai simply toddled off and went back to soaking up the sunlight.

She thought briefly about leaving. She could wander off and find another home. One cave was as good as another. Her reputation among the Synestryn would gain her shelter almost anywhere. And if it didn't, all she had to do was put on a little display, kill a few demons and make a show of it.

But what would that gain her? If she abandoned Mordecai, Vazel would hunt her down. Eventually, he'd find her and make good on his promise to eat her eyes first.

She could take Mordecai with her. He'd make a good hostage. Not only would a threat to him keep Vazel away, the child had to be useful to someone.

Maybe she could even go home, to Dabyr. Warn them of the danger speeding their way.

Maybe she could see Sibyl again and hug her one more time before the end.

Maura didn't realize she was crying until she felt Mordecai's gaze on her. A hint of sympathy shone in his golden eyes, and it was the first flicker of emotion she'd ever seen in him.

Maybe he was more demon than she suspected.

"Would you like to take a trip with me?" she asked. "Go someplace warm and sunny?"

Dabyr wasn't far. They could make it there before nightfall. He'd be safe there, even if she wasn't. No Sentinel would ever harm a small boy who looked human.

That was why the Synestryn had begun breeding offspring that looked human. They knew that their enemy would have trouble lopping off the heads of creatures who looked like those they were sworn to protect. And while the latest generation of demons had human faces, very few of them survived long enough to reproduce. The best they'd managed were the masses of gray-skinned creatures with plenty of loyalty, but not very many brains. But what they lacked in intelligence, they more than made up for in numbers.

Those creatures were going to be the downfall of Dabyr and every person it protected.

Unless she stopped it.

Mordecai turned his back, dismissing her offer to sweep him away from this place—the only home he'd ever known in his brief life.

Maura knew the attack on Dabyr was coming soon. Vazel didn't tell her much, but she heard things. Knew things—things she'd seen in the future but had never shared with her protector.

She'd know a lot more if she allowed herself to glimpse the future, but she didn't. If Maura passed the power of foresight to her sister, Sibyl would see what was coming. She'd see just how far Maura had fallen.

No, it was better to hold onto the power and hide from Sibyl what was coming. At least that way she'd die without knowing the monster Maura had become.

CHAPTER SIX

Justice didn't sleep.

She was tired. Her body felt heavy, as if she'd used up the last of her reserves. Still, sleep evaded her.

She'd met people who knew what she was—people with answers. It was possible they might even be able to help free her. All she had to do was rest and get strong enough for Ronan to try.

Her mind wouldn't cooperate. As tired as she was, her head kept spinning through everything that had happened over the last few hours.

She wasn't alone anymore—at least not right now.

Ronan's body was behind hers, pressing against her in spots. His sleep was deep, unnatural. He barely even breathed.

After an hour of hoping sleep would find her, she finally turned over and looked at him to make sure he was okay.

His complexion was pale, almost dusty. With his eyes closed he looked more like a marble statue of a man than he did flesh and blood. There was an artistic perfection in his features, as if they'd been carved by a master hand. His dark brows and hair gave him more life than if he'd been all stone, but even those strands seemed unnaturally still.

One arm was curled under his head to serve as a pillow. The other hand was tucked under his ribs as if to keep his fingers from straying.

His chest expanded as he breathed, but the act was so slow, it was almost hard to see. Even the pulse beating in his neck was spaced out so that she held her breath waiting for the next fleeting proof of life to show.

He was too beautiful for his own good. All the Sanguinar she'd met were. They all possessed an unearthly perfection that made them untouchable.

Justice wondered why, if she was what they thought she was, she didn't have the same trait. She was pretty enough, but nowhere near the level of Ronan or Hope.

The need to touch him raged through her. Would he be as smooth as he looked? As hard and cold as the marble statue he resembled?

With delicate care, she glided the tip of one finger along his cheekbone. He was smooth, his flesh firm, but not hard. His skin was cool to the touch, but not cold.

The need to snuggle close and warm him once again filled her thoughts.

What was it like to live without the warmth of the sun? She had always enjoyed her time in her convertible, driving with the top down during the summer, the wind in her hair and the sun turning her skin darker. That ball of fire was like an unblinking eye, staring down on her without judgment or blame. He blazed through the sky, doing his job, the way she tore through the country, doing hers. Neither of them had any choice—they went where the powers that be demanded they go. Her trajectory driven by the fates, his by physics.

She wondered if the sun hated his job as much as she hated hers.

Ronan shifted slightly in his sleep. It was more a deeper breath than a movement, but her hand was on his chest now—without permission—and she felt it all the same.

He had several blankets in his apartment, indicating he often got cold. Was he cold now? The heat of the van had faded, and the warehouse heaters were only running enough to keep the water from freezing. Even she was a bit chilly.

She scooted closer and pressed herself firmly against him.

Then she held her breath, waiting for him to react.

He didn't seem to notice from the depths of his sleep, which made her even bolder.

She wrapped her arms around his lean body and snuggled her head against his chest. His pulse was slow, but soothing. The hard press of his muscles against her softer contours was pleasant. She wasn't sure why, but she liked the feel of all that male flesh pressed up against hers.

A coil of need unfurled low in her belly, slow and languid. It stretched as if waking up from a long slumber and pulled in a deep breath.

Heat began to pour out of her, caressing every nerve ending as it went. Her skin seemed to hum wherever it touched his, and the feeling was so addictive, she found herself shoving his shirt up so she could feel more of him.

There were things a man could do to a woman to make her swoon. Justice knew this, even if she'd never felt it. She knew about sex and had even watched some online porn out of sheer curiosity.

Those naked bodies posing for the camera hadn't done much for her, but she finally saw in them what it was to want. She knew why people did the stupidest things in the hopes of getting laid.

Sex was a compulsion all its own, with incoherent demands that made people do things they didn't understand for an outcome they couldn't predict. As much as Justice might want to feel where all this shimmering heat would lead her, she had enough forces tugging on her to add one more.

She pulled her hands away and balled them into fists so she wouldn't touch him. Now was not the time to give into her fascination for Ronan. And that was all it was. She couldn't allow anything more than that—for his sake as well as hers.

She must have drifted off to sleep, because when she opened her eyes, she was stiff and needed to pee. There was no natural light in here to tell her how long she'd been out, but she was grateful for even a few minutes.

She slipped slowly from the mattress so she wouldn't

disturb Ronan, then eased past the closed curtains to get out through the front. The van's clock said she'd gotten a solid six hours, which was more than she'd had at one time in the past year.

After washing up, she went into the little office she kept here, fired up the laptop and checked the usual sites. Several of the black-market dealers she knew were offering up interesting trinkets, but as she scanned the lists, only one item caught the interest of the fates.

She made an aggressive bid, then switched over to a different site to check what job offers had come in.

There were only three, and the fates didn't find any of them interesting. She had plenty of cash, so the only jobs she took now were the ones demanded of her. The less she worked with the scumbags, the better.

She checked her email, but since she had no friends and no life other than her work, that didn't take long.

It was past lunch time, so she microwaved a frozen meal and forced herself to eat to keep up her strength. Ronan had said she was healing, but she didn't feel like it. She felt fine since she'd slept. Good, actually, especially considering she'd taken two rounds only yesterday.

He was handy to have around. Not that she was going to get used to it.

With nothing else to do to kill the hours until it was time to move again, she decided to go outside and catch a rare dose of fresh air.

The wind was winter cold, but the sky was clear and the sun was warm against her skin. She turned her face up to the heavens and simply breathed. As the minutes ticked by, she warmed and felt an odd kind of fullness just beneath her skin. It was pleasant. Almost a kind of satisfaction.

She mourned for Ronan because he could never feel what she did now.

When the sun dipped below the tops of the trees, she went back inside and started her search for Chester Gale. She didn't generally kill by choice, but for him, she was going to make an exception.

Buying and selling little girls simply couldn't go unpunished.

She was at her laptop with her fingers poised over the keys when the itching started.

She knew this respite was too good to be true, but the little bit of hope she'd managed to gather was crushed under the demanding heel of the fates.

It was time to obey.

"Fuck you," she whispered.

A tear slipped down her cheek, but she convinced herself it was squeezed out by the dry winter air, rather than a weak show of frustration.

Justice didn't do weakness. She couldn't afford to.

"Where now?" she demanded and waited for the compulsion to solidify.

The fates led her to the warehouse. She walked up and down the aisles until she found what she was looking for.

Stacked neatly under the pallet rack on the last row was sturdy metal shelving—the kind used to store heavy objects in a garage or workshop. Each one had five shelves six feet wide by two feet deep. A few weeks ago, she'd been compelled to buy every one the big box store had in stock, though she had no idea why.

Following the strong urging of the fates, she used her forklift to move the shelving up into the back of the semi-trailer she'd stolen. Once there, she began to put the shelving together. It would have been easier to do with help, but Ronan was still out until the sun went down and she was on her own.

After struggling with the first one, she figured out how to use the heavy corrugated box to prop up the pieces until she could assemble them. A couple of sweaty hours later, she had all the shelves assembled and attached to the walls of the trailer with heavy screws.

She surveyed her work and waited for the fates to complain. Two rows of shelving lined each long wall of the trailer. She didn't know what was going to go on them, but she was sure the fates would tell her when they felt like it.

With her luck, she'd be forced to steal live, poisonous snakes or yellow cake uranium.

When it was clear that she'd done her job to the satisfaction of the powers that controlled her, she decided to wash off the sweat and grime of her work.

Justice showered and dressed in a pair of worn blue jeans and a soft flannel shirt in muted green plaid that perfectly matched her eyes. She tucked Reba in the back of her jeans and stepped out of the tiny bathroom, right into Ronan's arms, colliding hard.

She was shocked to find him awake before sunset, but even more shocked by how her body lit up and warmed everywhere he touched.

His long fingers were strong bands around her upper arms. His chest grazed her nipples and made them pucker and lengthen to get closer to him. His thigh slid seamlessly between hers, weakening her knees in a way she'd never felt before—at least not without serious bodily injury involved.

Her brain swooped inside her skull, and she realized that this must be what it was like to swoon, like some kind of helpless Victorian maiden.

Fuck that.

She pushed against him to gain herself a few inches of personal space. His hands remained locked around her arms to steady her, but at least he wasn't rubbing against her nipples and her mound anymore.

She wasn't sure if that was an improvement or not.

"I thought you were asleep until sunset," she said in a voice too shaky to be her own.

"I woke a little early." His pale blue gaze slid across her face, all slow and sleepy.

He was too damn beautiful—too damn sexy—for her peace of mind. She didn't know why he affected her the way he did, making her insides melt and go all tingly, but she wished he'd stop.

His finger traced her cheek. "You look troubled. Is

everything okay?"

"Fine. You just surprised me. I thought you'd sleep longer."

"I was hungry."

"For people food?"

He grinned. "People food? You make me sound like a dog."

"You know what I mean."

"I do, and I refuse to be ashamed of what I am. I need blood, Justice. If you prefer not to see me feed, I understand, but I really have no choice." He stepped back, shedding some of the languid remains of sleep. "There's a gerai family not far from here. I'll go see them, then come back for you."

The instant, visceral reaction she had to that statement shocked her.

"Like hell," she said, though she wasn't sure if she was more upset by him leaving her behind or by the idea that he'd take blood from someone else. Maybe some other woman.

"You want to come with me?" he asked.

And then she knew the truth, because going along with him didn't fix the anger simmering in her gut. "I want you to take what you need from me."

He went unearthly still. His eyes lit up and cast a hungry glow onto her face. "You're still healing."

"You said even a few drops from me was like gallons from someone else. I don't see how that much could hurt me."

"It wouldn't. But with you, it's too easy to get carried away. I *crave* you, Justice. It's hard to know when to stop."

That shivery feeling in her limbs grew stronger, and she wished for a chair to sink into.

No man had ever looked at her like Ronan did. No man had ever craved her before—not even for her blood.

To be wanted like that was a powerful thing. It shimmered through her like magic, giving her strength and stealing it all at the same time.

There was no way she was letting him drink from someone else. The thought of his lips on the skin of another was abhorrent. It shoved dark urges buried deep inside her to the surface—the kind of urges that left a body count behind.

She unbuttoned the top button on her shirt and tugged the collar open. "You can have my blood, or none at all."

His eyes flared bright. He stepped closer, all lean predator now. His concern for her welfare had disappeared the second she'd bared herself to him.

The twin scars over her pulse throbbed.

"You're playing a dangerous game, Justice."

"I'm not playing at all. We had a deal. My blood for your help. Take what you need and do what you promised. Free me from the fates."

He lowered his head and pushed back her damp curls. His breath swept across her neck, making her shiver. One strong arm wrapped around her waist and pulled her tight against his body. The other pushed her head aside, exposing her neck.

Anticipation shimmered through her, growing hotter and fiercer until she thought she'd go mad. Every second stretched out, long and empty. Then his lips brushed her skin, almost but not quite a kiss.

In the next instant, there was a sharp sting and a release of pressure as his teeth broke through her skin. That fleeting second of pain dissipated, leaving behind a kind of pleasure she'd never felt before.

Her veins hummed and pulsed with energy. She felt like she was being caressed from the inside, out, like every part of her was bathing in the sun and stroked by a warm breeze. An intoxicating heat spread through her until her entire body went weak.

Ronan took her weight easily, holding her up with his strong arms. His lips moved over her skin and his tongue did a sinuous dance that made her dream of feeling the same thing against her nipples.

The desperate suction slowed until it was a leisurely suckling that was as close to a kiss as she could ever remember coming.

Too soon, the whole thing was over. She felt the intense

flush of magical healing, then after a few more swipes of his tongue, he was done.

Justice didn't move. She couldn't have if she'd tried. Her body was too relaxed and happy to do more than lay limp in his arms while he held her against his hard body.

He was warm now. Her blood was flowing through him, keeping him all toasty inside.

The idea was so intimate, she shivered at the power of it.

Ronan lifted his head and stared down at her. The hunger in his eyes was gone, but that bright glow was still going strong.

"I like you like this," he said, "all relaxed and pliant." His finger traced her brow, her temple, her cheek, then across her mouth.

Her lips parted, and her tongue darted out to taste his skin. Salt, magic and man. He tasted like her dreams, and she didn't know if she'd ever get enough.

He eased them to the floor with his back against the wall and her curled on his lap like a child. He cradled her as if she were as precious as one.

She'd never been precious to anyone. Important, perhaps. A necessary thing, like a tool or a weapon, but never a valued treasure.

If he didn't stop looking at her like that, she was going to start forgetting the way things were and go right along with this fantasy.

When reality returned, where would that leave her?

"Close your eyes, sweet," he said. "Relax and let me inside you."

Her pussy clenched at his words, but it wasn't her body that he was talking about sliding into, it was her mind.

Justice relaxed completely and let him take what he wanted.

She felt him there, right behind her eyes. His presence was strong and hot, and completely unmistakable. If she had a thousand vampires in her head, she'd know exactly which one was him. No other man could feel like he did—like he was woven from hopes and dreams and clothed in secret magic.

He was stronger than he'd ever been before with her. She didn't know much about what was happening, but she could feel his power throbbing within her, so deep that they were one.

She needed this—his presence. There were other things she needed, too, but having him within her was now as vital to her as air. She didn't know how she'd ever survive once he left.

"Shh," he said, his voice soothing her along with the stroke of his presence. "There's nothing to worry about. Everything is fine. Just relax and float. I've got you."

Relaxing wasn't her forte, but with Ronan, it was easy. She felt him moving within her and didn't try to stop him. She let him go where he wanted, seeing her mistakes and her victories alike. She let him see the parts of her that brought her pride and those that made her ashamed. She let him poke that foggy veil hiding her past, even though her head throbbed every time he did.

She knew he was trying to help free her from the fates, and as in medicine, sometimes the cure was as painful as the disease.

He pressed harder, and every time he did, she suffered a little more. After a few minutes, she was sweating and shaking from the pain. If he didn't stop, she was going to puke all over him.

She opened her mouth to say just that, but before she could, she felt him retreat. That glowing, powerful presence shifted out of her, leaving her feeling lonely, even though their bodies were pressed together.

She looked up to find him panting. His color was paler than usual, which was saying something. He seemed thinner, almost bony. The hollows under his cheekbones were more pronounced, and he had shadowy circles under his eyes.

"It didn't work, did it?" she asked.

He leaned his head back against the wall in defeat. "I'm sorry. I tried a few things, but none of them worked. There's definitely a presence inside you, but I couldn't cage it or pull it into me."

She sat up on his lap. "Pull it into you? You were going to free me by taking the fates for yourself? Are you nuts?"

"I've done it before, though only with demons."

Her jaw fell open in shock. "You took someone else's demons into yourself?"

"It was the only way. Others aren't as mentally strong as I am. It's better that I battle these creatures on their behalf."

Justice had no words to adequately respond to that. What kind of lunatic let himself be possessed—or whatever the correct term was—to save another?

"And you thought you could do that with the fates?" she asked, still reeling.

"It was worth a shot."

"Do you have any idea what you could have done to yourself? The fates don't give a shit about what time of day it is. They'd demand you do what they wanted, whether or not the sun was up. You would have killed yourself."

"I would have found a way to defeat them once they were my prisoner."

"Your prisoner? What about you being theirs?"

He gave his head a weak shake. "That wasn't part of my plan. Not that it matters. I wasn't strong enough to pull the presence in you out. It's almost like it's part of you."

"You think I'm doing this to myself?" she asked.

"No. It's definitely someone or something else enforcing their will on you, but whatever it is, it's so deeply entwined within you, there's no way for me to extract it. Even if it were possible, to do so would probably kill you."

Defeat landed heavily over her and shoved the air from her lungs. She struggled under the weight for several seconds before she managed to speak. "So I'm stuck. No cure."

"I didn't say that. I said I can't pull that presence out of you, but there are other things to try."

"Like what?"

"I could cage it or put it to sleep. Perhaps even kill it."

"But if we're so tightly bound, would that also kill me?"

He opened one eye, but barely. "I don't know yet. I ran out of strength before I could try."

He really did look wrung out, like a used dish rag, albeit a beautiful one.

"Take more of my blood."

"It's too soon to try to free you again."

"I didn't mean that. I meant you need to regain your strength. You used it all up and then some."

"It's too soon for that, too."

"Bullshit. I feel fine." She did, but the deeper truth was she wanted to feel his mouth on her skin again, moving as he fed from her. The thrill of it was both erotic and addictive.

Which only proved just how crazy she was. Who wanted a vampire sucking their blood, regardless of what he called himself?

"I'll be fine until we find someone else."

She wouldn't share him. Not like that. At least not yet. She knew she couldn't tie him to her for the rest of his life, but until she found a way to get over whatever spell he'd put her under, he was stuck with one food group. Her.

Justice pulled a pocket knife from her jeans and held it against the tingling scars he'd left behind a few weeks ago. "Your way is easier, but we can do it mine if you prefer."

His blue eyes lit up and a snarl covered his face. Sharp fangs elongated just behind his lips, gleaming white.

One second she was sitting between his open thighs, the next, she was lying on the concrete floor with his body covering hers.

He was stronger than she could have imagined, easily pinning her hands by her ears.

Reba bit into Justice's back, but she barely felt it. The hungry look on his face was all-consuming, driving every other thought from her mind.

"I am not weak," she snarled.

"You don't know what you're asking of me. You don't know how hard it is to resist you."

She tilted her head in a blatant dare. "Then don't."

She saw the moment she won the battle, but it wasn't defeat she saw in his expression, but something else. Something wild and untamed. Something hungry.

"Just remember," he said as he lowered his sharp teeth to her throat. "You asked for this."

CHAPTER SEVEN

Ronan was going to go too far this time. His efforts to free Justice from the presence haunting her had weakened him, leaving him as hungry as he'd been when he'd woken. Her possessive, almost belligerent offer to let him feed was too much temptation to resist.

If he hadn't seen in her mind how much she enjoyed him drinking from her, he might have been able to summon his willpower. But he had seen the pleasure his feeding brought her, and that was his undoing.

He so wanted to make her feel good.

His body pinned hers to the concrete floor. He wished they were in the van with a cushion beneath her back, but if she was uncomfortable, she wasn't complaining.

Her smell was intoxicating. Warm and honeyed, but with a hint of something herbal and clean. Beyond that was the scent of her arousal, so strong he didn't know how he was going to resist slicing off her jeans and giving her what her body so desperately craved.

As adept as he was at healing tissue and mending bone, he was even more skilled at making a woman's flesh obey his commands. He could easily slip into her mind and make her come with a mere thought. Her body would go where he led it, especially once he was buried inside her.

A raging rush of lust swept through him, so powerful it

left him shaking. His cock was hard and straining against his jeans. His skin was acutely sensitive, until even the slight shift of air in the room felt like a caress.

He had to fill his needs—food and sex. There was no denying both of them. He was already stretched too thin.

Ronan lifted his head and stared down at her.

Her shirt was open at the throat, revealing a tempting swath of flesh he wanted to kiss and taste. The swell of her breast peeked out above the green flannel, so soft and round his fingers clenched involuntarily. Her springy black curls were still wet from her shower and spread out around her head as another tactile treat for the senses.

She opened her eyes to reveal thin slivers of silvery-green behind thick, curling lashes.

There was want there. Desire. And maybe more than a hint of challenge.

He felt himself smile at that, so typically Justice. His fangs were still out, and he knew she'd be able to see them peeking out from his lips.

"What are you waiting for?" she asked. The way her lips moved, it felt like an invitation. They were full and plump and he knew he couldn't go one more minute without knowing how they felt against his own.

She saw his approach and froze.

She was willing to share her blood but not her kiss? He knew she wanted him. He could smell how aroused she was, hear her rapid pulse and see the flare of her nostrils as she pulled in his scent.

With the lightest of touches, he flitted into her thoughts, barely grazing the surface. Perhaps it was an intrusion of her privacy but he really didn't care. If he was about to make some giant mistake with her, he wanted to know.

Excitement and fear wared for supremacy in her mind. She was afraid to get too close because of another man she'd once known.

Had he hurt her? Broken her heart?

Ronan held Justice's gaze and dove deeper into her

memories until he found what he was looking for.

Noah. He'd befriended her shortly after she'd woken here, naked and alone. He'd helped her learn how to survive and how to find work. He'd introduced her to his contacts on the black market and been a good friend.

Then, one day, the fates had ordered her to kill him. She didn't know why and had tried to resist. Her disobedience had nearly killed her, but in the end, she'd done what she was ordered to do.

To this day, she still didn't know why she'd been forced to murder the only friend she had, but since then she'd never gotten close to anyone.

Until Ronan.

He understood now why he was a threat, why she had run from him. Him taking her blood the night they met was the most intimate thing she'd shared with anyone, and she was terrified she was going to be forced to kill him, too.

The sad truth was that she might. Until they drove the presence in her mind out, she was at the mercy of that powerful force, and if he tried to stop her from following orders, it would only cause her pain.

She stared at him, understandably caught between desire and fear. Now he knew why, and now he could push her in the direction he wanted her to go.

There was no question which he wanted her to feel.

Ronan moved in and kissed her. The instant his lips met hers, her whole demeanor changed, and she gave in with abandon.

She grabbed his shoulders and pulled him tighter against her. Her mouth opened and her tongue swept into his mouth, giving him a taste of heaven. She flirted with the sharp tips of his fangs, but he was careful not to let her draw blood.

Sanguinar were very careful about mixing blood and sex. It was too easy to get carried away as the frenzy of lust and hunger collided. If she ingested even a little of his blood, her body would become receptive to his sperm and she could become pregnant.

There wasn't enough blood to feed the Sanguinar they already had. Bringing another into the world would have been the height of irresponsibility. Even dreaming about having a child was something Ronan had forbade himself from doing.

He'd seen others of his kind take that first step and it had destroyed them. To want a child you could never have, or to have one and watch it suffer? None of them were strong enough for that.

Still, he couldn't seem to gain enough control to draw in his fangs, so being careful with them was the only thing he could do.

Her hands roamed his back, alternately clutching and petting as if she couldn't decide which she wanted to do. Soft sounds of hunger and pleasure drifted out of her in a musical chorus he'd never get tired of hearing.

Her kisses were as fierce as she was, with surprising moments of softness that always kept him guessing. By the time he started working to unbutton her shirt, he was strung so tight with lust he couldn't even think clearly.

Ronan spread the lapels of her flannel shirt to reveal the sweetest breasts he'd ever seen. Dark nipples showed clearly through the thin white bra she wore. The tips were tight, stabbing hard through the fabric. The shadowy valley that disappeared between her breasts was an invitation for his fingers and tongue to follow.

He lowered his head and kissed the swell of one breast, just above her heart. The organ fluttered in response to his nearness and pumped harder.

Hunger rampaged through his cells, overpowering his lust for a brief moment, but long enough for him to know there was no more time to wait. If he did, he'd forget himself as he had the first night he'd fed from her and be more animal than man.

She deserved better.

His lips met the smooth column of her neck. Her pulse leapt and she sucked in a tight breath. Beneath his weight, her hips squirmed and her back arched in anticipation. He didn't need to be in her mind to know this was what she wanted—almost as much as he did. He could feel it in the tension of her muscles and the catch in her breath.

Hunger prowled through him, demanding and impatient.

There was a time when feeding had been a leisurely thing, when Athanasian blood was far more plentiful and freely given than it was now. In his youth, men and women alike would come to offer him blood in exchange for good health and long lives. Sometimes they offered more, and sometimes he accepted.

He'd been so deeply hungry for so many years, that he'd almost forgotten what it was like to lust for the flesh. But even now, his body weak and desperate, he still wanted Justice.

She'd given him back desire, and for that he could never repay her.

Her fingers slid into his hair and held on tight. The tips of his fangs grazed her skin, catching on the little puckered marks he'd left on her neck.

She said something, but her words were too incoherent to understand. Instead, all he heard was a whimper of need that matched his own.

He promised himself he'd take only what he needed to regain his strength. He promised himself that he'd stop after just a few drops so her body could finish healing. He promised himself that no matter how much he wanted her after he fed, he wouldn't take her.

The instant his teeth pierced her skin, he knew he would break every one of those promises.

She was hot and sweet and filled with a roar of power. She tasted like victory after a fierce battle and unquenchable lust. No matter how much he drank, he'd never get his fill of her.

Her hands clenched in his hair, along his back. Short fingernails bit into his skin, but the slight pain only heightened his arousal.

Her power flowed into his mouth, and when it wasn't fast enough, he sucked at her throat, demanding she give him more.

He began to undress her as he fed, pulling free the button of her jeans.

Stop!

The alien command boomed in his mind, so loud he was shocked into stillness.

Had Justice said that? Had she somehow shoved that word into his thoughts?

Something about that didn't seem right. There was a strange vibration flowing through the command—one he didn't recognize.

Ronan willed her flesh closed so as not to waste a drop of her precious blood and lifted his head. There were still smears of blood on her skin, but he ignored them and looked around the small room for intruders.

They were alone. There were no sounds from outside and no smell of people, animals or demons nearby.

"What's wrong?" Justice asked, her voice languid and sleepy.

"Did you say something?" he asked.

"No." Her silvery-green eyes were bright, almost glowing. The sight was so beautiful he forgot all about the voice and simply drank her in.

"Did you get enough?" she asked.

"Of you? I'm not sure that's possible."

Her smile was hot and filled with womanly desire.

His thirst was quenched, but his hunger was far from sated. He was going to strip her bare and feast on her. Once he got her naked and learned how she liked to be touched, he was going to make her come until she was too spent to lift her head.

His lust for her had shoved its way to the front of the line and was now demanding to take its turn.

He unzipped her jeans, but before he could slide them down off those curvy hips, alarm covered her face.

"What is it?" he asked.

She scrambled away from him and started fastening her clothes. Her hands trembled on the buttons as she dressed. "I have to go."

"Now?"

He thought he might have seen tears glisten in her eyes but wasn't sure.

"Yes. Now." Her tone was curt, her movements sharp with irritation. "Fucking fates and their fucking bad timing."

Ronan closed his eyes and breathed deeply. It had been a long time since he'd had to deal with unsated lust and he wasn't sure he remembered exactly how to do it. His erection didn't seem to remember either.

"You don't need to tag along," she said. "I have a car stashed out back."

The idea of her leaving without him got his head back in the game.

He stood up and took her trembling hands in his. "If you think I'm going to let you slip away from me now, you're delusional."

"You've had my blood. You've tried to free me from the fates. It didn't work. Time to move on."

"Hardly. I'm far from done with you, Justice. I haven't even begun doing to you the things I want to do."

Her pupils flared and he smelled a wash of arousal flood out of her. The intoxicating scent didn't help him dampen his lust, but he still couldn't get enough of it.

He tilted her head up to look him in the eye. "We're not done. If you try to leave me, you may not like the way I react."

She took his statement as a challenge rather than a warning. He could tell by the flare of fire in her eyes. "Or I might like it a lot. I guess we won't know unless it happens. For now, your invitation to tag along is still good."

He loved that feisty side of her—the one that was fearless and never backed down.

"Where are we going?" he asked.

She tilted her head to the side as if listening. "I'm not one-hundred percent sure yet, but I think I need to visit a corpse."

***

Sibyl hadn't been on good terms with her mother since she was a child, but now that Gilda was dead, it was easy to forgive her for her mistakes. Somehow, death had a way of fogging over the bad and highlighting the good a person did.

The truth was, Sibyl often wondered if she wouldn't have made the same choices her mother had if she'd been in her shoes. Could she have watched her people suffer without working to end it? Could she have watched her children die, one after another, and not done something to stop it? Or would she have done anything to protect her babies, no matter how rash or foolish.

Sibyl hoped she never found out.

The Hall of the Fallen, which served as a place to remember the dead, was always quiet. Few people came here, and there were never gatherings. When one person came, etiquette required anyone already here leave to allow the newcomer to grieve in peace.

It was one of the few places other than her suite that Sibyl could come and think without being crowded by men who were desperate to see if she could save their lives.

She was an unbound female Theronai. She carried within her the power to save a man's life.

But only one.

After centuries of being trapped in a child's body too young to bond, one of the hardest parts of her rapid transition to womanhood was not her sudden, bizarre curves or bleeding once a month, but the burden of knowing she could save only one man when there were so many who deserved to live.

She wasn't ready for that responsibility yet. Soon, there would be no choice and she'd have to start testing the men to see who was compatible with her, but for now, they were all under orders from Joseph to give her a wide berth.

Sibyl took her father's sword from the mantle and settled into a soft, leather chair in front of the fire.

This room was small and cozy, decorated in soothing colors and filled with the pleasant scent of leather and lemon polish. In the room beyond this one, dozens of swords were on display to honor the men and women who'd given their lives to the war. But this smaller space was reserved for those who'd recently fallen.

Like her parents.

Her father's sword had been recovered from the cave that had collapsed in on him and her mother. Their bodies had been buried in the cemetery, but not their weapons.

Wrapped around the hilt of Angus's sword was the pale gray luceria her mother had worn since she was young. They'd bonded when they were all but children themselves and had remained that way until the day they died to save Maura.

After centuries of having her parents around, Sibyl still wasn't sure how to move on without them. Even Cain, who'd fostered her after she'd shunned her mother, was busy with his new life and new wife.

There was no one at Dabyr Sibyl could really talk to, so she came here and spoke to a sword and a necklace as if they could actually respond.

Silly. Childish. But comforting.

"I can't reach Maura," she whispered as she stroked the dented blade her father had wielded. "I keep trying, but she's completely shut me out. I know something bad is coming. I know she's involved. What I don't know is how to stop her."

Neither sword nor luceria answered, but Sibyl hadn't expected them to.

"I can't give up on her. Not yet. I worry that if she finds a male desperate enough to bond to her, she'll use his power to hurt people. I have to make her come back to us before that happens."

The carved wooden door leading into the Hall of the Fallen opened and Morgan Valens walked in.

He was a big man with light brown skin and matching eyes. His Egyptian heritage showed clearly in his features, and he was one of the few Theronai who had smile lines bracketing his mouth.

He was already in the room before he saw her curled up in the chair. He came to an abrupt stop and gave her a grin.

"Good to see you out and about, Sibyl. We've been wondering if you were ever going to come out of your room."

She shrugged in a move more casual than she felt. "People still aren't used to seeing me in this body. No sense in freaking them out."

Morgan winked. "No freaking out here. I'm over it."

She rose from her chair to leave, but he held up his hand. "Stay. I'll come back later."

"I was just leaving," she lied.

"Stay. Gilda and Angus were your parents. You get first dibs on visiting them."

"You came here for them, too?" she asked.

"Felt like I should pay my respects before I leave. Another time is fine." He turned to go.

Talking to someone—anyone felt good. And while Morgan was typically flirtatious with women, he wasn't with her. Like most of the men here, he still saw her as a little girl.

For now, she was glad for it.

"Where are you going?" she asked to get him to linger.

"Did you meet Serena?"

"Iain's betrothed?"

Morgan grimaced. "Yeah. Her. Joseph's been trying to get her to come back for months. Seems the men he's sent so far haven't been up to the task."

"They couldn't find her?"

"Oh, they found her all right. They just needed a Sanguinar to heal them once she was done with them."

"She *hurt* them?"

"Seems so. It's my turn to take a beating and try to bring her home. Joseph wants everyone who can help here to protect the babies."

"But if one of those babies is Iain's and his new bride's, and Serena was once betrothed to him, wouldn't having them all under one roof create some...awkwardness?"

Morgan laughed. "Who needs reality TV when we have so much going on right here?"

He made no move to come near her or touch her to see if

they were compatible. She knew that he was probably in pain from carrying around the power he housed, and there was a small chance she could be the one to ease his burden, but his total lack of interest in Sibyl gave her the courage to reach out.

She so desperately needed advice, and her father's sword was never going to give it.

"You are good with women, right?"

His laughter faded and he narrowed his eyes. "What?"

"I hear people talk. Everyone says you're a ladies' man. I assume that means you have experience with them."

His expression went skeptical. "Let's say I do. What's this about, Sibyl?"

"My sister. I don't know how to reach her."

His shoulders fell in relief and he let out a sigh. "For a second there, I thought you were going to tell me you wanted me to teach you about sex." He shook his head. "I'm sorry, honey, but I just don't think I can ever see you as anything but an eight-year-old."

Sibyl rolled her eyes. "First, I know about sex. I *have* been alive for a couple of centuries. Second, I know how you all see me—as the creepy little girl who can see the future and knows how everyone is going to die. Third, I'm not interested in any of you, either."

He winced. "Don't let the men hear you say that. You're giving them way too much hope right now to crush it. After everything we've been through, we all need a good dose of hope."

"Other than you and Joseph, I haven't spoken to any of the men. My secret is safe."

He nodded. "So what do you need to know?"

"How do you reach a woman who has no interest in speaking to you?"

"Hell if I know. I've never had that problem. Getting women to talk to me has never been a problem. How do you think I got the reputation for being a ladies' man?"

"You realize that's absolutely no help at all. This is my sister we're talking about. I *need* to get through to her and convince her to come home."

He let out a low whistle. "Good luck with that. I really doubt Joseph would let her through the gates, even if she did want to come in. And chances are she wouldn't live through the night after all the shit she's pulled."

"Everyone deserves forgiveness."

Morgan shook his head, his smile completely gone. "I'm sorry to be the one to break this to you, Sibyl, but you're wrong. Maura chose to side with our enemy. She killed a lot of good men. She killed her own parents. The only thing she deserves is a swift, painless death, light on the painless part."

***

After driving north for over an hour, Justice reached the destination the fates had in mind. Now all she had to do was figure out why she was standing over a freshly-dug grave in southern Iowa.

Cold winter air whipped around her, lashing her curls around her face. A few snowflakes danced in the air. In the distance, she could see the murky orange glow of a town's lights against the low clouds. Here, everything was dark beyond the single security light mounted high above the cemetery entrance.

Ronan stood beside her, silent, but still taking up most of her attention.

She could still feel his hands and mouth on her body, the way he touched her like part of her belonged to him.

Maybe it did.

The memory of his lips moving at her throat was enough to send an army of shivers marching down her back in tight formation.

She wanted more from him but didn't know how to get it. Did she ask, or simply take what she wanted? And if she did, what exactly would she take?

A slow, achy need simmered low in her belly. Her skin felt hot and tight, with an eager buzz humming just below the surface. Every cell in her body was attuned to him as if he were some sort of master conductor and they were all awaiting his cue to start playing.

"Any idea why we're here?" he asked in a soft, deep voice that cascaded over her senses like hot rain.

"Not a clue," she said. "But my guess is it's going to involve some digging. Do you happen to have a shovel in your van?"

He shook his dark head. "Medical supplies and weapons, yes. Gardening implements, no." He nodded toward the far side of the cemetery. "There's a small shed over there. I'll see what I can find."

She couldn't see that far in the dark but the fates always provided. If she needed a shovel, she would have been compelled to stop and buy one if there wasn't one here already. Besides, she trusted Ronan's ability to find what they needed. He had all sorts of uncanny abilities she didn't understand, like making her insides quiver just by looking at him.

Justice watched him walk away. His long, leather coat whipped around his calves. He'd pulled the collar up to shield his neck from the wind, but still looked cold.

The urge to warm him stretched through her, like some kind of dormant instinct waking up after a long slumber. She should have been cold out here as well but having him near kept her internal fires stoked and raging.

When he finally disappeared into the darkness, out of sight, she was able to turn her attention to the grave. Maybe, if she got lucky, she wouldn't have to dig at all.

She crouched in front of the headstone and read it in the dim light.

Martha Marie Oliver, beloved wife, mother and grandmother. Loved by all who knew her.

Justice Googled the woman and found her obituary in the local paper. The service had been earlier today. She'd died at the age of seventy-four of heart disease, leaving behind her elderly husband, three children and ten grandchildren. She'd been a devout Christian woman, who had made quilts for every baby born into her congregation for the last forty years. She had the state's biggest collection of sewing memorabilia, some of which was going to be donated to a nearby museum.

Justice didn't know what kind of things that collection might include since she'd never sewn a stitch in her life—at least not that she could remember.

"Okay," she whispered to the fates. "I'm going to need a little more to go on. I am *not* desecrating the grave of some sweet old grandma for the fun of it."

She kicked at a clump of freshly turned earth. It was already frozen into a hard lump—still diggable, but not easily.

Maybe she'd get lucky and not have to dig at all. Maybe whatever she was here for was not in that grave, but on the tombstone, or somewhere nearby.

As soon as the thought entered her mind, she knew it was wrong. She was going to have to dig.

Justice didn't get lucky.

There was a low, mechanical cough, then a rumble as an engine was fired up. A second later, she saw lights in the distance and Ronan, in the seat of a backhoe, heading toward her at a slow crawl.

A rush of emotion she didn't recognize welled up in her chest and spilled out her eyes. Maybe it was gratitude for his help or relief that she wasn't going to have to tear up her hands and back digging out a frozen grave. But whatever the feeling was, it was warm and happy.

He was helping her. She wasn't completely alone.

In the next heartbeat, all that warmth evaporated as she realized the truth.

The only time she'd ever had a friend, she'd had to kill him. She still didn't know why she'd been forced to do it, or what purpose his death had served. For all she knew it was a test to see if the control the fates had over her was absolute.

She wished she knew why Noah had been her target.

Maybe if she did, she'd finally be able to get over the guilt she carried.

Then again, maybe not. It wasn't like she was ever going to get convicted of the crime. Noah had been a street rat. No one was going to miss him. And she'd made sure his body would never be found. Acid was good like that.

The only punishment she'd ever suffer was the guilt she bore.

It wasn't enough. Not even close.

Ronan lined up the backhoe at the tail of the grave. "Do you want to do the honors, or shall I?"

Justice was shaking too hard to work the controls. For all she knew, once that hole was dug, she'd be throwing Ronan's body right in on top of Martha Marie Oliver.

Justice gave him a wave since her voice wasn't working and turned her back so he wouldn't see the shine of tears on her face.

She didn't cry—at least not where anyone could see. She wasn't about to start the bad habit now.

"I won't hurt him," she warned the fates. Maybe that declaration was tempting them to punish her, but she didn't care. Let them do their worst—make her head explode and her guts spew out her mouth. Ronan was off limits.

A small part of her wondered if she could ever be that strong. Torture could make even good people do bad things, and Justice wasn't all that good to begin with.

He made quick work of the dig, then jumped down and grabbed a shovel he'd tucked behind the seat. A few shovels full of dirt from the corners, and the coffin lid was clear. Dirty and scratched, but clear.

She shone a flashlight into the hole to help him see, though she doubted that he needed it as much as she did.

He opened the satin-lined lid.

Martha was a tiny woman, with little bird bones and a stiff helmet of blue-white curls. Her face was relaxed and lined, but with all the signs of the beauty she'd been when she was young. Her pale skin was creased and sagging in spots, but there were smile lines, too, as if she was thinking of an old joke.

She was dressed in a ruffled shirt under a suit jacket with a pale pink and gray floral pattern. Pearls dotted her ears and encircled her throat.

Ronan opened the lower half of the lid to reveal a coordinating suit skirt, a pair of pink heels and skinny legs clad in too-dark stockings.

He looked up at Justice with a look of expectation on his face. "Well? What now?"

There was something. She could feel it pulling at her but couldn't yet tell what it was.

She climbed down into the grave, being careful to walk on the rim of dirt around the edge of the coffin. As she got closer, an urgent hum hit the back of her skull.

Whatever the fates wanted, she'd nearly found it.

"I hate to do this, Mrs. Oliver," she said, "but I'm afraid I'm going to have to invade your personal space."

She handed Ronan the flashlight and knelt, straddling the woman's bird legs on either side. She felt around the slippery coffin lining.

There was nothing under the body but a chill, so she patted the woman's arms and legs, hoping for some kind of sign.

Ronan shifted the beam of light as she worked, and when she got to the woman's left arm, the light hit a brooch that had been camouflaged by the swirling floral print of her lapel.

It was silver, polished in some places and deeply tarnished in the crevices. Somewhere between a star shape and a flower, each of the eight protrusions were sinuous and twisted. In the center was a faceted crystal that gleamed with rainbow colors in the light.

As soon as Justice saw it, she felt a ping of recognition in the back of her brain and knew that this brooch was why she was here.

With cold fingers, she unfastened the pin holding it in place and said, "I've never robbed a grave before, but I'm glad you were my first. Sleep well, Martha."

She patted the woman's cold cheek, shoved the metal piece deep in her pocket, then scrambled out of the coffin.

"What is it?" Ronan asked.

"Who knows? I'm just glad she was wearing what we were after on the outside. This whole thing could have been so much worse if it had been something she'd swallowed."

He grunted in agreement. "Are we done, then?"

She nodded. "We'll put her back the way we found her, minus one ugly brooch. My guess is she won't miss it."

Ronan made quick work of filling in the hole, then rode off to put the backhoe wherever it was he'd found it. Justice waited for him, studying the brooch under the beam of the flashlight.

There was no maker's mark she could see. The back of the piece was rough, as if something had been broken off of it. The pin that had turned it into a brooch had clearly been added later. It was cheap, gold plated metal hot glued in place with a messy hand.

She used her pocket knife to pry the pin and glue off, hoping that if she got down to the original piece, her reason for stealing it would become clear.

The glue was cold and stubborn and she worried she'd damage the metal if she wasn't careful. If this was some priceless artifact like so many of the pieces she recovered, then she didn't want to be the one to devalue it.

Under the intense beam of the flashlight, the front side of the brooch was even more intricate than she'd first thought. There were tiny scores in each twisting petal that could have been decorations made by the metalsmith, some strange writing she didn't recognize, or the same rogue garbage disposal that had chewed on the ring she'd earned from Chester Gale.

As she stared, twisting the star-like flower this way and that, it seemed like some of those marks lined up to form new shapes with the marks on the adjacent petal.

Familiarity hummed along her spine, as if she should be able to read these marks. Maybe it was writing and she'd learned how to read it in the years she couldn't remember.

Justice was so wrapped up in studying the piece that she didn't see the demons until it was too late.

CHAPTER EIGHT

Ronan heard the excited heartbeats of Synestryn the instant he turned off the backhoe, but he was too far away from Justice to do more than shout a warning as the creatures charged.

There were three sgath charging her, their eyes glowing bright green with hungry light. Yellow saliva dripped from their too-wide jaws, leaving a smoking trail of singed grass behind them. Their heavy bodies were covered in thick, oily fur, and their powerful muscles rippled beneath the surface as they ran toward their prey.

He raced toward her, but he wasn't going to make it in time. The demons were too close to her for him to intercept them.

Justice drew her gun so fast, it appeared in her hand as if by magic. She fired at the closest sgath and hit its shoulder.

It yelped and stumbled before it regained its footing and rejoined the other two now in the lead.

Ronan ran harder, fueling his speed with a burst of magic.

She fired again and again. Each round hit her intended target and slowed them down, but little more.

No matter how many bullets she fired, she wasn't going to kill them before they reached her and tore her apart.

Ronan couldn't let that happen. He couldn't let her die.

He was still too far away, so he summoned his power—

power Justice's blood had given him—and lifted her from the ground. She flew upward, out of the reach of the demons just as they leapt to attack her.

She lost her balance and flailed against his efforts. Her wobbling made his job harder, but he held her aloft, out of harm's way, and kept running toward the demons.

His sword was at his side, but he was rusty, out of practice. And even if he hadn't been, a three-on-one fight wasn't the kind of thing he enjoyed.

Leave that to the Slayers who walked around naked in the cold and fought with their bare hands, grinning all the while.

The van was their only hope to outrun the sgath and it was parked at the entrance of the cemetery. Sgath this big could easily shred it to pieces, but it would take them some time— long enough for Ronan to get Justice the hell out of here.

Two of the demons leapt at Justice, trying to jump high enough to reach her, but the third was smarter than its kin. Bigger, too. It turned its head toward Ronan, fixing its glowing green stare on him. The eerie fire in its eyes flared brighter as it sighted new prey. Then it snarled, dug its claws into the frozen earth, and launched itself toward him.

Ronan pulled his sword as he ran and used another surge of magic to obscure his blade. Normally, it would become visible when drawn from its scabbard, but he needed every advantage he could find, and hiding his weapon was the only one his racing mind could find.

Usually, when it came to battle, he was far more careful, entering the fray only when there were plenty of Theronai to defend him. His magic was formidable, but limited, and he could already feel himself burning through the precious power Justice's blood had given him.

When that was gone, they were both as good as dead.

With that in mind, he calculated the fastest way through combat, and set his course.

The sgath drew ever closer. The frozen ground numbed his feet as they slapped hard against it. His breath billowed out in frosty plumes, and he could see the glow his eyes cast on the dead grass between him and the demon.

Just a few more feet...

A grin of victory stretched the sgath's mouth. Its jaws opened and a fierce snarl split the cold air. Powerful legs flexed as it launched itself for Ronan's throat.

He dropped low and slid under the beast, being careful to avoid its claws. His sword came up as he passed, ripping open a deep wound along its furry underbelly.

Black, oily blood spilled over Ronan's hands, and instantly, he could feel the tingle of poison searching for a way into his bloodstream.

The sgath landed hard and skidded over the ground where it came to land in a clumsy heap. It wasn't dead. Not even close. In fact, it had curled its body so it could lap up the blood flowing from its wound.

Within minutes, it would be fully restored.

Before that happened, Ronan needed to get Justice and himself out of here.

He turned his back on the beast and veered toward the van, dragging Justice's levitated body along with him.

She fired her gun as she went, knocking the demons back a few feet with every shot.

Poison numbed Ronan's fingers.

He didn't even have to think about his body's reaction to the toxin—it was as involuntary as his heartbeat. His skin sucked power from his cells and shoved the poison out through every pore it touched. He wanted to wipe it off, but there wasn't time for that now.

He couldn't feel his sword inside his numb grip, but somehow managed to keep it clenched in his fist.

Unlike the swords the Theronai carried, his didn't collect the essence of the things he killed. And even it if had, his kill list was woefully brief. He far preferred stealth to violence.

If not for the fact that the demons knew exactly where he and Justice were, he would have obscured their presence now. But it was too late for that. The sgath had their scent, and they weren't going to stop until they'd caught their prey.

There were a few feet between her and the demons now. She'd slowed them down a little with her weapon, but her gun was empty, and the sgath were quickly regaining ground.

"Hang on!" he shouted at her.

There was no way for him to communicate more information. No time. He had to act now, before his window of opportunity closed.

Ronan squeezed a burst of power from his blood and used it to fling Justice toward the van. She hit the side hard enough to leave a dent, but whatever damage he'd done was far better than what the sgath had in store for her.

Now that she was too far away to reach, the demons turned their attention on him, the far closer target.

His body grew weak from both exertion and fighting the poison eating away at his skin. He could once again feel his fingers, but that was not a blessing. They burned like they were on fire and someone tried to put it out with a mix of gasoline and acid.

He was slower now. There was no more energy to spare to speed his legs. Everything was going into keeping himself on his feet.

Justice shoved herself upright and shook her head as if stunned.

Relief at seeing he hadn't hurt her badly winged through him and gave him hope that she might make it out of this alive.

He, on the other hand, was not so fortunate.

The sgath were so close on his heels, he could smell their fetid breath and feel the humid heat of it on the back of his neck.

He couldn't turn and fight. He was too weak for that. But he couldn't outrun them either.

All he could do was buy Justice some time to run.

"Go!" he shouted to her. "Leave me!" He would have put a force of compulsion in his words if he'd had the strength.

She turned toward the sound of his voice. A few hundred yards separated them, but it might as well have been miles.

She was so beautiful. He wished he'd gotten more time

with her. He wished he'd spent more time kissing her and touching her soft skin. He wished he'd ripped down the veil to her past and gotten to know all of her. He wished that he'd been able to free her and give her back her life, her freedom. That was what he regretted the most.

There was no time for regrets now, only action.

Ronan made a sharp turn to his left and veered away from the van, luring the hungry demons along with him.

Justice was able to run now. At least he'd given her that much freedom.

***

Ronan was going to die and Justice had no idea how to stop it.

Reba was no match for these creatures, and there were two of them right on Ronan's heels. Another was not far away, licking up its own spilled blood.

Her head was still spinning from her wild ride and the very abrupt end where she slammed into the side wall of the van. Not that she was complaining. She would far rather have a physics lesson than be eaten by demons.

Since her gun was of little use, the only weapon she could think of was the one that had so recently rattled her brains.

If you can't shoot them, run them over.

She scrambled in behind the wheel and started the engine. The wheels spun on the frozen grass, but she managed to get the lumbering vehicle headed in the right direction.

As soon as the headlights hit Ronan, she knew she wasn't going to be fast enough. Not even her beloved Ricardo could accelerate fast enough to keep those teeth and claws off Ronan's back.

Still, with no other ideas, she gunned the engine and charged.

She was almost there when one wide paw raked across Ronan's back.

Panic exploded through her system. She screamed an

incoherent sound of denial. She'd just found him. He was her only hope. She couldn't lose him now. Not like this.

Blue sparks flew up from his coat where the sharp claws hit but didn't break through the leather.

He was still alive. Uninjured.

She didn't understand how, but she knew his luck couldn't last for long.

He was slowing down, running out of steam. There was so little space between him and the monsters she feared if she hit one, she'd hit him too.

It was almost too late to change course, but she angled the van slightly to the right and hoped she'd do no more than clip the back of his heels.

One of the demons hit the bumper hard and was sucked under the tire. The van lurched. The steering wheel was jerked from her hands.

She'd only hit one, and the other was lifting its huge paw for another swipe at Ronan's back.

A thought landed in her mind, heavy, solid, and fully formed. It wasn't her own. She didn't know where it had come from, but the frantic feel surrounding it made her follow orders.

She bit her wrist and used her other hand to shove the van door open.

Cold wind swooped in and grabbed the scent of her blood, fresh on her lips and skin.

Instantly, the demon turned its head toward her.

Sickly green light erupted from its eyes and froze her in place with fear. Her foot went limp on the gas. The van slowed drastically over the uneven ground.

Beneath her, she could hear the enraged howl of the demon she'd hit, and its frantic clawing at the underside of the floorboards.

It was alive, and it wanted a taste of her too.

The creature on Ronan's heels changed course and headed for the source of the blood it scented. As close as she was to it, she didn't think she'd even have time to close the door before it reached her.

There was something wrong with her body. The longer she stared at the thing, the slower she became, the more fear sank into her skin and sucked away her heat.

She needed to close the van door. She needed to reload Reba. She needed to survive.

Still, her body ignored her pleas, barely moving as she commanded.

The demon lifted its paws and opened its jaws as it lunged.

Her head was just the right size to fit all the way inside those giant jaws. One big bite, and her neck would be severed. Fast. Not painless, but fast.

No more fates, no more compulsions, no more worries.

No more Ronan.

That was the thought that jerked her out of her stupor.

She lifted her booted feet and shoved hard just as the monster reached the threshold of the door.

Before it could make contact, its head fell off. Just toppled off sideways.

It took her a second to realize that it had been severed.

Ronan stood behind the creature, sword in both hands, face pale but feral.

He'd killed the thing. Chopped its head clean off. How the hell had he done that?

Thick streams of black blood shot from the furry neck, several feet into the air. She shoved it away with her feet.

"Move over," Ronan ordered in a hard, cold voice.

Justice didn't argue. There were still two more of those things left alive, and she had no intention of seeing just how much closer to death she and Ronan could come.

He got in behind the wheel. "I need wipes."

He shut the door and drove off, taking care to drive over a low rock to scrape off the demon clinging to the van's undercarriage.

Justice went in back and found the plastic container of wet wipes. She pulled out several and handed them to him.

He cleaned his hands while he drove, then scrubbed the

wheel and door where he'd touched them. The oily black gunk went out the window, and she didn't even feel the slightest pang over his littering.

"Give me your wrist," he demanded. He was clearly angry, but as far as she was concerned, that was his problem, not hers.

She did as he asked and let him lick away her blood and heal the ragged wound closed.

After that, he seemed calmer, steadier, and far less pissed. Still pissed, though.

He gave her a quick glance—one filled with fire and fury. "The next time I tell you to run, you'd better fucking run."

She wasn't going to let him or anyone else push her around. She had enough of that from the fates. "I didn't realize you had the right to tell me to do anything."

"I was willing to die so you could live. That gives me the right."

Was that how things worked in his world? She didn't know. She hadn't been part of it for long. Still, she needed to make one thing perfectly clear. "I don't take orders from anyone but the fates, and them only because I have no choice. I hate them for pushing me around. If you keep pushing, I'll come to hate you too."

His jaw bunched. His cheekbones were more pronounced. He looked thinner, though not nearly as skinny as he'd been the night she'd met him.

He was hungry. He'd burned up a lot of magic saving her ass tonight, even if it had left her a little bruised on one side where she'd flown into the van. At least she was still breathing, rather than being digested in the gut of a monster.

He turned the wheel hard enough to slosh her around in her seat.

"Where are we going?" she asked.

"To see some people I know."

"For what purpose?"

He cast her a glowing blue glance. "To feed."

A rush of jealousy whipped through her, battering her insides until they were raw. "Feed on me."

"No."

"Why not? And don't say because I'm healing. I've told you I'm fine."

"You're injured. And even if you weren't, I still wouldn't take your blood."

"Why not?"

"Because I promised you I wouldn't hurt you again, and as angry as I am, that's exactly what I'd do."

"I don't believe you."

He gripped the wheel tighter. Blue light spilled across the dashboard. "Then you have no idea just how furious with you I am."

***

None of the Sanguinar took Nika's blood. It was far too dangerous, no matter how much simpler it would have made examining her.

Logan knelt beside the chair where Nika sat, her belly full and round with her child. She was still too thin for his liking, but she'd gained enough weight that he wasn't too worried. Besides, her husband Madoc was already in charge of nagging her to eat. He didn't need Logan's help in that department.

Thanks to Nika's nesting urge, their suite was as clean as an operating room. Every essential a newborn could need, and dozens of things they didn't, were here, awaiting the child's birth.

A girl. Nika and Madoc were going to have a baby girl any day now.

He laid a hand on her stomach and let his mind slip into her body to check on the health of mother and child.

"Is this going to take long?" Nika asked. "I want to rearrange the baby's closet."

"You've already done that three times," Madoc growled in his rough voice. "Just sit the fuck down and rest already."

Logan hid his grin. Madoc hovered over Nika, hardly letting her out of his sight. Since the day he learned he was going to be a father, he'd been a walking bundle of overprotective nerves.

This little girl was going to have her father wrapped around her finger almost as tightly as her mother did.

"I won't be long," Logan said.

His wife Hope stood behind him and laid a hand on his shoulder. Everything he did was so much easier with her in his life. Not only did her blood rid him of hunger and give him the kind of power he never dreamed he'd have again, she was also his rock. He couldn't imagine loving anyone more than he loved her.

She was his everything.

Nika's baby was healthy and growing. She'd turned so that she was head down now, kicking hard at her mother's ribs. Her life force was so strong, it was almost hard to touch. Intense and bright, like a star.

She had no idea how much joy and hope she was bringing to so many. If they weren't careful, she'd be spoiled beyond saving by her third birthday.

Logan retreated from Nika's body and back into his own.

She cocked her head to the side. Her white hair was longer now, falling past her shoulders. Madoc absently slid his fingers through it, petting his wife's head as if to calm her.

There was a time when Nika had needed that, but she was strong and steady now, thanks to him. His power had healed her splintered mind and made her whole again. It was a beautiful, amazing thing to behold.

"She's almost ready to be born," Nika said. "Just another day or two."

Madoc's heart rate jumped and his breathing sped. A fine sheen of nervous sweat covered his brow.

"How do you know?" Logan asked.

Nika blinked as if his question was a stupid one. "She told me."

Logan didn't understand the psychic link she and her daughter shared, but it intrigued him. He doubted that Madoc would ever let his daughter be the subject of study, but maybe when she was older....

"Let's hope she decides to come at night," Logan said. "I'd really like to be the one to welcome her into the world."

"She likes you," Nika said, then lowered her voice to a whisper. "But she likes Hope better."

Logan laughed. "So do I."

Hope shook her head as she grinned. "If we're done here, let's leave these two alone. Sounds like they're running out of nights where it's just the two of them."

Madoc paled and a look of fear rippled over his features.

Nika took his hand. "You're going to be fine. Best daddy ever."

He shook his head. "I'm not ready. I need more fucking time to prepare."

"Sorry, my love," Nika said, smiling, "but our daughter disagrees."

***

Chester Gale didn't mind working with demons. They paid well and always kept their promises. He did, however, dislike the visual raping he had to take whenever he gazed on the thing that called itself Vazel.

The demon was grotesque, with too much knobby skin and not nearly enough clothes to hide it all. His arms were overly long, and he was missing a couple of fingers on each hand.

Chester didn't know if they'd been removed or he'd never had them, but either way, his hands were just as ugly.

Their meeting place suited the creature. It was a dark and drippy industrial cave just east of Kansas City, and stank of old meat and chicken litter. The space had once been used as storage for corporate documents, but since the digital revolution, no one ever came here anymore. All the boxes were damp and sagging, some covered with fungus. Chester wasn't even sure the company that owned the storage space remembered it was here.

Fluorescent lights dangled from electrical conduit

overhead. A few were lit, but most of the bulbs had died years ago, leaving their survivors buzzing and flickering in grief.

There were new tunnels in the back of the space where no light reached. All Chester could see was a creature with two burned out eye sockets staring at him as if daring him to come closer.

He didn't.

"Did you bring it?" Vazel asked, spitting words through a mouth stuffed full of sharp teeth.

"I have the book. I lost the girl."

The demon's face was so fleshy and alien, Chester couldn't tell if his expression shifted to anger, or if he always looked like that.

Vazel held out his hand with only two fingers and twice as many joints in each as necessary. "Give it to me."

Chester handed over the book, carefully wrapped in tissue paper. He would have preferred one of his men do the job, but when it came to demons, they liked doing business face-to-face. He guessed it was so they could eat said face easier if they chose.

Vazel opened the paper and tossed it aside. The book he inspected, squinting his bulbous eyes as if trying to reach the intricate, swirling marks across the leather-bound surface.

"Is that writing?" Chester asked.

"To those who know how to read it."

"Do you?"

"I can read entrails, too. Would you like to know what yours say?"

Chester tried to keep his expression from giving away his sudden spurt of fear. By the creepy grin on Vazel's face, he'd failed.

He decided it was best to just stand there and let the creature finish whatever it needed to so he could get paid.

Finally, Vazel said, "It is the book I need. Would you like to know what it says?"

Instincts—the deep, animal kind that warned of impending danger—told him what to say. "No, thanks. I'm good. All I want is payment and a list of what else I can do for you."

"I wanted the girl."

"I truly am sorry about that. I've tried to find her, but my network of eyes and ears has no idea where she's gone."

"It's okay," Vazel said, waving that grotesque hand. "I know where she is. But I don't know where the one who stole her is."

"Justice, she calls herself," Chester offered. "She killed several of my men. She was shot, but rumor says she's popped up online, so she's not dead."

"I want you to find her. Bring her to me."

Chester nodded. No way was he going to deny this creature anything he wanted—at least not while he was within reach of those long arms.

"And the little girl Justice stole?" Chester asked. "Do you want me to send my men to get her back? If you tell me where she is, I will."

The demon grinned, as if anticipating a lavish dessert. "No need. I'll fetch her myself."

CHAPTER NINE

Ronan didn't normally jump to anger as his go-to emotion. He was usually more in control than that, saving his rage for the creatures he fought, rather than his allies.

Tonight, he was going to make an exception.

He couldn't believe that Justice had come back for him. What the hell had she been thinking?

Probably that he was going to die if she didn't intervene.

Maybe he would have.

He wished he were stronger. If he'd allowed himself to take more of her blood, he would have been, but no matter what she thought, she wasn't ready for that. If he let go of his control and drank his fill, he'd only end up hurting her, and that was something he couldn't allow.

He'd promised.

The need to free her from her compulsions was a powerful force beating at the back of his skull. She'd given him so much and yet he hadn't even figured out what was causing her to suffer.

It was a presence. That much he knew, but no more.

Or did he?

Something tickled his mind.

He'd heard a voice telling him to stop drinking her blood. That hadn't been his own internal warning system, much to his shame. And he didn't believe it had been hers, either.

Maybe the presence within her had spoken to him.

If it had, he could communicate with it and find out more—what it was, what it wanted, and how he could banish it.

Ronan drove to the home of Mr. and Mrs. William Pennyfort and woke them from a sound sleep. Once he explained his presence, the elderly couple welcomed him and Justice inside and offered their blood freely. As he fed, from William, he reversed the enlargement of the man's prostate so he could sleep soundly through the night without getting up to pee four times. His wife had a touch of sciatica, which Ronan also healed.

When all was said and done, the couple was in better health than he'd found them, and he was no longer starving. It was a fair, simple trade, and one he wished was more common.

Sadly, since one of his kind had turned traitor, many humans had begun guarding their blood jealously, as if the mere act of him feeding from them could make them turn against their own families and friends.

Justice watched the whole exchange but said nothing. When they were back in the van, she asked, "Do you feel better?"

"I do."

"As good as you would have after taking my blood?"

"Not even close."

A small, satisfied smile played around her mouth. "Good."

She was certainly a jealous thing, which he found he liked. It meant she wasn't planning on running off again—not if she wanted to be the only one he fed from.

He would use that to his advantage if the need arose.

She took the silver brooch from her pocket and turned it in her fingers.

"Any idea why you had to dig up an old woman's grave for that?" he asked.

"Not yet."

"Are your fates demanding anything of you now? Do we

need to raid a kitchen store for a pasta machine? Or perhaps get out pictures taken with the world's largest prairie dog?"

"No, but there is one thing I need to take care of."

"What's that?"

"Chester Gale. The man who took Pepper and killed her mother. Well, technically, I already killed that scumbag, but the man who ordered it done—the one who had some reason to buy a little girl—is still out there."

"The fates want you to kill him?"

"No, that's all me." She turned to face Ronan. The oncoming headlights flashed over her dark skin, highlighting just how serious she was about this. "Does that make me a bad person?"

"That you want to murder a man who destroys lives?" Ronan shrugged as he watched the road ahead for his exit. "I don't think so."

"He has wealth, power, and a vast network of people who work for him. Including me."

"He employs you?"

"I found objects for him a few times. I didn't know that he was into little girls until Pepper."

"What kind of objects?"

"A book, a dagger. Trinkets. Like this brooch. They all seem to have the same kind of marks on them. Maybe they were made by the same metalsmith and he's a collector." She shook her head. "The paychecks were always big enough to discourage a lot of questions."

"Were you compelled to find those trinkets the way you were this one?"

She was silent for a moment. "I thought the fates were simply funding my warehouses and my fast-paced lifestyle. You know, making it possible for me to have fast cars to get me where they wanted me to go and pay for all the speeding tickets that went along with them."

"And now? Do you think differently?"

"Why would they want me helping an asshole?"

"So, you think the fates are inherently good?"

"I think they're inherently irritating. I guess I always hoped that the things they had me do served some higher purpose. Like saving your life."

"Have you ever heard them speak?" he asked.

"No, but I've often hoped they could hear me. I've had plenty of things to say to them over the years."

"I just bet you have," he said.

He exited the highway and stopped at the top of the ramp to watch her expression. "I think the fates may have spoken to me. When I was feeding from you."

Her green eyes went wide. "What? Are you sure?"

"No, but if you'll let me, I can try to hear them again. Maybe even speak to them."

"Yes," she said without hesitation. "Do it now. Tell them to leave me the hell alone."

"I need to seek shelter from the sun first. The van is fine in a pinch, but I much prefer to be belowground during the day. There's a farmhouse a few miles south that has a basement. It's rustic, but dry. And the upstairs is quite nice. Comfortable beds, so I'm told."

Justice nodded but said nothing. He'd upset her somehow. He could smell the hurt coming from her in waves but had no idea what he'd done or said to cause it.

For a man who spent plenty of time in the minds of females of all kinds, Ronan still didn't understand what made them tick.

"Did I say something wrong?" he asked after a few miles of silence.

"No. It's fine," she said in a tone that meant it most definitely was not fine.

"I know you're upset. Tell me what's wrong."

After another few minutes of uncomfortable silence, she said, "Why wouldn't the fates speak to me? I mean, I've spent my entire life doing their bidding, jumping through every hoop they demanded, no matter how confusing or distasteful. I've *killed* for them. Why the fuck would they talk to you and not talk to me?"

"I'm not even sure if that's what happened, Justice. I heard something, but in our world, there are a lot of things that could have been."

"Like what?"

"I'm linked to those I've fed from. One of them may have been able to reach me if they possessed enough magic. And there's always the possibility that there was a psychic nearby who reached me without intending to do so. I know a woman, Rory, who was tormented by seeing things through the eyes of the people around her. She couldn't keep those visions out. Perhaps there's another female Theronai nearby who is unable to keep from projecting her thoughts to those around her. And let's not forget Brenya, who by all accounts is a magical badass of epic proportions. She's likely the one who sent you here. She may somehow still be linked to you and protecting you from being fed on by men like me."

"Hope mentioned her. Do you think she's the one making me do these things?"

Ronan shook his head. "I don't think so, but I could be wrong."

"Why don't you think it's her?"

"Because if everything I've heard is true, then she's got her hands full. We sent one critically ill woman to her for healing. Grace was beyond our help, but Brenya offered to try to save her. At the same time, she also took the young Theronai Tori, who had been raised by demons and tortured until she was little more than an angry mass of violent urges. On top of that, Hope says she's raising more Sanguinar to send here to aid our fight. I doubt she's got time to tell me when I've taken too much of your blood."

"That's what she said?"

"I don't know that it was a she, but the word I heard was *stop*."

"That's all. One word?"

"Believe me, one word was enough. There was power there. Lots of power."

Justice absently spun the brooch in her fingers. "That, at

least, makes me feel better."

"What does?"

"That the thing controlling me is powerful. I can't tell you how many times I've tried for fight the compulsions over the years. I never win. I'd always hoped it wasn't because I was weak."

He reached over and covered her hand with his. "I've been inside your mind, Justice. I've seen parts of you no one else has, likely including yourself. The very last word I'd use to describe you is *weak*."

She flipped her hand upright and slid her fingers between his. The way she clung to him went to his head and made him feel stronger than he had in a long time. She was counting on him. Depending on him to free her from her torture.

No matter what it took, he wasn't going to let her down.

By the time he pulled up to the old farmhouse, sunrise was still a couple of hours away. There was no garage, so he parked his van on the east side of the house, right up against the back steps.

"Planning to need a fast get-away?" Justice asked.

"Always. Let's hope it doesn't come to that."

"I don't know about you, but I'm starving."

"There should be food in the fridge. Help yourself. I'm going to call Dabyr and check on things at home."

He did a quick sweep of the house to make sure there were no nasty surprises lurking in the dark rooms. When he was sure they were free of visitors—both animal and Synestryn—he called Tynan, the Sanguinar the rest of them looked to as their leader.

"Are you still with the woman?" Tynan asked.

"I am."

"Is she like Hope?"

"I'm certain of it."

Tynan let out a long, relieved breath. "That's good news. When will you be home?"

"I don't know. The last time we were at Dabyr, she seemed to be blocked off from the presence controlling her."

"Then why not keep her here?"

"Because when she finally was connected to that presence again, it was...unpleasant for her. She worries that if she's cut off too long, it could possibly even kill her."

Tynan sighed. "We really need you home, Ronan. There are so many people packed inside the walls now. In addition to fights between the people inside Dabyr, there are skirmishes outside every night, as if the Synestryn are testing the walls for a weakness. Our fighters are holding them at bay, but the injuries are piling up and cracks are forming in the walls faster than Lexi can mend them. We're stretched thin, especially when it comes to the children who still need daily care. They miss you."

"I'm sorry I can't be there, but Justice and the power her blood holds has to be my priority. I have to find a way to free her."

"When you do, your next job must be to convince her to join us."

"Even if I do, she's not going to take well to following orders."

"She'll learn to obey. In time, we all do."

Tynan could say that only because he didn't know Justice. If he had, he never would have used the word *obey.*

"I suggest you don't voice your hypothesis where she can hear you," Ronan said.

"How much more time do you need?"

"I don't know. I'm going to try to reach the presence controlling her and communicate with it."

"The sun will be up soon. You'd better work fast."

"You as well, Tynan. Tell the children I miss them, will you?"

"Of course. Be safe." Tynan hung up.

Ronan turned to find her standing in the doorway to the farmhouse kitchen with a bowl cradled in her hands. Steam rose from the surface, along with the scent of onions and spices.

"Want some?" she asked. "I don't know what it's called,

but it's amazing."

He crossed the small living room and peered down into her bowl. Rice, beans, tomatoes and cilantro were mixed up and topped with a layer of golden cheese.

He picked up her fork and took a bite.

"You're right. It is good."

She handed it to him. "Have mine. I'll nuke another bowl. Nice of them to have it all laid out in individual servings. I could use elves like that myself. Eating on the road gets old fast. As in about eight years ago."

"You never cook for yourself?" he asked.

"Do microwave dinners count?"

He wrinkled his nose. "I think you know the answer to that without my help."

She pulled her bowl from the microwave and joined him at the little round table.

The kitchen was old, but clean. The white cabinets had been painted a few times, badly. The hinges were covered in layers of paint. Faded red roosters decorated the space, on the walls and on plates propped behind a rail above the cabinets.

The faucet dripped, and he made a mental note to turn in a repair request.

"There are two bedrooms," he said. "You can take your pick."

"Where will you sleep?"

"In the basement."

"Is there a bedroom down there?"

"No. Just a cot."

"Why no bed? Don't you deserve to be comfortable too?"

"I don't feel much once I'm asleep. Fortunately."

"Why do you say that?" she asked.

"Because most of the time, our kind are starving. Sleep is the only respite we have. That's why so many of our kind go to sleep for decades."

"What?"

"When the hunger gets too much to bear for one of our kind, we place them in a magically-enhanced sleep so they don't have to suffer. Plus, they use much less blood in that state, so it helps us conserve what we have available. We feed them when we can, but there's never enough."

"Where are they?"

"Beneath Dabyr. We have sleeping chambers behind several layers of security. Only a few of us have access."

"Why such tight security? What's someone going to do with a sleeping vampire."

He grimaced at the term. "It's not what they'd do with them, but to them. They're completely vulnerable. Even if someone were to hurt them, they won't wake without help, without blood."

She took another bite and chewed slowly, as if in thought. "I've spent the last ten years thinking that my life sucked worse than just about anyone's. But here you all are, unable to see the sun, starving, mistrusted, and still busting your asses to help everyone around you." She pointed at him with her fork. "I know you did something for the little old couple who fed you. And I know it cost you power you could have used in other ways."

Ronan shrugged. "No one exists alone in this world. We've learned that the golden rule is the only way we survive. If I had to get up four times a night to pee, I'd want someone to fix it."

She laughed. "What?"

"That's what I did for Mr. Pennyfort. Enlarged prostate. And yes, it cost me something to heal him, but I still came away with what I needed."

"Which was what?"

"Enough energy to get me to the next sunset."

She shook her curls. "Hope said that she and I are like you guys, but we're not. We're lucky."

"We all have our burdens to bear." He set his fork in his empty bowl. "If you're done eating, let's see what we can do about easing yours before the sun comes up."

He washed their bowls, then led her to the living room.

As in the kitchen, this space was clean but hadn't been

updated in decades. The furniture was 1980s beige plaid, to accentuate the beige carpet and walls to match. There was a lovely stone fireplace in the front wall, but it bore a sign that said it wasn't working properly.

This place really needed some attention.

"Get comfortable," he said. "This will be easier on both of us if you're relaxed."

"Are you sure you have the energy for this?"

"All I'm going to do is try to strike up a conversation. Nothing strenuous." He hoped.

Justice sat at one end of the couch and leaned back. Ronan sat next to her, close enough to smell her skin and feel her delicious heat.

He wanted to touch her again, kiss her. He wanted a lot more than that, but he was used to shoving his own desires aside for a bigger cause.

Freeing her from the presence haunting her was the only thing he could let matter right now. Later, when there was time, he promised himself he'd taste her again. This time, he would have more than just her blood. He'd taste every inch of her.

Already the idea was making him hard and agitated. He needed to find a way to calm down and center himself so he could focus on the task at hand.

"Just close your eyes and breathe," he told her. "If you hear anyone in your mind or feel any pain, let me know."

She nodded and laid her head back, eyes closed.

She was a stunning woman. Unearthly beautiful, with full, kissable lips and the smoothest skin he'd ever seen. The need to possess her in every way raged through him, but he shoved that all down and pulled in a deep breath.

Traces of her blood were still inside him. Her cells had become part of his, merging into his very flesh and bone. He could feel her essence in each of them and used that to attune himself with her mind.

Falling into her thoughts was easy now. She didn't resist him at all. One moment he was in his own body, and the next, he was in hers, coexisting beside her spirit as if he had always been here.

As stunning as she was on the outside, she was even more beautiful inside. Her warmth and strength radiated around him in welcome, like the hug of a long-lost friend.

Ronan swelled to fill as much of her as he could, to get as much contact with her essence as possible.

"Mmm," she moaned. "That feels nice."

Distantly, he felt his cock harden at the sound of her pleasure. She hadn't meant her words to be sexual, but his erection couldn't tell the difference. It wanted to make her feel good.

Lingering here with her like this for hours would have been easy but the weakness of day would force him to retreat from her mind soon. Before then, he had to find the presence compelling her. Make it speak to him again.

There was something familiar about her mental pathways, as if he'd walked along them a dozen times before. Often, this kind of journey was difficult and taxing, but with Justice, it was as easy as walking over smooth ground on a warm spring day.

He found the thick vein of duty that wove through every part of her and followed it back to that foggy curtain hiding her memories. Nothing here had changed. The wall was as thick and impenetrable as it had been before. Core parts of her, passed through it—duty, strength, courage—but when he tried to pass through as they did, it was as if the wall solidified to keep him out.

The presence he'd sensed within her was linked to this barrier. He didn't know if it had been erected by the entity, but he could feel a faint hint of intellect here.

Perhaps the fates were watching him.

"Can you hear me?" he asked, more with his mind than his mouth. The words may have left his lips, but he couldn't be sure.

His voice echoed from the other side of the fog, and for the first time, he got a sense of the vastness left hidden behind the wall.

A lot of Justice was trapped over there, cut off from her. And from him.

He didn't want that. He wanted to know all of her, to bask in everything she was and had been.

"Is anyone there?" he asked.

Again, all that came back was the echo of his voice.

A ripple of unease swept through Justice's thoughts and buffeted him.

"It's starting," she said.

"What is?"

And then he felt it—an itch at the base of her skull. The birth of a new compulsion.

"Focus on it," he said. "Lead me to it."

"I don't know how…. Oh. There."

A light began to glow in the distance. It was hazy at first, but as he raced through her mind toward it, it grew bigger and brighter. He followed the beam until he reached the end and saw what caused the itch.

A slender, silver thread, nearly too thin to see, glinted in the beam of light. It was kinked and tangled in places, rather than smooth and flowing like the rest of the elements in Justice's mind. As he watched, the strand seemed to pulse and shiver, almost like someone was pulling on one end, trying to jerk it free.

Was that Justice, or something else?

"Don't fight the compulsion," he told her. "Accept it. Embrace it."

She let out a soft groan, but he could feel her mind unclench around him as she relaxed and did as he asked.

"I have to go, Ronan. I can't stay here."

"Just a moment more."

He watched the strand, and while Justice was completely accepting in this moment, the silver thread still bucked and vibrated.

This wasn't a natural part of her. Someone had put it here, as they had the wall around her past.

Tentatively, Ronan reached out and brushed his essence across the thread.

Go! Go...now!

The presence. He'd found it, here in this strand of silver no thicker than spider silk.

A sense of excitement rushed through him. He didn't know if he could communicate with the being on the other end of this thread, but even if he couldn't, he now knew what to cut to destroy the link this presence had to Justice.

He wrapped himself around the strand and gathered a surge of power to fuel his efforts to reach the creature on the other end. "You must stop. You're hurting her."

A flicker of shock vibrated through the thread, along with an acute shift in awareness.

Whoever—whatever—it was, it was now focused completely on him.

Who...are...you? the presence asked.

"Ronan. Justice's friend. What you're doing is hurting her. You must stop."

Can...not. Danger. There were long pauses between the words, which were not truly words at all. They were more like momentary, flickering concepts than language, or instantaneous bursts of ideas surrounded by static.

"What danger?" he asked.

Coming...soon. Go!

"I can't wait, Ronan," Justice said through clenched teeth. "I have to go."

She was suffering. Her skin was burning, and a sense of desperation circled through her mind, over and over.

Whatever this presence was, it had the power to control her, and Ronan had no idea how to stop it.

He caught a flicker of her thoughts. She'd been sure he could help her—so sure she'd bargained with her blood. But he'd failed, and now disappointment battered her hope until it cowered back in its box, defeated.

"You have no right to control her!" he all but shouted at the presence.

Need.

Fury blasted through him as the flickering word filled Justice's head. He didn't give a fuck what this creature needed. All he cared about was Justice—her comfort, *her* needs.

He wasn't as strong as he had been when he'd entered her mind. Every moment he was here expended precious energy. Still, he had to try something. He couldn't let Justice lose hope in him. He couldn't face her if he failed.

He curled himself around that knotted, jerky strand and poured every bit of magic he could spare into severing it.

Heat blasted out of him, so strong Justice gasped. He could feel the presence retreating, lurching back away from the heat he shoved into the silver thread.

Retreat wasn't enough. He needed to sever the tie between them. Destroy it utterly.

As far as he could see in either direction, the strand began to turn a fiery red. Sparks flew up from it. The tangled knots quivered and hissed.

In the distance, he felt, more than heard, the presence scream in pain. It was long and high, like the dying howl of an animal. And then it stopped.

The silver thread crumbled to ash.

He felt as though he could do the same. He was brittle and weak from his efforts, with barely enough energy left to return to his own body.

The trip home was long and exhausting. When he finally landed in his own skin, all he could feel was hunger.

He opened his eyes to find Justice staring at him with tears behind her lashes. He was sprawled back on the couch with her straddling his lap. Her expression was an odd mix of fear and gratitude he was too spent to understand.

"Are you okay?" she asked, her voice soft and urgent.

He couldn't speak. Not yet. He wasn't yet settled in his own mind, much less in control of his speech. All he could do was let out what he hoped was an affirmative grunt.

He was alive. Weak. Starving. Spent. But alive.

"You did it," she whispered. Tears pooled in her eyes before spilling down onto her smooth cheeks. "The compulsion is gone. I'm free."

The smile she gave him was soggy, but beautiful. He'd never seen anything like it before and knew that he'd go through hell itself to see it again.

Hunger raged in his guts. He needed to sleep and block it out. There wasn't time before dawn to go hunting, and Justice had already given him so much. His only choice was to sleep through the worst of his pain and pray for sunset to come quickly.

Justice cupped his face in her hands. "I know what you did cost you. I can see your hunger blazing in your eyes. Let me feed you."

He wanted nothing more, and with each passing second, he was forgetting why it wasn't a good idea.

"No," he croaked out. "I'll sleep."

She unbuttoned the top two buttons of her shirt and peeled the collar away to expose the delicate curve of her throat.

"After what you did for me, I'm not letting you go to bed hungry. I promise to hydrate while you sleep."

Her vow was light and fragile, but as weak as he was, he still felt it settle heavily over his shoulders.

He wasn't going to be able to resist her. He was too hungry and exhausted. All he could do now was use what little willpower he had left to keep from taking too much, because once her blood began flowing into his mouth, he knew he'd never want to stop.

Justice lowered herself so that her pulse was aligned over his lips. She pulled her springy curls out of the way and whispered, "Drink."

***

Justice felt the moment Ronan gave into his hunger. There was a subtle shift in him that she could smell, like he'd become a little less man and a little more animal. Less thought, more emotion. Less logic, more passion.

She loved it.

There was a thrill in pushing him over the edge, in tempting him beyond his ability to resist. It made her feel desired and indestructible all at the same time, like some kind of goddess.

She knew he was worried about taking too much of her blood, but if he could feel what she did, he'd know his worry was a waste of time.

From the second his teeth pierced her skin, through the ferocious suckling against her neck, to the final moments, when he grudgingly pulled away from her, she felt powerful, filled with a shimmering kind of magic.

And now, she was free. No one was making her do anything. She was her own person, able to make her own decision and do as she pleased.

What she really wanted to do was Ronan.

She held his head against her throat as he fed and dug her fingers through this thick, silky hair. A rush of pleasure sped through her veins and vibrated through her bones. She quivered everywhere, like the sun was tickling her skin with warm fingers.

That's what he did to her when he drank her blood. He turned her into pure sensation and made her fly.

She felt his body change beneath her as he fed. His muscles filled out and hardened. His lethargy disappeared and he gripped her like he'd never let her go.

Between her spread thighs, his cock swelled and jerked. She could feel its hard length rubbing against her as she squirmed for deeper contact—the kind of contact she was only going to be able to get if they were both wearing a lot less clothes.

She shoved her hands between them to open his jeans. He grabbed her tighter and let out a growl of warning.

"I'm not trying to get away," she told him, panting. "I'm just trying to get more."

His tongue swirled across her neck. A warm tingle

bubbled over the twin wounds, sealing them closed. He lifted his head and stared at her with eyes that glowed a feral blue.

"I'll give you more," he said. "All you can take."

She wasn't sure what he meant, but she was more than ready to find out.

He kicked the coffee table hard. The few trinkets atop it clattered against the wall. The wood splintered against the stone fireplace. A second later, he flung her down onto the floor where the table had just been and pinned her there with his big body.

A shiver cascaded down her limbs, stealing her strength.

Sharp claws extended from his fingertips. He slid one down the center of her body, splitting open her clothing as he went. Her skin wasn't so much as scratched, but the fabric gave way and fell open to reveal a line of bare skin from her throat, down to her mound.

But he wasn't done yet.

Ronan grabbed the severed edges of her shirt and ripped them open until her breasts were bare and the tattered remains of flannel hung off her arms. Then he moved lower and pulled her jeans and shoes off in one clean move.

The blue glow from his eyes slid over her body, and she was sure she could feel the heat of it kiss her skin.

"Your turn," she said in a shaky voice.

A wicked grin lifted one corner of his beautiful mouth, then he stood and stripped out of his clothing so fast his motions blurred.

When he was done, he stood still for a moment, letting her drink him in.

The sheer male wonder of him left her speechless. He was perfect everywhere, lean and hard, rippling with muscles. His cock was long and thick and jutted out from his body like a dare—one she was more than willing to take.

He lowered himself over her, nudging her thighs open as he settled between them. His gaze was fixed on her face, alternating between her eyes and her mouth as if he couldn't decide which he liked more.

His skin against hers drove her wild. His bare chest teased her breasts with every breath they took and made her nipples stand up and ache. The scent of his body so close to hers made her head spin. Her pussy clenched and ached, and each time she wiggled to try to ease it, she felt a slick wetness building there.

He gave her all his weight, pinning her in place. The hard length of his erection pressed against her belly, and she knew that if she could just get him to lift up a little, she could find a way to get him inside her.

Normally, he wasn't overly warm, but right now, he was putting off waves of heat so intense, she thought she could see them shimmering in the light. But when his mouth met hers, she wasn't thinking about anything at all.

He forced her lips open to invade her mouth. The taste of her blood was on his tongue, but she didn't mind. In fact, she found it sweet and spicy.

Her hands roamed his back as she memorized every hard ridge and deep hollow. The line of his spine alone was a work of art, though she'd much rather feel it under her fingertips than look at it.

Ronan lifted his head to speak. His face was flushed and that feral light was still burning in his eyes.

"I'm going to fuck you," he said, his words a near growl. "If that's not what you want, then you'd better say so now, because once I start, you won't be able to stop me until I've had all of you."

Her chin lifted. "If I want to stop you, I will. I'm a big girl," she said. "You don't scare me."

He grinned, but it wasn't a comforting sight. It was the grin of a wolf spotting prey. His teeth lengthened to fangs and a flare of light spilled from his eyes. "Brave. Not smart, but brave."

Then he lowered his head to the curve of her breast, above her heart, and slid those sharp fangs into her skin.

Pain and pleasure swirled together until she couldn't tell where one stopped and the other began. She didn't understand why his feeding on her blood felt so fucking good—why it lit up her cells until they were dancing in ecstasy. All she knew was that she never wanted him to stop.

The familiar tingle of healing shimmered under his mouth, then his tongue cleaned away every trace of blood before he moved to her other breast. Again, his teeth bit into her, and again she gasped in a mix of pleasure and pain.

His fingers stroked her nipples, flicking and twisting as he fed. She wanted his mouth there too, but then she wanted his mouth everywhere.

As if he read her mind, he healed his bite and drew the peak of her breast into his hot mouth.

Lights danced behind her closed lids. As much as she'd enjoyed his fingers, they'd been a paltry substitute for his skilled lips and tongue. Soon she was panting and shaking, and a fine sheen of sweat covered her body.

Lust prowled just beneath her skin, growing more hungry and desperate with every passing second. She wanted to flip him over and mount him, to ride him until she tamed her wild need, but he was too strong. Every time she tried to shift his weight, he bore down on her with his, pinning her right where he wanted her.

When she didn't think she could take any more of his loving torture, he moved down her body, pushing her thighs wide as he went. His big hands were pale on her dark thighs as he held them open for his gaze.

"Such a pretty pussy," he purred. "I bet you're as tasty here as you are everywhere else."

Before she could formulate any kind of response—coherent or otherwise—his mouth covered her sex and his tongue set her world spinning.

She knew what a clitoris was. She knew she had one. She also knew that when she touched it, it felt nice. What she didn't know was that she'd been doing it all wrong, because nice did not even begin to describe what Ronan was doing to her now.

He was a magician, an artist. He worked some kind of dark

sorcery over her that made her whole world collapse into the tiny space where his tongue met her tight bundle of nerves. She had no clue what it was he did, but she knew that if he kept doing it for just a few more seconds, she was going to lose her fucking mind from the pleasure.

Before she could, he stopped. His fingertips petted her as if soothing her heated flesh.

"Do you want more?" he asked, his smug tone telling her he already knew the answer to that question.

"You know I do."

"That's good. I like you wanting like this. Panting and desperate, your hungry pussy dripping in anticipation."

She bucked her hips in an effort to get more pressure, but he was too fast for that. He pulled his hand away and deprived her of what she needed most.

"Tease."

"Hardly. I'm going to give you everything you want." He kissed the inside of her thigh, nipping at the skin, but not breaking it.

Justice's body clenched so hard, it shoved the air from her lungs. "When?"

He didn't answer. Instead, he found the pulse running along the inside of her thigh and scraped his fangs over it.

The need roiling inside Justice shifted, swirled and mixed. She could no longer tell if she wanted him to feed from her or fuck her.

"Both," she gasped. "I want both."

He froze, and that alone told her he knew what she meant.

Of course, he knew. He'd been so deep inside her mind he was practically part of her.

"Mixing sex and blood is dangerous," he warned. "I could lose control."

"I'm not afraid."

He peered up at her from between her splayed thighs. Blue light from his eyes spilled over her belly and breasts. "No, you aren't. I love that about you." He prowled up her body on all fours until his face was even with hers. "Be sure."

"Shut up and fuck me," she said.

Ronan's demeanor shifted, going darker. He grabbed her hair and pulled her head aside to bare her throat to him. His hips aligned with hers and the head of his cock slid along her labia, opening her slightly.

Everything inside of her held its breath in anticipation. She needed so badly, she ached. She was desperate for him to fill her, fuck her, bleed her.

There was a flicker of a presence inside her mind—his presence. He was with her to witness her need, and because of that, she felt it the moment he decided to take what she offered.

He moved, and in one blinding second, his erection glided up into her as his fangs pierced her skin.

She was filled, completely, utterly filled. He was in her mind, in her body. His cock was deep inside her, stretching her to make room for more. His teeth slid from her skin as his mouth worked against her neck. Each stroke, each sucking pull drove her higher, and in seconds, she was overwhelmed by it all.

Justice detonated. Pleasure unlike anything she could have imagined poured into her and flooded her. Every nerve strained to soak it all in. Every cell shuddered at the force of it. She could hear herself scream but couldn't do anything to stop it. Her body was no longer her own.

It was Ronan's.

Maybe it always had been. Maybe that's why she'd never before felt torn apart and put back together again, all at the same time. Only he could drive her to this magical place.

When she was certain that the sheer physical joy he gave her would kill her, it started to fade. She slipped down slowly on shuddering waves of warmth, only to be brought back up again every time his cock slid deep.

His mouth covered hers, and only then did she realize he'd stopped feeding. His kisses tasted like sweet spice and need— his need.

She stared up at him, loving the way the tendons in his

neck stood out, the way his broad shoulders blocked out the world and all its problems. She loved the power of his body and the way each thrust of his hips did something inside of her to make her feel like she was glowing.

Justice levered herself up enough to kiss his chest. His skin was taut and smooth and smelled amazing, like leather and midnight. She opened her mouth to taste him, and it was even better than she could have imagined. Earthy heat met her tongue and made her teeth tingle.

She wanted to bite him. Taste his blood as he did hers. Just a little. Just enough to carry him with her.

Hope was right. The idea was not disgusting. It was compelling, consuming.

Her teeth scraped the skin over his heart.

His muscles clenched and he let out a strangled noise of lust. Within her, his cock jerked and swelled until she felt stretched to the limit.

He wanted this, too, she realized. He wanted her to bite him.

She increased the pressure of her teeth on his skin, but before she could draw blood, he circled her neck with his hand and pushed her back to the floor.

"You must not take my blood."

"Why not?"

He didn't answer. Instead, he flipped her over onto her stomach, pulled her up to her knees, and buried his cock within her in one smooth stroke.

This new angle lit up all kinds of nerve endings that had never been awake before. Within seconds, she forgot all about his blood and let the new rise of need consume her.

He moved faster, each stroke harder than the last.

Justice gripped the beige carpet and held on tight. If she didn't, she knew what was coming for her would send her spinning away, too far to ever reach.

His presence flared in her mind. An instant later, he forced her to feel what he did—the feral need consuming him, the desire to give her pleasure.

He reached around her body and took her clit between his fingers. Whatever he did there made her erupt again, only this time she knew it was coming. She welcomed it with open arms and let her orgasm wash over her.

Ronan let out a harsh bellow. A hot flood of liquid spilled into her and somehow made her feel whole, connected. She was too swept away to understand why, but it hardly mattered. She was no longer in control, and for the first time in her life, she liked the feeling.

***

The rising sun forced Ronan downstairs after a quick shower. Justice had the luxury of lingering under the spray as the first rays of dawn broke through the bare trees outside.

She was still marveling over what he'd done to her, what he'd made her feel. Not only had he freed her from the fates, he'd made her feel things. She'd never known that kind of pleasure existed, but now that she did, she was going to wring more of it from him. Soon.

She could hardly wait for the sun to set. She wanted to see him again, to touch him. She'd been so lonely for so long, she'd lost all hope that she'd ever have any kind of meaningful relationship with anyone. Her life had stretched out in front of her, bleak and empty, with only the relentless drive to obey and inanimate objects to keep her company. Any other ties she had were superficial at best, because there was always that constant fear that the fates would betray her and make her kill again.

Until now.

Ronan had freed her, not just from her compulsions, but also from a life of utter isolation. She could finally be with people, and the top of the list of those she wanted to be with was him. She didn't care that he drank blood to survive, or that he was unconscious every day. She didn't even care that his life was filled with danger. He was a good man—the only one who'd ever helped her, and at great personal risk to himself.

Now that she had him in her life, she didn't know what she'd do without him. She needed to tell him that and let him know just how much his gift meant to her.

Already, she was trying to find a way to repay him, or at least find the words to express how lucky she felt to have him in her life.

Justice had just finished drying off when the itch at the base of her skull began.

All her happy excitement and hope for a future without loneliness shriveled to dust.

She wasn't free. Whatever Ronan had done had been temporary.

She clutched the edge of the sink to steady herself against the weight of her disappointment. Her lungs refused to open up and let in her next breath, as if they too were too devastated to carry on.

She wasn't free. The fates still controlled her, which meant no one was safe around her. Especially Ronan.

The itch progressed quickly to a slow burn, as if her tiny respite was somehow a punishable offense. Maybe it was. Maybe the fates were pissed that she'd found a way to reject their control, if only for a few minutes.

She dressed in fresh clothes as fast as she could. The fates weren't going to wait, and she feared that what Ronan had done would only make them angry.

Whatever they had in store for her, it wasn't going to be pleasant, and she didn't want to be anywhere near him when it happened.

It was far better to be alone than to carry the guilt of killing someone she cared about.

Justice found a scrap of paper in a kitchen drawer. Her hand hovered over the page, searching for words that would hold him at bay without hurting him.

She really didn't want to hurt him.

Finally, she settled on as few words as possible and

scrawled a note. Then she stole his van and took off into the glaring light of day. As she drove away, she told herself that her tears were due to the bright light, rather than what she'd lost.

How could she have lost something she never truly had?

The secret is out!

Shannon K. Butcher

is now writing as

Anna Argent

For a list of books available now
visit: www.AnnaArgent.com

CHAPTER TEN

Ronan woke mid-morning to the certain knowledge that something was wrong. He'd had this feeling many times before, and every time he'd been right.

Fatigue pulled at him, but not nearly as bad as it would have been without Justice's blood running through his veins.

He closed his eyes and concentrated on what had woken him.

Justice had left. He could feel her presence, but it was too far away—miles away.

She'd left him, but why? Was she in danger? Is that what had pulled him from a deep sleep?

He pushed himself to his feet on unsteady legs and went upstairs.

As soon as he cleared the basement door, sunlight blasted him. There were blinds on the windows, but some light still flowed inside to pool on the floor in parallel lines.

The glass in this house wasn't warded as far as he knew. If that light touched his skin, he would never see her again. No way could he win a battle against Warden with the weakness of day plaguing him.

"Justice?" he called out, even though he knew she wasn't here.

No one answered.

Had she been taken? Surely, she wouldn't have just left him without a word. Not after what they'd shared.

Unless it meant nothing to her.

Dark emotions roiled in his chest at the thought. He didn't know what to call them, but he knew that he had suddenly become very dangerous.

If someone had taken her, he was going to make them pay.

Careful not to step in any of the glowing puddles of sunlight dotting the floors, Ronan searched the house for signs of a struggle. Not only was everything in order—except for the broken coffee table—his van was gone.

He was trapped here until sunset.

She'd left and taken his only means of transportation with her? What would drive her to do such a thing?

He was so furious at her that he didn't see her note until his second sweep of the house. He pulled the paper from beneath the magnet on the fridge and read it twice.

I'm sorry I had to leave. It's better this way. Good luck.

What the fuck was that supposed to mean? And where had she gone? Had she left of her own free will? Had someone forced her to leave?

Then the truth hit him.

Ronan slumped into a kitchen chair, suddenly too weak to stand.

He'd freed her from her compulsions and she'd left him. She'd *used* him.

Anger suffused him. He wanted to lash out and smash his fists into walls, break glass and tear this house to the ground with his bare hands. He wanted to howl in betrayal.

He'd given her what she wanted most and she'd walked away as soon as she got it. She hadn't even written down her phone number so he could call and ask her why.

Another flutter of wrongness swept through him, but this time he ignored it. Justice was no longer his problem. She'd made it clear she didn't want to be.

He made it as far as the basement when he realized he couldn't let her suffer. Whatever trouble she was in, he had to help.

That was who he was, what he did, no matter how much it sucked.

He used his phone to find the only ally within a hundred miles and dialed.

Morgan Valens answered immediately. "You're up late."

"Are your car windows warded against the sun?"

"She's a truck, and yes, they are. Standard feature on all the new vehicles Joseph buys. Why do you ask?"

"I need a ride."

"I'm on a job for Joseph."

"Is it a matter of life and death?"

"I sure as hell hope not, 'cause if it is, she'll be the one to kill me, not the other way around. Heaven knows she's tried hard enough with the last few men Joseph has sent to fetch her."

"Who are you talking about?"

"Serena."

"Ah." Pieces clicked together in Ronan's sluggish mind.

Serena had been betrothed to Iain two centuries ago and locked inside a prison outside the normal flow of time. Everyone thought she was dead. When she'd finally been freed, Iain was with another woman, their bond permanent. Serena hadn't taken it well. She'd fled Dabyr and had been out on her own for months, refusing all attempts by Joseph to bring her back into the safety of compound's walls.

Logan and Hope had healed more than one man who'd tried to force Serena to obey Joseph's orders. Apparently, she had grown quite violent, even to her own kind.

"I'll help you," Ronan said. "I'll help you find Serena and bring her home. But I need you to help me first."

Morgan let out a heavy breath that was almost a sigh. "Sure. Okay. I'm one of the few people Joseph has let leave the compound, so your options are pretty slim. I'll head your way now."

The feeling of foreboding racing through Ronan solidified into cold, hard fear. "Please hurry."

"I will." Morgan hung up while Ronan prayed the Theronai wouldn't be too late.

***

Justice didn't mind stealing from assholes with more trinkets than honor. She didn't even mind stealing from emotionless organizations, like museums. But whenever the fates drove her to steal from those who had so little, she always felt a twinge of guilt. Maybe more than just a twinge.

Before meeting Ronan, such trivial things as emotions had always slid off her, leaving her untouched. She didn't feel much, and what she did feel was shallow and easily ignored.

But since the night they'd met, when he'd taken her blood, she'd been altered. Irrevocably changed.

Emotions plagued her constantly, even to the point of tears. What the hell was she supposed to do with tears? And how was guilt or loneliness going to help anyone?

She had no idea, but when she let herself into the little stone house in a small town she'd never heard of, she knew that what she was about to do was going to cause her eyes to leak all over again.

The woman who lived here was nearly deaf, judging from the volume on the TV. From Justice's vantage point inside the back door leading to the kitchen, she could see into the living room where a white-haired woman sat hunched in a recliner. She had hearing aids in both ears, and a floral housecoat faded from decades of washings.

Her gnarled hands rested in her lap, all knuckles, protruding blue veins and brown age spots. A cup of tea sat beside her, next to a half-finished crossword puzzle done in shaky handwriting.

Thick woolen socks protected her feet from the cold. The drafts flowing through the old house were so strong the sheers on the windows moved with every gust of wind outside. Inside, the temperature wasn't much higher, as if the woman couldn't afford to keep her small house toasty.

The carpet in here had been laid in the early seventies and

had stayed here since. The vinyl floor in the tiny kitchen was scuffed and dull with age. There were no doors on the cabinets, and the open shelving revealed too many mismatched dishes and not enough groceries.

Signs of poverty were everywhere, from the generic, store-brand labels on her canned goods, to the used plastic baggies washed and left to dry next to a cracked plate and chipped glass.

Justice walked to the fridge and peered inside. There was even less food here than on the bare shelves—just a quart of milk, a few restaurant packets of ketchup and mustard, a half-dozen eggs, and a pickle jar with one lone, shriveled cucumber floating inside.

The calendar on the fridge had a red circle around the first of the month with the label "check comes today." After that were the various due dates of bills the woman had to pay, half of which were listed as overdue.

The fates had sent Justice here to steal something from a woman who had nothing to spare. How the fuck could they do that?

She didn't have a lot of cash on her, but she took out most of it and tucked it under the eggs. She didn't know if that would even come close to covering the cost of whatever she was here to steal, but if not, she had the woman's address and would send her more.

Sadly, paying the old lady did nothing to ease her guilt, because whatever she was about to take, if the woman had wanted to part with it for cash, she would have long ago.

The commercial on the TV ended, and a talk show came back on. It was one of those trashy ones with angry guests and lots of curse words bleeped out. There was some young man saying that the baby couldn't possibly be his, and an even younger woman convinced that he was the father. Apparently, they were going to find out the results of a paternity test, but not before a few more family and friends with opinions were brought out to express them in raised fists and more bleeps.

Justice made a mental note to buy the old woman a cable

subscription so she'd have more choices of entertainment.

The fates were irritated with her diversion into the kitchen, and made their displeasure known in a spike of pain down her spine.

She sent them a silent message that would have needed its own lengthy bleep, then moved in the direction she was ordered to go.

A narrow stairway led up from one end of the kitchen. Justice followed her compulsion up the creaky stairs, wincing when the scream of the wood got too loud. She paused, waiting for the TV to be muted so the woman could listen for intruders, but the talk show droned on in a combination of shouts and beeps.

There were two bedrooms up here. One was set up as a sewing room, but from the thickness of the dust coating everything, it hadn't been used in a while. The second room was decorated in an explosion of pink roses, faded from the sun. The bed was meticulously made, with the pillows perfectly plumped. An embroidered pillow in the shape of a heart sat in the center, a treasured possession on open display.

A small dresser sat opposite the bed, topped with an array of children's photos in handmade frames and several porcelain nick knacks. Unlike the sewing room, everything in here was clean, tidy and dust-free.

She had no idea why she was here. She knew she had to find something, but she had no clue what. Eventually, something would catch her eye and the fates would let her know she'd hit the mark, but until then, all she could do was search.

She started with the small, low nightstand next to the bed. Atop it was an alarm clock set in a faceted glass cube, and a porcelain egg that, from the smell of it, had once held a bottle of expensive perfume. The single drawer held only a bible and a revolver, both well used.

Grandma had slept alone for a long time, judging by the sag on only one side of the bed. If there ever had been a grandpa, he'd been gone so long his clothes had been put away. There was no sign of a man hanging from the single rod or stacked on an overburdened shoe rack. That was filled with high heels that hadn't been worn in decades and purses so old their leather had cracked.

The only other obvious place to hide something was the narrow dresser opposite the bed, so Justice went there next before she started ripping up floorboards and slashing through floral wallpaper.

In the top drawer, next to a stack of voluminous, nylon underwear and overstretched bras, was a tray filled with costume jewelry, campaign pins for dead presidents, glass buttons, a couple of random bottle caps and something that lit up like Christmas as soon as Justice laid eyes on it.

She picked up the metal object in an effort to figure out what it was but found herself stumped, nonetheless.

A long, hexagonal shaft was connected to a swirling trio of loops on one end. On that was a bit of beaded chain, as if this object had once hung from a lamp. The chain was plated gold and tarnished with age. The hexagonal piece was made from a matte silver metal and inscribed with the same intricate markings as the brooch and ring she'd found. The other end of the shaft was blunt and rough, as if it had been broken off. Just like the back of the brooch.

She took the brooch from her pocket and held the new piece against it. The remnants of hot glue on the back obscured her view, but it seemed like the two rough edges might match.

Of course, if she put those pieces together, the whole thing would look vaguely like a highly decorative, miniature umbrella, which made no sense at all.

Still, the fates had fallen silent. The burning in her skull was gone, telling her she'd found what she'd come here to find.

Justice untwisted the bit of wire holding the tarnished beaded chain in place and left that behind in the tray. The rest—the six-inch long hexagonal cylinder and its looping end were coming with her. She shoved them into her pocket and turned to leave.

Standing in the bedroom doorway was Grandma in her faded housecoat and woolen socks. Her pale face was calm, resigned. In her gnarled hand was another revolver much like the one she kept in her bible drawer.

The barrel wavered, but not because of nerves or indecision. The hard look in her cloudy eyes told Justice all she needed to know.

If she so much as twitched, Grandma was going to pull the trigger.

CHAPTER ELEVEN

Justice had stared down the barrel of a gun three other times in her life, but never had she been as scared as she was now, on the business end of Grandma's revolver. Then again, she'd never felt things as deeply as she did now, nor had she ever cared too much about the outcome.

Pull the trigger. Don't pull the trigger. It was all the same to her.

She lived or died by the fates. There was no sense in getting upset if it was her time to go.

Only now, she *was* upset. She didn't want to die. It wasn't that she feared the pain or what came after. No, the thing that made her tremble in terror was the idea that she'd never again see Ronan. She'd never feel his touch or see the way his eyes glowed whenever she offered him her blood. She'd never give her body to him so he could make her very nerves dance with pleasure. She'd never see him smile or hear his laugh.

She'd thought she could walk away from him, but until this very moment, she didn't realize how wrong she'd been.

Justice had never meant much to anyone, including herself, but she meant a lot to Ronan.

He needed her, needed her blood. Because of that, she had to find a way to fight.

She kept her gaze on Grandma, then let Reba dangle from her forefinger and thumb. "I don't want to hurt you," she said.

The old woman's voice was deep, raspy, and overly loud, as if she could barely hear herself speak. "You don't think stealing from me hurts?"

"I left you cash. In your refrigerator."

The woman grunted. "Sure, you did. Let me just go down and check while you slip away." Her rheumy gaze hardened. "I'm within my rights to kill you where you stand."

"Please, don't. I really don't want to be here any more than you want me."

"Show me what you've stolen."

Justice reached into her pocket and pulled out the metal shaft with its looped end.

Frown lines creased her pale forehead. "That bit of old junk? It's been in my family for generations, though heaven knows why. It's not even real silver. What the hell do you want with that?"

"I don't know yet."

"So, you broke into my home and rifled through my things to steal a piece of junk you have no use for?"

There was no way to explain. "It's not for me."

"Who is it for, then?"

"I don't know that either."

The woman scoffed. "Liar. You're a little punk liar. What else did you take?"

Justice had to leave. The compulsion to move was tickling her brain, and the longer she stood here talking to this woman, the worse it was going to get.

"I'm going to go now," Justice said.

"No, you're going to wait right here while I call the police. Kids like you need to be taught a lesson."

Only someone as old as this woman would see Justice as a kid. Or maybe she couldn't see any better than she could hear.

"So, you're not going to shoot me?" Justice asked.

"Still might. I'd rather see you suffer in prison for a while, though."

"For stealing a piece of junk, as you called it?"

"You still broke in. Trespassed. With a gun. When I turn on the waterworks for the jury—sweet, little, traumatized, old lady—you'll be facing more than a slap on the wrist. Besides, punk like you probably has done this before. I bet this isn't your first time. If I don't stop you, it won't be your last, either."

Grandma had her there. Justice had never been caught, but she'd been close a couple of times. She was certain her prints were on file with the authorities for crimes in at least seven states.

"What can I do to walk out of here without any police involvement? Is it cash you want?"

"All I want is justice."

Justice laughed. She couldn't help it. She'd spent her whole life being used as a pawn in a game she didn't understand. Who was going to pay for *those* crimes—the crimes against her? "You and me both."

Tires screeched outside. Car doors thudded and heavy footsteps pounded on the pavement.

Justice leaned over and parted the pale pink sheers to see four suited thugs racing up to Grandma's house.

"Friends of yours?" Justice asked.

"My friends are all dead."

One of the men looked up. His beady eyes were set deep in his skull, and his nose listed off to the side as if it had been broken more than once.

She knew that man. He was one of Chester Gale's hired thugs.

Shock trickled through her, leaving an icy trail down her spine. Were these men also after the worthless junk Justice had been sent here by the fates to collect? That didn't seem right somehow, but she didn't have time to puzzle it out.

The man who'd looked up had seen her. He'd seen her and hadn't been surprised.

He'd known she was here. How could they have known?

Before she was able to figure out that riddle, she realized what this meant.

"You need to hide," she told the old woman as she put Reba back in her hand where she belonged. "Don't let these men see you."

"Like hell I'll hide in my own home. I'll send them all to jail right alongside you."

There was a deep crash as the front door was knocked in.

"You don't understand. They'll kill you."

Justice rushed toward the woman, planning to gather her up and shove her in a closet. Instead, Grandma's revolver fired.

Fire streaked across Justice's shoulder as the bullet grazed her flesh.

Before the woman could fire again, Justice jerked the revolver out of her hands.

Grandma's face paled to the color of skim milk.

Footsteps drummed on the stairs as at least two men approached.

"Hide," Justice whispered as she pushed the old woman away from the door. "Hide or die."

But it was too late. The first of Chester's thugs was here. His pistol cleared the railing, and before he could even see what he was aiming at, he began to fire.

Justice took a hit to the leg. Behind her, Grandma gasped.

Reba barked in her hand and took off the top of the head of the first guy in line. The second hesitated on the stairs, giving Justice time to step forward and fire again.

She didn't fuck around with these men. They were armed and deadly, and under orders from Chester that were not going to make Justice happy.

Whatever that child-stealing asshole wanted with her, it couldn't be good. The best she could hope for was a clean kill-shot. The worst, he'd make her death last for weeks before he finally gave it to her.

Assuming the fates didn't take care of her first.

As soon as she saw the sandy hair of the suited next thug in line, she aimed and fired.

Reba was as accurate as ever, but this man's skull was

thicker than the last. The bullet sliced through his scalp but didn't break through bone. He was still alive.

A strangled sound of pain came from the stairwell. Behind her, another similar cry rose from the old woman.

Justice ducked inside the bedroom doorway before she risked glancing behind her.

Grandma's faded housecoat was soaked with blood. Her bony fingers clutched at the chest wound, but they did no good. A river of blood flowed from her body, too fast to be anything but fatal.

Justice rushed to her side and grabbed up the edge of the pink floral bedding to staunch the flow of blood. Even before she could press the makeshift bandage against the wound, she knew it was a lost cause.

Her rheumy eyes met Justice's and in them was a deep kindness and fierce spirit of a life well-lived.

"Just hang on," Justice said, even though she knew there was no point.

"I'm not afraid," the woman rasped. Blood bubbled across her dentures, painting them red.

Something in Justice cracked as if it were about to break. She was both furious and sad. What right did she have to drag this poor woman into her fucked-up world? What right did she have to drag her problems into this woman's home? "I'm sorry I got you involved in this."

Grandma's gaze zoomed out, growing distant as if she were seeing something beyond the dingy ceiling and sagging roof. Something good. Something clean.

"I forgive you." The words were faint, but unmistakable.

In that moment, Justice felt a weight lift from her body and give her room to breathe. She'd never been forgiven before. She had no idea how good those three little words could feel. She was free. Saved.

The woman's arms went slack. Her hands fell to her sides. Her eyes lost focus.

One pulse of blood. Two. Then no more. Only a steady ooze with no force behind it. Her heart had stopped pumping.

Grandma was dead. Her last act on this planet had been to save Justice from the guilt that would doubtlessly have eaten her alive. The woman was dead because of Justice, but she'd forgiven her all the same.

Rage burned through Justice until she thought her skin would ignite. Red flooded her vision and a cold searing pain washed through her veins.

This woman had died because of her. Justice hadn't pulled the trigger, but she'd come here. Chester's men had followed her. She'd led them right to the frail, old lady who'd outlived so much, but couldn't survive one visit from Justice.

Still, she'd forgiven her. How was that even possible?

Justice jerked to her feet and stalked out of the room. There were three men left by her estimation, and she wasn't leaving until every one of them was dead.

The stairwell was empty except for a trail of blood the men she'd shot had left behind. There were two red splatters on the floral wallpaper, one far more satisfying than the other.

She tucked Grandma's revolver in the back of her jeans, barely feeling the sting of broken flesh along her shoulder as she moved. There'd be time for pain later. Now was only for revenge.

Justice heard someone breathing. Not far. At the base of the stairs.

She pressed her weight in the center of one of the steps hard enough to make it creak.

The man leaned out slightly to fire, but Justice was waiting for him. Before he had time to aim his gun, Reba lashed out and sank a round right through the man's eye.

He dropped like a rock.

There was a hushed whisper from below. A deeper voice responded.

Outside, dogs were barking and any minute, sirens would start to howl their warning.

"I'm right here," she said. "Fifth step up. Center of the stairwell. Come get me."

She braced her feet and held steady, gun raised and ready.

"Mr. Gale just wants to talk," said one of the thugs. His voice was muffled. He was in the living room, somewhere near the now-silent TV.

"If your boss wanted me alive, you wouldn't have come in firing. My guess is he doesn't care if I'm alive or dead."

"That was a mistake. He cares. He just wants to talk."

She eased down the stairs as the man spoke to limit his ability to hear her move. A shadow on her right told her that one of the attackers was in the kitchen, waiting for her to step out into sight.

She grabbed one of the framed photos on the wall and tossed it out at eye level.

A bullet ripped through the edge of the frame, sending the smiling toddler spinning.

So, they just wanted to talk, did they?

"Shit," said the man in the living room as he realized his lies no longer had a chance to work.

Plaster exploded next to Justice's head. Something sliced across her forehead, but she didn't know if it was a bullet or part of the wall that had cut her. Either way it stung like hell.

She let out a pained noise and fell into a crouch.

The shadow shifted as the man in the kitchen charged. He was fast. She'd barely managed to raise her gun to fire when he appeared. His aim was off. He'd thought she was higher up than she was, and that second it took to adjust his aim was the one that cost him his life.

Justice fired twice in quick succession—one through his chest, the other through his throat. Her shots must have severed something vital, because he went slack and crumpled to the floor. He wasn't dead, but that wasn't going to last for long the way he was bleeding.

The sound of footsteps in retreat came from the living room. A car engine started and tires squealed again as he drove off.

Distant sirens began to sing—a chorus of them. Police, ambulance, maybe even fire trucks. She couldn't tell because there were too many to separate.

Blood ran into her eye as she hurried down the last two steps to get the hell out of the crime scene before the authorities arrived. She'd just cleared the corner into the living room when she realized that her count had been wrong.

There had been five men, not four. And the one left behind was ready for her.

The first bullet plowed into her left arm and the second was screaming toward her. In her experience, when it came to professional killers, the aim of the second shot was always better.

Justice dropped to the floor and rolled.

Everything hurt, but she didn't have time to dwell on that. She had less than a second to live if she didn't make it count.

The man trying to kill her was a beefy blond with no neck and a double helping of shoulders. The extra muscles and the pull of his suit over his bulging frame made him slow enough to save Justice's life.

She rolled toward him fast. He didn't have time to adjust his shot before she was literally at his feet. Still dizzy and with blood stinging and blinding her left eye, Justice used his body as a guide to tell her where to shoot.

Her first bullet hit his chin, barely nicking it. His hands flew up instinctively to protect his face, and by the time he'd realized his mistake, she'd fired twice more, right between his legs.

The wicked, flesh-tearing bullets she used exited his back and left two bright splatters of blood on the white ceiling. The red spray patterns were so close, they looked like morbid butterfly wings from her position on the floor.

Sirens grew louder. There were voices outside now. Witnesses.

Justice grabbed a crocheted throw from the back of a chair and flung it over her head. She could easily see through the loops of colorful yarn, but they obscured her and Reba from being easily described by onlookers.

At least she hoped.

Half a dozen elderly people had gathered outside, gaping

from their porches. One wizened old woman had a pair of binoculars to her eyes, as if she always kept them handy, just in case of neighborhood shootings.

Blood smeared Justice's vision on one side. Her injured leg was weak and slow but she managed to fast-limp her way to the van parked around the corner. She climbed inside before any brave witnesses gathered the courage to stop her.

Perhaps these aging onlookers had lived so long because they weren't overly brave. Or perhaps they were just wise enough to know a killer when the saw one.

Justice sped off in a squeal of abused tires.

When she was a few blocks away, she ripped the blanket off her head and used it to wipe away the blood leaking from her forehead. A cop passed her going fast, but she was just a woman driving a van, not a gun-toting old lady killer.

Another two blocks and she saw an ambulance and a second cop. She covered the trickle of blood with her hand and gaped like any normal person would as she kept driving.

Her leg was the worst of her injuries, but even that wasn't fatal. She'd been injured worse—just a few days ago, in fact.

Only this time, Ronan wasn't coming to her rescue. Not only was it daylight, she'd stolen his ride and left him a note that made sure he knew they were done.

As the adrenaline wore off and pain settled in for a little quality time with her nerve endings, she almost wished she hadn't been so hasty to send him packing. But none of her physical pain could even hold a candle to her guilt.

The image of that old lady, dead in her own home, glared in Justice's mind. Violent. Accusing.

That was what happened to the people she got too close to. Even though she hadn't pulled the trigger, that woman's death was on her head as heavily as if she had.

Wherever Justice went, death followed. The idea of it finding Ronan was too much for her to stand. It was just as well she'd cut things off.

He'd find someone else with blood like hers. He didn't need her.

She'd been on her own for ten years before ever meeting him. She'd be fine on her own again. She knew how to stitch up wounds and how to treat gunshots. She didn't need magical healing or the hungry pull of his mouth at her throat. She didn't need his kiss or his touch. She didn't need *him*.

At least that's what she told herself and would continue to tell herself every second of every day until it was true.

One day it would be, and she couldn't wait for that day to come.

After putting a few miles between her and the bodies she'd left behind in Grandma's house, she pulled into a parking garage of an aging shopping mall and drove to the deepest bowels of the structure.

There were few cars down here, and the ones that were parked looked as though they hadn't been moved in weeks. Maybe longer.

Dust coated them, giving their windshields a foggy quality.

She moved to the back of the van and closed the heavy curtains. She had to flip on the dome light to see.

Her injuries needed tending, but there was something else that was even more important.

Those goons had found her in a place they never could have known she'd go. Even she didn't know that's where she'd end up today. That meant only one thing.

They had a way to track her.

Justice had thrown away all the bloody clothes and shoes she'd been wearing the day she'd met Chester Gale in the empty doctors' office. The cash and ring she'd earned were at Dabyr. She hadn't bothered to collect them when she'd left. It wasn't like she needed more money. She had stacks of the stuff in all her warehouses—payment for past jobs.

She wasn't in her beloved Maserati, and she hadn't been so much as touched when she was with Chester or his thugs. Nor had she consumed any food or drink. None of them could have planted any trackers in or on her body.

But there was one thing she had that was in their

possession, out of her sight. One thing she never went anywhere without.

Reba.

Justice unloaded and disassembled her Glock but found nothing. She emptied the last two rounds from the magazine to look for trackers hidden inside, but it was also clean. So were the bullets.

She studied the weapon she knew as well as her own hands. There was only one other place she could think to look.

On the back side of the grip was a hollow cavity that rounded out the backstrap. She'd inserted a plug in it years ago to keep dirt and debris out, but there was plenty of space in there for some kind of tracking device. Anyone who knew the weapon would know the open space was there.

Justice removed the plug and peered inside. A small metallic object the size of sugar cube cut in half had been hidden inside and adhered with mounting tape so it wouldn't rattle.

She searched through Ronan's stash of medical supplies for a tool to remove it. Small drawers and bins lined one wall of the van. There were no labels, so she had to go through each cubby to find what she was looking for.

She ripped open the sterile packaging around a pair of locking forceps and used them to pry out the small device.

There were no lights on it, no sound coming from it, but she knew what the thing was all the same.

She crushed the tracker under her heel, then shoved its remains into a bottle of water and tossed it out the door. Once Reba was reassembled and reloaded, she was finally free to deal with her next most pressing problem.

She found bandages and disinfectant and went to work patching herself up.

Her head was first, since she kept bleeding into her eyes. The wound wasn't deep. The scar it would leave behind would be easily hidden by her curls, which was nice, because scars were the kind of thing that made people stare at her. She really didn't want to draw any more notice than necessary, because there was no way to know when her life might depend on her anonymity.

Once she'd cleaned and bandaged her head, her leg was next.

She stripped out of her jeans and sat on the narrow mattress to inspect the damage.

The bullet hadn't gone clean through. It was still inside her and had to come out. At least the thugs had been kind enough to shoot her in a place she could reach to dig out the bullet herself. If she'd taken one in the ass, she'd be screwed.

Justice knew what came next. She knew the searing pain she'd have to inflict on herself. Been there, done that.

She was already queasy just thinking about it.

Her phone rang. The number was private, but she was more than happy to use the call as an excuse to put off the inevitable digging she was about to endure.

"That wasn't very nice of you to break my toys," said Chester Gale.

A feeling of disgust slid through her, cold and thick like sludge. "I haven't moved yet. Why don't you come find me? It will save me the trouble of tracking you down later."

"Miss me?" he asked, his tone nearly singsong.

"I never miss," she said. "Not when I'm aiming at an asshole like you."

Said asshole made a *tsking* sound. "Now, now, Justice. You really do need to learn to control that temper of yours. It's not attractive."

That only pissed her off more. "Neither is killing women to steal their children."

"Since when have you ever been sentimental? No one is going to miss one more mouthy child."

"No one is going to miss one more egotistical, entitled asshole."

There was the sound of an engine in the background of his call. Deep, throaty power and smooth shift of gears. German. Maybe Italian.

"As amusing as you are, my dear, I didn't call to chit chat.

I have a proposition to make."

"Does it involve me blowing a hole in your skull, because if it does, I'm in."

"Nothing so fanciful. No, I'd simply like to arrange a meeting between you and the...man who's most interested in my procurements."

His hesitation around the word *man* spoke volumes.

"Working with demons now, are we?"

Chester scoffed. "Who am I to exclude an entire group of beings? How very smallminded of you. Is their money not as green as humans'?"

"I'd say that I hope one of them eats your face off, but that would be a lie. I want to be the one to end your infection on this planet."

"So melodramatic. And honestly, you're not giving credit where it's due. Demons always keep their word, and they don't go stealing what's not theirs."

"Pepper was not yours to take or to keep."

"All is forgiven," Chester said. "Water under the bridge. Now, how much will an hour of your time cost me? I think ten-thousand is fair, don't you?"

"I'll give you the first five minutes for free if you send your goons away."

"Oh, it's not me who wants to meet you. It's this delightful creature I know. His name is Vazel."

"If you're not going to be there for me to kill, I'm not interested."

Chester laughed, the sound genuinely amused. "I've always loved that about you—how blunt an instrument you are. No lies or subterfuge. Just in-your-face honesty."

"I honestly want to kill you."

"I know, sweetheart, but it's good to want things we can't have. It builds character." He paused. "Twenty-thousand?"

"Not even close."

"I'll give you some time to think about it. Do try to get some sleep, will you? You're going to want to look pretty for your meeting with Vazel."

Chester hung up, leaving her fuming.

Condescending, arrogant asshole. Even if he hadn't killed a woman and stolen her child, the fucker deserved to die for his sheer ability to irritate Justice.

She couldn't stay here any longer. She had to get this bullet out and get back in motion. By the sound of Chester's ride, he wouldn't need long to get wherever it was he was going, and she was in no shape to face down the army of meat shields that would be in between Chester and the .40 caliber round with his name on it.

Justice opened a clean package of forceps and began to dig for the bullet in her leg.

CHAPTER TWELVE

Ronan followed the pull Justice had on him to the hangar-turned-warehouse she'd brought him to earlier. The sun had only recently set, and the exhaustion of daylight was finally fading.

There was no sign of his van outside, but he knew she was in there. He could feel her presence glowing against his skin.

He wanted to kiss her and shake her all at the same time.

"Are you sure you don't want me to stay?" Morgan asked.

"I've delayed you long enough. Thanks for the ride. And if you need any help with Serena...."

"I'll call. Let's hope she's in the mood to chat, rather than to fight."

"If not, I'll patch you up as good as new."

"Let's not borrow trouble there. What about Justice? What if she doesn't want to see you?"

Ronan had spent the better part of the ride here pondering just that and had decided on his answer. "I really don't care what she wants. We're all in this war together. Some of us dislike our roles in it more than others, but we still must play them. Justice is no different. She's one of us, whether or not she likes it."

"You told me she carries a gun."

"Yes, so?"

"So, I wouldn't say to her what you just said to me if I

were you. Not while she's armed."

"I'll take that under advisement. Good luck with Serena."

Morgan grimaced. "Thanks. At least she doesn't carry a gun."

Ronan stepped down from the truck and opened the back door to retrieve his bag. "I saw her practice with a sword once, before the attack, before her imprisonment."

"Oh yeah? How was she?"

"You're going to wish she carried a gun. It would be far less deadly."

Morgan sighed as he shook his dark head. "Women. Why do they have to be so damned difficult?"

"Because if they weren't, we wouldn't love them nearly as much."

Ronan shut the door and watched Morgan drive away. The Theronai had no idea what he was about to face, but Ronan didn't have the heart to warn him. All that would do was make the man lose sleep. In the end, the outcome would be the same. Serena would drive him away as she had the rest and leave him limping back to Dabyr to lick his wounds.

A woman as strong and stubborn as Serena was not coming home until she was good and ready, no matter how many times Joseph ordered her return. As good as he was with women, even Morgan wasn't going to change that. He'd be lucky to come back with all his parts intact.

Ronan turned toward the hangar and paused in front of the camera outside the door. "I'm coming in," he said. "We need to talk."

Justice's voice came over a speaker he couldn't see. "I said all I needed to say in that note."

"Well I didn't."

She let out a long breath. "Fine. Whatever. The door is open."

The second he walked through the door he could smell her blood. Sweet, intoxicating, powerful.

She stood in front of him, feet booted and braced apart. Her stance was hard and cold, like a stone wall he couldn't pass.

There was a bandage on her head and lumps under her clothing where more injuries were hidden. She looked tired, defeated. Sad. Even so, she was so beautiful he almost forgot to breathe as he stared at her.

"What happened?" he asked.

She shook her head. "Nothing important. Are you here for your van?"

"That, and an explanation."

"I only owe you the van."

He moved forward just one step. He knew if he took two, he'd be unable to stop himself from closing the distance and pulling her into his arms to reassure himself she really was okay.

"That's a lie and we both know it," he said.

She closed her eyes and let out a long breath. "I'm in the middle of something. Why don't you just go. We can talk about this again in a few days if you still want to."

If he'd still want to? Did she think he'd forget about her note so soon? About her walking out on him? Or did she think that he'd forget her altogether?

"Not a chance," he said. "I'm not leaving you like this, injured and bleeding."

"The bleeding stopped. The rest will heal. Please, just take your van and go. There are some very bad men looking for me. You don't want to be around when they find me."

"When, not if, they find you? You think that's going to get me to leave—that you're going to put me in danger? What about you? Who will be there for you when these very bad men find you?"

"No one. That's kind of the point. I can't have you hanging around, throwing off my groove."

He looked around the warehouse for whatever had forced her to leave—for the thing that was more important than him.

She'd parked the semi inside and had loaded boxes onto the shelving lining the walls. A large pallet of yoga mats blocked his view, but nothing he saw here seemed important or pressing.

Anger grew in his gut like a storm. "I see. Your groove."

"Clearly you don't see, or you wouldn't still be here."

"What about me freeing you from your compulsions? Did that mean nothing? You promised me blood in exchange for your freedom. I don't know how you think you'll escape your vow."

Unless...

"It didn't work, did it?" he asked.

Her silvery-green eyes closed. Her shoulders sagged. "It doesn't matter. You tried. I appreciate that."

Tried and failed. No wonder she'd left.

Disappointment calmed the storm of anger building inside him. He'd so wanted to free her, to be her hero.

What a silly thing for a man like him to want. He was no one's hero.

"So, you left because you're angry with me?" he asked with no heat in his tone. "Angry because my efforts failed?"

She was so surprised by his question, she actually jerked. "What? No. Of course, not. I left because I had no choice. The fates had plans for me. I wrote you the note because I didn't want you to worry or to follow me."

"Why not?" He stepped forward a little more but resisted the urge to reach for her.

Her eyes closed in defeat. "I don't want to get you killed."

"I've survived for a long time and have been in more than one dangerous situation. Our world is filled with nightmares. You don't bring any more to my doorstep than are already there."

"You don't understand."

"Then explain it. Make me understand."

Her eyes shimmered, but he couldn't tell if it was from tears or the industrial lights high overhead. "It's not the nightmares you have to worry about, Ronan. It's me."

"Are you planning to kill me?"

"No, but I'm not exactly the one planning my life. I've killed those who trusted me before. If the fates demand it, I will again." Her eyes shone with tears. "I couldn't live with myself if I hurt you."

This time he was certain he saw tears.

He couldn't see her suffer and not do something to ease her pain, so he crossed the space and gathered her in his arms. She was stiff at first, but quickly melted inside his embrace.

How horrible must it be for her to hold herself at a distance because she never knew who she'd be compelled to hurt next? How isolating. How lonely.

Ronan tipped up her chin so she'd see his eyes and know he was telling her the truth. "I won't stop trying to free you, Justice. I won't give up. Just because I failed once, doesn't mean we're defeated."

Her eyes were luminous and brimming with tears caught in her thick lashes. "What if I can't be freed? I don't want you wasting precious energy on a childish dream."

"Needing to be free isn't childish. And I've wasted a lot more magic on far less important goals. Besides," he said, offering her a small smile, "it gives me an excuse to be near you."

She shook her head. "But that's the problem. No one should be near me."

"Bullshit. You're an amazing woman. It's selfish of you to keep all that to yourself."

She stared at him in awe, as if no one had ever told her she was deserving of something as simple as companionship.

Maybe they never had.

"I'm not leaving you, Justice. And if you leave me again, I'll just follow. Until I find a way to free you, you're stuck with me."

There was relief in her expression, but also fear. He could smell it radiating out from her skin.

"I don't want to kill you, Ronan."

He slid his fingers into her curls. "You won't. I believe that. Whatever these fates of yours are, they don't bear the taint of Synestryn. Until we can free you from them, we're just going to have to trust that they know what they're doing."

She let out a hollow bark of laughter. "That's easier to say when you're not the one leaving destruction in your wake."

Something in her tone, in her expression told him she wasn't speaking of the past. "What happened?"

Her gaze slid to the floor. "An old woman died because of me today."

"You killed her?"

"Death by proximity. Just like what will happen to you if you don't leave."

He shook his head. "I'm not going anywhere."

"We can still meet. I'll still give you my blood."

Just the mention of it made his skin tingle with anticipation. His mouth watered and his fangs itched and began to lengthen.

Ronan shoved all of that down and concentrated only on Justice. "It's not about the blood. I care about you."

She flinched like he'd hit her. "Please, don't."

"Too late." He more than cared about her, but he wasn't yet ready to admit that, even to himself.

She pushed away from him and took several steps back. "I can't handle emotional ties, Ronan. Not with the life I lead."

"I can't handle using you for your blood. I'm not a monster."

"You use others that way."

"Not even close. What I offer is a fair trade. Blood for healing, longevity, children."

"You give people children?"

He shouldn't have said that. It was too close to revealing the existence of Project Lullaby. No one could know about that. It was too dangerous. Too volatile.

He covered up his mistake. "I help people conceive, sometimes. When they wish."

And even when they didn't, but he wouldn't tell her that.

He stepped toward her to close the distance. He didn't like being too far away from her to touch her.

"Do you have children?" she asked.

"No. Sanguinar don't breed. It would be too cruel to bring

a child into a world without enough blood to allow them to thrive."

She seemed to relax slightly. "I can never have a baby either. If I did, the fates might make me hurt her or abandon her."

The fact that Justice thought of her baby as a girl meant she had thought about it. Possibly even dreamed about it the way his kind did—in the way children dreamed of fairies and unicorns.

He moved another step closer. "If you let me try to free you again, then perhaps one day, you could become a mother."

She gave a tight shake of her head. "I won't think about that. I can't."

"I understand." And he did. Intimately.

He was close enough to touch her again and she hadn't run away. That was a good sign.

"Would you like me to try to free you again?" he asked.

Her green gaze met his. "I doubt I'll have much time before the fates send me on their next errand."

"I won't need much. I already learned where to find the connection to the fates. It won't take long for me to try to sever it again."

"That didn't work last time."

"Perhaps I didn't sever it close enough to the source. Or perhaps there were more than one connection and I didn't cut them all. I won't know until I try again."

"You're desperate for more blood, aren't you?"

"Not at all." Though the smell of it was definitely making it hard to think straight.

She had no idea what a temptation she was.

Her dark brows rose. "Really? Does that mean you won't care if I do this?" She tilted her head to the side and swept her hair away to display the pulse in her throat and the twin scars he'd left on her.

Everything inside of him clenched in need. He wasn't starving, but his need for her blood went far deeper than mere food or power. With her, feeding was an intimate tie that bound them together, and when it came to Justice, he wanted her bound to him as tight as he could get.

"Is that what you want, Justice? My teeth on your skin?"

"That's part of it."

"And the rest?"

Her gaze was direct, almost cold. "If you're going to stick around, I want you strong enough to stop me if I try to kill you."

Ronan didn't know if her concern was sweet or insulting. "Who says I'm not strong enough now?"

She pulled her Glock and aimed it at him. The move was planned, deliberate. "I say so."

"You think that because you have a gun aimed at me that I'm helpless?"

"Aren't you?"

Rather than answer, he simply acted. He used the power flowing through his veins to speed his movements, and in a blurry split second, he had her caged against the metal wall, her gun hand pinned high above her head.

"Hardly," he said.

A look of relief softened her features and relaxed the tension coiled in her body. She let out a long breath and sagged where he held her.

Her little display was over, but the animal inside Ronan was just getting started.

"Testing me isn't smart," he said in a low voice too close to a growl for his peace of mind.

"Neither is being near me."

He had no other choice. She compelled him as completely as the fates that controlled her. He could no more walk away from her now than she could simply decide to disobey her compulsions.

"You and I are both prisoners of our nature. I need your blood and that isn't going to change. It's about time you accepted that you're stuck with me."

"So, it is about my blood?" she asked.

"Does that make it easier for you to accept me staying with

you?"

Her chin jerked up, her expression became defiant. "I don't worry about what's easy and what isn't. Life isn't about easy."

"What's it about then?" he asked.

"Duty." The word popped out, automatic and without hesitation.

Something about that tickled the back of his mind as if it were a missing piece to a puzzle he was working on.

Before he could take the time to figure out where the piece went, she said, "If you're going to be near me, it's your duty to stay strong. Take my blood, Ronan. I need to know you're strong enough to defeat me if the fates make me hurt you."

He would never defeat her. Subdue her? Yes. But never defeat.

She was still pinned against the wall, her smaller body caged by his. She wasn't fighting his hold, but her stare was one-hundred percent challenge. If he didn't do as she asked, he had no doubt that she'd try to ditch him again.

That was the true danger. Not only would she be alone to face whatever came her way, but he didn't think he'd be able to contain his anger a second time.

If she tried to leave him again, he'd be forced to do something drastic. Possibly something unforgivable.

Even now, with her lithe body trapped by his hand, dark urges were surfacing inside him. He liked having her against him. He liked controlling her body. He loved knowing that she wasn't going anywhere unless he let her.

The animal side of him found her captivity arousing, consuming. His cold skin heated and a flush spread out through his limbs. Need prowled through his veins, entwining itself with the part of her that still lingered inside him.

He wanted more. So much more. He wanted to strip her bare and fuck her right here against the wall while he fed from her. Her blood was hottest between her thighs, sweet and heady with the taste of her arousal.

That's where he loved most to feed, with her naked and

splayed for his enjoyment.

Justice's hips surged against him. "Take me, Ronan. Whatever you want."

Such dark temptation was beyond him to resist. He could smell her sexual need entwining with his own, combining into a new, powerful scent that drove him mad with lust.

He eased the gun from her hand and tossed it aside. There was no soft bed here, but he didn't care. He wasn't in a bed kind of mood. The hard wall was just what he had in mind.

Before he lost himself in the haze of lust, his essence dove inside her body and used a sudden burst of power to heal her wounds all at once. He wasn't gentle about it, and when she cried out in pleasure or pain—he couldn't tell which—he covered her mouth with his and drank in the sound.

He freed her arms just long enough to strip off her jeans and open his own. His cock was throbbing and thick, the head slick with his need for her.

He lifted her body, wrapped her legs around his hips and surged inside her in one heavy thrust.

Paradise. Destiny. Home.

She felt like all those things and more. The hot grip of her slick body welcomed him inside. Her silvery-green gaze promised him impossible things.

Ronan shut his eyes to block it all out. He didn't want to think about what would happen next. All he wanted was to feel this moment with her and know that neither of them was completely alone.

As he moved inside of her, all thoughts were washed away on a wave of pleasure unlike anything he'd ever felt before. The woman he craved with every fiber of his being surrounded him. She wove through him, part of his very cells. After a lifetime of living half a life, he was finally made whole by her.

The pressure of his orgasm would not be denied. He was too far gone to hold back and make this moment last. Justice was far too potent for self-control.

Rather than dive into the fiery throes of climax alone, he sought out her mind and forced her to feel what he felt. Within seconds, she was right there with him, desperate and needy and gasping for one more breath before the tidal wave broke over them.

As the pleasure crashed inward, they were together, grasping onto each other as the only anchor in the storm.

His seed exploded out of him, flooding her. The feeling was so exquisite, he was left blind and deaf. He could feel her chest vibrating with her cries of release but couldn't hear the music. He could sense the way her body arched against his but couldn't see her beautiful face tense with her climax.

The intense sensations went on and on until there was no air left to breathe, no semen left to spill.

After his orgasm released his body back into his control, he felt oddly renewed, rather than spent. Justice's magic had wrapped itself around him and given him everything he could possibly need.

Well, almost everything.

He laid her gasping body on the ground, settled between her limp legs, lowered his head, and began to feed.

***

Justice had just drifted off into a satisfied sleep when she felt pressure behind her eyes.

She lay on the cold floor of her warehouse with Ronan's body cradling hers. His breathing was deep and even, but she could tell without looking that he was awake.

Part of him was inside her, weaving through her mind as if he could knit himself to her permanently. The way she was feeling now, with her body humming pleasantly and her muscles relaxed and loose, maybe he could. He certainly possessed enough magic to make her body do whatever he wanted it to.

Her thighs clenched together as she remembered the way he'd pulled orgasm after orgasm from her as he'd fed. Her throat was still sore from screaming.

"Just relax," he whispered into her hair. "Close your eyes

and relax."

If she was any more relaxed, she'd melt into a puddle and soak into the concrete floor.

"What are you doing?"

"Playing with the fates."

Whatever he was doing, it felt nice. There was a slight pressure, almost like her mind was stretching to hold more of him, but even that was an odd kind of pleasure. Much like her body stretching to hold the thickness of his cock.

"I think it's a single presence," he said.

"One fate?" she asked.

"Not fate. Not karma or God. Something else." His voice drifted off as the pressure behind her eyes warmed.

Justice floated and let him do what he wanted. She didn't try to shove him out or block him from seeing her thoughts. There were so few of them in her mind now, anyway.

Ronan had done a thorough job of fucking her brains out.

"It's a woman," he said, his voice faint and distant. "Powerful. She…." The warm band of Ronan flowing through her mind tightened as his arms flexed around her body. "She knows I'm here. She knows I'm trying to stop her."

Sharp, needlelike pain raced just below Justice's skull and made her cry out and clench her head. Her mind filled with a shrill buzzing sound. It wasn't words, but each vibration was filled with meaning she couldn't understand. Panic. Desperation. Fear. Everything was too jumbled to understand, but the emotions ricocheting through her were strong enough to steal her breath.

Ronan retreated instantly and gathered her up in his arms. As soon as he was gone from her mind, the pain began to ease. Only the echoes of desperation remained.

"Are you okay?" he asked.

Justice nodded rather than trusting her voice.

"What did you feel?"

"Pain. Panic."

"Yours?" he asked.

She wasn't sure anymore. Everything had bombarded her

at once, and she could no longer tell if what she'd felt was her own emotions, or those of someone else. "Maybe. Maybe not."

Ronan let out a resigned breath. "Whoever she was, she's far stronger than I am, even after I've fed. We're going to have to try something else."

"What does that mean?" she asked in a hoarse voice.

"It means I'm going to need help to evict her."

"What kind of help?"

"Logan. Maybe Tynan as well."

"You don't sound happy about that." She sure as hell wasn't looking forward to another attempt to evict the woman in her head.

He hesitated for a moment. "They'll have to take some of your blood. It's the only way they could connect to you deeply enough to do what must be done."

"So?"

"So, the idea of another Sanguinar feeding from you makes me feel quite violent. I love my brothers and wish them no harm, but I'm afraid of what I might do if they were to get their fangs anywhere near you."

She rolled over and faced him. Just the sight of his face had the power to calm her nerves and ease her fears.

He truly was a magical creature.

"Possessive, are we?" she asked in an effort to lighten his mood.

"Deeply. But for you, I'll get over it. We need my brothers' help to free you."

There were no more echoes of that pain now, just an empty kind of hum where it had once been. She felt hollowed out somehow, as if part of her had been removed and left empty. A vacuum.

"Who could she be?" Justice asked.

"I don't know, but I'm starting to get the feeling that you know her—or did, before your memories were stripped from you."

Justice chewed on that for a moment. "Hope told me that

her memories came back when she took some of Logan's blood. Do you think that would work for me? That your blood could restore my memories?"

"Perhaps, but it's too dangerous."

"Because of what I might remember?"

"Because my seed is still within you. If you ingest my blood, it will be possible for you to become pregnant. I won't sentence my child to a life of starvation."

She nodded. "Right. I agree. I forgot for a second." Besides, what the hell would she do with a kid? It's not like she could tote a baby across the planet while she followed the whims of the fates.

Or a single fate, as the case was.

Justice needed a better name for the woman who'd ruined her life. The bitch, maybe.

Something about that seemed off. Wrong. Disrespectful. As much as Justice hated being used, she hated even more being judged by those who didn't understand why she did the things she did.

She did bad things, so that made her bad. Only she didn't want to do them, so was she truly to blame? Justice had always held onto the idea that she wasn't evil. It was the only way she could live with herself.

What if this woman was in the same boat—being forced to torture Justice against her will for some reason? Maybe she was no more evil than Justice was.

As soon as that thought entered her mind, it expanded and settled into the cracks in her memory, as if mending them. She saw faces for a split second, but not long enough to name them. Before she could capture the image, it disappeared. There was a flicker of recognition and a thought that almost formed into a whole memory before falling to pieces once again.

She closed her eyes and let her head fall back to the concrete floor. As soon as she recovered from a pang of disappointment, she said, "I think that whoever is doing this to me doesn't like it any more than I do."

"What makes you say that?"

"I don't know. Just a feeling, I guess."

"A feeling is progress. We'll take it as a win."

"It doesn't seem like one, but I guess in a sea of losses, it's about as close as we're going to get to a win."

He stroked her temple with one long, tapered finger. His blue eyes slid across her features as if caressing them.

He was so handsome, she couldn't help but do a little staring of her own. Women everywhere would kill for one night with a man like him, and she'd already had him twice.

Now *that* was a win.

"Will you come back to Dabyr with me?" he asked.

"I don't think that's smart. There's something about that place that blocked the fates—the woman—from reaching me. I'm afraid if I'm there too long, the next time I leave, it might kill me."

"Joseph won't let any of the Sanguinar leave, not so close to the births. If we want help from Logan and Tynan, we'll have to go to them."

"Maybe they can help me once the babies are born?"

Ronan shook his head. "I don't want to wait that long. Every time this woman sends you on an errand, you're risking your life. You've been shot multiple times this week. We need to get rid of her before it's too late."

Before he'd finished speaking, the perimeter alarm guarding the warehouse began to scream. A second later, a hole exploded in the door where the lock used to be and armed men flooded the warehouse.

Ronan leapt to his feet, gloriously naked and predatory. His fangs lengthened, his fingernails grew into sharp claws. His blue eyes lit with angry fire as he lifted his hand toward the intruders.

A faint blue light began to spread out from his fingertips, but before it could grow into a protective shield, one of the men fired.

A bright, red hole bloomed in the middle of Ronan's chest. He flew back and landed hard on the concrete floor.

Denial billowed up inside Justice like giant dragon wings as she rushed to Ronan's side. She didn't care that the men might shoot her in the back. All she cared about was stopping the flow of blood spilling from Ronan's heart.

Before she could reach him, one of the men grabbed her foot and dragged her away from Ronan.

Something sharp jabbed into her calf, but she didn't care.

Panic fueled her strength but stole all ability to think clearly. She kicked and fought her attackers and all she gained was a few grunts of pain and several harsh curses.

Her body became heavy. Her vision fogged and shrank into a distant tunnel. At the end was Ronan, his blood pooling on the concrete beneath his still body, his sightless eyes staring toward heaven.

These men had killed him and the only comfort Justice could find was knowing she would soon follow him into death's embrace.

CHAPTER THIRTEEN

Nika found her husband pacing in front of the glass sliders leading out onto the wide, open grounds of Dabyr. Nervous energy spilled out of him and flooded the mental link they shared.

She'd tried to send him soothing thoughts to reassure him that everything with her and the baby was going to be fine, but his mind was too filled with all the things that could go wrong for her to have any effect.

Clearly, he'd read one too many medical textbook about delivery and what could go wrong.

"You're wearing out your shoes," she told him.

He turned away from the empty night as if startled to find her there.

Madoc was a big man, with wide shoulders and plenty of muscle. But lately, he'd lost weight, too worried about the birth of their daughter to eat.

His bright green eyes narrowed as he studied both her body and her mind.

"What's wrong?" he asked. "Is the baby okay?"

Nika stifled a frustrated sigh and gathered her patience. "We're fine. Everything is fine except you."

"I'm fine. You don't need to worry about me."

She nodded to the sword in his hand. "You're not exactly acting normal."

He turned back to look outside and growled, "I won't let those fuckers come for my baby."

"This is supposed to be a time of joy and excitement, Madoc. I really wish you could relax and enjoy it just a little."

"I'd enjoy killing something."

"You've been out of the field too long. Maybe you should go on patrol or something."

"And leave you undefended? Like fuck I will."

She shook her head. Her white hair had grown like a weed since she'd gotten pregnant, and now it hung nearly to her waist, getting in the way every time she moved. If not for how much Madoc seemed to like it, she would have cut it off months ago.

"I'm hardly defenseless," she said. "I've killed my share of demons since I've had access to your power."

"Killing is my job right now. You shouldn't be straining yourself in your condition."

"For heaven's sake, Madoc. I'm pregnant, not dying."

He stalked to her, grim and dangerous.

Her insides melted with need. It had been too long since they'd had sex. For both of them. No matter how many times she told him that it was perfectly safe for the baby, he refused—some remnant from his antiquated upbringing, she guessed.

Maybe if she fucked him, he'd lighten up a little, relax.

"You're not allowed to say the fucking d-word," he said.

"Dying?"

"Yes. That. I don't want to even think about it."

Her big, bad, warrior husband was afraid. No matter how many times the realization hit her, she was always shocked by it. The man battled snarling, poisonous demons for a living, and he was terrified by the idea of her giving birth.

She went to him and wrapped her arms around his body. The bulge of her pregnancy got in the way, but she didn't mind. This was her family now. Her whole life was right here, in her arms.

"Everything is going to be fine. Our little girl will be born any day now, and maybe once you hold her, you'll finally relax."

"Are you fucking kidding me?" he said, though with no heat in his words. "How can I relax when this little person needs me to keep her safe? When every snarly monster on the planet wants to eat her?"

"And that's not even counting all the boys who will want to date her," Nika added, just to distract him.

"Don't fucking remind me. I can't deal with that right now, Nika. I'm already losing it as it is without worrying about her dating."

Nika pulled back and reached up to cup his face in her hands. "We're going to be happy, damn it. So deliriously happy that you will smile all the time, even in your sleep."

"There's no time to smile. We need to prepare. Be ready to fight."

"But not tonight." She pulled his head down so she could kiss him. "Tonight, we should enjoy the last few hours we'll have alone." She opened her mind as she kissed him again so he could feel how much she needed him, how much she ached to have him inside her.

Madoc groaned into her mouth. His body clenched, and she could feel his arousal shimmering through their link.

She reached down and slid her hand over his erection. "It's your job to take care of me, isn't it?"

"Yes, of course."

"Provide for my needs?"

"Always."

"All of them?" she asked.

His hands tightened on her arms slightly. "But the baby—"

"Is fine." She slid her fingers into the top of his jeans, took his belt in her fist and pulled him toward the bedroom. "But I'm not. I need to come, Madoc, and it's your duty to make it happen."

She felt the moment he relented. His mind shifted from resistance to the rough, animalistic need she found so arousing in him.

"That's it," she crooned. "That's what I've been missing."

Then he swept her up into his strong arms and kissed her until there was no more breath left for her to speak.

***

Ronan's natural instincts saved his life.

As soon as the bullet severed the artery leading to his heart, his body shut down and began repairs. His heart stopped beating to prevent blood loss, and he went into a deep state of metabolic suspension much like hibernation.

Had it not been for the fresh infusion of power Justice's blood gave him, he wouldn't have survived. The damage was extensive, and it had taken most of his reserves to heal it.

As soon as he regained consciousness, he knew Justice was gone. He could feel her moving away from him fast, but he took heart in the fact that he could still feel her at all.

If he could feel her presence, then she was still alive. That was the thought that allowed him to stay where he was, naked and shivering on the concrete floor while his body finished knitting together the tissues that the bullet had ripped apart.

He had no idea who those men were or why they'd taken her. They weren't Synestryn—he could tell by the smell of them they were completely human—but they could be working for demons. He hadn't caught the scent of infection that came with long term exposure to Synestryn blood, but that didn't rule out them being new puppets, dorjan.

The list of reasons why they might want Justice was long, and one Ronan didn't dare let himself contemplate right now. All that mattered was that she was alive. As soon as he could stand, he would come for her and tear apart every one of the men who'd dared to threaten her.

He closed his eyes and willed his body to heal faster. He needed to taste the blood of his enemies. Soon.

***

Justice woke up, certain that she had been drugged. They'd injected her with something to disable her. That's what that sting had been—some kind of knock-out juice being shoved into her bloodstream.

She kept her eyes closed so as not to alert her abductors that she'd regained consciousness. Her head was still foggy, but as she willed it to clear, she felt her body working to do just that. It was an odd kind of bubbling sensation, like tiny minions washing away the drug with fire hoses spewing hydrogen peroxide.

She took stock of her body. Other than the drugs and a few bumps and bruises, she seemed unharmed. Naked, but unharmed. She was, however, tied up at her wrists and ankles. She couldn't tell if they'd used hand cuffs, zip ties or something else, but she was definitely bound and unwilling to test those bonds to see if she could break free. Not yet.

She was moving. The familiar sound of tires rolling over pavement told her she was in a vehicle. She had no idea what kind, but she wasn't scrunched up. She was on a seat with fabric cushioning her bare ass and behind her back.

There was heat on both sides of her body—men caging her in. She could smell their sweat and the greasy scent of gun oil and cordite.

One of these men had shot Ronan. Killed him.

Rage burned off the last bit of drugs fogging her brain. She was going to kill these fuckers for what they'd taken from her. She was going to steal their life the way they'd stolen his, but before she did, she was going to make them suffer. Make them beg her to kill them.

Ronan.

Just the thought of him lying there, bleeding and blind in death, was enough to crush the breath from her body. If he hadn't been with her, he'd still be alive.

She was as guilty for his death as the man who pulled the trigger. Nothing she did would ever change that.

She loved him and she'd killed him.

There were only two choices left to her now. She could

either let her grief have her and fall into a mass of sobbing, useless tears. Or, she could give into the rage that wanted to consume her and let it take over and turn her into a killing machine.

In the end, there was no choice. She'd never had much use for tears, and there were plenty of men who needed to die.

It was far easier to kill than it was to grieve.

The vehicle stopped. The engine shut off. One of the men beside her opened the door and got out. A second later, rough hands grabbed her under the arms and hauled her onto the cool ground.

There was little light. The ground was cool, but not cold enough for them to be outside. There was no wind, and an echo gave her the sense of an enclosed space.

She cracked her lashes open just enough to get a filtered view of rock walls and painted metal poles holding up a limestone ceiling.

They were in some kind of cave, like those used for storage and manufacturing around Kansas City.

She saw the legs of three men—two in combat dress and one in slacks.

"Is she damaged?" asked one of the men.

She knew that voice. Chester Gale, child thief, murderer and all-around entitled asshole.

"We were careful, like you said," one of the men replied from behind her.

Justice upped her impending murder count to four.

"Why is she naked?"

"She was fucking some guy."

"Where is he?"

"Dead."

"Where is the body?" Chester asked.

"We left it there. The warehouse is isolated. No one will smell him."

"Fine. We're in a hurry, anyway. Our client is impatient to meet her."

His client? Someone hired him to abduct her? Justice

racked her brain but had no idea who it could be. If she hadn't been with Ronan, she might have suspected him, but…

Ronan was dead. He hadn't hired anyone.

Pain and grief swelled in her chest and threatened to overwhelm her. She couldn't break down. Not now. Not here. Later, after she'd killed his murderers, she'd weep. But not now.

There was a shuffling sound in the distance, followed by a fetid smell of rot and feces. She struggled not to gag, as did the men surrounding her. One of them retched, and a splash of vomit hit the ground a few yards away from her.

"Vazel," Chester greeted. "Good to see you again."

"You brought the woman." It wasn't a question, but the greedy, wet tone was all too eager for Justice's comfort.

Vazel. The man Chester had offered her twenty-thousand dollars to meet.

This couldn't be good.

"I debated keeping her," Chester said. "She's caused me a lot of trouble. But I figured business is business. There's no profit in killing her myself. I'll let you have the pleasure."

"I'm not going to kill her."

"No? I assumed you would since she stole the girl you wanted."

So, this stinky fucker, Vazel was the one who wanted Pepper. That alone was enough for Justice to add him to her kill list.

"I have better uses for a woman of her talents."

One of Chester's men snickered. "I bet. She's hot."

The man's laugh was cut off suddenly and replaced with a chocking sound. A second later, there was a heavy thud of a body hitting the ground.

Vazel hadn't even moved.

"No one insults my future queen," Vazel said.

A new sense of foreboding gathered around Justice and stole what little warmth was left in her skin.

Whoever Vazel was, he wasn't human.

"She's awake," he said.

"Not for hours," Chester assured him. "The drugs—"

"Are for humans. Justice is far from that." He directed his next question to her. "Aren't you?"

No sense in playing possum now. At least if she could open her eyes, she'd be better able to take stock of her situation and figure out how to free herself and kill these fuckers one by one.

Too bad Reba was back in the warehouse, well out of reach. She was going to have to find a weapon or resort to bare hands.

Somewhere, deep in the primal part of her brain, that idea appealed to her far more than it should have.

Justice opened her eyes, and as soon as she saw Vazel, she wished she hadn't.

He was grotesque, all bulbous and fleshy, with too-long arms and misshapen hands. He was naked except for a dirty cloth around his waist. His flaccid cock and drooping balls hung below the short bit of fabric. Grime clung to patchy skin that was almost the color and texture of desert lizards. His mouth was stretched in a wide grin filled with pointed teeth.

Definitely not human.

Behind him, lurking deep in the shadowy recesses of a rough rock opening stood several tall, humanoid creatures with pale gray skin. They held rough, rusty weapons in their hands that looked more like hammered bits of scrap metal than swords. Still, as muscular as they were, she didn't doubt they could do some damage, even with the dull blades.

"I have no idea what I am," she told Vazel, "other than gonna kick your ass."

The demon laughed, the sound wet and phlegmy.

She gave her eyes a break from his abundance of ugly to look down at her bindings. Zip ties. Rough on the skin, but breakable. All she needed was a little time to herself.

"I enjoy a feisty woman," Vazel said. "My queen was like you. You will please me, my new queen."

Queen? Where the hell was this creature from?

Justice lifted her chin and sneered. "Untie me and we'll

see just how well I please you."

"As soon as I receive payment," Chester said, "she's all yours, to crown or fuck or kill—no judgment here. We all have our own path."

Justice's skin began to crawl as if it could get away from Vazel without her.

She struggled to her feet, certain she was giving the men behind her a hell of a show with her bare ass hanging out. "I'm not some *thing* to be bought and sold."

"Everyone has their price," Chester said. "Yours was quite steep. You should be proud."

Justice was not going to let this asshole get away with the things he'd done—to her, to Ronan, to Pepper and to God knew how many others.

She forced herself to look at Vazel. "You want me?" she told him. "Then prove it. Kill him for me. Kill the men who took the life of the man I loved."

Vazel grinned. Drool ran from the corner of his thin lips. "Bloodthirsty and feisty? I have chosen well. Our son will learn much from you."

Son? She had no clue what he was talking about.

"Wait a minute," Chester said as he backed away. "We had a deal."

"We did," Vazel agreed. "You bring me the woman. I pay you." He pulled free a small, dirty leather bag looped over his loincloth and tossed it to Chester.

The man opened the bag and poured out a pile of stones.

"Uncut diamonds. Now you are paid," Vazel said.

"I knew you were a man of your word."

Vazel lifted his too-long arm and pointed one misshapen hand at Chester. All the while, he stared at Justice with the most vicious grin on his face. "A gift for you, my queen."

The bald demons behind him began to hum in a low, almost reverent tone.

Chester's expression became one of confusion, then terror. A chocking sound erupted from his throat. He clawed at whatever invisible force had cut off his air, sending the diamonds scattering across the cave floor.

Chester's men shifted nervously. One of them rushed to his side. "Boss? Are you okay?"

One man turned tail and ran. Another lifted his assault rifle and aimed it at Vazel. "Let him go."

The demon flicked his wrist, and Chester's soldier went stiff, then fell back. His head hit the stone with a hollow thud, but he didn't so much as flinch in pain.

He was dead.

Justice stood there, shivering. Her ankles were bound. She couldn't run. She was barely able to balance against the remains of whatever drugs they'd used to knock her out.

When the last of Chester's gurgling death rattles quieted, Vazel came forward. He inspected each man, then leaned down and unbuttoned one of their shirts. He stripped it free of the dead body, then stood in front of her, offering it as if it were the finest silk gown.

Sadly, he smelled as bad as he looked, like rotting meat and unwashed flesh.

"For you, my queen."

She lifted her bound arms in the hopes that he might free her. "A little help?"

He had only two fingers on his hand, both tipped with sharp claws. He used one to slice through the thick plastic like it was tissue paper, then did the same with her ankles.

His complete lack of concern over cutting her bindings told her just how confident he was that she wasn't going to get away.

She took the dead man's shirt and put it on. It fell past her ass, but not nearly far enough. At least it helped ward off the chill of the cave.

Justice rubbed her wrists and looked around for a means of escape. The SUV was empty and all hers if she could find the keys. There was a second car, Chester's BMW not far away. She didn't know if he'd driven himself or had a driver who possessed the keys. Either way, she was going to have to dig through the pockets of dead men to find them.

She doubted Vazel would give her that much time before he squeezed the life out of her as he had the men scattered on the ground.

Behind Vazel was the rough opening in the cave wall where the other demons waited. She could tell that the entrance had been chiseled from the rock since this facility had been built. All around her were flat, paved floors, but inside that opening, the ground was jagged and uneven. The walls in here were painted, but none of that bright white coating went past the hole where the demons hovered.

"Where does that go?" she asked Vazel as she struggled to come up with a way out of this mess.

What she wouldn't have given for Reba right now, but she was back in the warehouse with Ronan.

Ronan.

The image of his lifeless body flared in her mind and stole her breath. A crushing weight of grief poured over her until she thought it would kill her. Tears threatened to spill, but she fought them back.

She couldn't crack now. She couldn't show weakness. If she did, this demon would eat her alive, possibly literally.

Vazel stared at her and cocked his head. "My love died too. Your pain will pass. Our son will help."

She grasped onto the distraction he offered. "What son? I don't have a son."

"When you see him, you will love him."

Justice pictured some slimy, squat version of Vazel with pointed teeth and body odor.

"You know I'm not going with you, right?" she asked. It only seemed fair to tell him the way things were since he'd been decent to her so far. Sure, he'd paid a man in diamonds to abduct her, but, demon or not, he was still far more civilized than Chester had ever been.

Vazel didn't seem surprised or upset. "You will try to run. I will stop you. As many times as it takes."

"Takes for what?"

"For you to accept your new life."

"Acceptance has never really been my strong suit. I'm more of a fight or die kind of girl."

He stepped toward her. She moved back, only he was faster. Her ass bumped up against the SUV which barred her path.

He pressed his reptilian body against hers, pinning her against the cold sheet metal.

"That is what makes a good queen. I can be patient. But just in case you are faster than me…." He grabbed her arm in his cold, claw-like hand and used one sharp fingernail to slit a cut across her wrist.

Blood flowed freely from the wound and dripped off her elbow. She tried to fight her way free, but he was too strong. All she did was gain a few bruises for her efforts.

Vazel bent and lick the drops of blood from her arm. The instant his tongue touched her skin, she started to tingle and itch, like she was having an allergic reaction.

Then again, being allergic to a hideous demon's tongue seemed pretty reasonable to her.

As he drank, he made the most disgusting slurping sound of enjoyment.

She was certain he was going to like what he tasted enough to tear into her throat with his teeth, but instead, he swiped his finger over the cut and closed the wound.

Blood coated his teeth as he spoke. "You are delicious. And powerful. But who is in there with you?"

Before she could respond, the scent of fresh blood reached the hovering demons, they began to shift and growl.

Vazel turned his head toward them and growled back. "*Mine.*"

The demons cowered and shuffled deeper into the shadows.

Justice used his moment of distraction to bring her knee up hard between his thighs. As much as she hated letting her bare skin touch that disgusting loin cloth and what lay beyond, it was her only hope of getting free.

But rather than doubling over in pain like any normal

creature, all he did was grunt and tighten his hold.

Her hand went numb. His hot, fetid breath swept over her face, gagging her with the smell of rotting meat. "There is nothing you can do now. You are inside me. If you fight, I will win. If you run, I will find you. There is no escape."

Except in death.

Justice had never had a death wish. She sometimes didn't care if she lived or died, but she wasn't suicidal. Still, with every life she took, it was getting harder for her to remember why she should keep fighting to survive.

She had no one who would miss her if she died. Perhaps Ronan would have, but he was gone now too. No one would grieve for her.

What was the point of surviving if she wasn't free? This creature might be able to hold her hostage, but he wouldn't be able to stop the fates—the woman—from compelling her to do things. If she was trapped and unable to obey, there was no question that she would die from the punishment inflicted upon her.

If she was going to die, better to do so here, fighting to be free, than underground, trapped and surrounded by monsters.

She glanced around at the ground littered with dead criminals, then to the line of creatures hiding in the shadows. As she did, a bubble of laughter escaped her lips.

Justice was fated to die surrounded by monsters no matter what she did. Might as well make a stand here. Go down fighting. Take one more demon down with her.

Maybe Ronan would find her in death the way he had in life.

A sense of peace settled over her and gave her the strength to smile at the demon. "I'm going to enjoy showing you just how wrong you are."

***

Ronan could still feel Justice's presence, but something was wrong. Terribly wrong.

If he didn't know her better, he would have said that the feeling he was getting from her was one of defeat. She was giving up.

Justice never gave up. She fought, she pushed, she clawed and scraped until she got whatever it was she wanted.

Or died trying.

Panic spread out through Ronan, bleak and insidious. She couldn't give up on him. She couldn't be suffering so much that she was willing to let go. Not his Justice.

He called Morgan for backup, then barreled his way down the interstate, practically pushing smaller cars out of his path as he went. He flashed his lights, blared his horn and sent out waves of fear so that everyone got the hell out of his way.

It still wasn't enough. A sense of doom pounded down on him with every tired beat of his heart.

He couldn't lose her. He needed her far too much to let her go, and not just for her blood. He needed that, too, but there was so much more. He needed her fire, her spirit, he needed her strength and beauty.

Ronan had endured a lot over his long life, but he didn't think he'd survive a life without Justice.

She was closer now. Her intense presence glowed like sunshine against his face, then slid to his right as he neared her.

He turned the van, nearly capsizing in his haste. A car behind him blasted its horn, but he didn't slow.

His phone rang. It was Morgan, answering his call for aid.

"I see your van," he said. "I'm right behind you."

Morgan Valens might have been a bit of a flirt, but when the chips were down, he was as dependable as they came. Thank God Joseph had let him leave Dabyr's walls to search for Serena, or Ronan would be going into a fight without backup.

Based on the desperate feelings coming out of Justice, Ronan was going to need all the help he could get.

Centuries of finding people through their blood helped him pinpoint her location before he passed his turn. The road led into an industrial area filled with caves turned into businesses and storage. He was familiar with the layout, but not yet able to tell which entrance he should use.

He pulled the van into the first parking area he could find, hopped out and ran back to Morgan's truck.

"That way," he said, pointing off to the leftmost entrance. "She's in there."

They drove through the gaping mouth of the cave, disguised with beams and posts to make it more palatable for the average visitor. As soon as they were inside the underground parking area, he smelled her blood and saw bodies scattered on the ground. Ugly yellow light flickered over the corpses and sent Ronan's heart into his throat.

"They're all men," Morgan said, his tone steady and reassuring. "Not her."

"She was here. I can smell her blood."

"All I smell is shit and rotting meat," Morgan said.

Ronan ignored all of that and singled out Justice's sweet scent. It led him to a puddle on the pavement near an abandoned SUV. It was still wet, fresh. She'd been here within the last few minutes.

Morgan bent over one of the dead men. "No sign of injury on this one."

"There were demons here." He inhaled deeply to gather their scents so he could memorize them. One stood out from the others. It was rancid, but there was something else to it— an innocence, like the creature had recently been in contact with a human child.

He followed his nose to a tunnel carved into the side wall of the industrial area. This had been opened recently from the look of it.

Ronan smelled more of Justice's blood and found a few drops of it next to a scuffle in the dirt floor of the cave. She was still fighting.

A sense of relief rounded out the sharp edges of his fear and made room for a cold, hard determination to take root. He was going to get her back. No demon was taking his Justice from him. Not today. Not ever.

"They took her this way," he said as he drew his sword.

The song of metal on metal answered behind him as Morgan did the same.

Noises echoed from the guts of the stone. Deep, resonant voices and a higher, sharper one.

Justice.

Ronan sped his pace.

"Slow down or they'll hear you coming," Morgan warned.

"Good. They should know death is on their heels so they can spend their last moments on this earth afraid."

The Theronai sighed. "That's where we are, huh? All logic out the window? Okay. If you insist. Brute force works for me."

There was a flicker of movement up ahead. Even though the caves were black, both he and Morgan had the ability to see, thanks to the magic flowing through their veins.

Ronan wondered if Justice had tapped into her ability to do the same, or if she was fighting in the dark.

Her voice rose in a shrill cry of pain, followed by, "Back off, you stinky fucker!"

The response was a roar of anger and a deep snarl from more than one creature. As soon as Ronan rounded the next turn, he could see just how bad things were.

Justice was beaten, bruised and bleeding. There were two scratches across her face, and a slick sheen of sickly sweat.

Even from here he could smell that she'd been poisoned.

She wore only a stiff, canvas shirt. No pants or shoes to protect her feet from the sharp rocks and bits of bone littering the tunnel floor.

There were at least a dozen tall, gray demons barring their path to Justice. They were all armed with rusty blades, and far stronger than they looked. While they didn't seem to carry the same poison as their more demonic kin, they were still deadly.

A tall, misshapen demon wearing only a loin cloth held her captive at the end of his long arm. His hand consisted of only two fingers and an oddly jointed thumb, but his grip was tight enough to keep her in check.

She swung a fist at his head, but the move was sloppy. Ronan didn't know if that was the ill effects of the poison in her system, or if she just couldn't see her target.

He wished like hell he were a Theronai and she his bonded mate. He could have touched her mind and told her he was here, that he'd come to rescue her and she didn't have to be afraid.

But he wasn't a Theronai, and the best he could do was act fast and save her from any more abuse.

"I have to go," she shouted. "The fates...you don't understand. I have to go!"

Ronan's throat tightened with fear.

Not a compulsion. Not now. They were already dealing with a deeply dangerous situation. If Justice risked herself to comply with the woman who compelled her...

Ronan lowered his voice so that only Morgan could hear. "Now."

The men charged the back of the horde, swords drawn, war cries echoing off stone walls. Every set of eyes turned their way, but the only ones he saw were Justice's.

She didn't focus on them. Her vision was off. She was blind down here in the darkness.

After healing himself, Ronan's reserves were slim. Every bit of power he used now was being wrung from his cells, leaving tiny, empty skeletons behind. He would grow weak, then skinny as his tissues were consumed to fuel his demands. Eventually, if he didn't stop, his body would shut down and refuse to sacrifice more of itself. He'd become mad with hunger and drain the blood of anyone unlucky enough to be nearby.

As he'd done with Justice the first night he'd met her.

He couldn't let himself go that far now. He had to hold something in reserve to undo the poison coursing through her system. If he didn't, she was as good as dead.

Morgan reached the first demon before Ronan. His sword sliced through flesh and bone, beheading the creature in one strike.

Dark red blood splattered the walls of the tunnel as well as the demons behind the dead one.

Ronan took down the next and the next. As each man cut his way through the mass of gray flesh, more demons replaced the ones that had fallen.

Through the chaotic swirl of bodies, Ronan could just make out Justice being dragged along by one arm, fighting with her bare hands every step of the way. She bit into the arm holding her hostage and raked her fingernails across the demon's twisted face.

"Justice!" Ronan called. "We're coming!"

He cut through another demon, but the next one in line got through his defenses. A rusty, dull blade sliced through his shoulder.

More of his dwindling reserves went to work closing the wound. The more he bled, the weaker he became.

"Ronan?" she said as though she didn't believe it.

"Hang on!"

He sped the pace of his blows, frantic to reach her. She fought just as hard, jabbing with elbows and knees.

"She's mine!" the demon holding her roared.

The creatures fighting stilled for a split second, as if terrified to move in the face of that angry tone.

That fraction of time was all he and Morgan needed to turn the tide of the battle.

Bodies fell at their feet. The back ranks of Synestryn began to turn and run as they realized that death was coming for them.

"Hold the line!" the demon in charge shouted, but even fear of him wasn't enough to get the deserters to stay and fight.

"We're coming for you," Ronan warned. Hot blood speckled his face. A blue glow beamed from his eyes and fell on his next victims.

He sliced his way through the demons by Morgan's side, both slashing and hacking like they were clearing jungle overgrowth.

"I see you!" Justice said. Then she jumped up onto the ugly demon, clamped her legs around it and began digging her thumbs into its eyes.

The Synestryn screamed in pain, grabbed her hair and flung her to the ground.

Black blood oozed from his eye sockets. His voice trembled with rage. "You could have been a queen."

Justice scrambled away like a crab, but her face was a fierce mix of defiance and the promise of more pain.

She refused to be defeated, which was one of the things Ronan loved about her.

"Instead, you will be sorry." The demon tucked his chin to his chest and began to hum a low note as he turned and walked away.

Instantly, the gray-skinned Synestryn fighting disengaged and began to hum the same note.

Ronan took down two more as he rushed forward toward Justice.

Morgan covered him, sword raised as he crouched beside her.

"You're alive," she said. "I thought you were dead."

"I'm sorry if I worried you."

"Worried?" she screeched. "I was scared shitless."

Morgan shifted beside them. "No time for this. We need to go, before they come back."

Ronan sheathed his sword and helped her to her feet. "As soon as we're out of here, I'll take care of that poison."

"Poison?" she asked, apparently unaware of the toxin sliding through her veins.

"You're going to be fine," Ronan assured her. "We've got time."

"I can't see. It's too dark without your eyes glowing."

He pulled his phone from his pocket, turned on a flashlight app and handed it to her. Then he picked her up so she wouldn't cut her feet worse and carried her out of the cave.

Justice laid her head against his chest. She was quivering, but he couldn't tell if it was from relief, adrenaline or something the poison had done to her.

"I have to go," she said. "The fates…"

He didn't ask if she was sure or berate her for the bad timing. None of this was her fault or in her control. So instead, he simply asked, "Where?"

Her tone was one of utter weariness. "Out of here." Then, after a pause. "This is what the rest of my life looks like, isn't it?"

"What?"

"Being pushed around by otherworldly powerful bullies and stinky monsters." Her grip around his neck weakened.

That was definitely the poison working through her.

"No, Justice. Things look worse than they are right now. That's all."

"I can't lose you again," she whispered.

"You won't. I pro—"

She covered his mouth with a weak hand. "Don't. Don't make promises you can't keep."

***

Morgan followed Ronan and the woman clinging to his neck. He was gentle with her, protective. Whatever was going on between them went deep. Morgan could see it in the way she breathed him in, and the way Ronan caressed her body as he carried her. Neither of them could get enough of the other.

Morgan missed that kind of intimacy. He hoped he'd been without it so long that he'd no longer crave it, but every time he saw one of his brothers happy in their bonded bliss with their mates, he remembered Femi and everything he'd lost.

God, how he missed her.

Even now, after all this time, there was a gaping hole where she'd once been. Nothing filled it. Nothing soothed the pain of that empty wound. No matter how many centuries he might live, his only true constant companion was going to be heartache.

His brothers thought they suffered. Like him, they carried

around the pain of holding in so much power with no way to release it. Every day that agony grew until some of them went mad. But Morgan knew the truth—a truth he held secret to protect his brothers.

No matter how much physical pain they bore, there was nothing that came even close to the torment of losing the woman they loved. If he could keep pulling in breath after breath with that agony riding him, then he could endure anything. Sadly, that meant there was no amount of pain that would kill him, no matter how much he might wish to escape it.

As always, Morgan hid his pain behind a grin and a wink. "You two lovebirds get in Ronan's van. I'll take you where you need to go."

"The semi," she said in a frantic voice. "We need to go back for the semi."

"Why?" Morgan asked.

"She doesn't know," Ronan answered. "Just drive. I'll show you where to go."

"We have to hurry," she said. "We're almost out of time to save them."

"Who?" Morgan asked. Then, before they could answer, he said, "Let me guess. She doesn't know."

Ronan glanced over his shoulder as they exited the tunnel. "Now you're catching on."

***

The van swayed and bumped over the road as Morgan sped toward the warehouse.

Ronan caught the poison before it had spread too far through Justice's system. He had to use precious energy to purge it from her system, but there was no other way. As he demanded his body give up more power, he felt himself wither slightly.

He was beyond hungry now—beyond blocking out the need to feed. Healing himself, fighting, and removing the poison had all taken little bits of him until he had nothing else to give.

"You can take what you need from me," Justice offered. "I can see how skinny you've gotten."

"I'm fine."

"You're not, but I appreciate you trying to protect me." Even her voice sounded tired. He couldn't remember the last time she'd eaten, and her blood supply was still low from the last time he had.

Ronan kept a supply of bottled water and snacks in his van. He found an energy bar and opened it before handing it to her. "Eat this."

She wrinkled her nose. "I need to clean up first. That Vazel asshole had some serious stank going on. I need to get him off me."

He handed her some wet wipes and let her scrub until she was satisfied that she'd rid herself of Vazel's stench and the dried blood coating her arm.

She hadn't been hurt anywhere else. The poison had entered her system through the wound. A brief glimpse at her memories told him how it had happened.

Ronan doubted she'd be able to get rid of that memory as easily as he had the poison.

Once she was clean, she took the bar and ate. He opened another and did the same. It did nothing for his hunger, but he hoped that it would make her feel better about him not taking her blood.

"Thanks for coming to help," she said. "I think I was in over my head."

"I'll always help you, Justice."

She let out a humorless laugh. "Not even death can stop you."

"I wasn't dead. It just seemed that way. My body shut down to heal before I lost too much blood."

"You had no pulse. You weren't breathing."

He winked at her. "Details."

She smiled, and the move cracked the tension riding along

her skin. "I'm glad you're not a detail-oriented kind of guy, then."

"Any more clarity on the compulsion front?"

She stared down at her water bottle. "The fates—the woman—she's frantic. I can feel her pounding at my skull to get me to hurry."

"Have you felt that before?"

"Yes, but not often."

"When?"

"The night I found you for one. I knew I was almost out of time."

He had been. He'd nearly died that night. A few more minutes and he might have.

"How long do we have?" he asked.

She shook her head. Her black curls were a riot of tangles, but she was still the most glorious woman he'd ever seen. No wonder that demon had wanted to claim her as his queen.

"I don't know," she said. "Not long."

"Any idea where we need to go once we get the semi?"

"Yeah. But you're not going to like it."

"Why not?"

"Because whatever shit is about to hit the fan, it's going to happen at Dabyr."

CHAPTER FOURTEEN

After hours in his office, Joseph had finally finished all the mundane work that demanded his attention. He'd almost reached his suite and the comforts of a sexy woman patiently waiting for him when he heard fast footsteps and heavy breathing coming down the hall.

He turned to see Sibyl, her long, blond hair flying out behind her. Her cheeks were flushed and a look of stark terror covered on her face.

"What's wrong?" he asked.

"Maura used our power," she panted.

"Okay. That's good right? It means it's your turn to see the future?"

"It is. It was. I already looked to see what she'd been hiding. Now I know why she stopped stalling."

"Why?"

"They've been planning this for a long time. She didn't want me to see."

"See what?"

"Synestryn are attacking Dabyr. Now. Tonight. Hordes of them."

"Are you sure."

Tears filled her eyes. "I am."

His phone rang. Nicholas.

"What's up?"

"I just got a call from Ronan. He has reason to believe we'll be attacked soon."

"How soon?"

"He didn't know," Nicholas said.

Sibyl grabbed his arm in a frantic fist. "It's too late. They're almost here."

**

Madoc had just left his sleeping wife to pace off some of his nervous energy just as sirens blared through Dabyr. Lights flashed in every suite and hallway, the red color warning the inhabitants that they were under attack.

He shut off the overhead lights and peered through the sliders as he drew his sword. The walls were still intact as far as he could see. There were no demons or signs of invasion of any kind.

Nika waddled into the living room, wearing only a sheet draped around her body. She rubbed at her eyes with one hand, her voice sleepy and confused. "What's happening?"

Madoc shook his head. "I don't know yet, but it's not a fucking drill. Joseph would never scare us like that with so many traumatized children here."

His cell phone chimed. He read the group text alert aloud. "Demons attacking the west wall. All fighters report for battle."

Nika's eyes went distant. He'd seen that look enough times to know she was seeking out the creatures who were unlucky enough to have ingested her blood.

After a moment, she said, "They're coming. With an army. Hundreds. Maybe thousands."

"Fuck!"

She turned around and fast-waddled back to the bedroom.

Madoc followed her. She was already pulling out battle leathers when he caught up with her. Hers, not his.

"What the fuck do you think you're doing?" he demanded.

"I'm reporting for battle."

"Like fuck you are. You're pregnant."

"I'm well aware of my condition, thank you. My boobs may be too big for the jackets and I doubt any of the pants will fit me at all. Maybe if I leave them unzipped..." Her voice trailed off as if thinking through her wardrobe options.

"You are not going into a fight."

"I don't know if you're aware or not, but it appears that the fight has come to us." She pulled a T-shirt over her head and struggled to get it to slide down across her enlarged breasts. "What I'm *not* going to do is stand around and wait for demons to come barging into our home."

"You can't risk the baby."

"The baby is fine. I'm not the first Theronai to channel magic while pregnant. Besides, our little girl might as well get a taste of what's to come for her. Maybe she'll learn a thing or two."

Madoc grabbed Nika's shoulders and resisted the urge to shake some sense into her. "We'll fight off the attack without you. Stay here. Stay safe."

"I will stay safe, but I'm going out there. Be as overprotective of me as you like on the battlefield, but don't keep me away. You know that the two of us may be the one thing that tips the battle in our favor."

"I'll go. You stay."

"You've seen what I can do." She cupped Madoc's face, her voice fervent. "Let me do it." She turned away and began struggling with her leathers again. "Besides, if you leave me here, I'm just going to sneak out once you're gone. Wouldn't you rather be at my side."

Frustration and fear ground him down until his insides were a pulpy mess of anxiety.

What choice did he have? Nika had always been able to get her way with him. That was the only reason he was still breathing—her damn stubborn relentlessness. He sure as fuck wasn't going to change her now.

"Fine. But you stay well back from combat."

Nika grinned. "That's where I do my best work anyway."

"And no shedding your body to go into the minds of the demons."

"Why not?"

"Because that body happens to be carrying our child. I want to know you're able to get her out of harm's way if something sneaks up on you."

Nika kissed his cheek. "Agreed. I'll stay with our daughter and teach her how to blow Synestryn to hell."

***

Justice had never felt more frantic in her life. She wasn't going to make it in time and people were going to die.

She pushed the semi hard through its gears, uncaring about the damage she might be doing to the rig. There wasn't time to slow down. Seconds counted.

Ronan was in front of her to keep any cops from seeing how fast they were going. Morgan had given him enough blood to keep him going. Justice didn't like sharing, but the situation was dire. Ronan had to be strong enough to protect himself.

She couldn't lose him again.

Morgan was bringing up the rear in case any Synestryn tried to stop them. She was in the middle, driving the clumsy semi with its 53-foot trailer filled with workout equipment and the other supplies the fates and demanded she bring. Her duffel bag of goodies sat on the seat beside her. She didn't understand what good a water bottle and resistance bands were going to do, but she knew better than to question the chaos.

Their short convoy raced over county roads, blowing through small towns. It was late enough that there was little traffic—so late it was now technically early morning. Snow flurries had begun to fall, and while the air was cold, it was thick with the humidity of an impending snowstorm.

Just what they needed.

Ronan called her cell. She put it on speaker to keep her

hands free to drive the unfamiliar rig.

"Any word from Dabyr?" she asked.

"All the Theronai are busy fighting. One of the humans answered, but she didn't know how things were going. The civilians are all in hiding belowground."

"We're going to be too late."

"We're not. You have to believe that."

"What about you? You're starving. The sun will be up in a few minutes. How are you holding up?"

"I've been worse."

"That's not exactly a reassuring answer."

"Morgan's blood helped."

"Enough to keep you on your feet?"

He changed the subject, which made her certain she was right. He was bad off.

"Any idea what we're supposed to do once we get there?" he asked.

"Nothing concrete. All I know is that there's something precious there we have to protect."

"There are many precious things at Dabyr. Children are at the top of that list."

For some reason, that didn't feel right—at least not like the thing she was after. "What else?"

"The Sentinel stones are a major target. With them, a powerful Synestryn might be able to break through the gate into Athanasia. We thought the Solarc had fused the gate shut, but enough Athanasians have come through to tell us that it's at least cracked open."

Stones? She ran that idea by the woman in her head and felt nothing—no resonance, no twitch of desperation. Nothing.

"Anything else?" Justice asked.

"The pregnant women."

She shook her head. "Maybe. What else?"

Ronan's voice was filled with dread. "The Hall of the Fallen."

"What's that?"

"It's the place where we honor our dead. The swords of the warriors we've lost hang there. If the Synestryn get their hands on those, they could find a way to release the essence of the demons killed by them."

If that wasn't filled with crazy-talk, she didn't know what was. "What? What does that even mean?"

"It means that we can't let them reach the swords. If they do, we'll have lost years, if not centuries, of fighting."

"Holy shit. Talk about a target-rich environment. No wonder the demons want in."

He took a turn ahead of her and when she followed, she recognized the area.

"We're close," he said. "I don't know what we'll face at the gates, but Joseph is supposed to clear the way for us to get in."

"Let's hope he has, because I'd hate to have to plow down that gate and give the demons an easy way in."

***

Despite the frigid temperatures, sweat dripped from Joseph's brow as he fought side-by-side with his fellow Theronai to hold the demons at bay.

There were so many Synestryn—an endless sea of those gray, human-looking demons with patchy fur and blunt, rusty swords. They'd breached the west wall and scaled the metal gate, forcing Joseph to split his troops in two locations or risk human casualties.

All the fragile lives of those he protected were inside the compound, hiding in safe rooms belowground. There were four large spaces, all stocked with supplies. Even if the demons made it inside, it would take them a while to locate them.

Unless one of the humans was bleeding.

As panicked as some of them had been, racing through the halls like mad, the chances that no one took a tumble and skinned a knee were pretty slim.

The garage was still secure, the vehicles intact. There was still a means of escape, but not a path. The only road leading through the gate was infested with demons—too many to count.

Ronan, Justice and Morgan were headed this way to help, but they needed a clear path inside the compound. Joseph had no idea how he was going to make that happen.

Madoc was on his left, screaming profanities as he fought. Paul was on his right, steady and silent in his killing.

Behind them, the women bound to them funneled power from their bodies and converted it into magic.

Nika's was the hardest to see, with no flashy light or fire to spill from her fingers. She could crawl inside the minds of demons and take control. Sometimes her power came through in a slight pause in the strike of the enemy's blade, but other times, she could make their heads explode. Literally.

Helen's power, on the other hand, was easy to see. It rushed out of her in torrents of flame, burning every demon it touched. She'd found higher ground in the lowest branch of a tree and was methodically burning down swaths of screaming demons behind the front ranks.

Lyka was the newest to her power, but still doing her fair share of damage. Bolts of lightning streaked low overhead, lifting the hair on his skin as they passed. Each hit sent shockwaves through the ranks of Synestryn and left dead bodies and the smell of ozone in its wake.

Behind the women roamed the displaced pack of Slayers that had been staying at Dabyr while they rebuilt their home. Andreas Phelan and his pack were deadly, picking off any demons who managed to slip past the front line of swords and magic. They fought with teeth and claws, some more animal than man.

There was a wild ferocity about them, as well as what seemed like sheer joy. Slayers loved the fight—whatever fight it might be—and they were deeply in their element tonight.

Joseph was glad they were on his side.

Still, it wasn't enough. With every passing minute, the

Theronai were being driven back, closer to the vulnerable humans hiding inside.

Beside him, Madoc hesitated as if something had happened. A rusty blade sliced across his arm and made him falter in his swing.

"It's time!" he shouted over the roar of combat. There was fear clinging to those two words.

"For what?" Joseph yelled.

"The baby. Nika's in labor."

While the Synestryn in front of them didn't speak in any language Joseph knew, they sure as hell seemed to understand what Madoc had just said. Every one of them smiled and began to fight harder.

That's what this whole attack was about. They wanted his baby.

CHAPTER FIFTEEN

Judging by the light show coming from Dabyr, the fight wasn't over yet.

Lightning and fire bathed the sky in a haze of orange and flashes of white. Smoke hung low, drifting lazily in the still night. The snowfall had picked up, and a pale coating now covered the grass lining the road.

Ronan turned the corner and saw just how bad things were.

This wasn't just an attack—some small skirmish. It was an all-out battle, with more demons in one place than he'd seen since the night most of their women had been slaughtered two hundred years ago.

There weren't enough bonded pairs of Theronai here to kill them all. Not even close. The only hope the Sentinels had of surviving this attack was holding out until the sun came up and drove the demons back into their dark hiding places.

Ronan knew the path of the sun as intimately as he knew the beat of his own heart. It would rise in less than an hour— the eastern horizon had already begun to lighten—but even that short time was too long for his allies to hold back the invading army.

They were losing.

All around Dabyr, demons beat at the walls with battering rams cut from nearby trees. Stones crumbled, grudgingly giving up their hold onto each other. Where Synestryn couldn't break through, they formed ladders with the bodies of the dead and climbed over on top of each other. Some of them were greeted immediately by the swords of Theronai or the teeth and claws of Slayers, but a few of them were able to slip through. As Ronan watched, one lanky, gray demon made it almost to a ground-floor window of the main building before being shot by a human on one of the upper floors.

A bullet wouldn't keep the creature down for long, and once it got up, there was little standing between it and the humans inside.

The paved road was covered with sword-wielding demons. There were too many for them to plow through with their vehicles, even the giant semi. And even if they could clear the road with the rig, the gate would be the next casualty, and if that failed, there was nothing to stop a flood of Synestryn from washing onto the grounds and taking over the compound completely.

He slowed and dialed Justice. "We can't push through."

"I have to get in there, Ronan. Now."

"If we do that, we'll kill everyone inside. The fighters are barely holding one line. They can't have demons attacking their backs, too."

Her voice was tense, as if she was in pain. "I have to go now. Can't wait."

"Okay. Just give me thirty seconds."

"I'll try."

"Back up so you can pick up enough speed to clear the gate fast. Then go. I'll make sure the gate is open."

Somehow.

Ronan called the number that went directly to whoever was manning the gate. Slade answered. Ronan gave him detailed instructions, then said. "Do not falter or we all die tonight."

"Got it," Said Slade. "On your go."

Ronan pulled his van off the paved road onto the snowy grass, then stopped. He used his teeth to score a deep scratch on the back of his hand, then got out of his van. Then he took off on foot, upwind from the demons at the gate.

As soon as they caught the scent of fresh blood, their heads turned in unison, as if the move had been choreographed.

Ronan used what little power he had left to fuel his frantic run into the woods and yelled into the phone. "Now!"

***

Justice sped the rig as fast as she could. There were so many damn gears in this truck, and no paddle shifter to make the job easier.

She missed Ricardo now more than ever. He could have accelerated so fast, the few lingering snowflakes swirling through the air would have made it look like she'd reached warp speed.

Still, what the semi lacked in zip, it made up for in mass.

A terrifying parade of blade-wielding demons raced after Ronan, along with other monsters that loped on four paws and some that lumbered along on spindly legs that looked like they'd been put on backward. Every one of them looked hungry.

They were all after his blood, and if the person manning the gate didn't time it right, there was going to be plenty of good-guy blood to go around.

Justice shifted gears again. By the time she'd reached forty miles per hour, Ronan's ploy had worked, and the majority of the demons clamoring at the gates had veered off to feast on his blood. A few creatures stayed behind, but as soon as the gates started to open, they were too distracted by the giant meal inside to realize that death was coming up behind them.

Justice ran over every one she could hit, veering dangerously over the paved road until she was certain the trailer was going to roll over and take her with it.

The trusty rig stayed upright as if it knew the stakes were high.

Tires slipped on blood. One of them rolled over sharp bones or metal and burst in a loud thud that sounded like a gunshot.

Justice didn't stop. She didn't slow. The large, stone building loomed ahead of her. Once she was through the gate, there wasn't much space for her to stop before slamming into the structure, but she had no choice but to keep going.

The woman compelling her was in the driver's seat now, forcing Justice's foot down on the accelerator.

A few demons made it through the gates without being squished by her truck. Those stragglers were already being cleaned up by the whirling swords wielded by the men inside. Two demons slipped past their reach but were quickly zapped like bugs by a bolt of blue-white lightning that flew from a woman's outstretched hand.

Justice sped through the opening. The gate on her right was so close, she could feel it scraping the side wall of the trailer as she passed. As soon as she and Morgan were clear of the gates, they began to close behind his truck.

Finally, the power compelling her forward eased up and let her slow down. But she wasn't done yet.

She turned the rig to the right, onto the snowy grass and up a slight incline. She had no idea where she was going, but the woman compelling her did.

The low overhang of clouds had begun to blow away, taking the storm with it. The sky had brightened enough that the outside security lights surrounding the compound automatically shut off.

Sunrise was coming soon, and Ronan was out there, a horde of demons on his ass with nowhere to hide from the coming dawn.

CHAPTER SIXTEEN

Vazel overlooked the devastation of Dabyr from his vantage point in the woods one ridge over. Things were going according to plan.

The thick walls had been breached in several spots where the magic that held the stones together had been weakened. His troops had flooded over and through the defenses and were now only feet away from reaching the building where the blooded humans were kept.

The female Theronai were running out of strength. Even from here he could see that their lethal blows were coming more sporadically now, each taking out fewer of his troops. As soon as one of the women fell, the others would have to take up the slack, and Vazel doubted that would end well for his enemies.

At least three of those women were pregnant. Perhaps more.

He'd always wanted to feed on the blood of a Theronai who carried the life of another inside her. He imagined the rush, the power, would be amazing. Such a thing might even fuel him for weeks.

But that wasn't the real prize, only a delicious side benefit to what he'd come here for.

Sunrise was coming. He could feel the sun's toxic light buffeting his skin as he oversaw the attack on Dabyr. Another few minutes was all he could stay, but that was all he needed to see the end of the show.

They were so close to victory now.

His troops would break into the building and take their time in seeking out the prey inside. The glass windows of Dabyr were warded against the sun and would protect his soldiers as well as it did the Sanguinar who roamed its halls, certain of their safety. His demons would feed all day and return to him tonight with whatever humans they hadn't eaten, the blades of fallen Theronai warriors and every Sentinel stone they'd kept hidden.

All of that was inevitable now, but still not the killing blow he knew would leave his enemy defeated, not just tonight, but forever.

Without healers, the warriors were doomed. They might live today or tomorrow, but eventually, they'd fall to injury or poison without the protection of the Sanguinar.

The healers were the key to Vazel's victory. All he had to do was destroy them and the rest of the Sentinels would fall.

Once they did, there would be no one to keep him out of Athanasia and the bounty that world held.

He crouched and dug his fingers into the earth at his feet. His troops were deep underground, waiting for his signal, for the time when the Sanguinar's allies were too busy defending their lives to save them.

That time was now. Even the few Sanguinar on the battlefield weren't strong enough to stop what was about to happen. This whole battle had been designed to ensure that weakness.

Vazel tucked his chin and let out a hum so low it was almost inaudible.

The rocks under his feet trembled. Snowflakes were shaken loose from the bare tree branches. His signal traveled fast, moving through dirt and stone until it reached his troops burrowed near the place where dozens of helpless Sanguinar rested in their magically-enhanced sleep. It didn't matter how much noise his troops made now moving the last few inches through the ground. The sound of battle would drown out whatever sound they made. And even if the Sentinels on the field heard, they were too busy to do anything about it. No one was there to stop what was about to happen.

All his demons had to do was kill the vulnerable Sanguinar while they slept and everything Vazel had worked for would be his.

***

There was so much chaos on the battlefield that Maura had no trouble slipping into Dabyr.

She'd been careful with her hair and dress, and put in blue contact lenses, so that anyone who saw her would think she was Sibyl.

Sometimes having an identical twin was handy.

She'd been inside this building before, years ago, before she'd left to join their enemy, before her parents had died, before she'd grown into a woman.

Maura didn't know why she'd come here. It was dangerous, foolish. Not only could she get killed by the demons who didn't realize who she was, she could also just as easily die by the hand of a Sentinel, put down like the traitor she was.

As close as she was to Sibyl now, she could feel her, like a familiar chord inside her had been struck.

Sibyl had to have felt it, too.

Why was Maura here? She didn't belong here. She wasn't one of the Sentinels anymore. None of them would want her here even if she did want to come home. She killed with a touch. No one could be close to her. No one could trust her.

So why was she here?

She couldn't let her sister die. That had to be it.

They'd always been a part of each other. They'd never been meant to be twins. Their separation wasn't some natural, biological miracle. Their mother had ripped them in two while they were still in the womb. She'd taken her innocent baby girl and torn her in half to aid the war. They needed more women, so their mother had cut them in two.

Maura had gotten the lion's share of power, but Sibyl had gotten all the goodness and light. She'd gotten the soul. She never had trouble making the right choice. She never struggled to do the right thing, even if it meant sacrificing her comfort or safety. Maura had no idea why she did it.

Except, maybe she did. She was here, after all, wasn't she? Sneaking through the hallways of Dabyr, looking for Sibyl to get her out before it was too late?

Was that goodness or self-defense?

The Sanguinar would fall tonight, just as the walls had. This building would be overrun by demons, and every human or Sentinel inside captured or killed. There would be nowhere to hide.

Not even for Sibyl.

Maura couldn't lose her other half like that. Part of her was terrified that if one of them died, the other wouldn't be far behind them. They were, after all, one being split in two. How could one half live without the other?

She crept along the halls, following the humming connection she had to her sister. It grew stronger and stronger with each step she took. As soon as she rounded the next corner, she saw Sibyl standing there, waiting for her.

She'd grown into a beautiful woman, with flowing blond hair and clear blue eyes. And while their faces were the same, somehow Sibyl was prettier, as if the soul she carried made her glow from the inside out.

Her sister was not happy to see her.

Sibyl's pretty face twisted in anger. "You betrayed us. You kept your attack a secret from me so I couldn't stop you."

"I did."

"Are you here to kill me?" Sibyl asked, chin raised in defiance, eyes narrowed with fury.

"I'm here to save you."

Sibyl's bark of laughter was hard and cold. "Seems an odd thing for someone to do when she was the cause of the attack to begin with."

"Vazel wasn't going to be stopped. With or without my help, this was going to happen."

"So why not just help kill your people, then, huh? Our destruction was inevitable, so why not join in the fun? Is that your logic?"

Maura ignored the barb and held out her gloved hand. "Come with me. I'll keep you safe."

Sibyl stared down at the black, leather glove. Her anger melted and a sad frown flickered across her mouth. "Your touch still kills?"

"You seem surprised."

"I thought that after what Gilda did to release us from our vow to her, your curse might have been destroyed too."

"Sorry to disappoint. My curse, as you call it, stems from me having no soul. I'm an abomination, so nature treats me as one."

Sibyl shook her head. "I've never believed you were born soulless. That's simply something you tell yourself as an excuse to behave badly."

Her prim sister had no idea just how wrong she was. "I'm not going to have an old argument with you all over again. We're running out of time. If you want to live through the night, then you have to come with me."

"And what? Join the Synestryn as you have?"

"They're stronger than the Sentinels. I would think you'd want to be on the winning side."

"That's where you always go wrong in your thinking. It's not about which side is stronger. It's about which side is right. And which is wrong."

"Victors are the ones who chose right and wrong after all the bodies have been buried. Or eaten."

Sibyl shook her head. "If you believe that, then I guess there really is no helping you see the truth, is there?"

"The truth is you're going to die tonight if you don't come with me."

"Then I die. But I'm going to die fighting for what I

believe in."

Maura let out a heavy sigh. "What I believe in is survival. You should too."

"Then help us fight. Help us protect the weak and the young."

"Not my style," Maura said. "But I will tell you this."

"What?"

"Everything going on out there…the demons, taking down the walls, trying to break into Dabyr—none of that is Vazel's real goal tonight."

"The babies? The Sentinel stones?"

Maura shook her head.

"Then why is he here? What does he want?"

"Your utter destruction, of course."

"Be more specific, Maura."

As much as she wanted to stay here and chat, she couldn't be caught by the good guys. She had to leave before it was too late. If one of those big, strapping warriors found her, they'd be compelled to take her captive, and if they did that, she would be forced to kill them.

Maura sighed. "The Sanguinar," she told her sister. "Without healers, you're all dead eventually. Once that happens, then all the swords, stones and humans are easy pickings. Vazel is investing in his future by taking out your healers. After that, all he has to do is bide his time while attrition marches through your ranks."

"But the Sanguinar are safe, underground."

"Are you sure?"

Maura turned and walked away. She'd betrayed so many people. Vazel would be just one more. Besides, it was already too late. She could feel the vibration under her feet. The attack had already begun.

***

Nika couldn't keep fighting. The labor pains were too strong, too close together.

She'd experienced this feeling before, but that time, she'd been hovering in her little sister's mind while she delivered her baby—a baby that hadn't survived its Synestryn parentage. This time, there was no way to blunt or escape the pain. The only way to get past it was to get through it.

She and Madoc had been in constant communication since the battle started. The magical connection they shared allowed them to be inside each other's minds, conversing in thoughts and feelings more than words.

But right now, the last thing she wanted was to share this gripping agony with him.

She had to leave. Find a safe place to strip off these leathers and welcome their little girl into the world.

Hope and Logan had been planning to be there when she delivered, but they were on the battlefield, healing injuries and shoving back Synestryn who tried to outflank the fighters.

Even Madoc couldn't be spared right now. His strong sword arm and relentless skill was necessary to hold the line.

Nika was on her own, and the only safe place she could think to go was down, underground where the earth would protect her and her baby on all sides. Just like the sleeping Sanguinar.

CHAPTER SEVENTEEN

Ronan used his dwindling power to speed his pace over the uneven ground. He didn't know how many demons were behind him but based on the hungry howls, snapping teeth and clanging swords, there were more than enough to kill him.

He used a burst of magic to gain a few yards but made sure he didn't put too much room between him and the hungry Synestryn. He couldn't have them giving up on the idea that he would be their next meal.

He closed the cut he'd used to bait them and licked away the remaining blood as he ran. Once he changed directions, he didn't want the Synestryn behind him able to smell where he'd gone, and if there were traces of blood on his skin, they would, no matter how well he shielded his presence with magic.

Assuming he had that much power left to manage the feat.

His muscles burned. His chest bellowed but couldn't find enough air to fill his aching lungs. He was growing weaker by the second but he couldn't stop yet.

The sun was just barely below the horizon. He could already feel it sapping his strength and warning him to burrow deep out of its reach.

The horde following him seemed to have no such problems with fatigue, though they were even more in danger from sunlight than he was. He might summon a Warden, but they would go up in flames.

Either way, they were all going to die out here if the sun came up before they reached shelter.

He veered deeper into the woods until the snowy branches of cedars blocked him from sight. Then he drew on his reserves and formed the thinnest film of invisibility around him possible. As soon as he was sure it was in place, he angled sharply to the left, back toward Dabyr's walls.

His cells screamed in agony as he forced them to sacrifice themselves to his demands. His jeans loosened around his waist, and he had to fist them in one hand to keep them from falling around his legs and tripping him.

His sword thumped against his thigh and felt heavier than it ever had before. He wanted to stop and pull it from his belt but couldn't afford to slow down for even a few seconds.

The demons were right behind him. He could hear them crashing through frozen branches and crunching over dead leaves.

Ronan did his best to dampen the noise he made but there was nothing he could do about the trail he was leaving behind in the dusting of snow.

He spared a quick glance behind him to see if his plan had worked.

Some of the Synestryn had continued on in a straight line after he'd disappeared, falling for his ruse, but a few of the smarter ones were still on his trail. They seemed confused that they could no longer see or smell him, but they could still see exactly where he'd gone in the tracking snow.

He couldn't lead them back to Dabyr, but he couldn't fight them here, so close to the other demons that would doubtlessly hear the combat and come searching for the smell of fresh blood.

Weariness bore down on his body and made his bones feel brittle. His skin was loose and dry, hanging on him like the wrappings of a mummy. Even the glow from his eyes was beginning to dim as he consumed his very flesh to fuel him.

A tree root caught his foot and tripped him. He fell to the cold forest floor, tasting snow and blood.

The demons were only two, maybe three seconds behind him. He had no time to stand and run. No energy.

Ronan ignored the burning in his joints and the stinging of his skin. He rolled off the path he'd been on and hid in the crook of roots at the base of a towering sycamore tree. Protected on one side by the tree, he then curled himself into the tightest ball possible and wrapped a shield around his body. He clamped his mouth closed to hold in a growl of hunger. He swallowed down the drops of blood leaking from the spot where his teeth had cut the inside of his lip. There was no energy left to heal the damage to his flesh. It was taking everything he had to hold the thin film of invisibility around his frail body.

A sgath was the first one to find the spot where he'd fallen. It skidded to a halt, digging thick, poisonous claws into the ground. Its furry body rippled with strength. Its glowing green eyes lit the scuffed earth as it sniffed and pawed where Ronan's body had just been.

Another sgath joined the first. They snarled and nipped at each other as they circled the area, looking for their lost prey.

Ronan wasn't going to be able to hold the magic around him for much longer. He was already starving, weak, aching to let go.

He didn't want to die like this. He didn't want to leave this earth before he'd found a way to free Justice. No one else would help her the way he would—until his dying breath. No one would be willing to sacrifice for her the way he would.

No one would love her the way he did.

Even the thought of her had the ability to strengthen his resolve. He placed her beautiful face in his mind and held it there like a talisman.

He could feel her nearby, just on the other side of the stone wall. Her presence sort of flickered in and out, as if the magic protecting the compound was still struggling to hold itself together.

The more he felt her, the more he knew the walls were failing. And if the walls failed, hundreds of innocents would die.

In the distance, somewhere close to Dabyr, a demon howled an eerie song of victory. More voices joined the chorus, calling their kind to join them.

The sgath hunting Ronan lifted their heads and answered the call. A moment later, they darted off into the thick woods.

He was safe for the moment, but a sgath howl like that could only mean one thing.

His allies—his friends—were now being feasted on by demons.

***

Joseph pulled his fighters back all the way to the front steps of Dabyr.

Sweat dripped from his hair. His muscles burned from cutting down an endless string of Synestryn. The magical conduit that connected him to Lyka heated as she siphoned off more and more power from him.

She was wearing out. Growing weak and exhausted from channeling so much magic.

She'd killed more demons with her wicked bolts of lighting and searing shards of fire than he had with his sword, but even she had her limits.

They all did.

His men were starting to falter. Their will—their resolve—was strong, but hours of battle had taken its toll on even the strongest of his warriors.

The few Slayers that had been at Dabyr when the attack started had held back from the fray, picking off the demons that slipped through the main offensive line of swords and magic. But even their sharp claws and savage teeth couldn't stop all of the stragglers. Even they were slowing as the endless flood of fresh, strong enemies slipped through the front line.

If the sun didn't come up soon and force the demons back into their caves, Dabyr was going to fall. It was only a matter of time and numbers now.

And even if they survived this night, tomorrow night was only hours away. The demons would come back. There was no time to rebuild the walls and rest his people for another fight like this one.

Joseph shoved that defeatist thought from his mind and found Lyka's presence glowing inside of him. She wasn't ready to give up. Not even close. And he wasn't ready to let her down. For her, he'd fight until there was no breath left in his body.

Behind him, screams of terror and pain echoed from inside the halls. The humans were all supposed to be hiding in safe rooms, guarded by some of his best men, but clearly, some humans had chosen not to follow orders.

He prayed it wasn't the teens, too rebellious to be smart and too certain of their immortality to even question how dangerous it was to fight demons with no magic to aid them.

The need to go in and rescue them warred with the need to stay here to keep the building from being overrun. If he and his men didn't hold this line, everyone inside would die. Once the demons made it inside Dabyr, all the magical enhancements that protected the Sanguinar from the sun would do the same for the Synestryn. They wouldn't have to hide anymore. They'd have everything they needed all in one place—protection from the sun that would kill them and all the food they could want flowing through the veins of the blooded humans inside.

Every Sentinel here would give their lives to stop that from happening. He prayed it didn't come to that.

Joseph's next blow was a fraction of a second too slow. One of the gray demons managed to get through his defenses and sliced a deep cut across his abdomen.

Pain flared bright, blinding him for a second.

Lyka's voice barked in his thoughts, easily heard over the roar of combat. *Duck!*

Joseph followed her mental instructions, forcing his body to bend exactly as she'd shown him.

He couldn't see the blade that would have taken off his head, but he felt it stir the hairs as it passed.

Joseph looked up to see Morgan standing next to him where Madoc had been earlier. He'd left to protect his wife while she brought their firstborn into the world.

Joseph hoped like hell that world was far more peaceful than the one they faced now.

A heavy clang of steel on steel rang just above him. Morgan had blocked another incoming blow that would have killed Joseph.

Morgan was fresh to the fight, incredibly strong, and as fierce a warrior as any Joseph had ever known. Maybe with his help, they could survive the last few minutes until sunrise.

Logan is stepping up behind you to heal you, Lyka whispered in his mind. Her voice wasn't as strong as before. Then again, none of them were.

Joseph kept his sword in front of his body and shifted his stance so that none of the demons in front of him could reach Logan.

If they lost their healers, the whole line would collapse as injury took them one by one.

Joseph knew from experience that in a situation like this, Logan wouldn't waste any energy blunting the pain of what he was about to do. While he could knit skin and bone with a touch, Joseph was going to have to endure every second of the pain of his recovery shoved into one very short, very agonizing moment.

Even though he'd experienced this before, even though he was braced for it, the searing torture of being healed hit him by surprise. It was like his mind couldn't face just how much it was possible to hurt, so it had blocked out the memory entirely.

Lyka's cooling presence eased him through the worst of it. Morgan's strong sword arm kept him safe from the blows that came flying his way. It only took Logan a few seconds to do the job, but it felt more like hours.

When it was finally over and the Sanguinar moved to find

the next injured warrior, Joseph was left a little weaker and slower than he'd been before.

Morgan and Lyka took up the slack while Joseph found a way to rally.

His people needed him. He couldn't stop. He couldn't fall. Because of that, he was going to find a way to make it until sunrise.

"Sorry I was late to the party," Morgan shouted over the din, grinning as he fought. "Glad you saved me some fun."

Joseph's voice was as weary as his body and as thin as his hope. "Have all the fun you want."

There was more than enough to go around.

* * *

Madoc found Nika in one of the lower levels of Dabyr, in one of the rooms Sanguinar used to treat patients. This room had been set up for the delivery, but the one piece of equipment that was missing was also the most important.

"Where the fuck are Hope and Logan?"

Nika's usually pale face was flushed and dotted with sweat. She crouched in a corner of the room, a short sword clenched in her fist.

Madoc loved that about his wife—that even when she was struggling through labor pains, she was still as protective of their child as she was fierce.

Their child. Their little girl. She was coming. Tonight. Now.

A wave of panic hit Madoc so hard he had to grip the edge of the door frame to keep from falling over.

He was going to be a dad. Holy fuck. How was that even possible? He wasn't father material. Not even close.

Nika panted through her contraction before answering. "Not coming. Battle before babies."

"Fuck!"

"I've done this before," she said. "Remember?"

"Your sister did this, not you. You might have been in her

head at the time, but that's not the same thing."

"I'm staying positive, love. You should try it."

Madoc closed and locked the door, then shoved a heavy cabinet in front of it. No way were demons getting in here to eat his family. And he was almost certain his hands were about to be full.

"How close are the contractions?" he asked.

She let out a low groan of pain. "Not watching a clock."

Madoc had read seven different books on labor and delivery. Thanks to his photographic memory, he was able to remember every word. All he had to do now was execute what he'd read and pray none of the complications haunting his nightmares would happen.

He glanced at the clock hanging over the head of the bed—the bed his wife was not on.

Madoc went to her, then stopped when he saw the blood on his hands. The shit the gray demons bled wasn't poisonous like some of the Synestryn, but he still didn't want it anywhere near his family.

As he washed, she hissed as the next contraction hit her.

He looked at the clock. Less than a minute had passed.

This was happening. Now.

Calm had never been Madoc's strong suit, but for his family, he found the strength to keep his tone even and level. "Nika, honey, I think it's time we got you out of those fighting leathers and up on the bed."

"Can't...move."

She was in too much pain to even stand, much less undress or climb up on a table.

Normally, Madoc would have found what was causing her pain and killed it, but in this case, his cock had been the thing that had gotten her into this condition. He had no one to kill but himself.

Still, seeing her suffer was tearing him apart. No man could be expected to endure their wife's labor without doing everything they could to ease her pain.

So that's what he did.

Madoc picked up his wife, laid her on the table, stripped off her leather pants and then found the tie that bound them together.

Their pipeline was usually wide open, so much so that they often shared the same mental space without even realizing it. Now, however, Nika had clamped it shut to save him from the pain she endured.

Not fucking likely.

He got between her legs and stared at her over her protruding belly, his expression telling her that he was about to get his way, whether or not she liked it.

"We're doing this together, Nika. You've carried the burden of this pregnancy most of the way. It's my turn to help."

"I don't want you to hurt," she said.

"Then open up and let me take some of your pain."

"No. I—" Her words broke off as the next contraction hit.

Madoc didn't even feel bad about shoving his way into her thoughts and finding the center of her labor pains.

They were intense, agonizing things that drove all thought from his head. But only for a minute.

He'd carried pain before. Nika had saved him from it. It was his turn to do the same for her.

Madoc gathered up his wife's torture and swallowed it whole. His body tried to convulse and reject it, but he told it to shut the fuck up and deal.

This was happening.

After a few seconds, he adjusted to his new reality and checked Nika's cervix.

"You're fully dilated, love," he told her, his voice rough with both profound pain and profound joy. "It's time to push."

CHAPTER EIGHTEEN

Justice grabbed her duffel bag from the semi and started to run. She didn't know where she was going or why, but she was no longer in control.

The woman who possessed her was frantic. Desperate. If Justice didn't run fast enough, she was certain she was going to be too late.

Ronan was going to die.

Justice ran faster.

She darted across the open area between the main building of Dabyr and the stone walls several hundred yards away. Most of the battle was raging on the west side of the building, but a few demons had managed to slip past the flashing swords and brilliant magic flashing in the distance.

Savage-looking men with elongated fangs and claws roamed the clearing, covered in black blood. They sought out the lone demons slinking around the grounds, then ripped them apart with their bare hands. Literally.

She'd heard about Slayers before but didn't think she'd ever seen one. She sure as hell hadn't seen one in battle, more animal than man. Some of them even seemed to have taken on animalistic traits—fur, widened jaws, the tendency to run on four legs that were more wolf than human.

Justice left the demon cleanup to them and made a beeline for the wall. She had no idea how she was going to get over it.

For all she knew, the fates would force her to dig her way through with her fingernails.

She could feel Ronan. She was getting closer, but not fast enough. She was going to be too late.

Her legs pounded, her heart hammered. Her breath billowed from her open mouth in a fog of mist that was swept past her as she ran. Tears cooled on her cheeks and streaked back over her temples into her hairline.

"Ronan!" she screamed, unable to hold his name inside her lips.

There was no answer, or if there was one, she couldn't hear it over the crash of battle.

She risked a quick glance back over her shoulder. A pair of four-legged demons with glowing eyes and barbed tails were heading right for her.

They were still yards away, and right now, that felt like an eternity. So much could happen in the time it would take them to cross the distance.

Ronan could breathe his last breath.

From her left, one of the savage Slayers intercepted the demons racing toward her.

Justice pushed herself even harder, ignoring the threat from behind. The one looming ahead of her was a big enough problem to consume her mind completely.

Ronan was nearby, but the wall stood between them. She caught herself against it and felt the cold mass of its surface sucking the heat from her cheek.

The stone was too smooth for her to climb. It was too thick for her to break through, even if she had some kind of sledgehammer.

She heard a low moan of pain float over the top of the wall. Even in torment, she recognized Ronan's voice instantly.

"Ronan! I'm here!" she yelled upward, hoping her words would reach him.

The only response she heard was an even weaker moan.

He was dying.

Hurry! The compulsion in her head was so strong it was

almost a language now.

Justice didn't even bother to figure out what the woman wanted. She simply opened herself completely and let the fates use her as a tool to save him. They'd done it once before, in that dark, damp basement. She'd been compelled to feed him and save his life. Tonight, she would do so again.

The duffel bag filled with sporting goods she'd hijacked fell from her shoulder and sagged on the ground. She ripped the zipper open and let the contents speak to her.

The two metal objects she'd stolen were in there, along with a wad of colorful resistance bands, a pocket knife, some spare magazines for Reba, an insulated water bottle, some grip tape and a small flashing LED light for nighttime joggers.

What the hell was she supposed to do with all that?

"Tell me what you want!" she shouted. "What do I do?"

The woman possessing Justice was slow to respond, but when she did, the knowledge was like a blowtorch to the surface of Justice's brain.

She knew exactly what to do.

Justice ripped open the flashing LED light and used the tape to adhere it to the side of the metal water bottle. She pulled the plastic tab covering the battery and the light began to flash red and blue. Next, she unscrewed the top of the bottle, opened the pocket knife and slit a deep cut along her wrist— the kind that bled fast enough to kill a person.

She held the bottle under the wound and bled into it for as long as she dared. Then she used one of the stretchy resistance bands to tourniquet her arm and wrapped the cut in more of the tape. It wasn't going to stop the demons from smelling her blood, but it might buy her a few more minutes of running away before she bled out.

The screw top went back on the bottle, smeared with her blood. Once she was sure it was secure, she stepped back from the wall and flung the bottle over the top.

"Find the bottle, Ronan!" she shouted loud enough to be heard over the sound of a Slayer ripping a demon's body in half. "Find my blood!"

She didn't know if he'd heard her or not, but there was no more time to talk. The scent of her blood had drawn the attention of several demons at the edge of the fray, and all those glowing green eyes were now aimed right at her.

Savage or not, there was no way one Slayer was going to be able to stop that mass of claws and teeth from reaching her.

Justice might have saved Ronan's life, but the move had cost her her own.

CHAPTER NINETEEN

Ronan slumped against the wall, too weak to draw a full breath. It had taken everything he had to crawl this far in the hopes that his body would be found by his allies before Synestryn could tear it apart.

Would a Warden be summoned if the sun hit his skin after he died? He wasn't sure. Either way, he guessed he would never know.

He was a sack of bones inside loose skin now. He'd burned all his fat and most of his muscle to get him this far. Sadly, his nerve endings hadn't also been consumed, because if they had, then he wouldn't have felt the excruciating pain of his starvation.

He thought he'd been hungry before. He'd thought he'd been near death. He'd never really known how close to death one of his kind could get before succumbing. No wonder so many of the Sanguinar sleeping beneath Dabyr could hold on for decades after they were nearly mad with hunger.

The sky lightened further, but he couldn't feel the growing weakness of day. He was already as weak as he could be, barely even breathing. His heart stuttered. There was so little blood left to pump through him.

At least he was going to die near Justice. He could feel her behind his back, just on the other side of the wall. She was the only warmth he had now, and like before, he found himself trying to turn so he could soak up as much of her as possible.

Her voice carried over the wall. He couldn't make out the words, but he could hear the frantic note she sang.

She knew he was dying too.

Ronan pressed his skeletal hand against the stone and tried to catch her warmth inside his grasp.

There was nothing there to hold. She was slipping through his fingers as surely as his last few seconds were.

"I love you," he whispered, wishing he'd told her before, when she could hear him. She was such a precious woman, she deserved to be told every day how much she was loved.

Ronan was a fool for waiting. He was a fool for not realizing how he felt sooner. And now she'd never know how he felt.

Something crashed through the trees over his head. At first, he thought it was a demon, but when no pain of teeth or claws came, he knew he must have been wrong.

"...bottle..." she yelled.

He didn't understand what she meant, but a second later, he smelled her blood and saw a flashing light in the leaf litter nearby. That light was attached to a gleaming metal cylinder smeared with her blood.

That's when he realized what she'd done. She'd sent him a bottle of her blood.

Animal desperation took over. He didn't think he had the strength to move, but that sweet, intoxicating scent drew him closer as if compelled.

He dragged himself over the ground, ignoring the scrape of sticks and rocks. His loose skin caught in places, but he jerked it free and kept crawling.

The light was closer. Her blood was almost in reach.

Demons still roamed the woods, and one of them must have smelled her blood too. Ronan heard it howl and knew that he was running out of time.

No way was he going to let some monster have Justice's precious blood.

He inched forward, each tiny fraction seeming like a mile.

Sticks tore at his face, breaking his thin skin. Tiny trickles of blood leaked down across his cheeks and over his lips. He licked them away, but there was no power left in his cells. They were utterly depleted.

He had to stop twice to catch his breath, but he was finally close enough to reach out and grasp the looped handle with one bony finger.

The bottle was cold and heavy. He was barely strong enough to pull it to him and open the top. On a growl of determination, the threads loosened and the top opened.

A wash of sweetly scented power erupted from the bottle. He put it to his mouth and gulped the blood down, frantic.

Justice's power slid through him in a trickle at first, then in a torrent. Her innate magic flooded his cells and restored his lost tissue. His eyes blazed blue across the forest. Even with the weakness of sunrise upon him, he felt stronger than he ever had before.

He consumed every drop he could coax from the bottle, then capped the lid to stop the smell from drawing demons to him.

Thanks to Justice, he wasn't going to die tonight—at least not because of starvation.

The sun was nearly up. One Warden could kill dozens, maybe more, and as much as the idea of setting one of those crystalline warriors loose on his enemy appealed to him, there was no way to keep such a creature from killing allies as well. He had to seek shelter, and the closest shelter he could find was right on the other side of the wall.

Justice was nearby, only a few feet away. All he wanted to do now was see her again, touch her again, and know she was safe.

A demon crashed through the trees, searching for Justice's blood.

Ronan gathered a burst of power and used it to lift himself up and over the thick stone wall. As soon as he reached the zenith and got a good view of the battlefield, every bit of victory he felt at escaping his fate died a cold, hard death.

Dabyr was ruined. The walls had fallen. Synestryn had broken through the ranks of warriors and managed to slip inside the main compound where the sun could not harm them.

Humans were inside. Children, elderly, injured. Even if the Sentinels who were surely inside to guard the weak and helpless managed to kill every monster inside, never again would any human feel completely safe within those walls.

Everything Ronan and his kind had worked for to ensure that blooded humans felt safe enough to have children was destroyed. Decades of careful planning and gallons of powerful blood were wasted. No sane parents would ever want to bring a child into a world filled with so much danger and terror. Without those children, the Sanguinar would starve.

So, even if the Sentinels cleared the battlefield and repaired the damage done here tonight, it wouldn't matter. The demons had already done irreparable damage.

A snarl of rage pulled his attention away from the devastation.

Eric Phelan was a few dozen yards from the wall, partially shifted into his wolf form. He was naked despite the cold. His dark hair was thick across his chest, arms and legs. His jaws were elongated and filled with sharp teeth. If not for his scent, Ronan might have not even recognized the man. His hands and feet were tipped with sharp, thick claws coated in black blood.

Only a Slayer could withstand the touch of that deadly poison.

As Ronan watched, Eric dug his claws into the body of a charging sgath and flipped it over onto its back. The demon locked its powerful jaws around Eric's upper arm, but the Slayer didn't relent. Sickly green light spilled across his distorted face, but there was no mistaking the pure hatred blazing in Eric's expression.

He ripped his arm free, tearing his flesh into ribbons as he did. Then he shoved the demon's chin up and tore into the furry throat with his teeth.

Black blood sprayed up in a grim arc to stain the dusting

of snow.

Eric kept pushing and chewing until the sgath's head finally ripped free of its body. Before the demon's eyes went dark, Eric was already looking for his next kill. His arm was bleeding badly but he didn't seem to notice or care.

Several more Synestryn were heading his way—or rather in his general direction.

Ronan looked down at the foot of the wall beneath him to the true target of the demons, and the person he saw standing there was Justice.

Her feet were braced apart, her gun steady in her hands. Three demons had made it past Eric and were charging her. There was no way she was going to be fast enough to shoot them all before they tore her apart. And even if she did, there was a limit to how much damage a single bullet could do to a creature who only died from fire or decapitation.

All she was going to do was make them angry.

***

Justice fired as soon as the first furry nightmare was in range. Even as she did, she knew she wasn't going to be fast enough.

After everything she'd survived, all the fights and thugs and monsters, after countless injuries from guns and knives, after years of compulsions and slavery to a power she didn't understand, this was how she was going to die. She was going to get eaten by demons.

If there was one thing she'd learned about herself in the last ten years of her life, it was that she was pathologically incapable of giving up. No matter how bad things got or how much she hated her lot in life, she never relented, she never stopped fighting. No pain, physical or emotional, was as abhorrent to her as the idea of surrender.

So, when these creatures came to kill her and she knew she was outclassed, the only thing she could think to do was keep fighting.

Her first round hit the shoulder of one of the demons. It tripped over its own foreleg and slid into a sloppy roll. She knew it wasn't dead—these things didn't go down easy—but she'd already turned her attention to the next most dire threat.

It opened its jaws as it lunged from the ground. Its equally terrifying, equally deadly, partner was right on its heels. Even if she took out one of them, the second one was going to get through. She couldn't fire that fast.

Before she'd finished pulling Reba's trigger, something came at her from above.

She instinctively turned her head to see what the threat was.

Ronan drew his sword as he swooped down from the air to intercept the demons. He lopped off each of their heads in one single blow, then landed gracefully on the ground as if he'd been set there by a giant hand.

He spun in a half-circle. The demon she'd shot went down under his blade, spine severed just above its powerful shoulders.

Justice blinked, unsure if what she was seeing was real.

Ronan could fly?

That was the only thought she could seem to find inside the jumbled chaos in her brain.

He'd never told her he could fly. Or that he knew how to fight like that.

He stalked toward her, lean and dark, like some kind of predator. His eyes glowed a bright blue so intense, she had trouble looking at them.

His face was bloody. His hair was tangled with sticks and leaves. His clothes were torn and dirty. Still, seeing him alive and well made her heart sing.

She raced toward him. He lifted the sword just in time for her to crash into his body without getting cut. She kissed him as soon as she was within range. Her mouth roamed over his lips, his cheeks, his jaw. She couldn't get enough of him, so she went back to his mouth and started all over again.

The familiar buzz of healing swept through her wounded

arm. He ripped the tourniquet away and held her tighter.

Her giddy sense of relief bubbled out of her in a laugh filled with tears. She could taste the salt of her tears slipping between their lips, along with a sweet, spicy…something she couldn't name.

Justice pulled back and licked her lips to gather more of the amazing flavor. Only then did she see that his face was flecked with blood from a dozen cuts along his cheeks. It had flowed onto his lips and hadn't been wiped away.

That's what she'd tasted—his blood.

It was amazing, unlike anything she'd ever experience before. The power of it soaked into her mouth, swept through her tongue and zinged down her spine where it spread out along her limbs. Tingling energy radiated out from her core and created a fizzing kind of warmth that drove away the cold.

She could feel her body changing, adapting to this new source of fuel as if it had been craving it all her life. And it was fuel. It was power, pure and undiluted.

The hairs on Justice's arms and neck lifted away from her body. The back of her skull started to itch as if she was going to be compelled, but then instead of that desperate, edgy feeling forcing her to obey, what she felt instead was a presence.

The woman.

Her presence was warm and safe. Comforting and familiar. She was also relentless and as determined as Justice had ever been about anything. No wonder this woman had pushed Justice to obey her so fiercely. She didn't know how to give in, how to give up. She won, period.

A surge of excitement made Justice's lungs swell. A noise of victory exploded from her mouth, but she was too busy focusing inward to worry about how strange she sounded.

Justice reached for this presence, diving into herself deeper and deeper until she found a thin tendril of energy connecting her to someone else.

They are dying, the woman said. Her urgency echoed in her tone, rippling with power. *Save them.*

Save who? Justice asked.

You can hear me? There was disbelief in her tone, along with a tremble of joy. *After all this time, you can finally hear me?*

Had this woman been trying to speak to her all these years? Had she been trying to communicate, but her words had somehow been lost, leaving behind only the compulsion to obey?

"Who are you?" Justice asked aloud.

There is no time. Save them. Save your people!

"I don't know what you want," Justice said. "I have no idea who my people are."

They're sleeping. Underground. The demons are nearly there! They come from below. Hurry!

"Who is sleeping underground?" she asked.

Distantly, she felt Ronan give her a small shake. "Are you talking about the Sanguinar?"

Justice repeated the question to the woman in her head.

Yes, the sleeping Sanguinar are under attack! Go!

The woman shoved Justice so hard, she was jolted out of thoughts and back into the here and now with Ronan.

He stared at her with worried eyes. "What the hell is going on?"

"The woman spoke to me. She says the Sanguinar are under attack."

Ronan turned around and looked. "No demons have breached that side of the compound that I can see."

"She says they're under attack."

"They're helpless. Asleep. We buried them deep below ground so they couldn't be reached while they were vulnerable. Even if demons did get inside, they'd never make it through all our layers of security."

"She said the demons were coming from below."

All the color drained from Ronan's face. "It can't be."

"She seems pretty sure."

He shook his head as if to hold the sad news at bay. "If that's true, then all is truly lost. Without enough Sanguinar to take turns facing our hunger, all the Sentinels will fall."

Justice absorbed that bleak prospect fast. "Then we'd better get our asses in there and save them."

She only hoped it wasn't already too late.

CHAPTER TWENTY

The ground rumbled under Ronan's feet, as if something huge was tearing its claws through dirt and rock several feet below.

As if the sound were some kind of pre-planned cue, the Synestryn pressing the front lines of Sentinels began to fight harder.

Joseph's voice rose over all the noise as he shouted orders to his men to tighten formation and hold the line.

More Theronai trickled from inside the main building to add more swords to the effort, but every one that left put those inside at more risk.

If the line of Theronai holding back the horde fell, Dabyr would be overrun. If too many men left the compound to hold the line, then the few demons who'd managed to slip into the building would be left to roam the halls, unchecked.

The balancing act was precarious. One wrong move and all would be lost.

Joseph was calling out more men for reinforcements, but he had no idea that there was another threat lurking below. They were being attacked from two sides.

"Hold on to my neck," Ronan said.

Justice scooped up the strap of her duffle bag and did as he asked.

He lifted them through the air, over the raging combat and onto the roof of Dabyr. Once there, he found the access hatch.

It was locked as a precaution against curious children with more courage than education in physics. As strong as he was right now, the lock was no match for him. He ripped it free of its hinges, then slid down the ladder leading to the top floor.

Justice was right behind him.

He took the nearest elevator down and sent a quick text to every Sanguinar here. *Sleeping chamber breached. Rescue the survivors.*

He doubted that with the battle raging, any one of the Sanguinar not already sleeping below would be free to check their phones, but at least this way, someone would know where to look for bodies.

A deep, rocky growl erupted from the earth again, but this time it was much closer. The lights in the elevator flickered, and the very air seemed to vibrate around them.

"She says we're almost out of time," Justice said.

"Did she tell you what's causing this? Or how to stop it?"

Justice closed her eyes as if listening. "The key. She says we have to assemble the key."

"What key?"

She rummaged in her duffel bag and pulled out two metal pieces. One was the brooch, the other was a hexagonal metal shaft with loops on one end.

"That looks like part of a key," he said, pointing to the shaft. "But where is the other end?"

"Here," Justice said.

She pried the gaudy crystal from the center. Some of the adhesive clung to the back. It was yellow with age, but Ronan could already see where the shaft might attach to the spot under the glue.

"They fit together," he said.

"I think so, but I don't have any way to fasten them."

"Let me try."

The elevator rumbled again. They were almost to the subbasement.

He shoved out one of his claws and used the sharp edge to scrape the glue residue away. As soon as he did, the two pieces fit perfectly.

"That's it!" she said. "The woman says that's the way it goes."

Ronan drove power to his fingertips and heated the metal until the two pieces of the key glowed red hot. He shoved them together and held them while he let the heat dissipate. As soon as it did, the key was welded together.

Justice held out her hand.

"It's still too hot for you to touch."

She covered her hand with her sleeve so she could handle it.

"What's it for?" he asked.

She shook her head. "I don't know yet."

The elevator doors opened on the lowest level of the south wing. Now that they were on the ground, he could feel just how violently the earth around them was shaking.

There was a long hallway leading to the sleeping chamber. No lights were on since the only people allowed down here could see in the dark.

Behind him, Justice stumbled.

"You can see in the dark, Justice. All you have to do is concentrate. Your eyes will shift and the spectrum of light you can see will widen."

"I don't know how to...oh. Wow." She held her hand up in front of her face and stared in awe. "That is amazing."

"I told you that you're like me. All you need is someone to teach you what that means."

"For now, I'll settle with getting this woman to shut the hell up. I thought being able to hear her speak might make my life a little less crazy, but now I'm not so sure. She's chatty and frantic."

Ronan swiped his ID and put his hand in the scanner so the machine could prick his skin and test his blood. Only a true Sanguinar could get past this door, and few of them were ever allowed entrance.

Ever since Connal had betrayed the Sentinels, Tynan had been careful with who he let have access to the weakest among them. One day they'd all take their turn sleeping, and it was important to believe that they were safe.

The ground shook again, and this time, sparks sprayed from overhead where electrical wires passed. Hairline cracks formed in the walls and floor. The steel door unlocked, but Ronan had to shove it hard it to get it to open.

Inside was a stone chamber where one of their kind usually sat guarding their sleeping kin. Today, it was empty as all available Sanguinar were needed to heal those wounded in battle.

The stagnant scent of rot and starvation was thick in the cool air. Every few days, they'd check to make sure that none of the weak had died, and far too often, that check would reveal that another one of them had passed.

He flipped on the lights to preserve his power.

There were too few of his kind left. Perhaps fifty sleeping in coffin-sized chambers along one stone wall. Their fronts were hinged glass panels that opened for access. Dim red lights inside each chamber came on to reveal the shriveled, shrunken remains of what had once been a strong, powerful people.

Most of the females had been killed two hundred years ago. The few who remained were wizened and gray, their hands curled in like hooks. The men fared little better, though they'd had more body mass to draw from in reserve. Still, they looked more like mummified corpses than people now.

In the opposite wall was a vault that held the most precious treasures the Sanguinar had found—artifacts that could heal or kill, tomes of knowledge that would have been long lost to the world if their kind hadn't saved them. Gold and gemstones to sustain them if the other races ever turned their backs.

Ronan hadn't been inside the vault in ages, but that key Justice had found made him wonder what else might be hiding in there now. It opened nothing he knew of, but that didn't mean there wasn't some locked chest or book inside the vault they needed to access.

The artifacts would have to wait. Right now, he was more

concerned with saving lives.

He pushed in a flat section of the wall—one that looked like one more chiseled rock than a button. Inside was a polished stone bowl that fed to a series of tubes that led to each of the sleeping Sanguinar. They didn't need much blood to survive, but they did need some. He and his brothers took turns feeding them, and because of his chase after Justice, he hadn't done his duty in too long.

Time to make up for that.

Justice stared at the Sanguinar, her mouth agape. "We have to get them out of here."

"We will."

"How?"

"I'm going to feed them, wake them. They'll have to walk, because we can't carry them."

"You think those dried up husks are going to be able to walk before whatever is trying to burrow in here reaches us?"

To punctuate her concern, the ground rumbled and dust began to fall from the joints between the stones.

She was right. It sometimes took days before a Sanguinar could move properly after a prolonged sleep. They sure as hell didn't have that long. They didn't even have hours.

"Do you have a better idea?" he asked.

"Not me. Her." She tapped her temple.

"She got us this far. What does she want us to do?"

"I don't know, but I think it has to do with these." She reached into her bag and pulled out a wad of what looked like giant rubber bands. They were a variety of colors and about six feet long.

"What are those?" he asked.

"Resistance bands. For exercise."

Ronan had no idea how one would exercise with such a thing, but there was time for fitness training later. "What are we going to do with them?"

"That floating thing you did to us? Do you think you could do that with them?" she asked, hooking a thumb toward the Sanguinar.

He did a quick calculation of the weight. Even dehydrated and shriveled, his kin would still be a considerable weight if he tried to lift them all together. And there wasn't time to do any less. They had a few minutes at most before the wall was breached.

"I could try."

"You need to do more than try. If we can't get them out of this tomb, we're going to end up being buried down here with them."

CHAPTER TWENTY-ONE

Joseph could no longer feel his arm, but he kept fighting. Lyka was in his mind, a constant reassurance that she was still safe—none of the demons that had broken through the line had reached her.

The sky glowed pink in the east. All he and his men had to do was hold steady for a few more minutes.

Morgan was still hacking away at the Synestryn who weren't smart enough to flee the rising sun. It was hard to tell over the din of combat, but Joseph thought the man might actually be singing as he fought.

All the other warriors were spent. They'd been fighting for hours, constantly facing rank after rank of fresh Synestryn troops. The wearier the Theronai became the more mistakes they made and the more hits they took. A split-second glance down the line told Joseph that his men were gaining injuries faster than the three Sanguinar left on the field could heal them.

In a few seconds, the healers were going to have to flee the sun and there'd be no one left to stop the flow of blood.

Lyka was behind them, taking a stance on higher ground. He used their telepathic link to tell her to give the order for the Sanguinar to go inside. They couldn't risk cutting it too close.

Her high, clear voice rose above the noise, issuing his order.

Now the fighters were alone.

Why weren't the remaining Synestryn fleeing? Certainly, they had to know the sun would fry their asses. Didn't all creatures of darkness know when their enemy, the sun, was approaching? It wasn't exactly a surprise.

Still, the demons kept fighting, their mouths pulled back in a grin like they had a secret.

That's when Joseph noticed. The demons remaining on the battlefield were different. Not much, but a little.

They had the same gray skin with patchy bits of fur. Their heads were bald, almost reptilian in texture. They were tall and strong and fought with swords, rather than teeth or claws.

But their eyes...their eyes were lighter. Not black. Red. And their blood, while dark, was not nearly as dark as those he'd killed earlier in the night.

Just as Joseph's fears about what that meant entered his head, the first rays of the sun rose in the east. Golden tendrils of light slipped through the trees and over the horizon to land on the demons before him.

They didn't scream. Their skin didn't smoke or light on fire. If anything, they squinted like they wished they'd brought sunglasses. But that was it.

The day was no longer the sole domain of the Theronai, humans or Slayers. Now it belonged to the demons, too.

***

Even with Madoc taking on much of her pain, Nika was struggling to deliver their little girl.

She thought she'd felt labor pain before, but now she realized that whatever she'd experienced through her sister's mind had been muted. Dulled. Either that, or she'd completely forgotten just how excruciating it was to shove a small person from one's body.

She was so tired. She'd used most of her strength in combat, trying to help her friends and family survive the night. She hadn't thought to save more for herself. She hadn't realized just how physically taxing this process was.

And now she was paying the price for her ignorance.

"You're doing great," Madoc said from between her spread thighs.

She wished he were there for a more pleasurable pursuit.

Nika didn't say anything. She didn't have to. He was a solid, glowing presence in her mind, hovering over her thoughts with that overprotective vibe she'd grown so used to since meeting him.

He knew just how close she was to the end of her strength.

She felt him pull sparks of power from the air and shove them in her direction, but she was too tired to even reach for them.

"No, you're not," he said. He came to the head of the bed and slipped his left hand around the back of her neck. The ring he wore connected to the necklace she wore, allowing the flow of power from him into her to move more easily.

The luceria hummed around her throat as if soaking him in.

She leaned her head against his arm, not caring about the sweat she left on his skin.

"You're doing great," he said. "Almost there."

Nika felt the demon's presence before she heard it.

"We have company," she said, but he was in her mind and already knew what she'd felt.

His sword was propped by the barricaded door, ready for use. They both looked toward it at the same time.

There was a sniffing sound under the door, then a scratching as something pawed to get in.

"It can't get in," Madoc whispered.

"It's strong. It has friends." She was panting, still not recovered from the last contraction. "And I'm too tired to blow it up."

"Don't worry about the furry fuckers outside the door. Focus on this. Right here, right now."

She didn't want to. She so preferred killing to labor.

The muscles in her body surged, then clamped down as

the next contraction hit. Pain gripped her hard and drove all thought from her mind. She knew she was supposed to push, but there was no more push left in her.

"The fuck there isn't," he said. He took her sweaty face in his hands and said, "We've been in worse situations than this. I know you're tired. I know demons are at the door. I know it hurts like a motherfucker, but none of that matters. Our baby needs you to dig deep, be strong. So that's what you're going to do. Now fucking push!"

CHAPTER TWENTY-TWO

Justice was surprised that touching these mummified vampires didn't creep her out at all. In fact, instead of disgust, what she felt toward them was a kind of kinship, and a shit-ton of pity.

How desperate had they been to choose this state over staying awake and being hungry? How much pain had they endured to make this kind of life the better option?

Justice couldn't even imagine, and she prayed she never would.

They'd found a few gurneys in one of the rooms used to store medical equipment. Ronan removed the feeding tubes snaking down each Sanguinar's nose and brought the bodies to her. On each gurney she created a precarious stack of mummified people.

They were stiff and dry, locking together like twigs. Some of them were more hydrated than the others, and those bodies were laid on the bottom of the stacks so they wouldn't hurt the brittle Sanguinar on top.

None of them moved or breathed. And they were so light.

"Are you sure they're still alive?" she asked.

"Yes," Ronan said. "Their sleep is magically enhanced. They only seem dead. I promise they are not."

"Is stacking them like this going to hurt them?"

"Not as much as whatever is trying to break through the

wall will."

Justice used the resistance bands to hold the bodies in place, making sure no stray arms or legs could slip free and catch a doorway.

They put as many of the Sanguinar on each gurney as they dared, then lashed the gurneys together with more of the stretchy bands.

The most gruesome train ever.

At the end of the long room, dirt began to trickle from a crack in the wall. The rumbling was so loud now, they had to shout to hear each other over it.

Any second, that wall was going to cave in, and a hungry horde of monsters was going to flood in here.

"Time to go," Ronan said.

Not yet! Use the key, said the woman in Justice's mind, her tone one of urgent fear.

"Where? How?"

The vault.

"We can't go yet." Justice glanced at the steel vault door set inside solid stone, then she looked at Ronan. "Tell me you can open it."

"I don't care about treasure. I only care about saving lives."

"She says we have to open it. She's been right all along."

He hesitated.

The wall began to buckle. More cracks formed. More dirt spilled inside.

"Now, Ronan!"

He ran to the vault, punched a series of numbers, pressed his hand against a panel and leaned close to the screen. A light passed over his eye, then a light turned green and there was a hiss of changing air pressure.

He pulled the door open enough for her to slip inside. Lights flickered on, casting the space in a brilliant glow.

The vault was a room about fifteen feet by twenty. On one side were stacks of gold bricks, tubes filled with gold coins, vials of glittering gemstones and a mountain of cash. There were ornate crowns and necklaces that had to have been hundreds of years old. On the other side were books and scrolls, and glass-lidded boxes displaying jewelry and daggers made from a dull silver metal. Many of them had the same intricate markings as the brooch and shaft they'd fused into a key.

Justice found it interesting that the artifacts on the right side, which looked to be of far less value than the gold and jewels on the left, were treated with far more respect and reverence. Each one had its own padded case and was labeled with a shiny silver plaque. There were names and dates that declared whose possession each had been and when and where that item had been found. In some cases, the purpose of the item was listed.

Cures blindness, binds demons, removes memories, slays the dead.

The list of bizarre uses continued, but Justice was out of time.

"What are we here for?" Ronan asked.

She lifted the key. "This."

He looked around. "What's it for?"

"I don't know."

Look down. Below your feet.

Justice did. In the center of the room was a small circle inscribed with more of the same marks on the key. Inside that circle was a depression, and in that depression was a hole that looked like the outline of the brooch.

She knelt down and saw that the hole went deeper than she could see.

Another loud boom shook the walls. A gold and gemstone necklace slithered from the table and hit the floor with a clatter.

"We need to go," Ronan said.

Justice slid the brooch into the hole until it wouldn't go any further, then she turned the looping end of the key. The metal spun easily, and she could feel a series of clicks vibrating through the shaft.

She wasn't sure what was supposed to happen, but nothing in the floor moved. Nothing popped open, no panel slid sideways to reveal some secret treasure.

"Do you know what this opens?" she asked.

He shook his head. "No idea. I didn't even realize that lock was there."

She saw something out of the corner of her eye—a flicker of movement on the far side of the room, behind Ronan.

A section of the vault wall eased down on a hinge. The opening was the same size as those where the Sanguinar had been stored, but this one had no glass front. In fact, if not for the key, she never would have known that this crypt was here.

Not a crypt, she reminded herself. A sleeping chamber.

Dust swirled as if the door to this chamber hadn't been opened in a very long time. Inside was another Sanguinar mummy, but this one was wrapped in heavy chains, locked at its wrists and ankles.

Ronan's face paled. He crossed to the Sanguinar as if worried it would lash out at him.

"Who is that?" she asked.

"It can't be. I thought he was dead. We all thought he was dead. Tynan said he'd killed him centuries ago."

"Killed who?"

"Sargon, the mad Sanguinar."

Bring him, said the woman. At the same time, Justice felt the strong compulsion to do just that. She was propelled forward on feet she didn't control and reached into the chamber with arms not her own.

"Don't touch him!" Ronan said.

"Too late." Justice pulled his feeding tube from his nose and reached into the alcove.

The mad Sanguinar was light, like the rest of the bodies she'd carried. He was taller than most, and a bit unwieldy, but she managed to get him out of the hole in the wall without dropping him.

Ronan took him from her arms. "This is a mistake."

"Maybe, but it's one we're going to make."

They piled the mad Sanguinar on top of the last gurney in the train, just as the first chunks of stone began crumbling into the room.

There was no more time. They had to go, now.

Ronan pulled on the first two gurneys while Justice brought up the end of the mummy train. They raced down the hall toward the elevator, which was large enough for at most a third of their convoy.

"We have to take the stairs," she said. "You can float them, right?"

He gave a tight nod, but she could sense his lack of certainty, even without seeing his face.

Even shriveled and dehydrated, there was still a lot of weight to move.

"I'll take some up the elevator," she said.

"No. We stay together. There's no telling what demons are roaming on the floors above. Too many broke through to risk it."

"It will mean more work for you. I can't help you float them up the stairs."

"I will manage."

Another loud boom shook the earth around them. More rocks crumbled from the wall in a deafening avalanche. She could hear snarls and howls now. The demons were nearly through.

Ronan opened the door leading to the stairwell. Justice took it from him and gave him a quick kiss on the cheek. "You can do this. If you get tired, I'm here for you. My blood is here for you."

"It's just the sun stealing my strength."

He jogged up to the first landing, then closed his eyes. A second later, the first gurney began to lift, staying perfectly flat and level. As soon as it reached the end of its tether, the second lifted, then the next. The whole string of beds rose and began making the awkward journey up the steps.

As soon as the last Sanguinar fingernail was clear of the stairwell door, Justice rushed past the beds and opened the door on the next floor.

They made it up one more level before Ronan set the gurneys in the hallway and sagged against the wall.

He was shaking. His face was gaunt. His skin had a sickly gray cast to it that worried the hell out of her.

They'd only gone up two flights. She hadn't counted how many levels down they were, but she knew they were deep. They still weren't past the secured floors to the area where Sanguinar treated patients and kept their quarters.

The pounding below had stopped, but that didn't make her feel any better. In fact, as soon as she heard a faint scratching, she knew what it meant.

"They've made it through the wall," she whispered.

Ronan's eyes blazed a bright blue. He pushed to his feet, using the wall for support.

"You can barely stand. How are you going to keep going?"

"Just get the door. Two more floors up and we'll find help."

Justice didn't argue. There wasn't time. There was a pile of monsters on their tail, and if they didn't hurry, every one of those helpless Sanguinar would become vampire jerky for demons.

She pulled the door open and watched as the man she loved found the strength to lift the gurneys and keep moving.

By the time they were halfway up the next flight of stairs, the door below burst open and a mass of fur and claws flooded into the stairwell.

"Go!" Justice shouted.

Ronan let out a painful groan and the convoy of beds flew through the door into the hallway of the floor above. They crashed against the wall in an uncontrolled rush, but there wasn't time to check on the passengers now.

Ronan was the last one through the door. He slammed it shut behind him, wrapped his hand around the lever and roared in fury and pain.

The handle turned red and sagged around his grip, welding it shut. He fell to the floor, panting from the effort.

On the other side of the door, demons yelped as they pawed at the hot metal. The sturdy steel rattled, but it held firm. At least for now.

Justice rushed to Ronan's side.

He was in bad shape, nearly as thin as the Sanguinar they were trying to rescue. His skin hung on his skull, pale gray and trembling.

A screech of bone on metal vibrated through the door.

The Synestryn were trying to claw their way through.

He couldn't keep going. Not like this.

Justice pulled her hair away from her neck and put her throat to his lips. "Drink. Now, before it's too late."

The fact that he didn't argue spoke volumes about just how hungry and desperate he was.

His fangs bit deep. The flash of pain melded into pleasure as his lips worked against her skin.

She licked her lips, tasting remnants of his blood clinging there from where she'd kissed his cheek. Inside that blood were memories.

Hers, not his.

In an instant, the curtain hiding her past opened. She saw a strange world with an orange sky and two suns blazing overhead. She remembered being raised with her sisters, learning from the older women there that—like her sisters— her life was to be forged from duty, that she had a purpose. A destiny.

She had been born to save the lives of the Sanguinar who could never feel the sun on their faces. She had been bred to rescue a race of selfless souls who fought, suffered and died so that others could live. She had been created to be more than just an individual, striving toward her own hopes and dreams.

Justice and her sisters were weapons. It was their duty to fight in whatever way was necessary to win the war against the Synestryn. And if that meant their deaths, then so be it.

On her nineteenth birthday, Justice had offered herself to the cause and sworn to do her duty to her sisters, her mother and her people. She'd bound herself to that duty, shunning all other purposes.

The final step toward proving her dedication had been to willingly give up her memories, her past, and her family so that she could step into the war and fight. If the enemy ever took her captive, they'd never be able to pry from her the secret location of her birth. Because if they did, then all the little girls on Temprocia would be at risk.

Justice had agreed without hesitation. She'd been the first of her age group to volunteer to give up everything to help her kind fight the war on earth. She'd been eager, excited.

She'd had no idea just how much the women who raised her were asking when they stripped away her past, but such was the nature of youth. She had believed she was wise, indestructible, invulnerable.

She'd been so very wrong.

And now that she had her past again, she knew who she was. *What* she was.

Justice was what the poor, shriveled souls on those gurneys should have been had they not been cursed at birth. She was free to walk in the sun and feel its warmth on her face. She would never need to drink blood for her strength. She would never be called vampire or monster. She would never be so hungry that she'd rather turn into a husk than stay awake and suffer.

These dried bodies were *her* people. They were the ones she'd been born to protect. They were the ones she'd been created to help, no matter the personal cost.

Ronan wasn't going to be able to save their people without more blood. There wasn't enough left in her for him to get the Sanguinar away from danger.

Unless he took it all.

She could sense his resistance to keep feeding even as his starvation and desperation urged him to continue. Any second now, he would stop, and if he did, they were all going to die down here.

The demons had nearly made it through the door. The metal was beginning to buckle. Here and there a black claw poked through, raking at the steel, fighting to rip it open.

They were all going to die down here if Ronan wasn't strong. If he wasn't fed.

She couldn't lift the gurneys. She couldn't fight with a sword and lop of the heads of the monsters hunting them. All she could do was her duty. Give her everything, as she'd been taught to do. As she'd vowed to do.

The distant voice of the woman in her head told her what she needed to know. The transfer of information was so fast, it was almost as if she was waking an instinct that had simply been sleeping.

Justice slipped seamlessly inside Ronan's mind and found the part of his thoughts she needed.

She whispered to him that she was healthy and strong. She had plenty of blood to spare. He could take all he needed and she'd be fine. There was nothing to worry about except drinking his fill so he could get their people to safety.

The subterfuge worked. He kept feeding while she weakened, while she became dizzy, while her heart fluttered. She was nearly empty now, but it was okay. Part of her would always be with Ronan. He'd hold her inside him forever and keep her close.

Justice had found her purpose. She'd fulfilled her destiny. She'd loved. As far as she was concerned, that was as full as any life could ever get.

Her final thoughts as she died were of how much she loved Ronan, and of how lucky she was to have lived a life that mattered.

CHAPTER TWENTY-THREE

Ronan didn't realize that he'd killed Justice until it was too late.

One second, he'd been sure she was fine, and the next, whatever veil had been cast over him had vanished, and he'd been holding her body in his arms.

Despair and guilt unlike anything he'd ever known fell over him and strangled the air from his lungs.

She had done this, he realized. She had sacrificed herself to save them all. If he'd stopped feeding from her while she was still safe, he never would have had the power he needed to rescue his people. Her people.

But now, her power rumbled through him like thunder. His muscles bulged with it. His mind burned with clear focus. Every spark of life she'd had was his now. He had everything he needed to save the sleeping Sanguinar.

The only person he wanted to save was Justice.

He held her close as he pressed his hand to her chest with the intent to restore her—give her back the life force she'd sacrificed.

He gathered her power inside him, ready to shove it back into her by force, but when he tried, her blood wouldn't cooperate. It wouldn't let him heal her.

Ronan let out a scream of feral rage. It echoed off the hallway walls and made the ravening demons gouging their way through the door back up a step. They yelped as if slapped.

How could she have done this to him? How could she have stolen herself away from him? Didn't she know he loved her?

Of course, she didn't. He'd never told her.

Ronan roared in pain again, and this time, the magic seething in his body came out. It shoved the buckling door inward and shattered the lightbulbs overhead.

He couldn't save Justice, but maybe another of his kind could.

He surged to his feet and pressed his hands against the door. The stairwell was the fastest way up, and with the way the electricity was sparking and flickering, he didn't trust the elevator. Nor would it hold all of the fragile souls he was determined to save—the souls Justice had sacrificed her life for.

Ronan gathered up a few precious drops of Justice's power and used it to bash in the heavy steel door.

Demons on the opposite side were crushed instantly. Their black blood splattered the walls and slickened the steps. Those that weren't killed, were shoved down and left to snarl and crawl over the backs of the dead.

He didn't give them a chance to recover. Instead, he pulled on Justice's power to light the whole furry, greasy, bloody mass of demons on fire.

They ignited in a whoosh of light and heat. Below, more demons howled as their fur caught fire.

If they wanted to reach him, they were going to have to burn to make it happen.

Before the temporary blockade burned out, Ronan levitated Justice and his brothers and pushed them up the stairs.

The strain of lifting so much weight, coupled with the lethargy of daylight weakened him faster than he would have thought possible.

Dark, slithering forms glided up the walls like giant centipedes with spiny backs. They dug long claws into the drywall, climbing up it as if the smooth finish was rough tree bark. Dozens of eyes in their segmented heads glowed a bright green. Their bodies bowed and arched as they kept sight of their levitated prey.

Ronan didn't have time or energy to fight them one at a time. His best bet was to get out of this stairwell and lock them all inside.

He'd managed to shove Justice's body and three of the gurneys through the door to the next level—the first one unsecured and open to humans and Theronai. This was the level where they treated injuries and tended the sick.

And it was filled with demons.

He could barely see through the nests of mummified arms and legs, but what he did see was the glowing green eyes of demons and plenty of teeth and claws.

Before they could feast on his family, Ronan shoved up a shield around each gurney and Justice.

The drain on his body was so strong, he felt himself sag.

He pushed harder, digging deeper. Finally, he got all the beds through the stairwell door. He shoved it closed and welded it shut as he'd done before.

Hot air rasped his lungs. His vision narrowed so that he could barely see. He was on the floor now, though he had no idea how he'd gotten here.

He pulled out his cell and dialed the emergency number.

Slade answered.

"Need...help. Infirmary," he panted.

Slade's voice was calm and even, despite his young age. "I have your location, Ronan. I'll send help your way. Just hang on."

"Need...blood. Justice...dying." Tears streamed down his face as he said the words. He could see her sprawled on the floor a few feet away from him, her pretty silver-green eyes staring back at him, lifeless. Empty.

He'd killed her. She'd let him. He loved her and he'd killed her.

How was he ever going to live with himself now?

The power she'd sacrificed herself to give him was fading. The blue shield around his allies began to flicker. Black, oily muzzles filled with rows of teeth began sniffing at the cracks, curious and hungry.

Ronan crawled across the floor toward Justice. The wheels of a gurney were in his way, but he reached for her with one skeletal hand. He had to hold himself together for just a few more minutes—let the magic eat his flesh and bone until help arrived.

He touched the tip of her cold finger. She was gone. He wanted to go with her. Be with her. But if he did that, his family would die.

She wouldn't want that. She'd given everything she had so that they could live.

His eyes fluttered shut. The shield fluttered with them. Demons growled and yipped in excitement.

Somewhere a few doors down the hall, a baby cried the raw, faint cry of a newborn.

Nika. She'd done it. She'd brought the next generation of Theronai into the world. If she could do that in the midst of death and destruction, then Ronan could hold on for just a few more seconds.

Then he would go to Justice and be with the woman he loved forever.

CHAPTER TWENTY-FOUR

Justice had never before seen the stunning woman standing in front of her, but she knew her instantly on sight.

She had long, black hair and pale green eyes that were filled with motion like spring leaves shivering on a soft breeze. Her gown shimmered with silver threads, and her neck and wrists were adorned with gleaming metal bands. Each of them was marked with the same strange marks as were on the key.

She was tall, with muscular arms bare from the shoulder down. Atop her black curls was a thin crown tipped with silver pearls and cut stones filled with light. Literally filled with light, as if someone had somehow captured the sun, liquefied it, then poured it into faceted crystal shells.

She was the most beautiful woman Justice had ever seen, and not only because she was Justice's mother.

"I am Celentia," she said. There was power in her voice— a power Justice knew all too well.

The woman. The fates. Her mother was the presence in her head, compelling her to act.

"You," Justice said. The word hovered somewhere between a question and an accusation.

She struggled to understand what was happening. Everything here was muted, diluted, as if she were experiencing it from a distance, outside of herself. She looked around but recognized nothing. She was in a dark place with moonlight streaming down from behind frosty clouds. There was a faint pink glow in the air, but it had no source. She could smell flowers nearby, but had no idea what they were, other than intoxicating. Almost spicy, like Ronan's skin, like his blood.

"Where am I?"

"Your mind is with me on Athanasia. Your body is dying on earth."

"Dying?"

"Dead, technically." The swirling green in her eyes blurred, but Justice couldn't tell if it was because of tears, or because her viewpoint seemed so distant.

"I don't understand."

"I know," the woman said, her tone dropping to a sad, minor chord. "There is too much to tell and not enough time."

"Then you'd better hurry."

Celentia smiled slightly, as if she found Justice cute. "I bound you too tightly to your duty. It hurt you. That was never my intent, but there was no undoing it. Until now."

"Duty?"

"I created you to aid the Sanguinar. I ordered you sent to Earth when you were ready, stripped of your memories to protect you."

"I chose to go." Justice remembered that now, clearly. She'd known what was going to happen to her if she left the comfort of her childhood village. She was going to be alone, stripped of her past, with only her instincts and her duty to guide her.

She'd been ready to go. Eager to serve. It was an honor few of her kind were tough enough and brave enough to receive. Only the strongest were allowed to serve. She'd been so proud to be given the honor.

"You chose to go because you were bred to choose duty over all else," Celentia said. "All my daughters were."

"I don't understand."

The woman stepped closer and pressed her warm hand

against Justice's cheek. "I so desperately wanted to stay with you, my sweet daughter." She stroked her temple. "Here, in your mind, but I see the folly of that desire now. Our times flow in two different rivers. Communication is painful for you. You suffered when I spoke."

"That was you?" Justice asked. "All this time, the compulsions—the fates—that was you trying to speak to me?"

Celentia nodded. "I never knew it would cause you pain. I am sorry, my child."

"You made me do things," Justice said, her tone sharp with accusation. "Horrible things. You made me *kill*."

"There is always death in war."

"And Noah? What about him? He wasn't shooting at me or hiding a knife behind his back. You forced me to kill him for no fucking reason!"

"There was good reason. He was not what he seemed. He was dorjan. Tainted."

"You don't know that."

"I do. I saw the poison raging through him, growing day by day. Time on your world was going by so fast. I feared if I slept, if I rested, he would destroy you." She shook her head and a tear spilled down her perfect cheek. "I tried to tell you why I commanded you to obey, but you could not hear me. I was not strong enough to shift the flow of time to speak so you could understand. I am so sorry for your pain. Sorry for your loneliness."

Justice still couldn't get over the idea that she was speaking to her mother. Even when she was growing up on Temprocia, she'd never met her. Celentia had given birth, then gone home, sacrificing her child to a war that was the only hope of survival for an entire world. Maybe more than one. Justice had known that from the time she was little.

"You abandoned me," Justice said. She felt like she should be angrier but couldn't seem to remember how to summon it.

"I left you in the only place you would be safe from the Solarc. I left you with women who raised you with strength and honor. I wish I could have done so myself and seen you grow into the powerful creature you are now, but such luxuries have never been mine. Too many lives rest in my hands."

"You could have stayed. You could have brought me back with you."

"You know that is untrue. The Solarc would kill you on sight. Even now, holding your spirit here, we are risking great danger to both you and your sisters and cousins."

"Then why bring me here at all? You clearly have no trouble justifying your abandonment of me."

"You are dying. I brought you here to give you a chance for life, for happiness." Her beautiful eyes slid shut as if in exhaustion. "There is little strength left in me after all I have given the war, but what I have is yours."

"I don't want anything else from you but to be left alone. If death is the only way to get that, then so be it."

Celentia bowed her head in defeat. The glowing gems of the crown nestled in her curls seemed to shift precariously to one side. "I free you. Go. Live your life unbound to me."

"It's too late for that. I'm dead, remember?" It was strange how Justice wasn't upset by the idea of being dead. There was a kind of fuzzy numbness around her emotions as there had been before she'd met Ronan. No fear or grief could touch her. But neither could joy. She was all logic and little feeling. Hollow.

Except for one little part—the part touched by Ronan. She missed him. She longed to be near him again. She didn't mind dying, but the idea of never seeing him again tore through her like sharp claws, ripping at her sanity.

She ached from his absence.

"That is how I feel for you," Celentia said. "Every moment I have missed watching you grow into the woman you are now. Every second of time lost. I will never know the pleasure of rocking you to sleep or telling you a story. I will never feel your small body crawl into my lap to hug me around my neck. I will never see your eyes light with joy from your first kiss or hear you whisper to me of your love for some young man. Your life is lost to me, lost to duty, both yours and mine."

"I'm just a tool, then." Justice said. "A weapon meant to win a war."

"You are as powerful as any weapon, but your purpose goes far beyond fighting."

"What then? If you so desperately wanted to be my mother, then why give me up? Why did all of the women like you give any of us up?"

"Did you want for anything as a child? Did you ever once question if you were loved, if you were safe, if you were important?"

She hadn't. Being raised in the village had been fun and exciting. Every girl there knew she was both wanted and necessary. Sure, they were taught how to fight and were told that someday they may be called to do so, but it hadn't been a bad way to grow up. She'd never been cold, hungry or neglected. She was never abused, and she was surrounded by the love of her family. She belonged.

She thrived.

Would it have been easier on Celentia to stay there and raise her daughter? Justice couldn't imagine ever leaving a child behind, but as she stared out over the balcony railing, across the dark countryside, she could see the signs of decay in the distance.

It reminded her of an old medieval setup with a towering castle surrounded by clogged city streets, ringed by homes growing less elegant and more modest as they stretched out toward the rolling countryside.

Rustic, earthen huts were vacant and crumbling. Farmland sat empty of crops. There were no sounds of laughter from the homes below, no children singing or crying as they raged against bedtime. There were no dogs barking or night birds singing.

"This place is dying, isn't it?" Justice asked.

Celentia bowed her head. "Yes, and it is taking everyone here with it. My brothers and sisters, my friends. It has already claimed my father in madness. My mother, Brenya, fled to find a way to fight back. You, Justice, are the only hope we have left. Not a weapon. Hope. That is your true purpose."

That's when Justice finally understood what would drive a woman to leave her child on another world by choice. Because having her here would mean her death. Nothing here lived for long. Nothing here thrived. Taking Justice to Temprocia was a gift, not abandonment. Her mother had made the ultimate sacrifice and left her child behind so that her people would have hope for survival, so that Justice would survive.

Celentia's regal shoulders sagged in relief. "You understand now."

"I do. You wanted a better life for me, for those trapped here."

"I would have given anything to watch you grow into the woman you have become."

"But doing so would put me at risk."

Celentia stroked Justice's hair. "I could not bear to never have borne you. The world needs you. Perhaps more than one world."

Justice considered that for a moment. Yes, her mother had left her behind, but Justice had known every day before her memories were stripped away that it wasn't because Celentia didn't love her. It was just the opposite. She loved her enough to give her a chance at survival, a chance to thrive and offer hope to those who had none. She hadn't been abandoned or forgotten.

In this moment, Justice remembered the little old lady who'd forgiven her with her last breath. She remembered how little she'd deserved the gift, but how much it had meant.

Justice wanted to give that same gift to her mother. It was the only way to truly honor the gift the old woman had given her.

"I forgive you," Justice said. "For all those years of not knowing who I was, for the headaches and lack of sleep and desperate races across the country to do things I didn't understand. I know that you never would have put me through that if there had been any other way. I understand why you did it and I forgive you. Please don't blame yourself."

Her mother smiled. Tears slipped from her verdant eyes. "You are as generous as you are strong. Brenya and the others did a fine job in raising you."

The unspoken words between them were that they both wished that it could have been different, that they could have been together all those lost years.

Celentia reached up to her crown and plucked one of the glowing gemstones from it. She closed her fist around it and whispered a few low, strange words. Then she held out the stone to Justice.

"You have done your duty well, child. But you are not finished. Take it. Swallow it."

"Why?"

"For hope. For happiness. For Ronan."

The mention of his name sent a stab of pain shooting through her—stark inside her foggy numbness. She missed him. Wanted to be near him. The idea of him suffering made her want to weep.

"What about him?" she asked, her tone stark and desperate.

"He believes he killed you. If you die, he will as well. If he dies, then all will be lost."

"He can't die," Justice said, her tone fierce, almost angry. "I tricked him into taking my blood. He should know that."

"He does know. It changes nothing. His guilt will consume him. Now. Tonight."

"Fix it!" Justice demanded. The woman standing in front of her was powerful and resolute. Chances were she could squish Justice like a bug and not even leave enough behind to bother scraping from her elegant shoe.

"I cannot reach him. You must. Save Ronan. Save Sargon. Both must live."

"Sargon? The mad Sanguinar?"

Celentia smiled. "Mad? Is that what they think he is?" She lifted the gemstone higher. On her hand was a ring exactly like the one Justice had been compelled to find. The surface was etched with the same strange marks.

"Go now," Celentia said. "My powers can only reach earth for a few more moments. You cannot be trapped here with the Solarc."

Justice picked up the stone. It was warm with secrets and pulsing with life.

"It will not hurt you. Now go and know that I will always love you. I will always be with you, even if you cannot hear me."

Justice hugged the regal woman who'd given her life. As she did, a feeling of love so deep and consuming it was almost impossible to bear sank into her. A mother's love. *Her* mother's love.

"Will we see each other again?" she asked.

Celentia shrugged one smooth shoulder. "If your people turn the tide of war, perhaps."

"And if not?"

She ignored the question. "There is no more time. Do your duty once more and save your people. Save yourself and be happy in your newfound freedom."

Justice did as her mother told her and swallowed the stone. As soon as it cleared her throat, the world—whichever one this was—went away.

CHAPTER TWENTY-FIVE

Madoc held his daughter in his arms, certain this couldn't be real. He couldn't be a father. He wasn't a good enough man to deserve the happiness he felt holding this little life in hands meant for killing.

He swallowed down the lump clogging his throat and gently handed his daughter to Nika.

She was crying openly, tears catching in the corners of her wide smile.

It didn't matter that the birth hadn't gone as planned, or that there were demons clawing at the door, fighting to get inside. It didn't matter that they'd suffered the pain of labor or the fear of what might happen. All that mattered was that they had shared this experience together. The two of them were now three. A family.

His daughter screamed in outrage at her new surroundings. Nika cradled her against her bare chest and cooed soft words of reassurance. "You're okay now. Everything is okay. Daddy's going to kill those nasty monsters and we're all going to be just fine."

The baby quieted and stared up at her mother with somber eyes, listening.

Madoc tied and cut the cord. Nika delivered the afterbirth without trouble. Her bleeding was minimal. Everything was normal, textbook. Even with the growling, howling demons at the door, inside this little delivery room, all was peaceful and perfect.

Nika looked up at him with eyes so full of love, he nearly wept at the sight. He could feel her pouring herself into him through their link, bringing with her a sliver of their daughter's innocent mind for him to see.

"She's amazing," he breathed. "She already knows me."

"Of course, she does. She's heard you talk and I've been telling her about you for months." She put her finger inside their baby's tiny grip. "She needed to know she was safe, that Daddy was strong and brave and deadly."

He laughed at that. "You've really built me up. Guess I'm going to have to prove you right and go kill some fuc— flipping demons so we can get out of here."

***

Justice crashed back into her body as if she'd been shot there by a cannon. Landing inside flesh and bone hurt, not only because of the sudden jarring sensation, but also because every ache and pain she'd endured before she'd died was right there, waiting for her to return.

She groaned and tried to focus her dry eyes. She had to blink a few times to get the fog to clear, but as soon as she did, she knew she was too late.

She was on the floor in one of the hallways of Dabyr. The lights overhead had gone out, but there was a faint blue glow surrounding her and the gurneys stacked with sleeping Sanguinar. On the outside of that glow were demons. Dozens of them, all staring at her with eerie green eyes lit from within.

They clawed and bit at the film of blue light, and every time they did, it flickered and faded slightly.

Ronan was dead. He had to be. He was too shriveled and used up to be anything else.

She screamed in denial, and the sound only managed to rile the hungry Synestryn more. They doubled their efforts to reach her.

Ronan opened his eyes. They were milky and shrunken in his head. There was no light within them. No life.

"Jus...tice." His voice was a weak thread of sound, barely audible over the snarls of demons.

He was alive! She wasn't too late, though she felt like she could lose him at any second.

"I'm here. Hang on."

She felt herself fill, swell. Whatever weakness she'd had dissipated. The aches and pains evaporated.

Whatever was in that crystal her mother had given her was potent medicine. In the space of a few seconds, she went from dead to feeling fine.

She belly-crawled under the gurneys to reach him. His hand was outstretched toward her, the fingers as thin as pencils. His skin was wrinkled and chalk white, just like the Sanguinar on the beds above them.

He was too weak to move. She wondered how he was still holding that protective light around them when he clearly had nothing left of himself to give.

Justice bit her tongue as she reached him, then covered his mouth with hers. His lips were dry and cold, but she didn't care. The man she loved was dying, and she refused to let that happen.

Her blood trickled into his mouth as she kissed him. Tears streamed down her face soaked into his cheeks. He didn't move. She couldn't even tell if he was breathing.

Something in her stomach began to heat. She felt that warmth travel up her throat and into Ronan's mouth. Light spilled from between their lips and splashed against the confines of the glowing blue shield. Every time the barrier flickered, some of that golden light spilled through the cracks where demon claws and teeth entered.

Synestryn screamed in pain and reared back away from the light. Their fur burned away and the skin began to sizzle everywhere the light had touched. They rolled on the ground and flailed against each other as if trying to wipe away the pain.

Several of them began to run, howling and yipping as they went, as if the devil himself were on their heels. Justice didn't lift her head to watch them go. Her sole focus was on Ronan and feeding him the blood he needed.

The hallway cleared of Synestryn. Only the stench of burning fur and the echo of pained cries was left behind.

Drops of her blood and golden light spilled from her lips to fill him. Soon, his body began to swell and his skin plumped. He moved a little—just enough to wrap his arms around her and kiss her back.

Their tongues danced. The sweet music of pleasure rose between them. His body warmed, as did hers, and soon he was strong enough to pull them up and drag her into his lap.

The light welling from her dimmed, then dissipated, but the power of it remained. It was in every one of her cells. In every one of his as well. Whatever magic her mother had gifted her with, it had been enough to save both her and the man she loved.

A door crashed open in the distance. Voices filled the stairwell, coming from above. A moment later, the hallway filled with men wielding swords, fresh from battle.

Ronan lifted his head and looked into her eyes, rather than at their visitors. "Before another second passes, you need to know how much I love you. I don't want to ever again face death without you knowing just how I feel."

Justice's whole world shifted and warmed around her, hugging her close. Happy tears stung her eyes, but she didn't care. Love didn't make her weak. It made her strong—strong enough to travel to another world and come back to save the man she loved.

She stared into his eyes and said, "I love you, too."

CHAPTER TWENTY-SIX

Theronai and Slayers roamed the halls of Dabyr, checking inside every room, in every closet, and under every bed for Synestryn. Humans moved the fragile, sleeping Sanguinar into the trailer of the semi Justice had driven. The shelving she'd installed in the back was the perfect size for the bodies, and the soft yoga mats served as cushions to protect the fragile bodies. Elastic bands were used to secure them in place so they could be transported to a safe location.

Wherever that was.

Ronan and his fellow Sanguinar healed the injured while humans lined up to feed them so they had the strength to do so.

Broken windows were boarded up, and the damage was assessed by Joseph and a small group of his trusted warriors.

Forty-nine people had died in the attack, most of them Theronai and Slayers. Only two human lives had been lost. Amazingly, one new life had been safely added to the ranks— Madoc and Nika's daughter.

The infant was still too new to have a name, but old enough to bring hope to everyone who saw her.

The next generation of Theronai had finally been born after two hundred years of waiting.

Ronan worked long past the time his brothers faded. Even Logan was exhausted now. Hope would return to him and replenish him soon, but she needed time in the sun before she was able to do so.

It wasn't until noon that the work was finally done. The worst of the injuries had been treated, though some of the minor ones would wait until nightfall, when the work was far easier on his kind.

Outside, both humans and Theronai were working frantically to repair damage to the outside wall around the compound.

Ronan slumped onto a stool in the now-empty examination room and let out a heavy breath.

Justice slipped inside and closed the door. "I got the final report from Joseph."

"How bad?" he asked.

"Pretty bad. The Sentinel stones and the Hall of the Fallen are safe, but the wall is completely compromised. Even with the work that's being done there's no way we'll keep the demons out tonight."

"I assume Joseph has a plan."

"He does. We're moving all valuable artifacts and anyone who can't fight out to your gerai houses—safe houses. Most of them have already been warded. Each one will be assigned at least one warrior for protection. I also offered up my warehouses, since they're stocked with enough food, water and beds to support dozens of people for months. They're set up with decent security too. It won't stop demons, but at least we'll know they're coming."

Ronan shook his head in wonder. Without her preparations, the coming night would have cost them so many lives. But now there were safe places for all to go, including his sleeping kin.

"He's going to rebuild, isn't he?" Ronan asked.

"His exact words were, 'this is our home, and they'll take it over our fucking corpses.' I think he's planning to take the fight to them by going down through the tunnel they dug into the sleeping chamber."

Ronan nodded. "Sounds like Joseph. Did your beloved car

survive the attack?"

"Ricardo?" she asked, as if the thought of her Maserati hadn't even crossed her mind. "I'm sure he's fine. And if not, I'll live. He's just a car."

Ronan didn't think she would have felt that way a few days ago, but he loved that she did. It meant the void Ricardo had filled was now full of something else—something he desperately hoped looked a lot like him.

"What about the sleeping Sanguinar?" he asked.

"Tynan is having them moved to one of my warehouses for now. You'll have to feed them one at a time, but it's manageable. Joseph has assigned a special detail to protect them."

"Sounds like we're going to be stretched thin," Ronan said.

"More Slayers are on the way. Joseph contacted some group called the Defenders and asked them to bring every man and every bit of explosives and firepower they could find. They'll be here before nightfall to help with what's coming."

The Defenders were dedicated and tough, but they were still human, no matter how many weapons or explosives they had at their disposal.

The casualties resulting from this night were not yet done mounting up. More would die before order was restored. Luckily, the Slayers would steeply tip the odds in their favor.

Justice pushed away from the door and crossed over to him. She was dirty and disheveled, but still absolutely stunning. Since coming back to life, she'd had a kind of glow about her, almost like an iridescence.

She'd told him that she loved him, but it wasn't enough. He wanted more of her. All of her.

She reached for him, and he found the strength to take her hand. As weary and worn out as he was, he still was nowhere close to being too tired to touch her.

"I spoke to my mother while I was dead," she said, her voice small. "She's some kind of alien royalty, I think. How weird is that?"

For some reason, the news that she'd spoken to alien royalty wasn't even in the top five most shocking things he'd seen in the past twenty-four hours.

"Definitely weird," he agreed. "What did she say?"

"She said that she was the one causing my compulsions. She didn't mean to hurt me, which I believe. She seems pretty cool, actually. Not really maternal, but definitely someone I could hang with, you know?"

Ronan laughed. "Next time she's in town, why don't we go out for a nice dinner?"

"Yeah. I get it. Not a lot of hanging with her likely to happen. Still, it was nice to finally meet the woman who gave me life."

"I hope I get to meet her someday, too. Especially if I don't have to die to do it. I want to thank her for giving the universe such an amazing woman."

Justice straddled his lap and draped her arms over his shoulders. He loved having her close like this, and reveled in how easily she touched him now, like they belonged together.

He was going to do everything in his power to ensure that they stayed that way.

Justice smiled. "My mother said that you were my gift for doing my duty. I think that means you belong to me now."

He grinned. "Is that what you think?"

"Well, she is royalty. You wouldn't want to insult her by ruining her gift to me, would you?"

"Never. I will happily belong to you for as long as you like."

Her brows shot up. "Oh, really? Are you sure about that? I'm kinda hard to get along with."

He cupped her face and kissed her, and in that instant, he knew that he could kiss her every day for a thousand years and never grow tired of her.

"I'm certain," he said.

All signs of humor fled her expression. "Promise me, Ronan. Promise me I won't have to be alone anymore."

His strong, confident Justice was as fragile and uncertain

as everyone else, but she never let that get in her way. He loved that about her as he did a hundred other things that made her such a treasure.

"You and I are meant to be together, Justice. I've known it since the night we met. And as difficult as you were to catch, I'm never letting you go again. I promise to be yours for as long as you'll have me."

The weight of his vow settled over him, warm and comforting. Right.

Justice shivered, then nodded, satisfied. "That's good, because I plan on having you as often as possible."

He liked the sound of that, no matter how tired he was.

She kissed him, slow and languid. "How about we clean up in one of those massive showers you have here and then get a few hours of down time before the sun sets. I have a feeling that our people are going to need us tonight. We need to be ready."

With her by his side, he was certain that the two of them would be ready for whatever came their way. Bring on the demons, the battles and the bloodshed. Their love was strong enough to withstand all of it. Whatever came their way, they'd face it, hand-in-hand, together.

About the Author

New York Times bestselling author Shannon K. Butcher (who now writes as Anna Argent) has written more than thirty titles since launching her career in 2007. She has three award-winning series, including the paranormal romance series *The Sentinel Wars,* the action-romance series *The Edge,* and the romantic suspense *Delta Force Trilogy.* Her alter ego also writes several series with a fresh and interesting spin on paranormal romance as well as a contemporary romance series. As a former engineer and current nerd, she frequently uses charts, graphs and tables to aid her in the mechanics of story design, world building and to keep track of all those pesky characters, magical powers and alternate worlds. An avid bead and glass artist, she spends her free time turning small sparkly bits into larger sparkly bits. She's rarely on social media, so the best place to find out news about upcoming releases under either name is via her newsletter. You can sign up at AnnaArgent.com.

Dear reader,

First, I want to apologize for the time it's taken me to write this book. I promise you won't have to wait so long for the next installment of the Sentinel Wars, which is well underway and features Morgan and Serena.

As you probably know by now, I've been secretly writing under another name for years—one I will be using for the majority of my work going forward. If you like the Sentinels, I think you'll love the stories I've written as Anna Argent. I'm especially fond of the *Lost Shards* series.

As always, I want to thank you for being the loyal readers you are, and for sticking with me through all the changes life has in store. I wish you much love and as many good books as you can stand.

Happy reading!
Shannon K. Butcher, now writing as Anna Argent

P.S. I'm rarely on social media so if you want the latest news and information (about both pen names), the best way to get it is through my newsletter. You can sign up at AnnaArgent.com.

Keep reading for a sneak peek of Anna Argent's book, SHARDS OF BLOOD AND SHADOW, book one of the *Lost Shards* series.

Chapter One

August 18, Cassadaga, Florida

As a professional psychic, Cleo Radella was used to handing out predictions about others, but the one she faced today was all about her. And it terrified her.

It was barely four in the morning, but she'd been awake since the stroke of midnight, knowing that the day of her mother's prediction—one given at the moment of Cleo's birth—was here. No more waiting. No more pretending today wouldn't come. No more certainty that her next breath was guaranteed.

No more time.

Despite the Florida heat, Cleo couldn't seem to get warm. A chill of foreboding wrapped around her, making goosebumps dance on her skin.

She wrapped a purple robe around her to ward away the chill and padded down the steep, narrow stairs, avoiding the third, the creaky one, so she wouldn't wake her aunt. But by the time Cleo had reached the kitchen, she realized her stealth had been unnecessary.

Her honorary aunt was already awake and bustling around the kitchen.

Delores Vail stood beneath a tarnished, antique glass light with a single bulb. The dim, golden glow was almost harsh in the darkness, making the cracked black-and-white floor tiles hurt Cleo's eyes.

"I thought you'd be up early," Delores said with a hint of worry in her tone.

A flowered apron was tied around her chubby middle, and a sad smile dulled her muddy brown eyes. She was closer to fifty than forty now. Her graying hair had once been a warm, soft brunette, but time was waging a battle within the short strands—one it would inevitably win. As soon as it had conquered her hair, it would spread its invasion across her body until there was no part of her left untouched.

Cleo couldn't stand to think about how the war would end. Today was already filled with enough fear.

Delores, while no actual blood relation, was the closest thing Cleo had to family. She'd been her mom's best friend since Cleo was little, and a constant fixture in her life. Now that Mom was gone, Delores was more than just her roommate and business partner. She was Cleo's anchor—the thing that kept her from spinning off into the darkness, adrift and alone.

If anything happened to Delores, Cleo knew she wouldn't survive it.

"Couldn't sleep," Cleo said. "You?"

Delores lifted the mixing bowl to display its contents. The smile she offered was genuine, but frail, as if it would crack if she exerted any more pressure on it. "I thought today called for a little fortification."

So sweet. Delores had always been kind. It was a tragedy that the universe had decided to give her such a heavy burden to bear.

Cleo felt a grin nibble away at her worry. "I hate to say it, but I don't think even chocolate chip pancakes have the power to make today not suck."

Delores's gaze softened. "It's a big day, but you'll get through it. *We'll* get through it together."

"I was hoping you'd forget what today was so you didn't have to worry. No sense in both of us having a day ruined."

"First, I'd never forget your birthday, especially not a landmark one like reaching a quarter of a century."

Cleo winced with cartoony exaggeration, which had the desired effect of making Delores chuckle.

"Second, your mom and I spent so many hours talking about this day that there's no way it would just slip my mind. She can't be here for you, but I can. And I will."

Cleo pulled out one of the mismatched chairs around the small kitchen table and slumped into it. Like everything else in the little house that also served as their fortune-telling business, it was faded and worn with use. No shiny stainless steel and gleaming granite for a couple of professional psychics in a town filled with them. There simply weren't enough clients—or their money—to go around.

Sometimes Cleo wondered if they'd be better off moving to a place where women like her and Delores were fewer and farther between.

Then again, no matter where she went, her mother's prediction would still follow. For all Cleo knew, if she hopped in her car right this second, she'd run right into the thing she was hoping to avoid.

No. Better to stand her ground, brace herself, and take it like a woman.

Delores poured the first pancakes into a cast iron skillet and sprinkled them with the darkest chocolate chips money could buy. "These may not make today fun, but maybe it will be a little easier with a bit of chocolate on board."

"You are as wise as you are kind," Cleo said.

"You're just saying that to earn extra chocolate chips."

The coffee pot let out a sputtering, hissing groan, indicating it was done with its chore. Cleo poured two cups, added a healthy spoon of honey to her aunt's, and a splash of milk to both.

"I think we should close the shop today," Cleo said.

Delores flipped the pancakes. "You know that won't do any good. Your mother's predictions always come true. Just like yours. There's no escaping it. Every action you take today will inevitably lead you closer to the thing you're hoping to avoid, so you might as well make some money while you're at it." She looked around the kitchen, which, while clean, was shabby in even the most optimistic light. "The house payment isn't going to make itself."

Cleo sighed in resignation and sipped her coffee.

Mom grinned at her from a photo on the refrigerator. When it was taken, she'd been standing in this very kitchen, baking Cleo's twenty-second birthday cake. There was a smear of chocolate on her chin and flour in her hair, but she was still so beautiful it made Cleo's chest ache.

She'd died twelve days later.

Cleo always wondered if she hadn't known she was going to die, or if she'd simply chosen not to tell anyone.

Sometimes it was better not knowing what the future held.

"I wish there was some kind of loophole in Mom's prediction," Cleo said.

Delores brought two plates topped with steaming pancakes to the table and set them down. Stuck in the top of Cleo's was a single birthday candle, it's flame bright and cheerful, as if it had no idea she was about to snuff it out.

Delores's voice was gentle. "Honey, your mother and I spent years turning her prediction around and looking at it from every angle. The only way through today is right down the middle. Be the smart, sweet, brave girl you've always been and you'll come out the other side just fine."

Cleo sure as hell hoped so. For twenty-five years, she'd always known that tomorrow would come. No matter what she did, or what risks she took, she knew she was going to be fine because her mother predicted that today would come. It couldn't come if Cleo was dead, so there was always a sense of peace in whatever decisions she made. But now…there were no more guarantees.

For the first time in her life, she wasn't sure whether or not she'd have another tomorrow. Even worse, darkness would enter her life today, and she wasn't entirely sure she'd survive it.

Cleo blew out the candle without bothering to make a

wish. Wishing would change nothing.

"Eat while they're hot," Delores said, then bustled off.

She returned a moment later with a long, narrow box wrapped in glittery unicorn paper.

Cleo's heart gave a little squeeze of nostalgia.

Mom always found a way to work unicorns into Cleo's birthday gifts, ever since she was a little girl. She'd had a unicorn-themed party at the impressionable age of five and had somehow connected birthdays and unicorns in her head. For years, no birthday had been complete without them, and when she grew older, her mom had delighted in finding creative ways to work them into every year's celebration. Now Delores was carrying on that tradition in Mom's absence.

Cleo blinked back a mist of tears and gave her aunt a big hug. "I don't know what I'd do without you. Thank you."

Delores didn't smile back. "Don't thank me until you open it."

Cleo tore into the paper, unconcerned about the glitter bomb she set off. A little bit of sparkle in her pancakes wouldn't kill her.

She lifted the lid of the box, and inside a foam cradle shaped to fit perfectly was a gleaming combat knife. She'd never seen anything like it before. It wasn't some mass-produced tool provided to the military or sold at gun stores. It was a unique, one-of-a-kind piece of art. Deadly art.

The handle was a beautiful piece of burled wood with an intricately swirling grain. It had been carved by hand and finished with loving attention until the surface was as smooth as glass. Rather than being thick and clunky, the stunning wooden handle was sized just for her grip.

The blade was a brilliant, polished silver, with twin grooves running down the length. It's mirror finish reflected her image—one pale blue eye and one emerald green eye, both wide with horror.

The overall design was simple and clean. Practical.

This was the kind of knife meant for only one thing.

Killing.

A cold chill fell over her and she dropped the box on the table like it was on fire.

Coffee sloshed out of the cups and the little birthday candle rolled to the floor.

Delores grabbed Cleo's hand, and only then did she realize that she'd knocked her chair over to scramble away from the weapon.

"Hear me out," Delores said.

Cleo jerked her hand away and hugged herself. "What the hell? Is this some kind of sick joke?"

"You need it."

She shook her head. "I don't want it. Take it back. I don't even want to touch it long enough to put it in the trash."

Delores sighed and shook her head. "You're keeping it. You need to be able to protect yourself. Especially today. I would have bought a gun, but—"

The feeling left Cleo's legs and she had to lean heavily against the kitchen counter to hold herself up. "I don't want a gun, either. I don't want any of this."

"It's only for self-defense."

No. No, it wasn't. A knife like that was meant to kill. She could see its intent shining in its pretty silver surface as easily as if it had been engraved there.

"I have pepper spray. That's all I need."

Delores's voice went hard. "That's not enough and you know it. Bad things are coming for you today and I'm not about to lose another daughter."

Her sharp tone cut through some of Cleo's shock.

"I'm not going to die today." It sounded more like a question than a statement.

"Not if you have a way to defend yourself, you won't."

"I can't take it." Her voice wavered and she felt tears form, hot behind her lashes. "I won't."

Delores got right in her face, putting on her sternest maternal expression. She pointed a thick, stubby finger at Cleo's nose and shook it. "I've already buried two children, a husband, and a best friend. I am *not* going to lose you, too.

You're going to take that knife and keep it on you all day. And then, after this whole awful day is over and the sun comes up tomorrow, you and I can sit down as discuss other options. But until then, you're going to carry the damn knife like it's the only thing standing between you and death. *Because it very well may be*. Understand?"

Cleo did. She understood that the woman she loved like a second mother was terrified out of her mind, and that if carrying some fucking knife was going to make her feel better today, then Cleo owed it to her to strap on the thing and tote it around.

It didn't mean she had to use it.

Cleo was not going to kill anyone today, no matter how clearly her mother's prediction had promised she would.

CHAPTER TWO

"**D**id you find her yet?"

Flint Skelton eyed the antique house from his nondescript rental car. Even though the sun had yet to rise, the thick heat was still stifling. He didn't dare open his windows to let in what passed for fresh air for fear of being noticed by a nosy, insomniac neighbor.

Cleopatra Radella's house was charming, with a wide, welcoming porch and lacy curtains in the windows. Great pains had been taken to make the front inviting, but he'd scouted the whole area on foot under the cover of dark and knew that the back had been left to fade and peel under the blazing Florida sun.

Appearances were apparently important to Radella.

"I found her," Flint told the woman on the phone.

"What do you think? Good guy or bad guy?" she asked.

Marvel Manning was a tech genius, a germaphobe, and a total chatterbox. While he appreciated her loyalty, ability, and work ethic, he did not want to get drawn into her conversational black hole.

"Don't know yet," he said. "She could have no shards at all."

"When will you know?" asked Marvel.

"These things take time. It's not like she has the answer stamped on her forehead."

"Starry told me to tell you to hurry. We're way behind on

bringing in the strays."

Flint suppressed his irritation. He owed Starry his life and would gladly repay her in full if she called on him to do so, but there were some things that were beyond his ability.

"Tell her it will take as long as it takes," he said. "I need to be sure before we send her to Eden."

Marvel sighed. "Yeah. I figured that's what you'd say. Problem is, my new program is spitting out names faster than we can find them. This Cleopatra chick has been out there for almost three years on her own. And if I can find her, so can the Vires."

Flint caught a fleeting glimpse of a woman through a window in the back corner of the house, in the kitchen. His vantage point wasn't great, but his eyes were good, and that little flash of movement was all it took to make out the features of a young woman: Average height, chin-length, straight blond hair, pretty features.

He couldn't tell more than that about her appearance, but her movements gave away much more to a man like him.

She was terrified.

The light in the kitchen winked out. A few seconds later, a light in an upstairs room came on. A shadow passed over the closed blinds, moving with jerky hesitance. Then she went still for a moment before her shadow shrank as she approached the window.

The cheap plastic blinds parted as she peered out and looked right at his car.

Flint froze.

He was good at staying hidden. People rarely noticed him, even when he wasn't using the magic coursing through his blood to enhance his ability to blend in.

Still, the blond woman looked right at him, as if able to see through the pre-dawn gloom, past the glare of streetlights hitting his car window, and into the shadows of the sedan's interior. He could feel her gaze on him, almost as if she'd known he'd be here.

He barely moved his mouth to speak to Marvel. "This

fancy program of yours…what does it tell you about the people it finds?"

"Not much. Most of the data is a bust. It's all based on obituaries. I set it up to track the people who have lost a parent or older siblings, and see if any weird news reports about them hit the 'net."

"Weird how?"

"You know, like manifestations of magical mojo—proof that they might have inherited shards."

Cleopatra's eyes stayed fixed on Flint's window as she squinted.

Cleopatra. What a ridiculous name for an American blonde.

"Does it tell you what abilities they might have?" he asked.

"Not really. I mean, we get hints sometimes, based on their parentage, but you know how fickle shards can be. The mix matters. This one time, I knew a dude whose dad could bench press a truck, but when he inherited the shards, he couldn't even—"

Flint cut Marvel off before he could be swept into her conversational vortex. "What about this woman? Does your program know what she can do?"

"Sure. She's a psychic. She lives with another psychic. Has a website and everything. You should check it out."

Flint relaxed. This woman was a charlatan. A con artist. Nothing more. He didn't have to worry about supernatural psionic blast rays coming from her eyes or a scream that could melt lead, like the last man he'd found.

Cleopatra Radella was simply a normal human preying on the gullible.

Too bad. For a thief and a liar, she was kind of cute. He just bet that had brought in more than one man for her to prey upon.

Her eyes disappeared as the blinds snapped back into place. Her shadow moved through the room, still jerky and unsettled, but she didn't appear to be coming out to see why he was sitting here, watching her house.

Like everyone else, she'd looked right past him and didn't even know he was there.

"Where's my next assignment?" Flint asked.

"You know the rules. I can't tell you until this one is done. No jumping ahead."

"It's done. There's nothing here. Time to move on."

"Are you sure?" asked Marvel, sounding disappointed. "The algorithm gave her a ninety-two percent chance of having inherited shards. That's unusually high."

"No one *advertises* that they have shards. That would be insane. She's just one more liar trying to make a buck by feeding into the delusions of the desperate."

Now Marvel's voice pitched up with irritation. "For the love of Odin! So, you're simply *guessing* that she's not one of ours based on pre-conceived notions?"

"Based on experience," he corrected.

"I don't have time to deal with your stubbornness. Hang on."

Flint was left with no choice but to wait for Marvel to send him his next target. As he did, he drove out of the aging neighborhood and headed toward a diner he'd spotted down the highway. He hadn't eaten in almost twenty-four hours—since before his hunt for Cleopatra had started—and he was starving.

The voice that came out through his headset was not the young, high-pitched voice of Marvel Manning, but instead, the low, sultry purr of another woman.

"Marvel tells me we have a problem," Starry Mandrake said.

Tattletale. Running to the boss because Marvel didn't like his decision was juvenile. Then again, she *was* young. He doubted she was even old enough to drink.

"No problems," Flint said. "Simply a difference of opinion."

Starry's voice had a bit of gravel in it, like Marvel had woken her from a deep sleep. "She says you're guessing that this woman has no shards, rather than being sure."

"She has a website hocking her wares. If she had shards and the ability to see into the future, she sure as hell wouldn't be stupid enough to tell the world what she could do."

"While your point is valid, you're missing one vital piece of information."

"Yeah? What's that?"

"Not everyone who holds shards knows what they carry inside of them."

"I know that. I've been doing this job for two years now."

"And I've been doing it for twenty."

"I'm not a novice," he insisted as irritation grated beneath his skin.

"No? Then why are you acting like one?" Starry asked. "The Flint I hired doesn't guess. He *knows*. You're one of the best scouts we have because you take nothing for granted. You're careful. Thorough."

Flint felt a ripple of pleasure at her praise, even as the shame of the truth killed it.

He *was* guessing. He hated liars, and his assumption she was one was clouding his judgment.

He let out a long sigh and pulled the sedan to the side of the street. "I'll go back. Make sure."

For Starry, he'd do anything. He owed her his life. Maybe more.

"Thank you," she said. "And if she is a vessel, I need you to bring her to Eden."

"That's not my job. Send Garrick or Wade."

"They're both busy."

"I'm a scout. I find them and verify that they have shards. That's all. Someone else can do the people stuff. I'm no good at it."

"I need you to figure it out, Flint. We're short-handed. It's time you got a promotion, anyway."

"I don't want a promotion. I like what I do."

"Then learn to like the touchy-feely stuff, too, because we need you to do this. *I* need you to."

And like a sucker, that was all it took to get Flint on board.

He breathed for a moment until his teeth unclenched enough for him to speak. "Any pointers?"

He could hear the smile of victory in Starry's voice. "Be friendly. Trust your instincts. If she has shards but doesn't want to play nice, then call and we'll figure out our next move. But you at least have to try. A little sweet talk might be all it takes to convince her to come in. If she's one of ours, we need her."

"And if she's one of theirs?"

"You were issued one of Marvel's guns, right?" Starry asked.

"Yes."

"Then use it."

BOOKS BY ANNA ARGENT
(formerly writing as Shannon K. Butcher)

THE LOST SHARDS
Shards of Blood and Shadow
Shards of Light (in The Secret She Keeps)
A Brush with Fate

THE TAKEN
Taken by Storm
Taken by Surprise
Taken by Force

THE WHISPER LAKE SERIES
The Longest Fall
The Sweetest Temptation
The Biggest Risk

THE STONE MEN
Made Flesh
Heart of Stone

CPSIA information can be obtained
at www.ICGtesting.com
Printed in the USA
LVHW092009220119
604821LV00002B/91/P

9 781945 292187